S0-CFG-792

UNHAPPY LANDINGS

Derek Lujan opened the hatch of the *Homeward Bound*'s shuttle and gazed out onto paradise. Dillon had shown him a library of reports on the projected fate of Earth. After five hundred years, Lujan had expected a wasteland of volcanic rock, a dust-clouded atmosphere, freezing temperatures, and a place devoid of vegetation.

But this—how could he keep this quiet?

Dazedly, Lujan stepped out into a wonderland of verdant green. Grass, trees, birds. And the sky! Clear and blue and beautiful, and the air sweet . . .

Damn! Dillon wasn't going to like this at all.

THE EARTH
IS ALL
THAT LASTS

Catherine Wells

A Del Rey Book
BALLANTINE BOOKS • NEW YORK

A Del Rey Book
Published by Ballantine Books

Copyright © 1991 by Catherine Wells Dimenstein

All rights reserved under International and Pan-American Copyright
Conventions. Published in the United States of America by Ballantine Books, a division of Random House, Inc., New York, and
simultaneously in Canada by Random House of Canada Limited,
Toronto.

Library of Congress Catalog Card Number: 91-91888

ISBN 0-345-37178-X

Manufactured in the United States of America

First Edition: August 1991

Cover Art by Richard Hescox

"It's a good day to die!
  Take courage, boy!
The earth is all that lasts!"
        —Black Elk,
          Oglala Sioux

PROLOGUE

And in the final days the Earth herself grew weary of Man's greed and stupidity and so decided to shake off this noisome infestation. With earthquakes, tidal waves, storms, and volcanic eruptions she assaulted his cities. Still he remained in great numbers. Then she drew her mightiest weapon—famine.

Some said it was the volcanic ash in the atmosphere blocking out the sun; others said simply that the earth had stopped producing. Whatever the reason, cold and drought settled over the globe, and crops everywhere failed year after year after miserable year . . .

Food was imported, of course, from the new colonial worlds, but it was never enough and always too expensive. The workers left first, to help harvest the new planets. Wars broke out—the rich fled to safety. Governments found it impractical to stay and moved their capitals to the distant stars. Finally the dry, dead, hostile Earth was not worth fighting over. The military evacuated what was left of the population; then they themselves broke camp, cursed, spit, and withdrew. The rape had ended.

Here and there pockets of humanity were left behind. The Earth, unsated, dealt cruelly with them, ending her drought with torrential rains and flooding. Few survived.

In the southwestern desert region of what had been the United States there were two exceptions. One was a group of Native Americans and their supporters who had refused to evacuate. Four thousand strong, they planted their heels and said that the Earth was their mother, and though she was angry now, her love for her children would return. They would wait for it.

The other group—scientists and technicians—trenched in high on a mountain in what had been a stellar observatory but was now a monitoring station to record the Earth's demise. Stocked with one last shipment of food from offworld, they settle down to record, transmit, and eventually die.

But they did not die. When the rains returned, their desperation hothouses became unnecessary, for the Earth began to produce again. High above floodwaters that devastated the region, they watched untouched as she washed herself clean. When at last the waters receded, it was a new generation of scientists that set forth in their aircraft to survey the awakening land.

Huddled in an ancient cliff dwelling just above the high-water mark, they found twenty-two survivors. The history, the culture of these Native Americans had died with their elders. They lived in near-animal fashion, clawing life from what native vegetation the reluctant Earth had permitted to live.

Being scientists and observers, the mountain dwellers elected not to bring the primitive people into their own technological society but instead to teach them the skills of their ancestors: hunting, harvesting, weaving, pottery. Every few years, they decided, they would send a teacher to live among the People and gradually impart to them the skills necessary to survive, to grow, and to flourish. They themselves would watch and record.

So the People developed a way of life that was old and yet new. They possessed the skills of their ancestors but created their own culture, their own legends, their own religion. Not surprisingly, their religion revolved around service to and harmony with the Mother Earth, for they knew all too well the meaning of her blessing—and her curse. Her favor was important to one and all.

It was most important to Coconino.

CHAPTER ONE

Coconino crouched in the brush, knife in hand, not ten paces from the tawny puma. The fronds of a desert broom clutched at his headband and the tangle of coal-black hair it held, but he ignored them, his dark eyes fastened on the big cat. A trickle of sweat snaked down his bare back, soaking unnoticed into his cotton loincloth. Carefully he put one foot forward, shifted his weight, took another step—

The cat's head snapped back, nostrils flaring, eyes startled as she found herself outflanked. Powerful muscles tensed, and she prepared to spring in this new direction. Coconino's hand tightened on the bone haft of his knife.

But the puma hesitated, and in that moment Coconino laughed. "What is wrong, Elder Sister?" he called, his eyes as mocking as his tone. "Did you think you could stalk your prey and not be stalked yourself? Be glad it is only me the Mother Earth sent to humble you. I will not injure more than your pride."

A moment longer she hesitated, then with a short snarl of irritation the great cat bounded off into the desert brush.

Behind Coconino, his friend Juan took a deep breath and eased off the tension on his bowstring. "*Aiiee*, Coconino," he grumbled. "You need a wife."

Coconino gave a short, bitter laugh. No one knew better than he how a wife would ease the tension in him and drive some of the craziness from his blood. But not just any wife, he thought, glancing toward the southern skies. No, not just any wife, for I can feel the thrumming of the Flying Machine in my loins. Soon my waiting will be over. Soon the Witch Woman will come.

"What do you suppose she was stalking?" Juan asked as they

1

turned their steps in the direction the puma had been leading them.

Coconino raised his eyes to the red buttes ahead, their sheer faces ablaze in the morning sun. At nineteen he was not unlike the rock himself: hard, rugged, and red-hued. He fingered the talisman that hung from his neck, a silver ornament set with blue-green stone in the shape of a bird—like his name, it was a relic of the Before Times. "I do not know what it was," he admitted, remembering the odd sense of expectancy he had felt when he had seen the big cat slinking through the tall weeds, intent upon its quarry. Had it been the voice of the Mother Earth that had called to him?

He shot a sideways glance at his companion, a wiry man with a bright red headband and a slightly flattened nose. "Whatever it is," Coconino informed him wisely, "it must be larger game than we have seen so far."

Juan grinned at him, a broad and ready grin that showed a mouthful of large white teeth. He and Coconino had wandered far from the Valley of the People in search of large game. Oh, there were rabbits and squirrels and quail to be had nearer the village, but after a winter of dried stores and small, bony animals, the young hunters had been eager to strike out in search of fleshier game. And besides, it was spring.

Spring came with a rush to this land, as sudden as the torrents of water that came tumbling down the thighs of the mountains to swell dry streams. Shivering, dancing, the water brought new life to the desert, causing wildflowers to erupt from the dormant earth in brilliant shades of blue, purple, and yellow.

So had spring rushed upon Coconino this year, more than any other. His heart pounded, and it seemed all his nerves lay exposed on the surface of his skin, waiting. The slightest breeze that brushed him, the bead of sweat that trickled down his cheek, roused him like a young animal. He felt himself filled with the potency of the waters, rushing headlong toward—what?

His fulfillment, of course. After all, was he not Coconino, son of a Man-on-the-Mountain by his Chosen Companion? Again he glanced at the southern skies, as though he could see to the mythical Mountain and its legendary inhabitants. Very soon now the Flying Machine would come, bringing its special cargo. Then all the village would know what he had decided, oh, so many years before.

Coconino would marry the Witch Woman.

He glanced covertly at his friend, wondering what Juan would think of the brash idea. Juan was older by three years and had married seven summers ago, a plump, happy woman named Cactus Flower. It would never occur to Juan that a Witch Woman might marry a man of the People.

But soon she will come, Coconino thought, and I will woo her as no Man-on-the-Mountain ever could. For as all Witch Women are Daughters of the Mother Earth, so I—I am her favorite son.

As the sun reached its peak they were still wandering among the outlying buttes of the Red Rock country, with no sign of whatever the puma had been tracking. Long ago this valley had been a lake bed, and the buttes, islands. Now their sheer rock faces were skirted by hard-packed rubble and their tops crowned by a few hardy shrubs.

They intended to go farther north to where they knew a stream ran, the laughing child of the waterway that had carved a deep canyon through the red stone. There, amid tall pine trees, they were likely to find mule deer or perhaps, along the upper reaches of the canyon walls, bighorn sheep.

But the sense of expectancy washed over Coconino again. Standing at the foot of one of the natural monoliths, he gazed hungrily up at its great height. A breeze touched his neck and he shivered inwardly.

"There could be bighorn up there," Coconino suggested.

"Very true," Juan agreed as he, too, gazed up the massive face. "Or perhaps an eagle's nest."

"The eagle is only a legend," Coconino replied. Then, "But if there were still such a bird, this is where he might be."

"A bighorn would be nice," Juan admitted. He looked at the vertical sides of the upper section and knew that nothing on four legs could climb it. "Yes, there might be bighorn at the top. Or an eagle's nest."

A grin split Coconino's coppery face. "Let's find out!"

This time Juan had no reservations about joining in the craziness. With bows slung across their backs, the young men challenged the red stone. Experienced hands and toes found invisible holds in the cliff wall, and carefully, gamely, they worked their way upward. Juan was smaller than his friend, more sinewy, and a little nimbler. "Your feet are too big!" he laughed as a rock broke loose under Coconino's foot and left him suspended momentarily, toes clawing for a better grip.

When he found it, he paused briefly, exhilarated by the rush of adrenaline and his consciousness of the Mother Earth's favor. "Bind me to your rock," he prayed silently. "Let me be one with the stone and the sky, and I shall climb this peak like a spider.''

As he started upward again, a breeze touched his sweaty cheek, stirred the strands of his coarse hair, and whispered his name. Coconino was not surprised; since he was a child the Mother Earth had spoken to him in this way.

But now another voice seemed to drift down to him. Who are you? it asked. Why do you come here, to my place? And how is it that you speak such gilded words, but without guile? For I would know guile, I would feel it . . .

A shiver ran through Coconino. Something waited for him atop the butte. With renewed vigor he scrambled after Juan and passed him. Coconino knew he must reach the top first, must find out what had called to him with no voice. Near the top a small piñon pine had taken root and a few cacti and other plants were clinging bravely to the steep slope. He grasped the pine and hauled himself the last few feet to the rim, just ahead of Juan. Reaching up, he seized the thorny shrubs that grew on the surface, wincing as they bit into his hands. Elbows found their purchase, then a knee, and then—

Coconino almost fell backward off the cliff. Watching him with curiosity was an animal that was neither bighorn, nor mule deer, nor any other beast he had ever seen enfleshed. It was barrel-chested with thick hooved forelegs and powerfully muscled rear quarters. Nearly twice the size of the legendary horse, it rippled with a powerful grace. Dappled red fur covered its sleek sides, but on its neck and withers were thick folds of skin, adding bulk to an already imposing form. The head was elongated like an antelope's, with a dished muzzle and black nose. Wise brown eyes studied Coconino from their slightly telescoped positions on either side of the head, and it showed no trace of apprehension; why should it fear? It knew what it was. And when Coconino saw the single braided horn crowning its majestic head, he knew, too.

This was Tala.

"*Aiiee!*" Coconino crowed in triumph.

At the sudden noise Tala jumped back, the darker color of his withers traveling outward as his hide transformed from red to deep brown. Startled by the creature's changing aspect, Coconino jumped, too, and his knee lost its purchase on the crumbling edge. He lurched his weight forward to keep from falling.

"What, what?" Juan called from below. "*Aaah*, watch out!"

he shouted as the dirt and rubble Coconino had dislodged rained down on him.

Coconino flattened himself on the ground and reached a hand back to pull Juan up. "It's Tala!" he cried. "Tala is here!"

Juan scrambled to the surface, and both men turned to gaze on the magnificent fable.

But it was gone.

"Where?" Juan asked suspiciously, wondering if he'd been had.

But Coconino's distress was genuine. The younger man paced the cliff top distractedly, looking for some evidence of his vision. "That's what the puma was hunting. And he was here, he was, just a moment ago—look!" Coconino dropped to his knees. "Here are hoof prints!"

Juan eyed the marks critically. Something had been there, but in the stony soil it was hard to say what.

Coconino ran across the butte top. The surface was not that large; where could Tala have gone? Dropped behind the shrubby growth, changing his color again to blend in with his surroundings? Coconino checked his headlong dash and searched the scant vegetation more carefully. No, there was not enough cover here to conceal such a large animal. Then where?

Over the side. It was the only place. Coconino reached the far edge and looked down, eyes scanning the steep sides. Surely no animal could descend such a rock face! But he had seen bighorn do impossible things, and Tala was no ordinary animal but a kachina, a spirit-animal.

Juan joined him. "Perhaps it was something else," he suggested. "A hawk sitting on—"

"It was Tala!" Coconino hissed, still searching the landscape below.

"A bighorn that—"

"Look!" Coconino cried in triumph, pointing out a creature moving on the valley floor. "There, you see?"

Juan squinted at what was only a blur of motion, a dappling of tan and brown running swiftly amid the jojoba and barberry. "It is . . . large," he said, trying to see the beast as his friend saw it. "It must be, to run so fast. And . . . it *could* be—"

"It is! It is Tala! I saw him!"

Juan looked back at the butte top, then down the steep sides. "But how did he get from here to there?" he asked.

Coconino was undaunted. "Come! We must go after him!"

Dropping to his belly, he swung his legs over the edge, searching for toeholds.

Reluctantly Juan took one last look at the dizzying drop. True, this side was not quite as steep as the other, but for a hooved creature to go down so quickly—or to have gone down at all! He did not think it likely.

But Coconino was Coconino, and who could argue with him? With a weary sigh Juan followed his friend down.

The cold water stung his bruised and scraped limbs, but Juan was glad of the chance to wash the dust from his throat and body. He had finally convinced Coconino to give up his pursuit of the elusive legend. "After all, Tala is Tala, eh? If he wants you to find him, you will. If he doesn't—what's the use?" Reluctantly the younger hunter had allowed himself to be persuaded.

They sat now on the broad, flat rocks that lined the stream deep in the canyon. Even under the glaring sun of midday it was cool there, the walls stretching hundreds of feet above them and trapping the cool air of nights that still dipped to near freezing. The scent of pine and musty, damp leaves reached them as they spread themselves on the rocks to rest.

Juan relaxed happily, enjoying the sound of the rushing stream and the sighing of a gentle breeze through the treetops. The warmth of the sun lay pleasantly on his brown skin, brushed off only rarely by a breath of the same breeze that found its way to the canyon floor.

But Coconino could not relax. Juan could feel his tension, his restlessness. Poor man, Juan thought. Who does he wait for that he has gone so long without taking a wife? Castle Rock? It must be. After all, she, like he, has a name from the Before Times, and her father also was a Man-on-the-Mountain. Well, she is fourteen now, a good age to marry, and Coconino better stop dragging his heels or some other man will have her.

Coconino tried to settle himself comfortably on the red, smooth stone, but he could not. To have seen Tala! And in this his twentieth spring. Surely it was a good omen, a great omen. Now the Witch Woman would come from the faraway Mountain, the Witch Woman with yellow hair and blue eyes and soft, pale skin . . .

He remembered the last Witch Woman, an astounding sight to a boy in the throes of adolescence. So wise, so gentle, with laughter like the sound of this brook gurgling so pleasantly—

"What was that?" He bolted into a sitting position.

"What?"

"I thought I heard the sound of a Flying Machine."

Juan laughed. "What you need is some of this cold water," he said, splashing a handful at the rigid youth.

Coconino scowled and splashed back. In a moment they were dousing each other merrily, then wrestling to see who could force whom into the shallow water.

Coconino won. Coconino always won and had since he was twelve and surpassed the older boy in height. But he took Juan's advice and rolled off into the frigid water himself. Truly the Witch Woman must come this year, he thought. Otherwise I may die.

The watchman high on the wall of the Ancients saw the young hunters approach and sent up a cry that brought the village children dancing out to meet them and their travois laden with fresh venison. Late the previous day they had come upon three young does drinking at the stream. Two arrows loosed simultaneously had dropped two deer where they stood; the third doe had bounded for the safety of the pines but had gotten no more than twenty yards, twin shafts buried in her neck.

Juan and Coconino had argued good-naturedly all evening over whose arrow had struck first as they roasted fresh liver and lashed together two travois to carry their kill home. At dawn they had begun the laborious trek out of the old lake bed over rolling hills that led eventually to this: the Valley of the People.

Coming down from the northwest as they did, their home was hidden until they rounded one last hill and angled southwest. Then suddenly they could see the Village of the Ancients seemingly carved into the buff-colored cliff face above their village, tier upon tier of stone cubicles like an ancient fortress looming halfway up the mountain.

In truth, it was built in a natural cave in the limestone, a shallow depression that provided a sheltering overhang and solid footing. Stone retaining walls were cemented with the same adobe plaster of which the houses were made. Ladders led upward from one natural stone shelf to another and finally to a low area in the retaining wall that was the entrance to the first level. Here one- and two-story houses butted against each other, rising from different floor levels and offering rooftops as walkways while seeming to present an unbroken mass.

The rooftops of these front houses gave access by ladder to a second series of chambers set farther back into the cave. The rear houses reached to three stories and were crowned by a short wall on which a vigilant lookout was always perched. The wall also fenced in a large common area. Here, in the heat of the summer, the women might come with their sewing and their basketry to work and gossip in the cool shade.

The cliffside fortress was a sight that filled Coconino with wonder still. Through floods and drought and tremblings of the ground, through black clouds and endless rains, this stone fortress had clung to its moorings and provided shelter for the last remnant of the People. In the Year That the Men-on-the-Mountain First Came, they had found the swirling floodwaters only a few feet below the base of the retaining wall and a tattered band of decimated people, twenty-two in all, clinging to life inside the crumbling shelter.

That had been long ago. The shallow brook splashing through the valley now was hundreds of feet from the foot of the cliff. Wickiups dotted the intervening ground, and it was there that the People lived now, not in the cliff houses. Upstream, nestled in a great loop of the creek, were farmlands rich with silt. Soon corn, beans, cotton, and squash would poke tentative sprouts through the dusty soil, watered by irrigation trenches.

From the first ragged band, the People had grown and prospered to a community of over seventy persons, relearning many of the Old Ways forgotten during a century of deprivation. They hunted, farmed, wove cotton, tanned hides, baked pottery, and carved implements from bone and wood. All those crafts had been taught them by the Men-on-the-Mountain, who sent Teachers to restore to the People the skills by which their ancestors had survived.

Now the village boys yipped excitedly as they reached the returning hunters and saw the magnificent kill. Surely there would be a feast tonight! Good roasted meat and the tender flower stalks of sotol as well as steamed cholla buds. Truly the Mother Earth was to be praised for her bounty!

Some of the boys wore loincloths like their elders, but most ran naked in the manner of children. They all wanted to help drag the travois back to the village. Coconino and Juan feigned great reluctance at surrendering their prize, but they were glad enough to be relieved of the burden and to swagger ahead.

Once a road had led to this place, but floodwaters had broken it up and covered it over with silt. Now it was only a broad flat place, good for walking. They followed its windings to an especially wide clearing just above the village; then they turned aside and sought the small stream that sustained their community. The water was high with spring runoff and cold; they drank sparingly and continued walking, bathing their dusty feet occasionally in the sparkling water.

Just at the path to the village someone waited on the bank.

Coconino growled when he saw her. She was dressed in a light cotton skirt, knee-length and knotted at her hip, its hem embroidered in black and red designs. The deep heat of summer was a long way off, so she wore a blouse of simple, straight cut, fastened with a drawstring at the neck. Her long black hair was combed and held in place by a muslin tie not unlike Coconino's but daintily embroidered to match the skirt. Her blossoming figure pressed against the thin fabric in a most appealing way, and the smile on her round face was flirtatious.

"Oh! Hello, Coconino. Juan." Castle Rock pretended mild surprise at meeting them there. On her shoulder was a large clay water jar. "You are back from your hunt, I see. Where is your kill?"

Coconino jerked a thumb back in the direction of the village children, but Juan was inclined to be more expansive. "*Aiiee!* It is a story you will tell your children," he asserted. "Three deer, three arrows—*thwck, thwck, thwck,* as though the Mother Earth had called them to herself and they dropped in obedience."

"Four arrows," Coconino corrected him sourly. Then he made a right angle to climb up the hill away from the girl.

But Juan caught his arm. "Don't be in a hurry, Coconino. Let's wait for the children to come a little closer with our kill. Everyone will want to see it. Let's quench our thirst here at the stream." He grinned at the girl and gave Coconino a gentle shove toward the water.

Coconino grumbled and sloshed into the brook, ignoring the girl, who followed daintily with her water jar. She managed to keep just within his peripheral vision, swaying slightly as she walked with the jar on her arm. "The sun shines upon the Valley of the People," she lilted, "now that Coconino—and Juan— walk once more upon her paths."

"The sun would shine with or without us," Coconino growled. Did she think he could be softened by such clumsy flattery? Her elders had spoiled her, fussing over her beauty and her manners and the fact that she was the daughter of a Man-on-the-Mountain. They even whispered, he knew, that he waited for her—and she believed it! The smug smile on her face told him. She believed he had stayed wifeless for season upon season only to have her when she came of age. Ha! Well, you are of age now, he thought. Why do you suppose I have not yet brought gifts to your mother's door? Why do you suppose, at your coming-of-age ceremony, I took careful pains to be out of the village?

"Ho! There is Cactus Flower!" Juan lied, pointing up the bank. "Excuse me, I must go and tell my wife how lucky she is to be married to such a superb hunter. *Aiiee!* She will grow even fatter eating the choice portion of so many kills!" And before Coconino could object, Juan scrambled up the hill toward the village.

Coconino scowled after his friend, knowing his fate was sealed. There was nothing to do but walk up from the river with Castle Rock beside him for all the village to see. Then they would smile their knowing smiles and nod their heads, and no one would notice how furious he was at having been tricked into this awkward position.

Her jar filled, Castle Rock returned to the bank and stood— no, she posed—watching him. "The People are fortunate to have such a skillful hunter as Coconino," she purred.

"And Juan."

"And Juan." She set the jar down and clasped her hands behind her back, the better to show off her figure.

It worked.

It's not fair, Coconino cursed to himself, splashing water over his face and arms. She is so smug and arrogant, so full of her own importance, so childish in her thinking, and yet I can't take my eyes off her. And she knows it.

Castle Rock turned profile and lifted her face to the Village of the Ancients, high on the cliff wall behind the village. Though the People no longer lived in the cliff houses, they did not forget how the Mother Earth had sheltered them in the hollow of her mountain. They kept the dwellings in repair and held their most solemn ceremonies in them. Here were coming-of-age rituals played out; here were marriages consummated; here the Mother met with her Council . . .

Castle Rock looked back at the young man in the stream, wondering if he had noticed what was going on in that stone village and the one below. Indeed he had not; he was too busy ignoring her, brushing drops of water from his chest and arms, trying not to shiver as a breeze touched him. "See how the children decorate our village," she called to him.

Coconino looked up at the ramadas whose poles were adorned with clusters of wildflowers. His gaze traveled up the slope to where the ladders accessing the Village of the Ancients had also been festively wrapped. Then he saw it; high on the third level a puff of smoke escaped from the Council Chamber.

"What has happened?" he demanded of the saucy girl on the bank. "Why does the Council meet?"

"Council business is not my business. Ask your mother."

She knew, but she was not telling him! Coconino sloshed out of the stream and grabbed her arm roughly, then immediately regretted it, for she did not resist but was soft and yielding in his grasp. He let go as though she were a hot stone.

"Tell me!"

She smiled, too near him, her head tilted up to meet his blazing eyes. Coconino backed off a step, wondering how to get away from her without seeming to turn tail and run, how to find out the reason for the Council meeting, how to—

Suddenly he laughed. Of course! It was all so simple. If only he had listened to the brook at his feet, it would have told him. The hawk soaring near the cliff top would have squawked the answer if only he had listened. Even Tala had spoken it with his eyes! "They arrived today, didn't they?" he asked.

Castle Rock's eyes widened, but she forced innocence into her voice. "Who arrived?"

Again he laughed and strode a few feet downstream, his eyes on the puff of smoke from the Council fire. "They who meet now with the Mother and her Council. They who arrived in a Flying Machine. The new Teacher—and the Witch Woman."

Castle Rock could not keep the surprise off her face now. He might have guessed about the Teacher, but the Witch Woman? "How did you know?" she gasped. Perhaps the stories were true; perhaps Coconino could speak with the Mother Earth.

He turned derisive eyes on her. "I will tell you something else I know," he taunted. "I will marry this Witch Woman. What then for your fine plans, Castle Rock?" And laughing, he scrambled up the bank to seek his destiny.

Castle Rock sat on the stream bank in utter despair. She did not hear the birds chirping happily in the sycamore trees that grew along the bank and shaded the village. All she heard was the mocking tone of Coconino's voice and the awful import of his words: He would court the Witch Woman—not her.

But why? What was a Witch Woman? They were strange—all

the people who dwelled on that faraway mountain were strange. They dressed oddly, they spoke oddly, they laughed at things that were not funny. Why should he want a Witch Woman?

Slowly her despair turned to anger. What nerve! To court a Witch Woman! No one was allowed to court a Witch Woman; they were all to return to their Mountain. Who did he think he was? So his mother had been the Chosen Companion of a Man-on-the-Mountain. So had hers! And what if his mother was high in the Council of the Mother; that did not put either of them outside the Way of the People. And the Way of the People was that Witch Women did not marry men of the village.

He is proud, unduly proud! she pouted, stamping her bare foot on the ground. Then she sighed. And unduly handsome, she thought. Leaning back on the bank, she gazed sightlessly at the vivid blue sky, untouched by even one cloud. For years she had watched Coconino laughing with his friends, swaggering into the village with fresh game slung across his shoulder, earning the respect of the People, young and old. Even the Mother, she thought, smiles on him with pride. As a child she, Castle Rock, had admired him greatly.

Now that she was of age, her interest had become more specific. Other young men had smiled at her, cast admiring looks her way, praised her beauty to their friends. But the only whispers that pleased her were the ones concerning Coconino. How fine a husband he would be. How lucky the girl he finally favored. How he must be waiting for someone special. Even his mother, Two Moons, had indicated that she would not be displeased if her son brought gifts to Castle Rock's door. And Juan, his best friend, had grinned and left them alone together by the stream.

He toys with me! she decided suddenly, sitting bolt upright. He pretends to want another so that I will pine for him, weep foolishly, and be ever so joyous and thankful when he finally brings his gifts to my door. Marry the Witch Woman! Did he really think I would believe such a lie?

Oh, you will be sorry, Coconino, she thought, for trying to hurt me with your lie. There will be consequences for your rash statement, do not doubt it. And I shall laugh last.

Then, her self-confidence restored, Castle Rock climbed back up to the village, plotting how to get even with her annoying suitor.

CHAPTER TWO

Heart pounding, Coconino waited in a courtyard just below the Council Chamber. It was on the edge of the pueblo, its second-floor entrance protected by the crumbling northwest wall of the cave. A short ladder stretched from a small shelf above the courtyard to a broken-walled antechamber that hid the three-foot doorway. Like all the other doorways in the village, it was T-shaped to allow better ventilation and provide handholds for crawling in and out. The Council door was marked, however, by three symbols painted around it: on the right a great eagle, on the left a two-armed saguaro cactus, and above it a single human figure that knelt with empty hands uplifted and wept. He was the Mourner for Things That Will Not Live Again.

From inside the dried mud chamber came the low murmur of voices, and though he waited circumspectly in the courtyard that was the entryway to the village, Coconino's ears strained to hear unfamiliar tones amid the voices that drifted down occasionally from the room. The hard, clipped speech patterns of the Men-on-the-Mountain should be easy to distinguish from the melodious, resonant intonation of the People.

Excited children frolicked in and about the lower level of a two-story house on the other side of the small courtyard. They hoped to catch a glimpse of the new Teacher and speculated among themselves what magic this Witch Woman would have. Coconino scowled at them when their noise became disrespectful, but mostly he waited and remembered the last Witch Woman . . .

"But why must you leave?" asked the dirty-faced boy.

Gentle blue eyes smiled at him. "Because someone waits for me," she answered. *"He will be my husband, and we will have children who must grow up on the Mountain."*

13

"*But why?*" *he persisted, his chin set stubbornly.* "*Why can't you take a husband from the People and raise your children here?*"

"*Because,*" *she explained patiently,* "*as you are promised to the People, though your father is not one of them, so my children are promised to the Mountain. That is the Way Things Are.*" *The boy had scowled to hide his hurt and stalked away in anger that fooled no one.*

But though the young man who waited now still tended to scowl, he had learned much, much that even the Witch Woman could not teach him. He had learned that the Way Things Are could be changed.

A feminine giggle stirred Coconino from his reverie. The maidens of the People were coming up the ladders to the Village of the Ancients, hoping not so much to see as to be seen by the Man-on-the-Mountain. They had scrubbed themselves clean, combed and braided their hair, and put on their finest clothes. Each one hoped that she, among all the maidens of the village, might become this honored guest's Chosen Companion. But they eyed Coconino as well, casting shy looks and small smiles in his direction as they climbed over the wall into the courtyard, brushing the dust from their bare legs and arms and giggling together.

To hide his discomfort at being the object of their attention, Coconino ducked into the house where the children played and climbed to its second level. This was called the Gatehouse because without ladders, one had to pass through it to get to the rest of the Village of the Ancients. The children drew back as he entered, wondering if his sharp look was meant for them. But Coconino ignored them and hoisted himself through the empty smoke/ladder hole to its roof.

He liked this vantage point much better. Leaning against the sun-warmed adobe of the back tier of houses, he could study the maidens in detail, and if they wanted to admire him, at least he could pretend not to notice.

They were small and dark, each one, with long hair and round faces. There the similarity ended. Nina was bony, with a large crooked nose; she was also the oldest at seventeen. Bright Morning was round in body, her nose more flattened and a small gap between her front teeth. Too Pretty was in between, her body more pleasing and her face even-featured. She was a rival for Castle Rock in beauty but also a rival for any harpy in the sharpness of her tongue. Coconino shuddered reflexively. She was only fifteen. Perhaps when she was seventeen like Nina and still had no husband, she would learn to control that tongue.

Then there was Brook. Brook was unremarkable for size or beauty, but she had blue eyes. Both of her grandfathers had been Men-on-the-Mountain, and so, it was said, magic was strong within her and gave her blue eyes. Coconino did not put much stock in this, for the Witch Woman had told him once that when the People had first been found by the Men-on-the-Mountain, several had had blue eyes and some had even had light hair.

But light-haired babies sickened and died, and so after many generations they became fewer and fewer. Now only three of the People boasted hair that was not jet black or, at the very least, a rich brown. One was the child Little Dove, whose mother constantly fussed with oils and berry juice, staining her daughter's skin and keeping her out of the sun. The old man Snowy Mountain was said to have been blond as a child also, though now his hair was as white as his name implied. And then, of course, there was Corn Hair.

Coconino turned his gaze down to the village to see if he could spot her. Yes, there she was, standing in front of her wickiup, shading her eyes and looking eastward. Ha! he thought. Probably waiting for good-for-nothing Lame Rabbit to return from hunting.

Beside her a two-year-old danced in the dust. His older brother was probably here with the other children waiting to gape at the Teachers. It was lucky, Coconino thought, that harvest and hunt were shared among the People or surely the two boys would have starved to death long ago. Poor Corn Hair, you deserve so much better . . .

They had grown up together, born in the same summer, their mothers good friends. Because of her blond hair he had teased her that she must have had a Witch Woman for an ancestor. She had laughed and said to be careful or she would cast a spell over him, for it was well known that each Witch Woman had a powerful magic of some sort. "Then," she had laughed, "I will make you take me to faraway places the hunters tell of: the Red Rock Country to the west, the Black Lands to the north—and perhaps even to the Great Canyon beyond the Mountains that only the Men-on-the-Mountain have ever seen." And there was a time when Coconino had believed her.

But he had been too young and too much like a brother when young men had begun bringing gifts to her door. So he had watched with unexplained sadness as she had followed Lame

Rabbit up the ladders to the Village of the Ancients, to a wedding chamber in that blessed place. And he remembered still, like a knife thrust in his heart, how just before she had entered the festively decorated house she had turned and given Coconino one last, desolate look—

"*Aiiee!* Here they come!"

The children stopped their scuffling, the maidens whispered together, and Coconino bolted for the smoke hole, for he could not see the Council door from here. He dropped through to the top floor of the house, then took two steps on the ladder and jumped down to the next floor. Two more steps brought him crouching to the doorway; he ducked through and—

He tripped over a six-year-old and sprawled headlong in the dirt. Though he rolled immediately to a sitting position, it was not in time to save his dignity.

The children backed away, afraid they would be scolded. The maidens tittered. The members of the Council as they descended the ladder smiled and chuckled, and perched on the stone shelf at the foot the ladder the Witch Woman—

Coconino thought at first that the fall had impaired his vision. This tall creature could not be the new Witch Woman. She was thin as a sapling, all long arms and legs, and her skin was as dark, her hair as black, as his own. Her countenance was hard as she stood above him, her stance unyielding. And to make matters worse, she threw back her head and laughed raucously.

Anger flashed in Coconino's eyes, and he came quickly to his feet, brushing the dust from his hands and arms. He set his jaw and said nothing but glared at the Witch Woman.

The Mother intervened. The first out of the Council Chamber, she stood now in the courtyard with the maidens and the children. She was a squat woman, leather-faced, her hair gone white with age, but her mind was quick and her eyes sparkled. "Dust Devil," she addressed the child, "are you hurt?"

"Dust Devil sounds like a good name for him," the Witch Woman said, her voice dry and hard as an old corncob. "And what about this one?" She stepped down and crossed to Coconino. "What's his name?"

Coconino met her mocking eyes and drew himself up proudly. "I am Coconino," he replied haughtily.

A puzzled look flickered across her face. "Coconino? I don't know what that word means."

"No one does," he told her, barely managing to keep the sneer out of his voice. "It is from the Before Times."

To his surprise, she bristled dangerously. ''Is that supposed to make it special?'' she asked icily.

He tried to forgive her ignorance because Witch Women were not expected to know the Way of the People. ''Only the child of a Man-on-the-Mountain may have such a name,'' he explained patiently. ''My grandfather found writing from the Before Times and brought it home to my mother while she carried me. It is a great omen.''

Her eyes narrowed, and he wondered why such cold anger lurked there just below the surface. ''Bear in mind, Coconino,'' she warned, ''that there is a difference between a great omen and a good one.''

Here the Man-on-the-Mountain broke in. He was a burly man with a round face and dark curling hair. He wore a mustache and sported crooked teeth. ''What's that coming into the village?'' he asked, pointing toward the northeast, where the young boys were carefully guiding the heavy travois down the steep embankment to the village.

''Ah.'' The Mother nodded, pleased. ''The Mother Earth favors you, Coconino. How many animals do you bring us? Two?''

''Three,'' he replied. ''We can make a great feast tonight in honor of our guests.''

''So we shall. Come, Teacher, Witch Woman—as soon as the animals are prepared, we will help you build your wickiups.''

''Wickiups?'' the Witch Woman echoed. ''I'd rather live here in one of these.'' She crossed to the Gatehouse and peered inside.

There was a collective gasp from the Council, but the Mother appeared to be considering the idea. She watched as the tall woman stooped and climbed inside, checking the ladder to the second level. ''The rooms are small,'' the Mother cautioned.

''I don't need much.''

Coconino wondered what the Mother would do. Everyone knew it was *moh-ohnak* to live in a wickiup; other shelters were only for temporary use. But the Witch Woman was not everyone, and who knew what was *moh-ohnak* for her? Perhaps for her it was fitting to live here in this place of communion with the Mother Earth, this place of Council gatherings, solemn celebrations and marriages—

Marriages! Suddenly Coconino's chest tightened and his head began to ring. He had lost more than his pride when the Witch Woman had laughed; in that moment a dream had died as well.

For so long he had waited for another Witch Woman, for golden hair and blue eyes—but this tall, ungainly creature folding herself to fit back out through the doorway appealed to him far less than Castle Rock did. Marry that? He shuddered. Yet there would be no other Witch Woman for many years, and he would not be allowed to wait. He must either surrender his dream or . . .

"Yes," the Mother was saying. "You may have the corner house, there on the second level." She pointed toward the opposite end of the pueblo. "It has its own entrance and a smaller room attached. The front chamber will have more light, the back more privacy. I will have Muddy Hands make sure the roof is well repaired."

"Good, I'll bring my things up," the Witch Woman agreed, brushing the dust from her hands. Then she followed the Mother over the retaining wall and down the series of ladders to the village below.

Coconino watched as the entourage followed, one by one, down the sturdy wood ladder away from the stone fortress: the Council, the children, the maidens. But as they went, he saw one girl pause and look back at him: Castle Rock. Her eyes mocked him without pity.

"The Witch Woman is too tall."

Castle Rock had strolled casually to where Coconino and his friends squatted on a slight rise, sharing their feast. Falling Star, Coconino's brother-in-law, was elaborating on his discussion with a rattlesnake over who had the right to a narrow pathway through a particularly thick stand of cholla. Finally Falling Star had found the skeletal remains of a large piece of the cactus and had used that stick to prod the lazy snake into seeking some other place to sun itself. It was an amusing story, with the young man relating the snake's words as well as his own, and for a moment Coconino had forgotten his desolation.

Now it came stabbing back with Castle Rock's calculated words. He stopped chewing the tender venison and stole a glance at his companions. They were watching Castle Rock but said nothing. Perhaps she would go away.

"And too thin."

Now he saw some smiles of amusement as his friends cast glances at the Witch Woman. She sat with the other Teacher, Gonzales, on a flat stone not far from the Elvira, the ceremonial fire, in the center of the village. She said little, which was a blessing, for although she spoke some of the language of the People, she clipped her words, and her speech was always freely laced with euphemisms he did not recognize. He suspected they were disrespectful.

Even in the rosy firelight her complexion was amber—not fair, as the other Witch Woman had been, and lacking a healthy glow. Her face looked pinched and tired, although she was not old. In that way she was like Corn Hair, but with the mark of bitterness Corn Hair never bore. In her tight, heavy cotton trousers and a sleeveless leather shirt she looked especially thin, with spindly arms and an awkward amount of leg bent at the knee. Like a cricket, Coconino thought. She has legs like a cricket.

"Perhaps they are hungry on the Mountain," Loves the Dust suggested. He was a young farmer with large biceps and a hint of chestnut brown to his hair. "Perhaps the Mother Earth does not bless them as she blesses the People."

"But see the Teacher," Juan pointed out. "He has not gone hungry! Though you would never know by the way he eats tonight."

"He eats almost as much as you," Falling Star said.

"I work hard, though. See?" Juan patted his flat stomach. "I have no time to get fat, I am always working."

"Yes—on your elbows," Loves the Dust smirked.

Juan grinned at the ribald jest. "That is the best kind of work! It keeps a man thin and happy, and it pleases the Mother Earth, for so she gives us children!"

Castle Rock was not pleased that the conversation had drifted away from her topic. She brought it carefully back. "But that cannot be why the Witch Woman is so thin. Such activity makes a woman round and beautiful, not thin and ugly."

Coconino's back stiffened, but he did not rise to the Witch Woman's defense. After all, she was thin. And—well, not beautiful.

"Can you imagine," Juan picked up, "making children with such a woman?"

"Not you, certainly," Falling Star replied. "Your legs would rub together and start a fire!"

They all laughed heartily, except Coconino. Castle Rock smiled, pleased. This was what she had hoped for. And now, Coconino, she thought, to repay you for your contempt this morning! She posed herself prettily, innocently, and said, "But there is one among you who wishes to marry this Witch Woman."

Coconino froze, his mouth full of tortilla that was suddenly too dry to chew, let alone swallow. His friends had stopped eating, too, and were staring mostly at Castle Rock, although some eyes had found their way to him. He felt a prickling at the back of his neck.

"Perhaps you heard wrong," Falling Star suggested. "Perhaps he said *a* Witch Woman, not *this* Witch Woman."

"He said *this* one," she replied definitely.

More eyes found Coconino.

"It was a joke," Juan said, laughing. "That was it. You were being teased, Castle Rock. No one marries a Witch Woman." The others murmured their agreement.

Her eyes slid slyly to Coconino now, relishing his discomfort. "Was it a joke, Coconino?"

Slowly he finished chewing his tortilla and with great difficulty forced it down his constricted throat. It would be easy to lie, and yet if he did . . .

"Be careful of such teasing," Loves the Dust advised him. "This pretty creature may take you seriously and offer her charms to another man."

It was more than Coconino could bear. His eyes flashed and his jaw tightened, his anger barely controlled. "To marry a Witch Woman," he said, "would be a great honor."

His friends stopped laughing, unsure again. "Yes, a great honor," Juan agreed. "But to marry such a bony one could be a great pain."

Their laughter was tense; Coconino cut them off. "All Witch Woman are Daughters of the Mother Earth," he declared.

"But some are a meadow," Falling Star said, "and some are a stone."

"Is a stone less than a meadow?" Coconino snapped. "You have been to the Red Rock Country; you have seen how the rocks soar above the land, how they touch the Father Sky. The hawk nests in them, and the river sings to their feet. There Mother Earth shows her strength and courage. Can you say such stone is less worthy of praise than some meadow?"

Just then the Witch Woman rose from her seat, rubbing her bare arms against the night chill. Their eyes followed her as she started up the slope toward the Village of the Ancients. "But you cannot marry her, Coconino," Falling Star protested. "Witch Women do not marry men of the People."

"That is up to the Witch Woman," he replied. "Not to fools who think that a woman's value lies in her girth." Then he strode away after the Witch Woman.

The trouble is, Coconino thought as he scrambled up the rocky slope toward the first ladder, I am just such a fool. For years I have measured every girl in the village by standards such as theirs. Though I refused to marry one, still I considered them all, burning sometimes. Burning most times, he admitted. Yet this Witch Woman does not kindle the slightest flame in me. Furthermore, I have no wish to change that.

He had pondered his dilemma all afternoon. On the pretext of rabbit hunting he had left the village alone to roam the hills to the south and west. But in truth, he had spent most of his time sitting on a rock outcropping, watching the southern horizon and begging the Mother Earth for an answer. If not this Witch Woman, then no Witch Woman. But this Witch Woman *was* no Witch Woman—at least, not the kind he had expected.

He closed his eyes and remembered her. Blond hair gleamed golden in the light as she stepped from the Flying Machine. Blue eyes sparked like jewels in her pale face, and she looked too delicate to touch. Yet how warm and sure her laugh had been, how mellow her voice! And as she had looked at the faces of the children who had stood gawking at her, a smile had radiated from within her and come to rest, finally, on him. "And what is your name?"

Aloof, alone, pretending not to care, he had stationed himself near a mesquite tree, for what was a Flying Machine? He had seen them before. And what was a Man-on-the-Mountain? None of them could hunt as well as his stepfather, Made of Stone. Such curiosity was for children, and he was almost twelve.

But when her smile had washed over him, all his pretense had vanished. She was the most beautiful creature he had ever seen, lithe and graceful as a doe, and she had asked his name. His. No one else's.

"Coconino," he had stammered. "Here, I will carry your bag for you."

Through the magical spring he had followed her like a puppy, his own mother laughing at what a good "son" the Witch Woman had. He had sweated away the long, hot summer at her feet, struggling to learn the impossible lessons, because that was what she asked of him. She shared with him her magic, the magic of marks in the dust, of charcoal on stone, and finally gave to him the keys that could unlock the mysteries of the Before Times.

Then autumn came. The nights grew chill, the harvest ended, and the village readied itself for the winter rains. On a gray, chilly morning the sound of engines whining out of the south sent arrows of sorrow stabbing through his chest. He wanted to run away to his secret place across the stream or into the hills where no one could see his tears. But she had asked him to carry her bag again.

He put on his sternest face, trying to turn it to stone, for stones did not cry. He went to her wickiup and wordlessly took the canvas bag from her. They walked in silence to the tableland above the village where the Flying Machine waited. There were official good-byes and thanks and gifts. The Witch Woman said nothing to him, but just before she stepped into the Machine, she took a cord from around her neck—the one with the blue-green bird set in silver—and placed it around his.

And then she was gone.

He touched the stone now. He had forgotten the name of the bird, but he knew its story. It had risen from its own ashes to live again, Life springing from Death, the People rising from extinction, Hope born of Despair . . .

"Witch Woman," he called softly.

The dark-haired woman ahead of him jumped and turned back, startled not only by his voice but by the fact that he had spoken to her in English. She strained to see him in the deep shadow of the cliff. They were on a rock shelf just above the second ladder, about halfway to the adobe village. The sudden dusk of the desert had descended, and it was a moment before she recognized him. "Oh, it's you," she grumbled. "Young Hercules. Where'd you learn to speak English?"

Coconino bridled. "My mother thought it fitting that I should know the language of my father," he told her; there was also that other, that golden one for whom he would have learned the language of hell itself. "And I am not Hercules," he corrected, "I am Coconino."

"You mentioned that."

"I am of the People," he said pointedly. "Hercules was Greek."

Again she was surprised. "You know about Hercules?"

"He strangled snakes," Coconino replied proudly. "It is a great story. I know many great stories."

Where in the world would he learn Greek myths? she wondered. "Did you hear them from the Mother?" she asked.

But he shook his head. "The Mother only tells the stories of the People. She does not like the others," he confided.

She studied him now in the fast-fading light: a man-boy, not unlike a dozen man-boys she knew and usually scorned on the Mountain. There was more to him, she decided, than she had first thought. This afternoon he had been only a puffed-up, swaggering hunter full of his own importance. Did he know how foolish he had looked trying to regain his feet and his dignity? And then, drawing himself up so proudly, with dirt smudged on his nose and chin and rubbing more grime onto his chest with his dusty hands.

Now he did not look foolish at all. In the deepening shadows, the angular lines of his face were dramatic and the well-muscled body commanding. Here in the twilight, away from the crowd, he was not swaggering. In fact, there was a simplicity, almost a vulnerability about him now, and her old frustration returned. Why did they try so hard to be men? Didn't they know it was these moments of betrayal, when they gave up trying to impress anyone, that so touched a woman? An older woman, anyway.

"Where did you learn the stories?" she asked.

Like a child with a secret, he tried not to smile, and he leaned toward her slightly as he whispered, "Books."

For that had been her magic, that other Witch Woman, to teach the children the baffling shapes of Letters and how to read the ancient books. But the Mother had been opposed to such magic. "We have no need of your alphabet," she had told the Witch Woman. "In time we will create our own, one that is *moh-ohnak* for the People. Tell me, what language shall they read in, these children you teach? English? Spanish? O'odam? Hopi? Apache? The language of the People has borrowed from all of these others. Where is there written a book that we can read?"

"I will write books for the children in their own language," the Witch Woman had assured her. "Besides, you need someone who can record things, someone who can set down the stories of the People, their history, their way of life for future generations. Who will do that?"

"You will," the Mother replied. "You and all the Teachers who come after you. As for the People, we will speak our heritage to our children, and they to theirs; so shall the People always learn to listen." A small smile played on the old woman's lips. "And our heritage shall grow richer with each telling, eh?"

But only Coconino had struggled to master the strange symbols; only he had learned to read the writing of the Before Times. As the Mother had foretold, there were few of the ancient books he could actually read; he was confounded in English by his limited vocabulary, in Spanish by its deviation from the spoken language of the People. But he struggled through some with the Witch Woman's help. She even transcribed some books especially for him in his native tongue, laboring over hide scrolls or clay tablets. Some still lay hidden away in his mother's wicki-up.

So now he waited for the new Witch Woman's reaction to this startling news, the news that he, Coconino, could read books. A breeze rustled the ash leaves below; a whippoorwill called softly—and the Witch Woman began to laugh. It was not laughter like a brook but like a coyote, harsh and unkind. Coconino was confused as she turned and started away toward the next ladder.

"Why do you laugh?" he demanded.

He was close enough to see the derisive sparkle in her eyes as she turned back. "You are not what I expected, Coconino."

The irony was too much for him. "Much the same could be said for you."

"Oh?" There was a definite edge to her voice. Even had she not been the victim of numerous verbal slurs in the past, she could have recognized such a poorly veiled one.

Coconino knew then that he should have kept silent, but there was no calling back the words already spoken. Instead he struggled to find some truth to elaborate that would not offend the Witch Woman. "A rock," he began, falling back on his earlier rhetoric, "is not a meadow, but both—"

"And I'm the rock, right? Thanks a lot, *chue*!" she snapped, turning on her heel.

His own anger surged, and he reached for her, not thinking. But as he spun her around to face him, the white-hot fury in her eyes blasted him like a raging desert wind, and he realized what he had done. This was a Witch Woman he held by the arms, and he quailed at his own recklessness.

Yet he did not let her go. Instead he faced those burning eyes as best he could, his momentary anger purged in their heat. If she cursed him, she cursed him, but not until he had said what he had started to say.

"But both," he continued quietly, "are Daughters of the Mother Earth, and as such they are due all honor and respect." He let go then, carefully, and backed away. The darkness was cool against his face and chest after the heat of her wrath. Somewhere across the river an owl hooted, staking out his territory, and in the distance another owl answered.

Coconino did not hear the owls as he left the stone shelf and started down the ladder. He was aware only of a heaviness in his stomach where the roasted meat would not digest. Ah, Coconino, what have you done? he asked himself. So proud to think you might marry a Witch Woman! So rash to speak of it to Castle Rock. And so foolish to suggest to the Witch Woman that she does not fulfill your dreams. It is the Mother Earth's punishment that this woman is so hard and cold and stirs not one drop of your blood, but it is your own fault, your own, if you have made an enemy of her.

What does it matter, though? he thought bitterly. If she hates me, it is only the scorn of a woman, no more than Castle Rock's or any other maiden's, for she is no Witch Woman to me. In all my lifetime there will only be one Witch Woman, and she has gone.

In eight long years Coconino had never felt so alone.

In the center of the village the drums began to sound the strong compelling beat that resounded in the bowels of the People and called them to Elvira, the ceremonial fire. Soon the dancers would begin their rhythmic retelling of the Survival, and the children would watch—as once their parents had watched—with shining eyes and open mouths. They would hear the chanting, see the dancers, and feel the story within their bodies as it melded with their bones, throbbed in their veins, and became them. The stories of the People had shaped the People as much as they had shaped the stories. Young and old alike were always called by the drums.

Coconino felt them reverberate in his chest and his loins. "You are of the People," they said. "You belong to the Mother Earth," and though he felt little like joining the crowd, still the drums touched him and he went. The solemn tones of the drums filled the empty space within him, crowded out the pain and the hurt and the disappointment.

High on the cliff face, within her house of stone, the Witch Woman did not hear the drums at first. She sat on the dirt floor in utter darkness, her arms wrapped around her knees, staring at nothing. Her anger crashed against the adobe walls in great waves and then lashed back even harder on herself. In her misery she did not reason what had triggered her anger; she only felt it engulf her, batter her, suck her deeper toward a fathomless ocean of despair. Panic seized her, and she trembled. Oh, God, don't abandon me to myself! Even I don't deserve that. Unconsciously she squeezed her eyes shut, and two small tears slipped down her cheeks. Her breath came in small, strangled sobs.

But from the close, rough walls and the hard-packed dirt floor, strength began to seep back into her. She clutched it like a floating log and forced her eyes open. Fixing them on the far wall, she willed herself to take slow, regular breaths, drinking deeply of the coolness and the dust around her. Gradually the panic was forced back, out of her body, beyond the walls of her room. Then consciously, one by one, she relaxed her muscles from her toes up to her scalp. Finally, weak but in control again, she got to her knees.

She had tossed her bag carelessly in a corner of this outer room of her two-room "apartment." Crawling to it, she rummaged through the contents and found the long-sleeved shirt she had come after, pulling it on over her leather vest.

Not what you expected, she thought sourly. No, not at all what you expected! You expected the Mother to be warm and welcoming, not hostile and suspicious. You expected the primitives to be tall and willowy, not short and squat. You expected to fit in, not feel like an alien.

She had thought the People would be not just different but better than the narrow-minded idiots of her Mountain. But were they? Would they be more charitable, more understanding, than their technological counterparts? Or had life in a harsh and unforgiving land made them harsh and unforgiving also? Would this place on which she had pinned all her hopes be, in the final analysis, "not what she expected"?

She shook herself. No. She would not surrender to pessimism. She would carve her place here, she would fit, as once she had carved her place in the machine shop on the Mountain. Below her the People stood chanting words she could not distinguish, the colorful dancers jigging and bobbing to the rhythm of the drums—drums! How long had they been playing?

With a sigh she knotted her shirttails and her resolve and ducked out the doorway, into the night.

The panorama of the night sky exploded before her, and she caught her breath. Even on her Mountain the stars did not seem this bright. Here on the cliff face she felt as if she were suspended among them, and she and her troubles were dwarfed by the immensity of the sky.

She groped her way through the Gatehouse and down one last level to emerge into the entry courtyard. There she stopped and gazed once more at the brilliant points of light that bedizened the heavens. Somewhere out there circling those specks of light, she knew, were other worlds, worlds to which the rest of humankind had fled and taken their culture, their civilization, their medicine . . . Cowards, she called to them. Cowards! We survived. It wasn't easy, but we survived. You could at least come back to check. Why, in five hundred years, did you never bother to check?

Turning her back to her deserters, the Witch Woman eased herself over the short wall and started to back down the ladder. There she stopped, her foot poised on the first rung. This was not the way the People descended. Cautiously she turned herself so that she faced out once more into the occupied heavens. This time she really was suspended, clinging like an insect to a twig, caught between heaven and earth. If I fall, she begged her distant cousins, will you catch me? For a moment she was too terrified to move.

Then she felt the radiant heat of the sun-warmed cliff at her back. Knowing it was there put strength back into her limbs, and she groped carefully with her foot for the next rung. No need for anyone to catch her. In time, she promised herself, she would make this work. She would master this technique and all the others. In time.

CHAPTER THREE

Clayton Winthrop sat in the kitchen of his sprawling ranch-style house on Juno, sipping his morning coffee and reading the news. Friends thought it odd that a spacecraft captain should want such a large, rambling estate on a backwater farm planet; wouldn't he rather have a tidy apartment near a major spaceport?

Clayton stretched luxuriously and slumped his long frame in a boyish fashion, hooking one knee over the arm of the chair. The pose was incongruous with his dignified features, the creases of fifty-eight years that lined his face and heightened a look of wisdom. His dark hair, graying nicely at the temples, was as smooth and neat as the work smock he wore, and he had already shaved. But he was off today, and he was relaxing in a way few of his friends ever saw.

His consumption of the news was another idiosyncrasy others found hard to understand. Instead of picking up network transmissions or enjoying dramatic re-creations, Clayton preferred to read. One whole wall of the kitchen was a screen, and from the controls in the table he could flip through page after electronic page, skimming through each article, lingering over those which interested him. The technique was called "random viewing," and even his wife shook her head over it.

Suddenly a light began flashing over one of the articles, and Clayton straightened up. He had programmed the light to cue him when articles on certain subjects appeared, just to make sure he didn't miss one in his leisurely perusal. He isolated and enlarged the piece—a short notice with a modest headline—and saw the phrase that had triggered his pointer: TERRAN RESEARCH COALITION.

Clayton was a notorious Terraphile. He called his estate Terra

28

Firma, and he was a frequent visitor to the Earth Room of the Interplanetary Museum of Art on Argo. His prize possession was a battery-operated device called a calculator that dated back to before the Evacuation. Never mind that no batteries existed; he understood the concept behind them and hoped one day, when he retired, to turn his attention to the manufacture of replicas that would power his antique.

Nor was he alone in his fascination with Terran artifacts. People on the colonial planets had not forgotten about Earth; it was just that life had gone on without it for so long . . . In the beginning there had been great curiosity about what had happened to the birthplace of humankind. Reports had come from the research team left behind, relayed from a warp terminal on Earth's moon, for the first five years. People wept when they read them, realizing that their home planet was dying; so, too, was the valiant research team. Each message seemed bleaker than the ones before: bitter cold, razor winds, and nothing would grow, not even in their hydroponic gardens. Equipment failed; crops failed; and finally, the transmissions failed.

Someone should have gone back for them, Clayton knew, to find out why. But then, it was too easy to guess why. Besides, the newly colonized planets had troubles of their own. Of those governments which had survived the natural calamities of Earth, few had survived the transfer to new worlds. New governments for new situations, people said. It took sixty years for internal strife to die down, another hundred to settle boundary disputes. By then Earth and its problems had faded into legend.

Then one day, nearly ten years ago, on the outer fringes of the Cyrus system, an old-style radio message had been picked up. It was fragmentary, garbled, its origin unknown, but it seemed to say, "Out of the depths I cry to Thee . . ."

Most critics dismissed it as an elaborate hoax. Some thought it must be a robot transmission, repeating an archaic plea long after its makers had expired. But there were some who thought it worth investigation: archaeologists, historians, romantics . . .

Clayton was one of the romantics.

For ten years now the Terran Research Coalition had been trying to scrape up financial support. Governments and industry were not interested. What could Earth offer that anyone would want? In the Cyrus and DeBane systems there was land in abundance, natural resources to be squandered once more. Technology, although it had backslid during the years of unrest and civil strife, had advanced to a state far beyond anything represented by the relics of Earth. There was simply no hope of economic gain from such an expedition.

So the project had to be funded with donations. Clayton had wanted to invest, but before he could talk his wife into it, there had been a scandal: fraud, embezzlement, nasty tax complications. A practical man, Clayton had opted to sit back and watch; an impatient man, he had gone on to other projects.

But now here was this notice: TERRAN RESEARCH COALITION SEEKS EXPERIENCED CREW FOR EXPEDITION TO EARTH. There was an address; Clayton called it and requested more information. He was just signing off when Jacqueline walked in.

She was lugging a basket of clean laundry. "Maid's day off?" he teased. Jacqueline shot him a dark look; for the few days each month they actually inhabited their gracious home, she patently refused to hire domestic help. Clayton suspected that in a perverse way she enjoyed the menial chores. Here in the backwoods, the woman who ordered orderlies and controlled catastrophes could lose herself in the mindless work of feeding soiled clothing into a scrub chute.

Jacqueline plopped the basket on the table and straightened up, hands supporting her stiff lower back. She was five years older than Clayton, and though her face was somewhat smoother, her neck showed the difference. Loose skin was beginning to soften a jaw that had always been square and hard. Her hair, drawn back in an efficient bun, had gone completely white, but the eyes still gleamed a dangerous blue. She fastened them on the screen, where the TRC article was still isolated. "Hrmph. They still around?" was her gruff comment. Then she picked up her basket and started for the bedroom.

Clayton followed her, his cup of coffee still in hand. "Rumor has it Jamis did their legal work. When he was through, the government owed *them* money."

She snorted. "Not as much as they owed Jamis."

"Well, they must have gotten money from somewhere," he told her. "They're looking for a crew." A wicked grin stole across his face. "Want to sign up?"

Jacqueline dropped the basket on their bed and turned to face him, hands on hips. Dressed in a straight-cut jumpsuit, she was imposing, for although she was not tall, she was big-boned. She had struck that same stance the day he had met her: hard-bitten, cynical, tough as nails. He hadn't believed it then, either.

"A *crew*!" she retorted. "That will give new meaning to the phrase 'ship of fools.' "

Clayton laughed and slipped his arms around her, being careful not to spill his coffee. "Ah, yes, all the great fools of history," he chided. "Columbus, Einstein, Yuko, Hamad-ja . . ."

"Edison," she murmured, correcting the familiar litany as she returned his embrace. "You left out Edison. 'Columbus, *Edison*, Einstein, Yuko . . .' "

Beside the bed a panel chimed, and Clayton reluctantly withdrew his arms. "Mazie: show," he called firmly, and the panel cleared to become a screen. It was the information he had requested from the Terran Research Coalition.

"Mazie: page, speed three." A page of information appeared; in a moment it was replaced by another. "Mazie: hold. Hm." His brow furrowed as he glanced through the data, noting the names of officers, consultants, underwriters. "Interesting. Jamis has something to do with it. He's listed as one of the directors. Not like him to invest in a not-for-profit venture." He looked up, a wry smile quirking his lips. "Do you suppose he's a Terraphile, too?"

Jacqueline was stacking clothing neatly in their drawers. "Could be; they turn up in the strangest places."

"Mazie: go." New information welled up on the screen, and Clayton let out a low whistle. "That's an ambitious timeline."

"What?"

"They intend to select crew over the next three weeks and leave Argo in six months."

Jacqueline closed the drawer she had just filled and leaned back against the dresser. Her eyes were not sharp now as she studied her husband. Twenty-eight years of command sat well on him; his graceful posture capitalized on each inch of his six-foot frame, making him seem taller than he was. He did not look young, he simply looked fine. Very fine. Jacqueline shook her head slightly. "It's a rush job, Clay," she said gently, her voice rich and mellow and very serious. "Rush jobs are sloppy."

Clayton arched an eyebrow. "They've had ten years to plan; I'd hardly call that a rush job."

"But for what?" Her brow was furrowed with genuine concern. "What do they expect to find back there?" She was a woman who hated waste in all its forms.

He shrugged. "People?"

"If there are, they've done fine without us so far."

Clayton shook his head. "This is not for them, Jacqueline, I know that." He settled back on the arm of a chair near the panel, his cup still in one hand, the large master bed separating them. The distance between them had never mattered; they were accustomed to communicating over light-years. "They're where we came from, Jackie. And they're what we could be, if we had to. They're a connection to our past and a, a—" He groped for the right word. "An affirmation of our essence. *Did* they live? And how? What is it in the human race that makes us all survivors?"

Jacqueline exhaled slowly and collapsed her basket, folding it deftly into a three-inch cube, which she tossed in a drawer. "It's arrogance, Clayton," she told him. "We never know when we're licked. Look at my patients: living when they've no right to. Look at the Terran Research Coalition: they've fleeced money from gullible investors to make a costly voyage to a dead planet, when it can only end in disappointment—and possibly disaster. But they'll go, Clayton. They'll go anyway. Because we never know when to quit."

For a moment they sat in silence, hearing only the comforting whisper of the environmental control unit. Clayton started to sip at his coffee, but it was cold. He hated cold coffee. So he only stared into the murky liquid and wondered about those faraway people who might have sent out a message four hundred years before. Out of the depths I cry to Thee . . .

Finally Jacqueline rose, stretched, and turned to begin straightening the holograph stands on the dresser behind her. There was one of Clayton in his dress uniform from his service days; another of Chelsea and Cin at ages five and seven on Shetland ponies; and of course, Chelsea's high school graduation holo. "Mazie: interrupt. Letter, to Arthur Petite, AAJ Enterprises, Ltd. Message: Dear Art, regret Captain Winthrop and I must cancel contract, thirty days' notice hereby given. Thanks for ten years. Sincerely, J. E. Winthrop. Mazie: Send."

Clayton looked up incredulously. "Jacqueline—did you just quit our jobs?"

"You wanted to retire anyway."

He was dumbfounded. This was a perfect contract, both of them on the same ship, a straight-dealing company, excellent benefits. "But we're going to the DeBane system in three weeks," he protested, "I was going to look up Heinrich—"

"DeBane system, my left cheek," she grumbled. "You know as well as I do we're going to Earth."

*   *   *

The planet of Argo boasted the largest and finest museum anywhere in the colonial worlds. In his office in the Interplanetary Museum of Art, Oswald Dillon sat at his antique desk, admiring the rich polished wood that seemed to glow from within. It was oak, brought from Earth before the Evacuation had begun, and was some seven centuries old. The golden tones were almost sensuous in their beauty, and his face reflected his pleasure in it. The woman across from him recognized the look and allowed him a moment to indulge in his appreciation. Then she cleared her throat.

Dillon looked up. He was a dapper man with steel-gray hair and a mysterious half smile. As well designed and carefully groomed as one of his art treasures, he gave the impression of being always amused with something or someone.

"Your SDI, sir," she began. "You asked me to let you know—"

He brushed her introduction off with an impatient but still bemused gesture, as though it amused him that she thought she had to explain why she had come. This was her job, the selected dissemination of information: SDI. It was why he had hired her. She hoped.

"The Terran Research Coalition has advertised for a crew. They have an embarkation date in six months."

Abruptly Dillon's eyes narrowed, and the half smile dropped from his face. He steepled his fingers, and his attention faded into deep thought. The woman waited patiently for his return.

"Is Carmine Ferro still on their board?" he asked finally.

"Yes, sir."

"What major contributions have they received in the last six weeks?"

The woman crossed to an info-unit and tapped its keys. It was faster for her than speaking, since she could jump past the layers of programming necessary for parsing human speech and translating it into something the machine understood. "The Noah Isaacson Estate in its entirety, Misha Trablinski for six million, Francoise—"

Again he cut her off with a gentle wave of his hand. "Thank you, I'll take care of it."

She stopped, deflated, as she always felt deflated when he dismissed her. It was as though her service were—flotsam. Something that had washed up on the beach, to be sifted through carefully and then left to bleach in the sun. To her, information was exciting: finding useful items was like finding gold. To Dillon, it was part of life. He had built his extensive empire on information, and he trod its gold now like grains of sand.

But even as she turned to go, he rose from his oaken desk and crossed to intercept her. "How long have you been with us now, Camilla?" he inquired politely.

"About five months, sir." She suspected he knew that very well.

"Have you seen our Earth Room yet?" he asked in that same polite, carefully controlled tone.

Camilla was thirty-two; she had spent ten years in research jobs and had been exposed to a variety of subject areas, but this was her first encounter with art. She knew there was work waiting on her desk, but if Dillon was offering . . . "No, I haven't, sir," she replied.

"I think you'll have a greater appreciation for your work," he suggested, "if you become acquainted with some Terran creations." He smiled and gestured for her to precede him out of the office.

There were no enclosed elevators in the Museum; every conveyance was open to the sights, sounds, and smells of the collection. As they rode up seven floors, they traversed the height of a sculpture by Sotwan, bathed in the light and fragrance of a Pearl Jhetti, and experienced a re-creation of a Mozart symphony. By the time they stepped off in the Gallery Galactic, Camilla felt a bit giddy. Dillon took her arm gently and escorted her toward the archway whose sign declared EARTH ROOM.

Inside the great exhibit hall was the most impressive collection of Terran art and artifacts in all the colonial planets. The *Mona Lisa* hung in an environmentally controlled display case; the *Pietà* stood on a dais near the center of the room; a perfectly preserved 1997 Mercedes-Benz glistened toward the back. They entered to strains of *Also Sprach Zarathustra*, but as they circled the perimeter, Camilla recognized bits of *Das Rheingold* near the Frankenweil collection and *Les Miserables* as they passed the Picasso display.

The Evacuation Era Exhibit was at the very rear of the hall, and it was to this exhibit that Dillon guided her. The audio-olfactory recordings of Genesis accompanied several of the foam sculptures and plastic castings that perched like giant chess pieces on their tiered stands. Camilla stopped, gawking, in front of one gleaming white lump that depicted a gaunt child in the jaws of an eyeless canine. "Frightening, isn't it?" Dillon murmured. "And yet fascinating. Humanity's worst nightmare. It's a theme that dominates the work of the period. I have a Muñoz in my portico that shows a mother eating her own child. Quite ghastly, but so passionate! So passionate!"

Camilla turned to look at her employer. It was the most emotion she had ever heard from him. "You have a Muñoz?" she asked. "At home? Aren't they quite rare?"

His bemused expression returned. "Yes, quite. There are only three in existence; I own them all. Along with two first editions of Lewis Carroll and nine of the thirteen M'Burras known to have survived. By the end of the year I hope to make it ten."

Camilla was suitably impressed. "And they are all here?" she asked. "In the Museum?"

Dillon contemplated the work before him, but he was thinking of his palatial estate high in the mountains above the city. It was neo-Grecian, with porticoes and alcoves and acres of gardens. "No," he said softly. "No, not all."

They strolled from display to display, Camilla enrapt in the dramatic visuals, the subtly seductive scents and sounds. She reminded Dillon of the fine oak desk; her hair was the same golden color, her skin and nails gleamed in the same polished way. He admired the curve of her neck, the graceful arch of her back, the smooth, supple way she moved. He had selected her carefully from among many candidates, but it was not until this moment that he knew he had chosen correctly. When she gazed on these expressions of human suffering and was moved, her allure took on the depth he craved. The difference between a beautiful object and a work of art, he mused, was the latter's ability to express emotion.

"Consider it part of your duties to come here often," he told her. "Immerse yourself in the culture of our Terran ancestors. And let me know every piece, every particle of information you can extract on the Terran Research Coalition."

"Mother, you're not!" Chelsea Winthrop exclaimed, horrified. She had come home for midterm vacation, expecting to do some horseback riding and atmospheric flying and perhaps warp over to Newamerica City to visit John. Life at Terra Firma was always lazy, comfortable, like stepping off a moving conveyor to stand motionless for a time. She had not expected this bombshell.

Jacqueline flicked the sheet across the bed to her daughter, and together they tucked it into place. "I am," she replied briskly. "Why shouldn't I?"

"Because it's crazy!"

"So is your father," Jacqueline responded.

"Oh, now, don't go blaming this on Dad," Chelsea protested. "You could stop him if you wanted to, and you know it."

"I suppose I could," Jacqueline admitted, shaking out a blanket with a practiced hand. A quick snap sent the material floating into place and Chelsea's long hair swirling in the draft. "I could also replace a man's eye with a golf ball; why would I want to do that?"

Chelsea felt like stamping her foot; Jacqueline's similes had confounded her all her twenty-one years, and they were never fair. But she was never able to refute them, either. So she tried a new tack. "Have you told Cincinnati yet?"

The hesitation in Jacqueline's deft motions was painful to see. Her oldest child—named for the ancestral city of the Winthrops—had been a charmer from the day he was born, blessed with his father's smile and his mother's capacity for love. It had been a bitter pill for Jacqueline that his brain had not been fully developed and he was mentally deficient. "Cincinnati knows we go away for long trips," she said. "To him this is just another long trip."

"Oh, great, and if you don't come back, I get to tell him what happened?" Chelsea knew she was hurting her mother, but it seemed the only weapon she had.

"This venture is not dangerous," Jacqueline said grimly. "Foolish but not dangerous. It's no different than warping over to Regus or Curio."

"Right, and that's why you have to have five months of training."

Jacqueline flipped a pillowcase at her daughter. "It's a research mission, Chelsea. It takes planning." With a pillow tucked under her chin she shook out another pillowcase herself and began to fight the pillow into it.

"Oh, Mother, let me," Chelsea groused, snatching the pillow away from her. "You never did have the knack."

Jacqueline watched as her daughter slid the case easily over the pillow. She was an attractive girl; not beautiful, for she had inherited Jacqueline's square chin and high forehead, but she was fresh and exuberant, with long blond hair curled in thick masses. The curl was artificial, of course. Cin's hair was naturally wavy and dark, like Clay's. A wistful smile brushed Jacqueline's lips. "Your brother has a girlfriend."

Chelsea looked out of the corner of her eye as she finished with the pillow. "Only one?" she asked, giving the pillow a last shake. "Last Christmas he was talking about three or four. They flock to him; he's the only one in that place who dresses with any style."

"No, I mean a sort of serious one. She lives in his building at the Center."

"Uh oh, watch out for Cin," Chelsea warned, tossing the pillow into place on the bed. "She'll be living in his apartment before long."

Jacqueline scowled. "They don't allow that, Chelsea. He has to be independent; it's one of the rules." Jacqueline watched as Chelsea swung her bulging suitcase easily onto the newly made bed. "Unless he gets married."

Chelsea stopped with her hand on the latch. "You think he might?" she asked in surprise. Jacqueline only shrugged. "Wow, that's a thought." Chelsea chewed on that as she keyed the lock and the suitcase sprang open. "He's always been such a heartbreaker, it's hard to imagine him . . ." She sat down on the bed suddenly.

A sardonic smile slid across Jacqueline's face as she watched her daughter. "First time, isn't it?" she asked.

Chelsea looked up blankly. "First time for what?"

"First time you realized the people you love evolve. Especially when you're not there."

But Chelsea shook her head. "No, it's not the first time," she responded. "But this is such a good thing, and I still feel . . ."

"Cheated?"

Again she shook her head. "Just left out. Really left out."

"Ah." Jacqueline nodded wisely. "Life goes on whether we're there or not."

"Will you miss my graduation?" Chelsea pouted.

"Not for worlds."

"Bring Cin?"

"He wouldn't miss it, either."

"And his girl?"

Jacqueline laughed. "If he still has the same one. You know your brother."

Suddenly they were hugging, tears slipping down both their faces. "Don't stay away long, Mom, okay?" Chelsea asked.

"Oh, Chelsea," her mother sighed, "not nearly as long as you will."

In his office in the Museum, Dillon smiled and pushed a plain white envelope across his desk, watching his visitor with a beneficent smile.

On the other side of the desk an obsequious little ferret of a man with a round face and a great deal of perspiration on his bald head reached uncertainly for the envelope. Carmine Ferro had been on the board of the Terran Research Coalition for ten years, and powerful people like Dillon made him very nervous. They could be the making or the breaking of this venture. He peeked inside. "Oh, my," he squeaked, quite taken aback by the amount on the draft. "Oh, my, Mr. Dillon. If I had known . . . the media . . ."

The dapper man waved this off graciously. "The Earth venture is, of course, of great interest to me."

"Yes, of course," Ferro agreed. "What with your interest in Terran art, I can see where— What's this?" he asked as he fished a small piece of paper from the envelope."

"Just a name," Dillon assured him. "And a rank. Among the applicants for berths on this venture you may come across that name. The rank is . . . a suggestion."

"Oh. Oh!" exclaimed Ferro as the light dawned. "Of course. Yes, I understand." Spacecraft were not cheap; crew members, however, were a dime a dozen. They had been flooded with qualified applicants. "Your suggestions are valued. Highly valued."

Dillon only smiled and pointed to the door.

CHAPTER FOUR

While the Witch Woman sat in her stone house, fighting off her panic and despair, Coconino danced with the others. Not as one of the feature dancers with costume and headdress decked in ribbons and feathers but as one of the People. Eyes closed, he felt the rhythms pulsing up from the ground through the soles of his feet, seeing the feature dancers in his mind, becoming one with them and with the legend they told. "Long ago, at the beginning of the Time That Is, the People stood on the edge of the world . . ." His voice had joined the others in chanting the story, phrase by phrase, as he slipped away from this place and stood with his ancestors on a rain-slashed hill, searching for shelter from the torrential storm. He was Alfonso, He With Faith; he was Chico, the Unbeliever. He was Ernestina, wife of Alfonso, She Who Also Had Faith; he was Tanya, the Child Who Died Anyway. One by one they were named and remembered as the People moved to the rhythms of the Earth Drums.

"Then the Mother Earth spoke to Him With Faith and told him of the Village below his feet. 'Aiiee' laughed the Unbeliever. 'There is no village in the mountain. There is only water, water, and you will be washed away.' "

Beat by beat they stamped out Alfonso's daring venture: lowering himself over the edge of the cliff on a rope during the wild rainstorm to discover the Village of the Ancients. Coconino could feel the rain whipping him, feel himself suspended on the slippery rope, eyes searching through the veil of water to see what he knew must be there. He felt the elation of the Survivors as they touched their feet to the solid roofs of the third level and slid inside the houses to welcome respite. He stood with them, was one of them, on the following morning as they gazed out from the walls of their fortress and praised the Mother Earth for their deliverance . . .

The last note of the chant echoed away, and still the People stood, caught in their trance. Children moved first; then slowly their elders began to stir, to come back from their time voyage to stand again on the hard-packed earth of their village, the flames of the Elvira crackling and throwing weird shadows across them.

Coconino was the last to open his eyes. He felt renewed, infused with the spirit of the Mother Earth. He had no problems now; there was no emptiness within him, no longing. He stood motionless, trying to preserve the feeling as long as possible.

But they were calling his name. They wanted a story, a story of the People, a story of his hunt to catch the mule deer.

"I will tell you a story," he agreed, moving closer to the fire, and the People were glad. Like his mother, Two Moons, Coconino was a good storyteller. "I will tell you of this hunt and of the strange and wondrous thing I saw."

The Witch Woman joined the fringes of the crowd as the story began. It was a moment before she recognized the speaker, but when she did, she pushed a little closer. His voice was rich and resonant, and it seemed to reverberate through her chest like the call of a puma through a mountain canyon. Macho hunter, she thought at first. Look at him eating up their attention. But then she saw the enrapt faces of his listeners, and she listened, too.

". . . rocks that flame like the sunset," he was saying. "Great giants that sweep the sky with their fingertips to chase the clouds away." Well, he could talk, she'd give him that. And the firelight on his face—she shook herself. Don't get hungry for a young one like that, she warned herself. Among his people he may be pushing middle age, but by your standards he's still a cub. What does he know of feelings, of the way people deal with each other, of mind games—

". . . it sprang from its roots deep in the Mother Earth, stretching upward, ever upward. A breeze whispered to us of eagles at its top, and the rock itself called us. So we laid our hands upon the living soil and began to climb."

Oh, sure you did, she thought, having recognized his description of the river canyon to the northwest. I've flown over that canyon, I've seen those buttes. You couldn't possibly climb up their faces.

Then she glanced back at the mud houses plastered against the cliff wall. Or could you?

". . . and saw what had called my name. His brown eyes were full of knowledge, his head proud, and he nodded to me, saying, 'You are brother to me, Coconino. You are brother—to Tala.' "

A ripple ran through the crowd, and eyes widened in amazement. The Witch Woman was confused. What was Tala? A bird? A mountain lion? A snake? She racked her brain but could not remember ever hearing the word. A glance at Gonzales told her he did not know, either, and he had spent far more time than she studying their culture and the peculiarities in their dialect.

"He watched me as a coyote would, curious but unafraid. His body was powerful and well muscled, like that of a fine ram, but his fur was sleek like a deer's. He was red, the color of the rock when it is dappled with sunlight, and he had shining black hooves and a black nose. His shoulders and neck were covered with thick folds of skin, darker than the rest of him, as though his strength rode upon him like a magic serape." Thick folds of darker skin . . . the back of the Witch Woman's neck began to prickle. ". . . larger than any two mule deer or even the Great Antelope of the Black Lands. His eyes stood out from his head, and upon his brow he wore the single horn—"

She jumped. My God, she thought, he's talking about— No, it can't be. It's some legend they've concocted from pictures, and he's making this up to impress his friends.

"Did you, too, see Tala?" the Mother asked Juan.

"I saw—something," Juan replied unhappily. "But it was too far away by then."

Ha! There, you see? Liar. Liar, liar—

Suddenly Coconino's eyes caught hers, and the Witch Woman realized she had pushed her way to the very front of the crowd. Liar, liar! her thoughts sang, but they were not the eyes of a liar. A knowledge that welled up from her toes through her entire body told her that Coconino, at least, truly believed what he had seen.

The young man read the accusation in her face, and all his will came to bear on her, a will strengthened and focused by the Mother Earth. *I have seen what I have seen, Witch Woman,* he thought fiercely. *Not your disbelief, nor Juan's, nor even that of the Mother can change the truth of it. I have seen Tala. He showed himself to me.*

"Then what?" Falling Star prompted.

Coconino looked back at his brother-in-law. *Yes, he believes,* Coconino thought. *And Once a Wolf, and Pedro, and Twisted*

Branch. They all believed. Juan wants to believe. And the
Mother . . .

The old woman was watching him carefully, weighing him.
She had the power to dismiss his story and his credibility or to
accept them. But now Coconino was unconcerned, for the challenge of the Witch Woman had steeled him. Let others think
what they might, he knew the truth of his story. He turned to
answer Falling Star.

"Then what, indeed?" Coconino echoed with a trace of irony.
"Once one has looked into the face of Tala, what can follow?"

"Good hunting!" Juan chimed in, and the crowd laughed.
Even Coconino smiled. Then the Mother spoke.

"From your birth, Coconino, the Mother Earth has favored
you," she said. "Never forget that you are in her special grace.
And never forget that you are of the People." With a sweeping
gesture she began a chant of praise to the Mother Earth.

Coconino slipped quietly away from the fire, vindicated.

Heart pounding, Castle Rock watched him go, proud and
handsome in the firelight. Ah, my love! she thought. In all the
village there is no one like you! Perhaps in all of the Time That
Is there never has been. You must have a wife and children.
They will be a great blessing to the People, like their father. Yes,
you must have a wife to bear you strong, beautiful children, to
love you and gladden your heart—

Her brow furrowed as she watched the Witch Woman turn and
leave the fire also. What kind of children could she give him?
Skinny, ugly children who would sicken and die. Or children
with strange magic, perverted magic. She was so thin, perhaps
she could not bear children at all, and all his seed would be
wasted.

To say nothing of his smile.

Quickly Castle Rock detached herself from the crowd and
followed the Witch Woman. Yes, the skinny woman was going
after Coconino. What if she cast a spell on him? Perhaps she
already had, and that was why he'd said—but no. No, the look
on his face when he'd first seen the Witch Woman told Castle
Rock there was no spell. Not yet. And someone must see that
there never was. Who better than the maiden who loved him
dearly?

Castle Rock hurried her steps and called her smile into place,
the smile she always used on her parents when she wanted some-

thing. "Witch Woman," she called. "Excuse me, Witch Woman, may I speak with you?"

"Coconino is the best storyteller in our village."

Corn Hair, too, had hurried her steps, but to catch Coconino. She shifted her two-year-old in her arms; the boy did not awaken.

"Ah, the mighty hunter has run his quarry down," Coconino observed, touching the child's hair.

"His brother might do likewise," she teased, "were it not that a certain hunter keeps him agog with tales of red rocks and living legends."

Coconino grinned, and they walked on together.

"Oh, Coconino," she sighed happily, "when I hear you speak, I feel as if I am really there, amid the towering cliffs, or hearing the wind sing through the tall pines. Truly you have a marvelous gift."

"The Mother Earth blesses each with a gift of some kind," he replied.

"Oh? And what is mine, I'd like to know."

He detected the trace of melancholy in her irony, and it saddened him. "Yours are too many to number," he told her honestly.

"Flatterer!" she accused, but the melancholy was gone and Coconino was glad he had said it, hoped that she believed it. "Perhaps," Corn Hair suggested, "my gift is putting up with your teasing."

"It used to be." Privately he thought, Perhaps it is putting up with a worthless husband. To her he said, "Perhaps it is raising two fine, strong sons who will be a credit to the People. And to their mother."

In the pale starlight her face seemed to shine a little more. "More likely my gift is not going crazy while they grow!" she replied.

"See?" he jested back. "So many gifts you have."

"Yes. So many." But her voice was sad now. "Too bad choosing a good husband was not one of them."

Coconino swallowed. It was not like her to make such a comment. Always she made the best of things, looked for the good in others, especially in Lame Rabbit. Always she hid her pain—this was not like her at all.

And almost immediately her gentle good humor returned.

"My mother always said my smile was my gift from the Mother Earth," she said, showing it off for him.

They had stopped in front of her wickiup, where the faint light of her cook fire cast its glow on her face. "So it is," Coconino agreed. "And so is your hair." He touched a strand of the blond, silky hair. Stop! a voice warned him. You tread dangerous ground. This is spring, and that is another man's wife. But his compliments were so welcome, he could see it in her face. All she wanted was kind words. Words he could give her, words in plenty. "And your eyes—"

"Ah, Coconino," she sighed sadly, "but my eyes are not blue."

No. Not blue. And he had teased her once as she had fussed and tried to look just right for the coming of a new Man-on-the-Mountain, that if only she had blue eyes, he would marry her himself. If she only had blue eyes.

Fool, Coconino, had chided. Would you have married her even then? For you were so sure that you would win a Witch Woman.

"Hey, Hercules!"

Coconino jumped, startled by the Witch Woman's harsh voice and disconcerted at being found in a private moment with Corn Hair. He drew his hand back quickly and turned to see the Witch Woman storming up to him, Castle Rock trailing behind.

Her eyes were living coals as she planted herself in front of them. "The *chiquilla* here tells me an interesting story," she snarled, jerking her head toward Castle Rock. "Something about you bragging to your friends you were going to marry the new Witch Woman."

Coconino's stomach rose to his throat and stuck there.

"Is that true?" she demanded.

Corn hair ducked quickly into the wickiup with her child. Coconino tried to swallow, but his mouth was too dry. "I only said—that it would be an honor for any man, and . . ."

"But by the river, Coconino," Castle Rock spoke up in her most innocent voice, "did you not say you would marry this Witch Woman?"

Ah, Castle Rock, for what you have done to me this day I should like to stake you to a honey tree and wait for the bees to come home. "I only meant that—"

The Witch Woman exploded in a series of epithets he had never heard before but whose meaning he could well guess. "Listen, *chue!*" she roared. "Let's get one thing straight right now. I'm no one's prize, I'm no one's property, and I'm no one's Chosen Companion. I'm a Witch Woman, *comprende?* That means I'm forbidden fruit to you and every other horny jackass in this village. Is that clear?''

She stalked off. Coconino watched her go, once more feeling the night cool in the wake of her wrath. Then he turned burning eyes on Castle Rock.

"I'm so sorry, Coconino," she apologized with false contrition. "I thought when you went to her earlier, in the Village of the Ancients, that you had spoken your heart." He took a menacing step toward her, and she faded back. "After all, it is a place of marriages, is it not? Why else did she choose to live there, if not to wait for a husband?" He took another step, and she prepared for flight. "And so fine a hunter as yourself deserves such a sweet-tempered wife—"

He lunged, and she fled back toward the center of the village, laughing. At least, he thought bitterly, she had not cornered him in front of his friends again. That would have been a humiliation beyond bearing.

Inside her wickiup Corn Hair had knelt where she could see the stupid girl, but neither of them could see her. When Castle Rock had gone, she meant to come out, only to touch Coconino's arm and say nothing, but a small noise stopped her. Across the way Juan's wife, Cactus Flower, was just coming out of her wickiup.

Corn Hair wanted to weep. Cactus Flower was a pleasant, round woman with two chins, merry eyes, and quite possibly the loosest tongue in the village. She could not have helped but overhear the Witch Woman's verbal scourging. By tomorrow the whole village would have heard as well, with suitable embellishment. Oh, don't look up, Coconino, don't know, don't—

But the young man turned at the noise, and his eyes met Cactus Flower's across the path. Corn Hair wanted to shriek at the unfairness of this twist of fate. Mother Earth, could you not have stopped her ears? Was this humiliation necessary?

Then Coconino stepped back and melted silently into the darkness.

"Fool, Coconino. See what comes of pride."

On the far bank of the stream there was a spot where, as a child, Coconino had gone with his dreams and disappointments. He had found it again now, in a stand of willows, a place that in the brightness of day was well shaded and with the night became

invisible. The powdery earth where he dropped his weary frame
had been cleared of stones during his adolescent visits. Here he
had brought his coveted books, here he had wept when the other
Witch Woman had left. Here he had first dreamed of the coming
of the new Witch Woman, the one who would be his, who would
never leave him but keep his wickiup and bear his children—
blond children—

"Fool!" he cursed himself. "Fool, fool—"

"Coconino?"

He froze, knowing the intruder could not see him. Just keep
still and she will go away, go away . . .

Corn Hair stood on the bank of the creek, the faint starlight
illuminating her form, edging her forehead and cheek in silver.
The short skirt knotted at her waist seemed almost iridescent in
the night. She had slipped a light jacket on against the night
chill, but it was not fastened, and underneath her blouse was
nothing more than a strip of soft cotton knotted between her
breasts. He wished that she would only stand there, starlight and
shadows, a slender form to desire but never touch.

"Coconino, please, I know you are here somewhere," she
whispered. "Don't hide from me." She moved several steps,
her thigh flashing through the slit in her skirt.

Hide from you? he thought. Hide from her, hide from the
village, hide from myself—why not from you? You whom I
want so much at this moment, you whom I can never have . . .

"What do you want?" he growled.

She jumped, as much from his unexpected closeness as from
the tone of his voice. But she composed herself, turning toward
the darkness of the willow grove, willing herself to pick him out
from among the shadows. "I knew you would be here," she said
softly. "This was always where you came to escape the world,
to sink into yourself."

Slowly he stood up so that she could make out his form, still
only a shadow among shadows. "If you know this is a place for
aloneness," he said less harshly, "why not leave me alone in
it?"

Her chin came up. Boldly she took two steps into the grove,
into the deeper darkness that the starlight did not pierce. Though
she was closer, he could not see her as well. But he could feel
her. "Aloneness is not what you need this night."

His blood surged. Slowly he took a deep breath and tried to
calm his pounding heart. "We are not children," he told her.

"For a man and a woman to be together so—the Mother would frown on this."

"The Mother does not know of it." She glided another step toward him, so close now that he could feel the warmth of her body only inches away from his. "Nor will she. No one saw me come. My children are asleep, and my husband is gone. Everyone else is still gathered at the ceremonial fire."

Music drifted across the stream, faint voices and the throbbing of the drums that Coconino could feel in his loins. She was no child and no fool; she did not come to him in innocence. Yet he hesitated. "The Way of the People is wise—" he began.

But she silenced him with a finger on his lips. "The Way of the People is cautious in the making of children," she replied. "There will be no children made this night, for Lame Rabbit's child already sleeps within me."

The whole willow grove seemed to sigh then and draw closer around them. As their bodies melted together, the night birds and the insects wove a sweet cocoon of sound around them, and the incense of blossoms drifted through the trees. All the yearning, all the longing that Coconino had known for season upon season rose up within him, and he loved her urgently, recklessly, and in great haste. But in the great calm that followed she came to him again, gently, her body warm with its own kindled fire.

This time he stopped to savor her touch. He felt her body respond to his caress as she had to his compliments, felt his own desire return like the trickle of a stream after a dry winter, growing and swelling with each moment. Her lips were warm, her hands gentle, and he found at last the tenderness he had craved. Gratefully he drew her again to his dusty bed.

There the Mother Earth hid them, cushioned them in her fragrant bower, cloaked with her soft mantle of darkness.

The Witch Woman stood on the sun-drenched retaining wall at the entrance to the Village of the Ancients, just above the ladder. She had been standing there for half an hour, willing away any vestige of vertigo, determined to be as easy and confident on those heights as the People. But she had not been there all morning. No, indeed she had not.

She had joined the group of women in the village below who were processing the remainder of the mule deer. She was eager to learn how they dried the meat, cured the hides, used the sinew and the bones and the antlers. It was not long, however, before she noticed them whispering and casting looks her way. At first she thought it was curiosity, shyness. But she could hear smothered giggles, see dancing eyes.

They were laughing at her.

She walked up to two middle-aged women who were hanging strips of meat on a rack over a smoky fire. Middle-aged—why, they're probably no more than thirty, just my age, she thought. But their faces are lined, their hair is graying— "What's so funny?" she demanded.

Instantly they sobered. "Pardon, Witch Woman?"

"You were laughing. What's so funny?"

They exchanged a look. "Laughing, Witch Woman?"

"You were laughing and looking at me, and I want to know why!"

"Oh, we were not laughing at you, Witch Woman," the taller one replied with some relief. "No, we were laughing at Coconino."

Now, perched on the wall, she scowled as she watched them go about their work. Men and women toiled in the fields to the northeast, tending the irrigation trenches, pulling weeds, transplanting seedlings. Some of the younger men had gone out earlier in search of the proper woods for new arrows, but Coconino had not gone with them. Instead he had taken up his polished throwing club and gone off alone to hunt rabbits. The smiles and snickers that had followed him had been poorly disguised.

I didn't mean to cause him trouble, she thought sourly. I just wanted him to leave me alone. She set him up, that simpering little adolescent. She set him up and used me to— But he deserved it, didn't he? That arrogant young— I'm ten years older than he and a world different . . . and "not what he expected." I'll bet I'm not! What was he expecting, a cute little thing that giggles and jiggles and—

Stop it, she chided herself. You're projecting. Each man has enough faults of his own, you don't need to give him someone else's. So I'm not what he expected—well, I didn't ask for this body and all its problems, but it's what I've got. And if you don't like it, young Hercules, that's too bad.

She brushed a stray hair from her face in annoyance. You shouldn't have bragged about your intentions ahead of time, Coconino. But I—I should have known that my scorching would not go unrelated. Yes I, of all people, should have known there would be whispers, and looks, and snickers . . .

He came into the village then from the west. She watched as the heads turned, watched him stalk past with his jaw set, his chin high. Well, you asked for it, she thought. Next time you'll think twice. Next time you won't open your cocky mouth before you know what you're talking about. But this time . . .

She sighed and started down the ladder. This time I'll help you out. Because no one should have to live with whispers and looks.

Coconino stopped in front of his mother's wickiup. Two Moons was painting an intricate design on a ceramic bowl. Nothing pleased her more than spending hours shaping the mud and imbuing it with mystic patterns. She was known throughout the village for her beautiful pottery. But she put the bowl aside as Coconino approached.

Two Moons was beautiful still, her son thought—round and soft, her long hair now white at the roots. Such a sweet face and gentle eyes could not help but beguile a Man-on-the-Mountain. It was no wonder she had been Chosen. And when that Man had left her with his infant son, it was no wonder that the young men of the village had fought over the privilege of taking her to wife.

The cotton dress she wore was embroidered with the emblems of the Council. She smiled up at her son. "What have you brought me, Coconino?"

He cleared his throat and used a voice just a bit louder than necessary. "Only a rabbit, my mother, and a small one."

Her eyes flicked immediately to the wickiup across the way, where Corn Hair's mother, Rosa, was spreading yucca leaves to dry in the sun. "Not so small, my son," she replied, also in a too-loud voice. "But I still have meat in plenty from yesterday. The choice part of your kill was mine, you remember, and it is roasting now."

Rosa had barely paused in her work.

"Then what shall I do with this rabbit?" Coconino asked.

"Leave it there by the fire and fetch me a basket of sotol pods," she suggested, "for that is what I would like today."

Coconino draped the animal carelessly on a large flat stone near the fire. "It is not good to waste," he sighed.

Behind him Rosa cleared her throat. "Do you have a basket, Coconino," she asked, "to collect sotol?"

"I have none," he confessed.

She crawled into her wickiup and returned a moment later

with a large, shallow basket woven from yucca fibers. "A basket like this is what you need," she told him gravely.

"Yes, a basket like that would be good," he agreed.

The old woman thrust it toward him. "Use this one."

"But, good neighbor," he protested, "I—"

"*Aiiee*, what are neighbors for?" She waved him off. "Use the basket."

Coconino reached for the basket but stopped, looked around him, and spied the rabbit with feigned surprise. "Ah!" he exclaimed. "You have a basket I need, and I have a rabbit I cannot use. Here." He offered her the rabbit with one hand and accepted the basket with the other.

Her wrinkled hand trembled slightly as she took the rabbit. "It is not good to waste," she agreed, and turned back to stir up her cook fire.

Two Moons smiled inwardly. With such graceful games her son had been providing for the old widow for several years. It was, of course, Lame Rabbit's responsibility to supplement the common harvest and group kills with small game and other food gleaned from the Mother Earth. But Corn Hair's worthless husband could seldom provide enough for his own children, let alone his mother-in-law. So Coconino saw that his mother's friend did not want either for food or for dignity.

Now he hesitated, the basket in his hands. "I was so busy hunting the rabbit," he said, "I did not notice where sotol was growing."

Rosa turned back from her fire. "My grandson will know," she offered. "I'll fetch him for you."

As she waddled off, Coconino allowed himself a sly wink at his mother. The boy would help him gather the sotol, and when the basket was returned, it would not be empty.

"*Ea*. Coconino."

He turned in dismay at the sound of the Witch Woman's voice. It was dry and brittle like the breaking of a dead branch, and there was no music in it. It also brought back the memory of their last meeting, of Castle Rock's treachery and the fool he had been made to look. His back steeled, his chin lifted, and he glared at her.

She stopped ten paces from him on the path between the wickiups and planted her feet wide, arms akimbo. Her gaze was level and cool but not angry, he noticed. Her long hair was gathered, as usual, at the nape of her neck and fell almost to her waist. She wore heavy, tight trousers and her favorite sleeveless leather shirt with its deeply scooped neckline. She looked like a spindly cholla.

"I wanted to ask you about that, that thing you saw," she said flatly. "Tala."

"Tala is not a thing," he flared. "He is a kachina, a special child of the Mother Earth."

"Whatever." She folded her arms across her chest and sauntered a step or two closer, pausing with her hip cocked, one long leg stretched to the side. "This horn, what did it look like?"

"Like two horns twisted together, as a rope is twisted, and very straight." He measured eighteen inches on his arm. "Maybe this long."

She nodded her head. "Mm, that sounds right."

He was surprised. "You have seen Tala?"

"No, but I've heard about it." A covert glance told her that others were listening now. "Actually, it's an animal from—" She hesitated. "From the Before Times. We didn't know any still lived." She wasn't sure she should get into its offworld origins. "Where exactly did you see it?"

"In the Red Rock country." He waved a hand northward. "Not far from the old city."

"How far is that from here?"

He shrugged. "That depends on how fast you run."

"Not very."

"Perhaps a day, then, perhaps less."

She considered, trying not to watch the watchers. How far do I have to take this, she wondered, to gain back a little respect for him? Oh, hell, he's just a puppy, she decided, and I'm a Witch Woman to him. How dangerous can he be? "I'd like to see this place," she said. "Someday. Maybe you'd take me."

Something glimmered in his eyes. "To search for Tala?" he asked.

The Witch Woman balked. That wasn't what she had intended. But maybe . . . "Well, none of my people have ever seen one. If I could prove that these creatures survived—well, then I'd have honor among my people." She glanced around. "As Coconino has honor among his."

That's enough, she thought as neighbors began to put their heads together. I embarrassed him last night, I've acknowledged his honor today. Now I can go about the business of learning how to survive here, to make pots and weave baskets and scratch a living from the soil—

"It is a hard trip for a woman," Coconino said. "Much

climbing and a long distance if one follows the waterways to the creek that runs through the Red Rock country. I think it would be too difficult for you.''

She froze in the motion of turning away. Slowly she looked back at him, her eyes dangerous. ''I'm a lot tougher than you think.''

''Of course, a Witch Woman may be different from the women of the People,'' he added hastily. ''But to search the Red Rocks for Tala would be a challenge even for a hunter.''

I didn't say I wanted to scour the rocks! she wanted to shriek. Instead she said, ''Maybe later this summer I'll take you up on that challenge.'' Once more she started to turn away.

''The Mother may not want you to leave the village.''

Now she stiffened and turned her full attention back to him. ''If I want to leave the village,'' she said coldly, ''I'll leave. I'm not a prisoner here.''

Coconino shifted uneasily, not accustomed to having the Mother's authority slighted. Then he was seized with an idea. ''I could bring Tala back to you.''

Don't! she wanted to wail. I just pulled you out of a hole, don't jump back in! ''That's not necessary,'' she told him. ''If we go, we'll go together.''

''He may not be in the Red Rock country anymore, and then we would have to journey on. It is an arduous task requiring great strength. If I went alone—''

''Together!'' she snapped.

''Very well.'' He shifted the basket in his hands as Corn Hair's older son came running up. ''I will ask the Mother tonight, and if she allows it, we will go in search of Tala.'' He turned and, with the small boy leading, started out of the village.

Inwardly groaning, the Witch Woman turned back toward her cliffside retreat. Idiot! she chastised herself. Now who's jumped into a hole?

CHAPTER FIVE

Seated at the great loom outside her wickiup, the Mother watched as the new Witch Woman paced restlessly along the rooftops of the Village of the Ancients, climbing from one level to the next. Each day the woman spent an hour or more simply climbing through the dwellings, over the roofs, through the doorways, along the walls, up and down the ladders, trying to burn the restlessness from her soul. Too bitter, the Mother thought, too bitter! Why did they send her? She will teach the People nothing but will poison them with her bitterness. Already they avoid her, fearful of her sharp tongue. No. It was a mistake to send her here simply because the Mountain could do nothing for her.

"She's taking it bad, Mother," Gonzales had told her privately. "Like it was personal. But it's the Code, you know. Everyone felt bad, but what could we do? So when she asked to come out here, they said sure, why not? New environment, new faces—maybe it'll help. Time is the great healer, and out here you've got plenty of time."

"Time is time," the Mother had replied, "here or on the Mountain. But what can she teach us? You are to send us Teachers, not invalids."

Gonzales shrugged. "Simple machines, maybe? Block and tackle. I know you don't have much use for mechanics, but . . . Some new tools, maybe. Scissors or—"

"You could do all these things."

"Yes, but—"

"Then what can *she* teach us?"

Gonzales spread his hands. "Patience?"

Patience. The Mother watched as now the Witch Woman scuttled down a ladder toward the valley floor, facing out from

53

the cliff in the manner of the People. It is not the People who need to learn patience, she thought. But there was something to Gonzales's half-jesting remark. As a wickiup is not truly tested until the storms come, perhaps the value of the Way of the People is not truly tested except by such as the Witch Woman. Perhaps now I will find out if all I have striven to preserve, to protect, is indeed superior to what I have sought to protect it from.

She glanced to the northeast to find out what had brought the Witch Woman down from her lofty perch and saw Coconino and Juan returning from ''hunting'' with Juan's young son and several of the other village boys. Frowning, she saw the Witch Woman turn south, heading out of the village. It had been so for several days; when Coconino returned to the village from his day's activities, the Witch Woman would leave. There could be many reasons for this, the Mother knew, and she did not like any of them.

Back and forth went her hands over the loom, back and forth went the shuttles, now the one with red thread, now the one with black. Word of Coconino's proposed quest had reached her ears long before the young man had presented himself at her wickiup. She had stalled him, but soon she would have to answer him. Had he requested to go on such a journey with Juan or Falling Star or any of the other village men, she would have agreed at once. Coconino's dreams were always larger than anyone else's, and because of that, so were his achievements.

But the Witch Woman—how had she gotten involved in this? Everything she touched became complicated. To send an unmarried man off with a Witch Woman would not raise any eyebrows in the village, for a Witch Woman's business was her own and none would question it. But to send *this* Witch Woman, and with Coconino . . .

Red thread, black thread, white thread, yellow—the pattern was woven one strand at a time.

The Witch Woman was trotting now, along the river path out of the village. In an hour or so she would return, sweaty, winded, to plunge into the cold of the swollen stream. It was the same every day. Then she would join the People at their work again until deep darkness. Finally, with no torch to light her way, she would climb the ladders to her adobe house, her demon exorcised—until morning.

Send you with Coconino? You in whom such a storm rages?

Of all who call me Mother, if I had to pick one who best represented what the People are and can be, I would choose Coconino. Oh, he is arrogant at times and stubborn as the gila monster, but his ways are the Way of the People, and the Mother Earth speaks to him. Yet he is so vulnerable, for he has never known your kind of tempest. How will his wickiup stand?

With a great sigh she set down a shuttle. Red, yellow, black, they all dangled from the great loom, waiting for her hands to set them in motion. Very well, Witch Woman, she thought, I will try my wickiup against your storm. But if it shows signs of damage, your storm will stop. I will see that it does.

The Witch Woman broke the surface sputtering and slinging water from her hair and arms. The late March sun was hot, but the stream was ice-cold. It always looked so inviting after her run, but the shock of her plunge left her gasping for breath, thrashing and rubbing her limbs to warm her blood again. After a moment she wiped the water from her eyes and turned toward the bank.

Coconino stood watching her. Her anger flared as it always did when she saw him, and he wore the hard, set face he always wore when he confronted her. They stood like two stags warily watching each other, each waiting for the other to make a move.

"You can swim?" he asked.

"Sure. There's a catch basin on the Mountain; kids like to go there in the summer." Not just kids, she thought, remembering her father's insistence that she join him in the frigid waters and practice her strokes.

He nodded. "Good."

Well, thank you very much, I'm so glad you approve, she thought. Now, if this stream were more than waist deep, I'd challenge you to a race.

"You run every day?" he asked then.

"Since I got here." Since you challenged me.

"How far?"

"Till I'm tired. Then I run back."

"That does not tell me how far."

"What difference does it make?" she demanded.

He shifted his stance and his eyes, gazing upstream as though he could see around the hills to the fields where the People were tending young seedlings. "The Mother said we may search for Tala."

Oh, yippee, she thought. *Just what I want to do, go chasing through the hills in search of the last survivor of a breed of animal that probably died out five hundred years ago.*

"I wanted to know how strong you are, how much distance we can cover in a day. I need to know how many canteens to carry, which route to take so that you do not collapse and I have to carry you."

"You won't carry me, *chue*," she told him, wading back to the shore.

He watched her as she stood on the bank, chest heaving, her sodden clothes clinging to her frame. Her leg muscles seemed well developed in spite of her thinness, and the ribs in her chest were visible but not prominent. Neither were her breasts, he thought with contempt. But she did not need those to run, and that was what concerned him now.

"Tomorrow we will run together," he informed her, "so that I will know."

"Really? If I flunk the test, am I reprieved or is there a make-up exam?"

He blinked. "Please?"

She almost laughed, he looked so puzzled. But she kept a straight face and rephrased herself. "If I don't run well enough for you, do you test me again in a few days, or do we call off the whole thing?"

"There will be some time before we can leave," he answered. "It may be you will grow stronger."

"How much time?"

He shrugged. "That is up to the Teacher."

"Gonzales? What's he got to do with this?"

"The Mother said we may not leave until after his Choosing."

Please, Gonzales, don't be a lecherous old goat, she begged silently. *Take your time. This cocksure whelp has decided to make me look incompetent because he doesn't want me along any more than I want to be there. But I'm not going to give him the satisfaction of rejecting me; no one does that to me ever again. No, I'll go with him to his Red Rock country to search for his mythical Tala. And if he wants to go on from there, then he'll go alone. But I'll quit when it's* my *choice, not his.*

I need more time, though, to get in shape. So look the girls over carefully, Gonzales. Very carefully. It'll take at least another week for my wind to improve.

She watched as Coconino climbed the trail toward the village, his muscles rippling with catlike grace and latent strength. Her body stirred, and she yanked it back. You won't find your life along dead-end trails, she reminded herself.

Oh, please, Gonzales. Take a year.

Ben Gonzales was forty-three years old. He had a wife, six children, and two grandchildren with a third on the way. But for years he'd had in mind that he wanted to spend some time among the primitives, helping them with their agriculture. Now that his children were older and Maria had plenty of company and help, he had decided it was time to offer his services.

He'd brought new seeds with him, vegetables that he would show them how to raise. And he would observe their irrigation practices, find out which crops they rotated on the same land, and share with them better ways of making their tools. He would stay through the harvest, or perhaps until spring, among the People.

Since his plan had been some time in the works, he had had a chance to study the culture he was walking into, speak with former Teachers, learn some of the peculiarities of the language. Their customs impressed him as being basically logical, the product of both convenience and necessity.

The custom of the Chosen Companion bothered him. He was a married man, and in a community as small as the mountain installation he had never risked hurting Maria by an indiscretion with another woman. It troubled him that Maria, too, knew what was expected of him here in this village. Most of all it troubled him that the maidens were so young.

My daughter Elise is this age, he would think when a shy young thing smiled at him. They are all children, fourteen, fifteen years old. The oldest here is seventeen, and it is whispered that if I do not choose her, she will go to live in the village on the cliff until some man takes pity on her and marries her, or at least impregnates her, so that she will have a child to fulfill her womanhood.

For that was their prime concern: the survival and propagation of their race. Where half the children didn't survive infancy and most adults died before age forty, the young were all expected to marry and have children, lots and lots of children. And any visiting Man-on-the-Mountain was expected to do his part. Such children were especially prized because they represented new blood and reduced the risks of inbreeding among the People.

But the girls were all so young! And so innocent. He watched their shining faces, some coy, some bashful, but all reflecting their hope that he would favor them. Him! Big-bellied, leather-faced, clumsy forty-three-year-old Ben Gonzales. They all wanted to be his choice.

Once he had resolved to decline. But their eyes were so bright, their bearing so hopeful, he knew they would be crushed to think he preferred celibacy to one of them. And in truth, he did not relish celibacy.

So for his need as well as theirs he knew he would choose, although he would never tell Maria. She had not spoken of it before he had left; he knew she would not speak of it when he returned.

But whom to choose? Of course it should be Nina, the older girl who needed a husband so badly. She had a large, crooked nose and an awkward, bony body, but what of that? He was no prize. This was duty more than pleasure; he sought harmony more than excitement. And she was older.

But as he sat in the evenings eating frijoles and listening to the stories of the People, there was one other maiden who always caught his eye.

The sun rose almost directly over a bend in the creek, its rays sending spikes of gold along the dancing waters. The Witch Woman had met Coconino while it was still dark, glad of his suggestion that they run before the day turned hot. She slapped her bare legs, knowing she would be glad later that she wore shorts and not trousers, but it was cold now in air as yet un-touched by the golden fire in the east. Her long-sleeved cotton shirt was welcome.

Clad only in his loincloth, Coconino eyed her garb suspi-ciously, but what did he know? Perhaps it was more comfortable than it looked. He handed her a gourd canteen filled with water from the stream. "Here. We will each carry one."

She nodded and tied the thongs of its carrying net to her belt. "How far are we going?" she asked.

"Not far. Only to the Well and back."

"The Well? How far is that?"

"It is that way," he said evasively, waving a hand northward.

The Witch Woman tried not to quail visibly. Not only was the young hunter purposefully vague about the distance, but the direction in which he pointed was away from the creek. She swallowed back her apprehension. "Should we carry some food?" she asked.

"Food!" he laughed. "It is spring. Food is all around us." With that, he took a mouthful of water and trotted off.

"The rope is gone," Coconino told her with a helpless shrug.

The Witch Woman forced herself into a sitting position on the large, flat stones at the rim of the Well and looked, Coconino noted with a smirk, appalled. "What?" she demanded with the little breath she had left. "How am I going to get down there?"

The Well was a circular pit in the limestone some four hundred feet across with a spring-fed lake at the bottom—a veritable pool in the desert. But its surface lay seventy feet below the rim of the pit, and the sides, while jagged with rock layers, were nearly vertical.

"I will go down and fetch water for you," Coconino offered.

"No-o-o!" she protested, her voice a comical groan. The giddiness of exhaustion had sapped all her anger, bringing out a side of her Coconino had never seen. "There's shade down there. I can see it, I can *smell* it . . ."

Coconino had set a moderate pace—not one he used with the village children but not one designed to weed out weak hunters, either. And the Witch Woman had held up surprisingly well for the first five miles. Then she had faded quickly, and they had been forced to stop and walk awhile. She had gamely declined to turn back, however, insisting she wanted to see this well.

So they had walked until she got her wind back. "You should hold water in your mouth while you run," he advised her, "so you will breathe properly."

"If I hold water in my mouth, I'll drown."

He did not try to argue. It did not seem to him that arguing with the Witch Woman would be profitable. Instead he offered another suggestion. "If you chant to the Mother Earth, she will give you strength."

"Chant? With water in my mouth?" she quipped.

"Chant silently," he admonished. "In your mind. She will still hear you."

"You chant," she replied. "I gave up my religion even before I gave up my virginity. Let's go."

So they had run on. Now, two walking breaks and both canteens later, they had reached the lake in a hill. The People, Coconino told her, always left a coil of rope under a rock here so that weary travelers could get down to the water. He had let her sprawl, exhausted, on the flat limestone boulders of the rim while he got the rope from its cache. He was genuinely surprised not to find it there.

Now he pulled her into a sitting position. "Don't lie still," he warned her. "Your muscles will knot like old bowstrings."

"My muscles," she panted, "haven't got that much energy."

"Give me your canteen. I will go down and fill it for you," he said. "There are many hand- and footholds; it will be easy for a good climber like me."

"I'll go down, too," she insisted.

"You can't," he protested with vivid visions of her falling to her death. "It's too steep!"

"But I want to drown myself in that lake," she moaned. "My whole body, top to bottom, wants to be in that water."

"Someday perhaps you *will* drown yourself in it," he replied, "but while you are with me, you will take no such chance with your life. I'll bring you water to drink. Stay here. And keep moving." He dragged her to her feet, though he knew she would collapse the minute he was over the edge, then gave her a gentle shove away from the rim. As quickly as possible he lowered himself over the side and climbed the ragged wall downward.

He found the rope at the bottom on the natural rock lip that surrounded the pool. Someone dropped it, he thought, some young hunter who didn't want to bother climbing down to retrieve it. Or perhaps, he thought with contempt, it was Lame Rabbit, who hadn't the skill in climbing. Perhaps that was how he had twisted his ankle.

Lame Rabbit had limped back into the village the day after the feast. His presence had churned Coconino's stomach, and he was glad of the distraction the Witch Woman had provided with her suggestion that they search for Tala. He had let that consume him, avoiding the village and its one most irritating inhabitant.

He avoided Corn Hair, too, but not out of shame or lack of respect. No, he was afraid that if their eyes met, their secret would show on his face. He was afraid that if he heard her voice, he would want her too much and take some foolish risk to be alone with her again. He was afraid that the thought of Lame Rabbit's child growing within her would drive him wild with anger and despair.

So instead he had spent his time with the village children, with her son, Dreams of Hawks. By teaching the boy to snare rabbits and look for tracks in the earth, he hoped to convey to her his respect, his gratitude, for what they had shared.

Now he filled a canteen and climbed quickly back to the top with the rope. As he had suspected, the Witch Woman had stretched herself on the rocks again. "I'm moving, I'm moving," she groused when she saw him, weakly waving a leg in the air. Had she not been the Witch Woman, he would have laughed out loud.

"Here, drink," he said, handing her the canteen. "I found the rope at the bottom. Now you can get down to the shade."

She gulped the cool water while he secured the rope around a large rock. "Not so fast," he cautioned. "You'll get sick." She obligingly slowed her drinking to small sips, which she rolled around her mouth and allowed to slide down her throat with obvious relish. Coconino smiled at her exaggerated expressions, pleased that this one time, at least, she had listened to his advice.

Then he helped her to her feet, and with one arm around her waist and the rope around them both, he began to back down the cliff.

Though she had virtually no strength left, she tried her best to hold her own weight and to facilitate their descent. They slipped once, but not badly, and soon they stood on the rock ledge below with the dark, placid water at their feet.

"Oh, glory," the Witch Woman sighed as she knelt and immersed her head in the liquid, heedless of the plants and algae floating on the surface. A moment later she came up, slinging water from her long hair and gasping for breath.

Coconino sat back in the shade, reclining against the layered rock wall of the pit, and watched her with some amusement. If the arduous run had not taken the fight out of her, it had certainly taken the poison out of her fight. With the anger gone from her demeanor, she looked at this moment very like a wet coyote, shaking itself but looking no less bedraggled for it.

"You should keep moving," he reminded her.

"I intend to," she panted, and, sliding her legs over the edge, slipped into the water. Its temperature made her gasp, for at that time of year the spring-fed water was not much warmer than the creek, but she pushed off bravely and swam a few strokes out before returning to drag herself up onto a sun-warmed section of the ledge.

Coconino considered helping her out of the pool but decided against it. Although it was a struggle, it was within her capability, and he had come to the conclusion that she needed to push herself as far as possible on her own. The run had stretched her but not to breaking, and it seemed to have improved her personality. Besides, it was amusing to watch her flopping like a beached fish.

"There are some berries here," he offered, pointing to nearby bushes.

"Even if they flew off the bushes," she panted, stretching out on her back, "and into my mouth, I haven't got the strength to chew them."

He smiled and helped himself to the fruit.

After a moment, her breathing slowed down and a peaceful look settled onto her face. It looked very much like a face of the People, Coconino decided, with high cheekbones and a slight tilt to the eyes—although it was not as round as it should be. Were it not so thin, it might even be attractive with its finely molded bones and even features. It was easier to see that now as she rested. Their run had not achieved what he had originally hoped it would, but perhaps it had achieved something better. "You ran very well," he told her.

"At first."

"Even at last," he admitted. "To go on when you were so tired—you have great determination. A hunter needs that."

"Anyone needs that to survive."

He considered that a moment. "Yes, I believe that's true," he replied. "I do not like farming, but those who do it must have great determination."

The Witch Woman opened her eyes and tilted her head so she could see him. She said nothing, only watched him a moment and turned back.

"We will not push so hard on our way to the Red Rock Country," he told her.

"Why not?"

He shifted uncomfortably. "It won't be necessary."

"Now that you've figured out you can't kill me off."

His eyes flashed, but he pulled his temper back. She was right, after all. "I did not try to kill you," he said calmly. "But I did want to know how you would hold up. And I wanted you to know how hard the journey would be." He hesitated. "I thought you would want to turn back."

She opened her eyes again and studied him longer this time. He met her gaze and let the searching dark eyes find what they could. Finally she turned away again. "Now I could chew some of those berries," she said.

For some reason she reminded him of Juan, and he smiled, as he often smiled at his friend when Juan was not looking. Then he plucked a handful of berries and crossed to squat beside her in the sun. The water she had splashed over the rocks was drying already, with small pools gathering in shallow depressions. Her sodden hair lay in tangles about her head. Her eyes were closed, but her lips were slightly parted; he slipped a berry between them.

The Witch Woman murmured a small laugh—a pleasant sound, not at all like her coyote laugh—and chewed the berry. "Delicious," she said, and opened her mouth for more. "You aren't Dionysius in disguise, are you?"

"Dionysius was fat," he replied. "And he made wine. The making of wine is forbidden by the Mother."

She was surprised. "Why is that?"

He sat down and stretched one heavily muscled leg out in front of him, resting his elbow on the other as he fed her the remaining berries. "Long ago, in the Before Times," he told her, "the ancestors of the People were nearly destroyed by wine and whiskey and all manner of spirit waters. It made them sick, and they could not care for their families, yet they could not stop, for there was a powerful spirit in the drink that possessed them and would not let them go. So now the Mother has forbidden such evil drinks to pass the lips of the People."

"I only had time for the short course before I came," the Witch Woman said. "They didn't tell me about that."

"Well, it is so." A prickling sensation traveled along his spine. "You did not bring any such thing with you from the Mountain, did you?" he asked uneasily.

Her eyes sprang open again at his tone. "No. Why?"

He fed her the last berry from his hand before replying. "Long ago," he said, "when the Mother was young—before she was the Mother—a Man-on-the-Mountain came to us who brought the evil whiskey. He gave some to the harvesters after the corn was brought in, as part of the celebration. It made a crazy spirit come upon them. One fell into the fire, and another—another took up a knife in anger and killed his friend.

"The People did not know at that time of spirits that can live in such drinks, and they were greatly distressed. But the Mother is wise, and she discerned the source of the spirit. The Council met then and decided that a strong message must be sent to the Man-on-the-Mountain that spirit waters must never be brought among the People again. It was decided that the Teacher who brought the evil must carry the message back.'' He paused. ''But only part of him.''

The Witch Woman jumped. ''What?''

Coconino gazed levelly into her startled eyes. ''When the Flying Machine came to get him in the spring, only his hand carried the empty bottle back to the Mountain. The rest of him was never found.''

The Witch Woman struggled to a sitting position and stared at him. ''You're lying,'' she guessed. ''We've never lost a person out here; they would have told me.''

''Perhaps it was not in your 'short course,' '' he suggested innocently.

''You're making that up to scare me,'' she insisted. ''Plenty of people tried to talk me out of this; they would have used that if they could have.''

''If they knew.''

''Listen, we don't have to send Teachers out here. All it would take is one time, one, when a Teacher didn't return safely and—''

''And yet there have been two.'' A dark gleam crept into his eyes. ''And one was a Witch Woman.''

''You lie!'' she spit.

''Coconino does not lie,'' he told her sharply. ''Indeed, two Teachers did not return to their Mountain: the one I told you of and the Witch Woman named Margaret.'' The gleam became a grin. ''Why do you suppose Witch Women come so seldom and stay only a few months?'' Her discomfiture pleased him. ''That was not in your short course, either, was it?''

The Witch Woman strained to remember. In truth, she had not paid much attention to parts of the training, since they seemed to have no bearing on her purpose. Had they actually talked about her predecessors? ''What happened to her?'' she asked uncertainly.

Coconino reached over to the pool and washed the berry juice from his hand. ''That is a good story,'' he said, wiping his hand on a brown thigh. ''I will tell it to you sometime. It is one of the stories of the People.'' He retreated into the shade farther back from the pool.

''But it's just a story, isn't it?'' she demanded, following him.

His smile was smug now as he leaned back against the stone. ''Is any story just a story?'' he asked obliquely. Then, arms folded across his chest, he shut his eyes and ended the conversation.

The Witch Woman watched him, fuming. He was toying with her, of course, baiting her. But—her thoughts churned. The legends of the People were not old and most probably were rooted in fact. She had believed the story about the liquor right up to where it got violent.

For these are not a violent people, her mind protested. Their life is based on harmony: with the Earth, with each other. They only kill animals for food. Life is cherished here; the young are cherished for their promise, the old for their wisdom. There is nothing in these people capable of hacking up a man whose only crime was ignorance or perhaps poor judgment.

And yet . . .

What would they do if they felt their way of life, the Way of the People, threatened? Look at Coconino—would he stand idly by while someone jeopardized the harmony of his village? And what was it that nagged at the back of her mind, something she'd been told once about some previous problem with a Witch Woman? Something that had not mattered to her at the time . . .

"Witch Woman."

She stirred and wondered why Dick was waking her and why he called her that. Then she opened her eyes, saw Coconino, and remembered. "Oh, it's you," she grumbled.

He grinned. "I'm glad you're so pleased to see me." She looked up sharply, but there was no malice in his eyes. "It is time to climb back up. Come, stretch out your muscles," he instructed, reaching out a hand to help her to her feet. Then, with condescension, he added, "The sun is fierce; we will walk on the way back."

"You're the boss," she said, blessing whatever deities had reprieved her from any more running that day. Every muscle in her shrieked as he hauled her to her feet. Her neck was stiff and sore from the position she'd slept in; she massaged it a moment, then rolled it in a careful circle, first left, then right. Her legs felt tight, and her joints rubbery. Slowly she stretched forward, to the sides, then diagonally to pull on the hamstring muscles. Finally she crossed to the pool to drink and splash the cool water onto her sleep-numbed face.

Coconino tested the rope as he waited for her to wake her reluctant body. It was still securely fastened, but he knew that getting the Witch Woman back up would be harder than getting her down had been. He had brought his half brother Flint here once, but the boy was of the People and, once rested, had climbed out on his own, not needing the rope.

She came up behind him as he frowned at the rope. "What's the matter?"

"You go first," he said, "and I will——"

"You'll stand right there and anchor the rope," she told him, "till I get to the top. I grew up on a mountain. I know something about climbing." Okay, Dad, she thought, all those tricks you taught me better work or I'm going to look like an absolute fool.

Coconino watched to find that she did, indeed, climb well. Her legs were still weak from their exertion, but she stepped with authority, and her long arms hauled bravely on the rope. In a few moments she was at the top. He followed her quickly.

She was breathing hard but not panting when he climbed over the rim and untied the rope. And her eyes sparkled with pride. "Fooled you, didn't I, Tonto?" she gloated.

"Why do you call me by such strange names?" he asked in exasperation as he coiled the rope. "I am Coconino."

"Well, you never call me by *my* name," she countered.

He was puzzled. "I call you Witch Woman. What else should I call you?"

"My name," she informed him, "is Debbie."

"Debbie." He looked her up and down as he considered the strange word. She stood erect, hands on hips, thin and strong with the sun gleaming off her jet-black hair. He tried the name again, trying to associate it with what he saw, then shook his head. "That is no name for a Witch Woman," he decided, stowing the coil of rope in its place under the rock.

"Oh?" The caustic edge had returned to her voice. "And just what would you suggest?"

He thought about that for a minute as he squatted beside the rock. Idly he plucked a blade of grass that had managed to take hold there and put it in his mouth. "You should have a name from the Before Times," he concluded. "An ancient name, one with great power like mine. The kind that men wrote on metal and anchored in the earth. I found such a name once, as my grandfather found mine. But I did not have to bring it to the village, for I could read it myself," he said proudly. "I have been saving it here, in my head, till it was needed. I think it is needed now."

He stood up, turned his palms toward the earth, and chanted a series of words that were foreign to her. They were guttural and seemed to vibrate through her abdomen and chest, expanding her ribs to accommodate them. Then he turned toward her and with great solemnity announced, "I will call you Foh-ee-nix."

She blinked as the word landed empty on her ear. Then suddenly she understood and began to laugh.

"What?" he asked, offended.

"It's 'Phoenix,' " she told him. "The *o* is silent. Fee-nix."

"Phoenix," he repeated, embarrassed that his pronunciation had been imperfect.

"Everyone has trouble with that one," she assured him.

"Is it Greek?" he asked suspiciously.

"It's—uh—gosh, I don't really know," she admitted. "But you're wearing one around your neck."

He touched the medallion, surprised. "Then it is a name of the People!" he exclaimed. She doubted it but said nothing. "It is a good name, the name of a bird that rose from its own ashes to live again. So have the People done."

It was true, though she had never thought of it before. It was true of the Earth as a whole, and it is true, she thought, of me. "I like this name," she said softly.

Hearing the unaccustomed sincerity in her voice, Coconino looked at her—at a woman who was somehow not the same one with whom he had begun this journey. "Yes," he agreed, nodding. "It is *moh-ohnak*."

Then he turned his steps eastward. "Hey, isn't that the wrong way?" she asked. "Or am I really confused?"

"It is not the way we came," he told her, "but it is the way we will go home."

"It's an easier way, right?" she accused.

"The creek is just over this hill. It is usually easier to travel along its bank."

"The creek?" she demanded. "The *creek*? You made me climb all the way down to that lake when the creek is just over the hill?"

"Ah, but now you can say you have been to the Well," he replied with a grin. "All the village boys will envy you. And you will not tell them, will you, that the creek is just over the hill?"

"Are you kidding?" she snapped as she fell into step beside him. "Do you think I'd admit to being such a damn fool?"

CHAPTER SIX

The Terran Research Coalition's doctor was no fool; he saw the angry bruise the young woman had tried to cover with makeup. "Is your husband also applying for a berth on the Earth venture, Ms. Reichert?" he asked conversationally.

"I'm not married." The tonelessness of Karen Reichert's voice spoke volumes. So did the silence that followed.

"Off on your own, then, are you?" he persisted. She was anemic; he could hold her back. It depended on who else was going.

"Yes. On my own."

The doctor nodded. A good decision. Not a final step, unfortunately, but one with possibilities. "Well, you're in good physical shape," he said as he jotted notes on her chart. "Except for that low red count, but a few vitamins will fix that up. Eat more chicken," he advised. And, he thought, stay away from whoever the hell is beating you.

"Thank you, Doctor."

Her wide-set blue eyes were so lifeless, the delicate, china-doll face so somber, that he wondered then if it had really been her decision. Was someone else forcing her into this trip? "Looking forward to the venture?" he asked casually.

Then he saw it, just a glimmer in her eyes, almost lost beneath the fashionably long, wispy dark bangs. "I've studied a lot about Earth," was all she said.

He handed her the chart, reassured that his decision was also a good one. "Just give this to the clerk," he told her, "and tell them I said to sign you up." Sign you up and get you away from him. "Good luck, Ms. Reichert!" He smiled as he left, but inside he was thinking, You'll need it. Because over half this crew will be male, and all too often women like you leave one sadist only to find another.

There are so many men, Ms. Reichert, on this world and on others. Find one who belongs to the human race.

"Oh, good!" the motherly clerk exclaimed when she saw the approval stamped on Karen's papers. "We have another communications technician signed, but his credentials aren't nearly as impressive as yours. Welcome aboard, Ms. Reichert!" She handed Karen an electronic badge. "This will give you access to the compound when you come back with your things. You can bring any personal items you like to the compound; it's only when you move onto the ship that there will be limitations. You'll need to supply your own uniforms. Here's the address of the uniform shop. We have three styles to choose from; they'll know which ones. We'll expect you in forty-eight hours."

"I'll be there," Karen replied, turning to walk down the long corridor to the reception room. I'll be here sooner than that, she thought. Forty minutes to get home, twenty to pack, forty to return, and then—

She leaned up against the wall as a wave of relief washed over her. Giddily she thought, I am going to Earth, I am going to Earth, I am going to Earth . . .

Earth had been in her dreams since she was eight. It was the year they had begun to study ancient history in school and she had discovered that all the bright heroes whose names had slipped like shadows past her ears were real people. There *was* a Madame Curie, who discovered radium. There *was* a Mahatma Gandhi, a man of peace. There *was* a Yuri Gagarin, the first man to leave his planet in a tiny capsule.

Even the men of war fascinated her. Alexander, Caesar, Napoleon, Hitler: love them or hate them, they had been empire builders. And the women: Eleanor of Aquitaine, who led her women on crusade; Catherine the Great, ruler of all the Russias; "Dynamite" Wu, the democratic reformer . . .

Karen shook herself and moved down the hallway again. Of course they were dead and gone, and Earth was probably dead, too. No garden. No blue skies and green grass, just gray haze and dusty rock. Only a child would imagine it otherwise. Only a child would imagine stepping out into an alpine meadow to be greeted by a tall, handsome man on horseback. Only a child would believe he would lift her easily to the front of his saddle, settle his arms around her, and gallop off with her. Only a—

"Pass, please."

Karen stifled a gasp as she was wrenched from her daydream. She looked up into the piglike face of a man perhaps forty-five whose dark hair was cut short, giving his head a square look. His body looked square, too, as deep as it was broad, though he had just enough height to carry it off. He was not massive, but he was solid, and the hammy hand he shoved at her was well callused.

Karen fumbled for her temporary pass, edging slightly away from the man. He took the tag, checked it against his electronic clipboard, and handed it back. "Turn it in at the gate," he told her. Then he saw the permanent pass clutched in her other hand. "I see you made it."

She stared dumbly at the pass, then back at the square man before his comment registered as a separate thought. "Oh. Yes. I'll be joining the crew."

The pig face split into a smile. "Tony Hanson," the man rasped, sticking out his hand. "Second officer. Also quartermaster. All supply requisitions go through me."

Hesitantly Karen shook his hand. It was both clammy and rough. "Karen Reichert," she said faintly. "Communications."

"Comm tech. Good," he barked. His beady eyes narrowed a bit. "How much experience you have?"

She swallowed. "Five years. I've been at—" Why was this man grilling her? Did she have to answer to him? "At Motes-Org. Field coordinator."

Tony Hanson grunted. Did that mean he was impressed? "Well, that's more like it," he grumbled. "The other fellow they accepted is fresh out of school. No experience under fire, if you know what I mean. When I was in the service—"

Just then a bell chimed pleasantly from his wrist unit. " 'Scuse me," he said gruffly. Karen slipped gratefully away but checked her urge to flee the last five yards into the reception room. Earth would be dead. There would be no people left; there would only be a long journey with men like Tony Hanson, and in the end she would have to come back home.

Derek Lujan sat in the conference room, Captain Winthrop on his left, Tony Hanson on his right. Across the crescent-shaped table sat Jacqueline Winthrop, the ship's doctor, and Rita Zleboton, the chief engineer. Sitting attentively in stiff DeBanese chairs were the remaining thirty-two men and women of the crew of the *Homeward Bound*.

They're all young, Derek thought as he looked over the crew. All under thirty, except for the people at this table. Like the crew of the *Aladdin* had been: young, energetic, sharp—a good crew.

Derek himself was twenty-five.

A member of the Board of Directors of the Terran Research Coalition was addressing them. She was going on at length about how proud they were of this crew, how positive they were that history was being made, and how many wonderful people were at work behind the scenes. She proceeded to name them all.

Lujan looked across at Jacqueline Winthrop, who appeared just as bored as he was. In her gray jumpsuit, with her white hair pulled back in its efficient bun, she looked every inch the competent physician her file said she was. Wise choice, he thought. But as Jacqueline caught his eyes, the stare she returned had a cold edge to it. She doesn't trust me, he thought. Having been in the Merchant Fleet herself, she's heard about my exploits on the *Aladdin*, and it's made her suspicious. I don't look like that kind of commander.

People tended not to take Derek seriously at first. His light brown hair rippled in thick waves, short as it was, and his light blue eyes were habitually mild. "An Ashley Wilkes of a man," his mother used to say, much to his embarrassment, for he fancied himself more of a Rhett Butler. His profile hearkened back to some Greek ancestor, straight of nose and strong of brow, and a trim brown mustache graced his upper lip. No wonder people had trouble believing he had three degrees in five-dimensional physics. No wonder they couldn't believe he was the hero of the *Aladdin* catastrophe.

Derek smiled at Jacqueline, his most ingenuous, sparkling white smile. She looked momentarily disconcerted; then she turned back to watch the speaker. I'll win her over, Derek thought. She's tough, but she's pragmatic. Eventually she'll give over to logic, and I'll earn her respect.

There was polite applause as the director sat down, and Captain Winthrop rose to his feet. Derek liked the cut of the man's navy blue uniform: double-breasted with slightly padded shoulders. It heightened his authoritative bearing, complementing the years of experience that had written themselves in the lines of his face. His cheeks were blue-black with the shadow of a heavy

beard; the man probably shaved at least twice a day. Derek
stroked his own mustache, knowing his beard would never match
its fullness.

"I want to introduce you to someone," Winthrop began. He
spoke with the easy confidence of a man accustomed to addressing large groups. He did not try to be suave or lighthearted; he
felt no need to impress his listeners. He simply told them what
he had to say. "I want you to meet a specialist, someone with a
number of years of experience, someone with the respect of both
peers and leaders in a field that is critical to our mission."

Beside him, Lujan could feel Tony Hanson sitting a little
straighter, expanding his chest, trying his best to look the part.

"This person came to us," Winthrop went on, "taking a loss
in personal income to join this venture, agreeing to work as just
one member of a team."

Lujan controlled an urge to smirk as Hanson puffed himself up
even more. He's talking about his wife, you idiot, Lujan thought.
Can you really be so self-important as to believe it's you?

"This person has my admiration and my respect," Winthrop
told them, "and deserves nothing less from you. This person—is
sitting in the chair next to you."

A sigh of laughter swept the room, and even Lujan had to
smile at the captain's cleverness. Crew members were looking at
one another, seeing under the various exteriors a competent,
skilled professional. Then there was an indrawing of breath as
each realized that someone in the room was looking at him or
her.

With a start, Lujan realized that he was looking at Tony Hanson. He smiled his ingenuous smile with the flair of much practice, but it was not returned, and he thought, Not you. I find it
hard to believe that you are here for any noble reason or that you
are worthy of much respect. You're a petty little bureaucrat, and
I intend to find out just how you got accepted on this crew.

"Now that we've introduced ourselves," Winthrop continued
with a momentary twinkle in his eye, "let's talk about the mission." A hologram of Sol and its planets appeared in the curve
of the table. Earth was easy to spot in its traditional form of a
blue and white sphere.

"We'll come out of our spatial warp here," Winthrop explained, indicating the spot with a light pen. "Because of the
vagaries of spatial warping and the position of Earth's moon, we
need to arrive on its backside—that is, it will be moving away
from us in its orbit. We'll be entering the warp under full thrust,

so we'll be coming out of it at the same speed; we don't want suddenly to find the moon in our faces.''

A hand shot up from the crew. ''Why enter under full thrust?'' a man asked. ''Wouldn't it be safer to come to a stop before warping?''

''That's the normal procedure,'' Winthrop said, ''but it requires a great deal of fuel to stop and then restart our motion. We're traveling light; just enough fuel to do what we have to do and get home. By warping under thrust and letting our inertia carry us when we come out on the other side, we'll save 240 tons.''

''And the price of the fuel,'' Jacqueline grumbled.

Clayton ignored her. ''With the kind of distance we're warping, the margin for error is about seven hundred miles. Our target is to come out three hundred thousand miles beyond lunar orbit, sufficiently removed from the strongest effects of the magnetic fields of both Earth and Moon. Even if the margin goes the other way and we arrive farther from lunar orbit, we'll reach Earth orbit in a matter of hours. Time we have in plenty; fuel is another matter.''

The hologram changed; Earth was now at the center of the display, and a tiny ship orbited her. ''We'll fix the ship directly above the area where the research team was left behind, here in the southwestern desert of North America. We have one probe— it can tell us whether the atmosphere is breathable, what the temperature is, other things it would be nice to know before we set foot on the surface. We won't try to land on the mountain itself; unless nature has made some violent changes, there should be plenty of flatland nearby. The shuttle will go down first; we'll set up a warp terminal in its cargo bay. We're trying to talk our good friends on the Board''—here he clapped a hand on the director's shoulder—''into at least one mini-shuttle as an emergency backup. It would be a shame to get all the way to Earth, then have to come back empty-handed because of a system failure on the ground and no way to get to it. Once the terminal is established, we have several jet packs, landcrawlers, and fliers to get us up the mountain or anywhere else we may decide to search for life.''

Another hand shot up. ''Captain, seven hundred miles seems like an awfully broad margin. Just how dangerous is this jump?''

Winthrop turned to his first officer. ''Mr. Lujan, would you care to explain?''

''I'd be happy to, Captain,'' Derek replied, coming to his feet with a smile. He stood facing Winthrop for a moment, enjoying the fact that he was two or three inches taller than the captain. Winthrop had broader shoulders, of course, even without the uniform; that was why Derek had chosen a more tapered style for himself, to accentuate the athletic trim of his body. Still, he doubted he could take Winthrop in a wrestling match, even a friendly one.

The captain sat down, and Derek smiled out at his audience. "If you'll bear with me, I'd like to start with a basic explanation of Yuko's law," he began. Turning to the screen on the wall behind him, he activated his light pen and drew a line. "We start with one dimension," he said. "In order to achieve another dimension, we have to square it." He drew three other lines to make a square. "Now we have two dimensions: height and breadth. If we square it again, we have three dimensions." He expanded this drawing into a cube, with straight lines angling back from the original square to another square sketched behind it.

Derek checked his listeners to make sure they were following. He loved doing this demonstration; it always got a good reaction. For a while he had considered teaching as a profession, but it didn't pay nearly enough. And there were only so many ways a teacher could supplement his income.

"So what happens if we square the cube?" he asked.

"You have a tesseract," someone in the front row replied.

"Exactly. And the tesseract is the basic unit involved in Yuko's law, which states that the shortest distance between two points is *not* a straight line; it's a bend. A warp."

They were shifting in their seats now, not sure they followed him. It was time for the pièce de résistance. "Let's see, this cube is roughly—" He measured the lines of the original square between his hands. "—fifteen inches. Now, if I'm standing on the front of the cube," he proposed, drawing a stick figure atop the front square, "and I want to get to the back of this cube," and he drew a circle on the back square, "how far do I have to travel?"

There was a moment of hesitation. "Fifteen inches," someone replied.

"Really?" Lujan drew a straight line from his stick figure to the circle just behind it. "Looks like about four inches to me."

From the corner of his eye he caught Captain Winthrop smiling.

"But your drawing isn't in three dimensions," someone objected finally. "It's in two. It wouldn't be four inches in a hologram."

"Exactly," Lujan agreed. "By forcing three dimensions into two, I've showed you a shorter route. Essentially, Yuko's law does the same thing, but going the other way. The mathematics get complicated, but when you apply the theory to a three-dimensional object, and factor in time as the fourth dimension, it pushes you up one dimension, from four to five. The result is a shortcut.

"Unfortunately," he went on, perching casually on the edge of the table, "I can't make you a visual model of five dimensions; if I could, I'd have a VanKurtz Prize. But I can tell you that despite what you were taught in school, five dimensions are not unstable." He put on his most serious expression, then cracked a smile. "It's our calculations that waver a bit. We've redefined the formula far beyond what it was at the time of the Evacuation, but we still need to allow a margin of about two miles for the jump from here to, say, Aunt Shelby's." The mention of this notorious pleasure planet in the next system drew the expected smiles. "And the margin increases exponentially with distance."

Another hand went up, and Lujan nodded toward it. "Isn't it also a bending of time?" a woman inquired. "So that, no matter how great the distance, you still arrive only seconds after you left? If all goes according to plan."

Lujan grinned. "You must be our other warp technician," he accused. "You're right, of course. Yuko's theory postulates that in five-D, time and space are essentially identical, similar to the way matter and energy are interchangeable. There are a lot of variables involved, like velocity, acceleration, distance traveled, and the strength of the warp field, and as the variables increase in magnitude, the results can get pretty mind-boggling, but in theory, if you could bend space far enough, you'd arrive before you left."

"Or fifty years later," someone offered darkly.

Lujan's smile faded a bit. "That's the only real danger in warp travel," he acknowledged. "When the *Betsy Ross* arrived fifty years after she left—a passage of seconds for the crew— she'd gone into warp in an area where massive stellar flares were causing electrical disturbances. We don't yet know why, or how, electromagnetic disturbances and strong gravitational fields affect the warp equation, but we know enough to avoid them. We learned the hard way." Besides the *Betsy Ross*, several ships had come out of warp in the wrong place: One crashed into an asteroid, another was vaporized by the proximity of a star, and two others had been far enough off course to run out of fuel while making corrections.

"So you see, we're not taking any chances," Lujan continued, lightening his tone. "We enter warp well beyond the magnetic field of Argo, and we come out well beyond the pull of Earth. And when it comes to ship-to-surface travel, we send a shuttle down to establish a warp terminal. Having a terminal at each end takes away the margin of error; we don't have to worry about coming out of warp with our feet six inches below ground level." There was a nervous titter from his listeners. "And don't worry—I test everything on myself first."

The captain rose. "Thank you, Mr. Lujan," he said gravely. Lujan took his cue and sat back down. Winthrop went on then about the twofold purpose of the mission: to see if human life had survived and to report on the current status of Earth from geological and meteorological standpoints.

Lujan only half listened; the officers had been briefed earlier. Instead he watched the crew, trying to fit faces with names he had read on the crew roster. One by one he went down the rows, testing himself, until he came to Karen Reichert.

Karen. There was something odd about her, something both haunted and haunting. She was lovely with an almost mannequinlike perfection, but when he looked at her, he felt he was seeing a person with no soul.

Her medical file hinted at something. That information was confidential, of course, and there was a security lock on it, but such devices were no barrier to a man of Lujan's skills. He knew a good deal more than warp physics. And as first officer he intended to know everything there was to know about his crew, including personal and confidential histories. He had bypassed the lock without compunction.

But the TRC doctor had not been explicit. "Subject shows no physiological evidence of stress . . ." Was there another kind of evidence? "I recommend that the subject not be allowed visitors once she returns to the barracks. This will afford her a tranquil adjustment period and uninterrupted concentration on the task at hand." It sounded as though she were in an addiction recovery program. Who was the visitor the doctor was afraid would show up? A domineering mother? An old boyfriend? A hit man?

You are a mystery, Karen Reichert, Lujan thought, and I like mysteries. I like them very much.

Derek put on his most charming smile as he entered the Health Center. "Good morning, Doctor," he greeted. "Good morning, Chief."

Jacqueline was leaning on a counter, chatting companionably with Rita Zleboton. Both women looked up as he spoke, hostility in their eyes. There was a tense moment; then Jacqueline turned to an array of instruments she had spread on the counter. "Wipe the smile off your face, Lujan," she told him, "and come right to the point."

Aha. Every bit as blunt as her reputation. "I'm concerned about one of the crew members," he said, stripping every vestige of cajolery from his voice. There was no point trying to manipulate a woman who could spot manipulation a mile away. "If someone has a problem that might affect her work performance, I think the officers ought to know."

Jacqueline exchanged a glance with Rita, who excused herself tersely. She brushed past Derek without a word, and her heavy step was heard retreating down the corridor. When she had gone, Jacqueline turned around and cocked an eyebrow at him. "Her?" she prompted.

He gave a wry grin. "Well, I'm not above a little self-interest," he admitted. Was that what she wanted to hear? "But it really is a bit disconcerting to see one of my crew walking around like a zombie."

"Karen Reichert." Jacqueline frowned and turned back to her instruments.

"What's wrong with her, Doctor?" Derek pursued.

"You mean besides the fact that she's been physically assaulted on a regular basis?"

Lujan's jaw dropped. "Beaten?"

"Among other things."

That's not in her record, he found himself thinking. "How do you know?"

Jacqueline sighed and opened another cabinet door. "I know the symptoms; I interned in a women's clinic on Darius. Their culture still approves of submissive women. Give me the fleet any day; at least the women know how to fight back."

"Who?" Derek asked, both repulsed and intrigued.

But Jacqueline only shrugged. "Monsters come in assorted

packages. Anyway, it won't affect her work, if that was really your concern.''

"One of them," he replied. "Thank you, Doctor. I appreciate your candor." He started for the door.

"Lujan!" Jacqueline called after him. "Be kind to her. Be very, very kind." There was a warning tone in her voice.

"I wanna see my daughter!" Winston Reichert raged.

The receptionist at the Coalition's training center inched his chair back from the console, ready to put distance between himself and the burly, red-faced man. "I'm sorry, sir, the mission team is involved in a class right now. There will be a free period at—"

Reichert slammed his huge hands down on the desk, sending the receptionist skittering backward in his chair. "She's my daughter," Reichert growled, "and I want to see her *now*."

"I'm sorry, sir," the receptionist stammered, his numb brain unable to think of any clever subterfuge to use against a man who obviously had forty pounds and a great deal of adrenaline on him. "I can't reach her just now. She's in class—"

"Then I'll find her myself," Reichert snarled, starting around the console for the door.

The receptionist hesitated, weighing the merits of physical intervention versus waiting for Security—the man must have crashed the gate, and Security should be on its way already—

"Can I help you?" came an arresting voice.

Derek Lujan stood in the doorway facing Reichert, fixed in an imposing stance the receptionist had never seen him use before. But it was not his bearing so much as the steely cold edge to his voice that stopped Winston Reichert, if only for a moment.

"I'm here to get my daughter," Reichert growled, and made to go past the young officer.

Lujan's restraining hand was firm, though his tone was carefully polite. "What's your daughter's name?" he asked, blue eyes glinting like ice.

"Karen Reichert."

Blood rushed in Lujan's ears as Jacqueline's words came back to him: beaten—among other things. So this was the monster. He smiled with grim satisfaction. "I'm sorry, Mr. Reichert," he said in the same polite, dangerous tone, "this area is restricted. You'll have to leave."

Reichert shoved his face to within inches of Lujan's. His

breath reeked of stale tobacco as he glared menacingly at the young man and promised, "Not without my daughter."

Eyes locked, they weighed each other. Reichert sneered belligerently. Lujan's mustache twitched; he held up his hands in a gesture of capitulation; then he slammed his knee upward with brutal force. Reichert doubled over in agony, and Lujan landed a crushing right on the point of the big man's jaw. With a sickening thud Reichert dropped to the floor and did not move.

There was a moment of silence. Then two security guards burst through the door. Lujan smiled at them. "Ah, gentlemen," he greeted them. "Kindly remove this refuse from the lobby." He massaged his right hand gingerly and wondered how many bones he had cracked. "And Larry," he told the receptionist, "if it shows up again, do call me. For now, I'll—" He winced. "—be in the Health Center."

"I offered to teach this class as a means of building up our physical strength before we embark on this mission," Derek lied smoothly. But it was all right; every one of the twenty-six people in the gym knew he was lying. They also knew why his right hand was bandaged and why the captain had supported the idea of a class in self-defense. "We don't know what we might find on Earth, and it behooves us to be in good physical condition, with sharp reflexes."

Karen Reichert watched the handsome, athletic officer and wondered again at his behavior. She had expected, after the episode with her father, that Derek Lujan would come knocking on her door to receive her thanks, but he hadn't. She had seen him at mess two or three times since then, and if his eyes chanced to meet hers—which somehow they always did—he would smile that disarming smile of his and she could feel a blush rising to her cheeks. But he never approached her.

I should say something, Karen thought for the hundredth time. I should just go up and say, "I heard about what you did, and I just wanted to thank you." But how could she thank him? Sooner or later she would have to go home. How could Derek Lujan protect her then?

Perhaps she wouldn't go home. Perhaps when the mission was over, she would go somewhere else. Maybe she could convince TRC to lose her records, or change them just a little, or say she had died while she was there. Then she could really go somewhere else and not be followed. She wondered where Derek was from . . .

"Unfortunately, I can't demonstrate this technique at the moment," Lujan was saying without so much as a glance at his injured hand. "Perhaps Mr. Hanson would do us the honor."

Tony Hanson swaggered to the front of the class. He struck the stance Lujan had spoken of, showing surprising suppleness for his bulk. "I'll be your guinea pig, Tony," Derek offered, taking up a position opposite him. "Now watch as I come at Tony with my right—my left hand, how he pivots and—" With a swift move Hanson flipped the younger officer to the mat. Derek gave a small *oof*. "And uses my own momentum against me. Did you catch that?"

His gaze swept the class, and Karen was sure it stopped to rest on her. "Let's do it one more time. Tony?"

Tony helped him to his feet, and they squared off once again. They were an odd pair of combatants, one square and grizzled, the other sleek and youthful. Derek moved faster this time, a lunging strike. Tony caught his leading left arm and began to pivot, but suddenly Lujan could not resist; he countered with his right foot and threw the second officer off balance, causing him to crash heavily to the mat.

Hanson scrambled to his knees, eyes blazing, and Lujan wondered if he hadn't made a serious mistake. "Come on, Tony, it was a joke," he said softly. "A demonstration for the class. Take a poke at me later if you want."

Tony restrained himself, but the hardness did not disappear from his eyes.

"And that," Derek said to the class, "is the countermove. Lesson number two: Every move has a countermove."

Tony Hanson got to his feet with as much good grace as he could muster and returned to the sidelines, his ears burning. Arrogant, cocksure young bastard, he thought. Think you've got it all over older guys like me. But wait and see, Mr. First Officer, sir. It's a long way to Earth and back.

Karen watched Derek as he moved among the pairs of students, correcting their postures and their grips as they tried out the maneuver. Not until he got to her did their eyes meet and he smile at her. Now he's going to say something, she thought. Now he's going to make some reference to my father, to his cracked knuckles . . .

"Spread your feet a little wider," was all he said to her. "Not too much . . . that's good. Now pivot. No, with your whole body." He demonstrated for her; why didn't he mold his body around hers and show her that way? It was a ploy that had been used before. But he stood apart. She tried again to imitate the move.

"Excellent. Now try it with your partner."

What, no offer to be her partner? No taking advantage of the opportunity to be in physical contact with her? Perhaps she was mistaken. Perhaps he smiled at everyone like that. She looked up into his eyes.

No, not like that. He did not look at everyone like that. Then why do you keep your distance, Derek Lujan? Are you waiting for me to come to you? I don't know how.

"Excellent, excellent," Derek murmured as she executed the maneuver. "Practice it a few more times, then change places." He started toward the next pair of students.

But as he passed her, his left hand wrapped gently around her upper arm. "I need to ask you a favor," he whispered without looking at her. "Can I stop by your quarters tonight?"

"Sure," Karen murmured, and her thumping heart slowed down somewhat. He would come by her quarters. Of course. Sooner or later it was bound to happen.

This is only another space voyage, she told herself. Just another ship with carbonite walls and close, stale air. Nothing but hard work and routine and someone who wanted favors from her. Derek Lujan was, after all, only a man.

Oswald Dillon turned from his guests and smiled at Camilla. "Yes?"

"The Terran Research Coalition," she whispered as he took her arm and led her several steps away, toward the statue of Ari Yuko. "Their permission to embark was just granted by the Confederated Transportation Commission."

"I feared it would be," he replied mildly. "It is well that I took other steps."

"Other steps?" Camilla's stomach tightened; she wondered just what other kinds of steps a man like Dillon would take to stop the Earth venture.

"Oh, don't worry, my dear," he laughed, seeing her concern. "I have merely placed an agent in the crew. He will cause things to happen in accordance with my will—without endangering the crew, since that includes himself. He is a greedy man but not a foolish one." Camilla felt her tension lessen. Dillon turned to lead her back toward the waiting knot of people. "Come meet my guests. They are people it would be well for you to know."

CHAPTER SEVEN

Castle Rock smiled smugly to herself as she patted the corn-meal mixture into a flat tortilla and set it on a hot stone to bake. Two Moons had just stopped by to visit with Castle Rock's mother and had mentioned rather pointedly that Coconino could not leave on his great adventure until after the Choosing. The Mother had said so.

And I know why, Castle Rock thought. Yes, I know why. Because Coconino is so slow to choose a wife, the Mother wants to impress upon him that his choice may soon be narrowed. It is a clever plan, and because the Mother thought of it, it must work. But I will do my part to help it along.

Carefully she turned the tortilla. The problem, she decided, is that Coconino thinks I will always be here, that I will turn other men from my door while I wait for him to change his mind. He scorns me because I am such easy prey. A hunter wants to be challenged. A hunter wants to feel he has cunningly tracked his quarry and, with a swift and skillful shot, brought it down. Most of all, a hunter likes to think his arrow was swifter and truer than that of another man who shot at the same time.

So I will make him track me. I will let him think he must compete for my favor, and with a worthy adversary. I will let him believe he was the hunter.

And after we are married, I will tell him the truth.

There was no reason for Coconino to be happy. Lame Rabbit would be village-bound until his twisted ankle healed. His own dreams of marrying a Witch Woman were shattered, and now there would be pressure for him to choose one of the village girls. Juan had decided not to join him on his quest for Tala, and though he would have left immediately, he had been forbidden to go until after the Choosing, which time was indefinite, to say the least.

Yet Coconino was happy. He lounged contentedly on the ground in front of Falling Star's wickiup, watching his half sister Talia as she bent over the cook fire to spoon stew into a bowl for her husband. She looked very much like their mother, especially now that her middle swelled with the child she carried. It would arrive at the end of summer, one year after she and Falling Star had been married. Talia was fifteen.

Lulled by a full stomach and Falling Star's account of his day's hunt, Coconino drifted as peacefully as the scent of mesquite blossoms on the breeze. The sun was sliding down the edge of the cliff face southwest of the village; soon twilight would creep upon them, followed by the sudden velvet blackness of the desert night. Stars would shine clear and cold in the cloudless sky, specks of light shimmering like frost on a smooth, black bowl overturned on the mountain peaks.

The men and women returned now from their fields, trudging up the path from the creek. Their faces were dusty and tired but happy, for the young plants breaking the ground were numerous and the depth of the creek promised a good water supply well into the growing season. The Mother Earth seemed pleased with her children, and all was well.

Gonzales came with them, smiling and conversing with Loves the Dust. They paused at the stream to wash their faces and hands, then continued up the slope and into the village. Several mothers of eligible maidens called to Gonzales to come and join them for supper, but Gonzales smiled and begged off, heading for his own wickiup at the far end of the village.

Just beyond Falling Star's wickiup Castle Rock was coming up the path, a bowl of steamed sotol and fresh roasted quail in her hands. Coconino thought that she was a long way from her wickiup and wondered what she was plotting now. But, he thought tolerantly, tonight even she cannot spoil my mood. It is good to be of the People and a favored son of the Mother Earth!

But it was not Coconino she sought out. Instead she approached the Teacher shyly, raising her downcast eyes only occasionally to look at him from beneath long lashes. Coconino could not hear what she said, for she spoke softly, but the music of her voice carried to him and her purpose was obvious. Gracefully—but modestly—she offered Gonzales the bowl of food. Gonzales hesitated, then took the bowl from her hand. She flashed him a smile that was sunshine breaking through clouds and started to skip away.

"Wait!" the Teacher called. He came slowly to where she stood; then the two of them continued down the path together, she looking up at his great height with bright eyes.

Coconino turned away to find Falling Star watching him. "What?" he growled.

"I think the Choosing may not be so far off as you think," Falling Star suggested.

"Good."

Falling Star grinned. "Good for the Teacher."

Coconino considered that a moment. "Castle Rock is very pretty," he admitted. "She has a sweet face and a smile that— you saw how she smiled at him. Such a smile could warm a man on a cold winter day. And her eyes? Her eyes can be soft as cotton or shiny as stars. She is young and filled with life, and her voice is like the voice of a brook laughing in summer. Yes. I could marry her myself," he said, rising to his feet. "If her charm were not all by design and she so calculating. As it is, I wish the Teacher good luck. He will need it." Then he grinned at his brother-in-law and strolled away.

Yes, Coconino was very happy.

The Witch Woman Phoenix sat on the hardened mud bank of the stream, drying herself in the sun. The creek was getting shallower now, and the kiss of the sun at midday was a fiery one. Her muddy racial heritage had blessed her with skin pigment almost as dark as the People's—thank goodness for that, she thought. A lighter person would burn to a crisp out here. But she had never worried about the sun; of course, on the mountain, her work seldom took her out into it. It had been years since she had been this brown.

"What is your magic?" Coconino had asked her once.

"Haven't figured that out yet."

"What was it on the Mountain?"

"Keeping three-hundred-year-old machines running on spit and candle wax and whatever spare parts I could manufacture in the metal shop. Unfortunately, you don't have much use for machines out here."

"Fortunately," he corrected her. "I do not like machines."

She looked at him curiously. "Why not?"

"They stink," he said flatly. "And make noise. Phoenix, how can you hear the Mother Earth through all that clatter?"

Phoenix. It still sounded foreign, but he was right, the name suited her. Rising up from ashes, hard and charred—or new and tender? And having become Phoenix, would she ever be Debbie again? Even to herself?

Now she reached out a hand to a patch of soft caked sand that the receding waters had left on the bank. It was warm and smooth and fell into loose grains as she brushed it with her palm. Like a slate, she thought, unmarked and waiting . . . Slowly she drew the outline of a bird with her finger.

A shadow crossed her sandy sketch pad, and she looked up to see Coconino standing over her. "God, you're quiet," she muttered. "The deer don't stand a chance with you around."

"What is that?" he asked, pointing to her marks in the sand.

"It's supposed to be a phoenix," she said, "but I'm not much of an artist."

Kneeling beside her, he deftly added flames at the feet of the bird and a stroke or two to indicate motion. "Not bad," she admitted. Then an idea occurred to her. "Can you draw Tala?"

"In the pictures of the People, Tala is shown like this," he told her, making a curved stick figure with four legs, an arched neck, and a single horn. It was graceful and stylish. "But what I saw looked more like this." With a few strokes he outlined a quadruped deep in the chest, lean in the flank, with a bulky neck and withers deeply textured. The horn he indicated as a curlicue.

"What do the stories of the People say about him?" Phoenix asked.

"That he is a kachina, one of the spirits which come in the form of human or animal, a special child of the Mother Earth. What do the Men-on-the-Mountain say about him?"

"That he died in the Before Times." She saw the dark look cross his face and wished she had not been quite so glib. "Well, that's what we thought, because we hadn't seen any—but once we thought all the People had died, too, until we found them here in the Village of the Ancients. Have any others among the People seen Tala?"

Coconino shrugged. "None that live now. The People rarely go as far north as the Black Lands."

"The Black Lands? Is that where they say he lives?" she asked with greater interest. Coconino nodded. "Well, that would make sense, because the original herd was just northeast of there, up in Colorado."

"Original herd?"

"Well . . ." Phoenix hesitated, wondering how much of the

story he could grasp. "You know about the other planets, right?"

He pointed skyward. "The Sisters of the Mother Earth? Out there?"

"Right. Other worlds. And people from Earth went there to live. On one of them there were all kinds of animals: six-legged cats and birds with four wings . . . Well, when the Earth was struck with famine, there was a man in Colorado who imported some of these unicorns—that's what people called them, although their real name was *Celux* something or other—as livestock. They were very hardy, and he thought they could survive on less fodder than beef cattle.

"But people started poaching his breeding stock right away. They say he sat there with a disrupter trying to protect his herd, but hungry people will go to dangerous extremes. He was found impaled on the horn of a dead unicorn—or actually, the severed head, which was all that was left. The herd scattered; it was generally assumed they were all hunted down and eaten. Not much escaped the butcher knife in those days."

Coconino frowned uneasily and gently brushed his marks out of the sand. He did not like stories about the Before Times; they were filled with much senseless violence and a blatant disregard for the Mother Earth. Why She had not struck back sooner he did not know, for he had seen the wounds, the scars, that lay upon her body still. Though She had purged herself with wind and fire and floods, yet were there places the sight of which made him grieve. There was ground where nothing would grow yet, waters which five hundred years later could still make one sick.

Truly the people of the Before Times had no respect.

Slowly he scooped up a handful of sand and let it slip through his fingers. The image of Tala's noble head frozen in death, severed from the powerful body, was nauseating. "To take the life of Tala," he said softly, "to rub out his existence like the eagle and the beaver—this is a great wickedness."

"So was starving to death," she pointed out.

But the image was too powerful for him. "It was their own fault!" he snarled, fist clenched on the last grains of sand. "They tortured the Mother Earth till she cried, 'Enough!' And she shook their cities so that they tumbled down, and sent black clouds to blot out the sun, and rained fire upon their evil to drive it out."

The Witch Woman eyed him a moment. "Well, that's one way to put it," she observed dryly. "Hey, don't worry about it, all right? It was before our time. We're the product, not the cause. What can we do?''

He relaxed a little and stood up, brushing the sand from his palm. ''We can search for Tala,'' he said, ''and declare to all the People, and to the Men-on-the-Mountain, that he lives to mock the Before Times. To say that the Mother Earth can save whom she chooses despite the cruelty of those Others, those ones who lived Before.'' A smile touched his lips. ''And we can leave soon. I just spoke with the Mother. The Choosing will be tomorrow night.''

Phoenix exhaled deeply, surprised to find she had been holding her breath. She shook out her hair, almost dry now, glad that Coconino's moment of environmental passion was over. Its intensity had surprised her and had left seeds of concern that she did not want to dwell on. ''Will he choose Nina, do you think?'' she asked, grateful for the change of subject.

Coconino shook his head. ''*I* would not choose Nina,'' he said flatly.

''I know that,'' she laughed, ''but you're young and vain. Ben is neither.''

''It doesn't matter,'' he told her. ''Men-on-the-Mountain always choose beautiful maidens.''

''Always?''

''Always. They only stay a year, maybe two—there is no time to grow too deeply in love or too much to hate. Why should a man not have what pleases his eye, since it will not last forever?''

The words bit into her, and she scowled. ''I could make a man's life miserable for a year,'' she said darkly.

Again Coconino shrugged. ''If the girl ceases to please him, he is free to abandon her and choose another.''

''What!''

''But that has only happened once. Among the People it is a great honor to be a Chosen Companion. Few have been unhappy.''

''You'd never catch me agreeing to it,'' she growled.

''But you are not of the People,'' he pointed out. ''Imagine this, though: If any man in the village was yours for the asking and honored to be your choice—and only this one time!—what kind of man would you choose?''

Phoenix stood up, brushing herself off. ''I don't know,'' she grumbled. ''I'm just ornery enough to pick the fellow who least expected it.'' But she thought, Would I really? Or would I pick the sexiest one in the bunch and find out, just once, what it was like to be wanted by the kind of gorgeous man I always dreamed of but knew I could never have? Am I selfish enough to do that?

You bet your sweet ass I am.

Together they trudged up the bank toward the village. Phoenix watched Coconino from the corner of her eye as he moved with casual grace, no swagger to detract from the natural working of his body. Certainly his choice of maidens would not be restricted, either—had not been, for in the customs of the People he could have married three, even four years ago. A question that had bothered her recurred. "Hey, Coconino," she asked finally, her voice intentionally brassy. "When I first came, why did you want to marry me?"

He jumped. A blush would have been difficult to see in his dark skin, but his eyes were, as always, a window to his emotions. God help you, she thought, if you ever have to deceive someone. It's not that you *don't* lie—you *can't*.

Coconino swallowed once. "For years," he said, "I dreamed of marrying a Witch Woman. When I knew that you had arrived, I thought that time had come."

"That's what I thought," she rasped. "I knew it couldn't be my personal magnetism."

He looked at her hard face as she marched beside him, nearly his height, arms dangling from the sleeveless shirt. "It was forward of me, I know," he said, hoping to avoid the true thrust of her comment, "and you were right to rebuke me for my arrogance."

She nailed him with eyes that said she knew full well he was sidestepping. Coconino swallowed again and stared down at the path. "It would still be an honor," he said, "if you ever wish to reconsider."

Angrily she whirled on him. "Look! If and when I'm in the market for male companionship, *I'll* do the asking. *I'm* the Witch Woman. And until that time, if you so much as mention the subject again, I'll stuff your silly marriage proposal down your silly throat and I'll roast your eyeballs for lunch! *Comprende?*" Then she stormed off toward her cliff home.

Coconino drew a deep breath and turned down the path toward his mother's wickiup. Somehow he had done it again, raised the Witch Woman' incredible fury. But he was baffled at the predicament he'd found himself in: to say nothing would have been to admit he found her undesirable, a thing that obviously hurt her. Yet to say that he would marry her had again brought down her wrath, her rejection, and a bitterness that seemed so much deeper than it should have been.

Like choosing between falling on cactus and falling on stones, he thought. Like choosing between celibacy and Castle Rock. It was no choice at all.

As though to mock his dilemma, Castle Rock stepped out from behind a wickiup to confront him on the path. "Coconino, may I walk with you?" she asked.

He halted. "The path is the path, and any may walk upon it," he growled.

"Coconino, please." Her voice was soft and anguished. Coconino looked at her in surprise. There was no arrogance in her face, no smug smile or mocking eyes. For a moment she looked very like the child she was.

"Very well," he said more gently. "Let us walk." What harm could it do anymore?

For a while they walked in silence. In the center of the village the open space around the Elvira was deserted. Those men and women who were not in the fields were hunting or gathering the fruits of desert plants or tending small children in the shadow of the cliff. For all purposes, Coconino and Castle Rock were alone.

She stopped near the unlit fire. "There will be a Choosing tomorrow," she began.

"The Mother told me."

She raised pleading eyes to his. "And it means nothing to you?"

There was a mocking edge to his voice. "It means I can leave to search for Tala."

She dropped her eyes then. "It means something to me," she murmured.

"I should imagine it means a great deal to you," he replied. "A great honor, another bead on your string of pride. Who then will be able to resist your charms?" He had not meant to be quite so sarcastic, but once begun, the words had tumbled out.

The hurt on her face was obvious, but she blinked away her tears and continued. "It is a great honor, isn't it?" she said. "To be Chosen by a Man-on-the-Mountain, of all the maidens in the Village. It is indeed an honor." She swallowed. "But Coconino, I do not want to be Chosen!"

"Then you should not have played the sweet young maid," he told her. "If you play the game, you must pay the wager."

"You are heartless, Coconino!" she cried, tears escaping now and trickling down her cheeks.

"I am tired," he retorted. "Tired of your wheedling, tired of your ploys, tired of you trying to use me to please yourself. You can't always have what you want. It can't always be your own way. It is a painful lesson, but until you learn it, you are still a child, a spoiled child." But even as he spoke, he knew the words were as much to himself as to her.

"I just don't understand," she sobbed. "What is so terrible about me?"

He softened then. Her tears were genuine, and he was touched by them. "You are not terrible," he conceded. "You are annoying, but you are not terrible. Except perhaps—" And here he smiled wryly. "—when you told the Witch Woman I planned to marry her."

Castle Rock hung her head. "I'm sorry. But you mocked me so by the stream that day—"

"As you mocked me," he told her. "That day and a hundred others when you assumed that of course it was you I'd marry, as though I had no mind or feelings of my own." He tilted her tear-stained chin up with a crooked finger. "You are not terrible, Castle Rock. But you are not perfection, either."

She tried to blink away some of the tears. "Why don't you want me?" she asked, bewildered.

The irony struck him, for at that moment he wanted her very much. Her soft and sensuous body was close to his; her pride was gone, and in its place was a vulnerability he found most alluring. Had this been a private place, away from the eyes of the village, he would have gladly drawn that body much closer, dried the tears with his kisses, let her willing eagerness fuel the fire in him till it consumed them both. But he was saved from his own desire by the nearness of the women on the rock shelf below the cliff, the maidens bringing water up from the creek. "Perhaps," he mused aloud, "in a year, after the Man-on-the-Mountain has gone and you are a little older—"

"But I don't *want* to wait a year," she whined. "And I *don't* want to be his Chosen Companion, not even for a week!"

Coconino drew his hand away in surprise. "Why not?" he asked.

"Because he's *ugly*," she hissed. "He grows the hair on his lip, and he's old and dull, and he works all day in the field—"

"Then refuse him!" Coconino challenged, his sympathy vanishing with her returned pettiness. "It is your right. But don't cry to me to save you from the wickiup you have built yourself!" He stalked angrily away from her.

He headed for his mother's wickiup, thinking to take his bow and quiver and go out in search of quail or fox or anything else foolish enough to cross his path just so he could prove to it that he was the best hunter in the village and not to be trifled with. But as he passed near one wickiup, a gentle voice called to him. "Coconino."

He spun to face Corn Hair, his blood still hot from the encounter with Castle Rock. She stood beside her cook fire, graceful as a willow, her blond hair pulled to one side of her neck and falling nearly to her waist. The memory of their time together in his secret place rushed back, and he longed for night. Somehow he would sneak her away from Lame Rabbit, away from her children, away from the Village—

She met his burning eyes, but her own brown eyes were soft and liquid. "There will be a Choosing tomorrow."

Why did they all feel they had to tell him that? "What has that to do with me?" he snapped.

She blinked at his tone but let it slide, turning her attention to the quail she had spitted, giving it a quarter turn. "It is said that you will leave our village the day after," she continued.

He relaxed then, flexing his shoulders and realizing how tense he had been. "I did not mean to be sharp," he apologized. "Yes, I will leave the day after to search for Tala."

"With the Witch Woman."

"Yes."

She looked back at him. "Has she changed her mind about you?"

Coconino shifted uncomfortably. "In what way?"

It was a moment before Corn Hair replied. "Does she consider you for a—a Companion?"

He felt the heat creeping up his neck and into his face. "She does not desire me, and I do not desire her," he said simply. "It works very well."

Corn Hair nodded and added another stick to her fire. "That is as I thought." She watched the flames lick at the new wood, test it, sear it, till finally it yielded and was consumed like the others. "You need a wife, Coconino."

He sighed. "That I know."

She poked at the fire with another stick. "And tomorrow there will be a Choosing and one less maiden in the village. Then you will leave, and by the time you return a second may be gone and a third. Will you take what is left, Coconino?''

He shifted again. ''I have asked myself this question, Corn Hair. I do not know the answer. I will have to wait and see.''

''You may wait, of course,'' she agreed, ''although that seems to me a great waste.'' His blood surged again; blessed Mother Earth, cloak us with your mantle of darkness once more! ''As long as you realize that I am not a temporary solution to your problem.''

Suddenly he felt as though something had sucked all the air from his lungs. ''Not a . . .'' He tried to make it mean something else. ''No, I did not think you so transient, to be used for a time and—''

''One time,'' she corrected him. ''There was just one time. There will not be another.''

He swallowed hard. ''Never?''

She adjusted a stick in the fire, then put her poker aside. ''Whenever I hear the drums,'' she said, ''I am filled with such sweet sorrow, such longing as I . . . It is the drums. So it was the night I accepted Lame Rabbit.'' She sighed. ''And then there was your sorrow—that bright-eyed little viper Castle Rock!—and the Witch Woman and your broken dreams . . .'' She smiled sadly, remembering. ''I do not regret it. I will never regret it. But it is gone and will not come again.''

''That is for the Mother Earth to say,'' Coconino replied.

Corn Hair laughed. ''Perhaps, Coconino,'' she admitted. ''But listen well to what *I* say, for I would hate for there to be a misunderstanding between us. We have been such good friends. Let it remain so.''

Good friends, yes, he thought, but didn't you know how I— But of course you did. You knew it before I did. You were always just a little wiser, though we were born the same summer . . . And perhaps it is your wisdom now that says no more nights together. But more likely it is just your careful logic, the logic by which you chose Lame Rabbit, the logic which is not always right. There was more than friendship in the willow grove that night. There was more than my need; there was yours, too—I have not forgotten. So you can say it is over and will not come again.

But when the drums sound again, then we will know.

CHAPTER EIGHT

"You look like hell," Phoenix told Coconino.

They had slowed their pace to a walk, but Coconino still held water in his mouth, so he said nothing.

"What's the matter with you, anyway?" she pursued. "We're finally on our way, on our quest; you're supposed to be ecstatic. You look like your mother just died."

He spit the water out angrily. "Don't say such a thing!" he snarled.

"*Ooo,* my, aren't we touchy!"

"It is a black and evil thought; don't even think it!"

"Okay, okay. Hey, it's just an expression; I didn't mean anything by it. What's your problem, anyway?"

"I have no problem," he snapped. Then after a moment, "I have many problems, all related, but I can do nothing about any of them, so they do not bear thinking about; therefore, I have no problem."

She studied the stormy face. "That's the most twisted piece of logic I ever heard," she said flatly.

"It is the logic of the People."

"I don't doubt it." They continued in silence for a while. Then Phoenix spoke again. "I take it you weren't delirious about the Choosing."

"What has this Choosing to do with me?" he exploded. "Everyone I know came to tell me there would be a Choosing, then watched me like a hawk watches a rattlesnake. What did they expect to see? Horns sprouting from my head? Wings growing from my back? It was a Choosing, like a dozen others I have seen. What did they think?"

"They thought you would marry Castle Rock," she said dryly.

93

"I would rather marry a wounded puma."

Phoenix could not suppress a smile. "Well, she's not my favorite person, either," she admitted. "But that's because I think she's a conniving little weasel. What's your reason?"

He glanced at her finally just to be sure she was not mocking him. "She is a conniving little weasel," he agreed.

"But a cute one."

"A puma kitten is also cute."

"True." She sighed. "Well, maybe in a year or so she'll be less obnoxious."

"I will worry about that in a year or so."

She studied him again. "Then what is it that's gotten you so upset?"

He trudged on, avoiding her eyes. "I didn't sleep well," he told her, and it was the truth. But he could not explain to her why he had slept so badly. The evening had started off well enough: There had been a great feast and much music and storytelling. Coconino had laughed to himself to see all the curious eyes watching him and searching for some sign of jealousy or regret but finding none. He had laughed, too, as Castle Rock contemptuously refused to look at him, sparing him only the barest of scathing glances when their eyes chanced to meet. She pretended such joy and modesty at being Chosen, but inside, he knew, she was seething because he had not succumbed to her machinations.

When the time had come, though, for her to return with the Man-on-the-Mountain to his wickiup—for this was not a marriage and therefore was not consummated in a Wedding Chamber on the cliff—she had not needed to search the crowd to find Coconino. She knew exactly where he was, flanked by Juan on one side and Falling Star on the other. She cast one last, long look his way, and it was not scathing or contemptuous. Yet this look raised the hair on the back of his neck and knotted his stomach, for it was a look he had seen before.

It was the look Corn Hair had given him on the night she was wed.

So Coconino spent the night in silent cursing at the irony of his situation. The one woman he could have had but did not want; the other he wanted but could not have. His problem, as Phoenix had called it, was that desire was ever present within him yet his deepest desire could never be satisfied. For when all was said and done, Coconino still wanted a Witch Woman.

It was not something he could tell Phoenix. He glanced at her now to see if his comment had satisfied her. It had not, but she seemed inclined to let the subject drop.

They traveled without stopping, alternately running and walking, downstream to where the creek flowed into a larger river, then back up that river to the northeast till they reached the mouth of the creek that flowed out of the Red Rock country. Here they stopped to eat, and after a quick dunking in the stream, Phoenix stretched herself on the riverbank to rest.

Coconino, however, was restless. He searched the area for animal tracks but found nothing unusual. That only fueled his restlessness; he wanted signs, portents—not this ordinary, everyday experience. Soon he roused his companion to continue their journey upstream.

"In this heat?" she protested.

"Soon we will be among the cliffs," he told her. "It will be cooler."

"Easy for you to say," she grumbled. "You're running around in a loincloth."

"You may do the same."

She gave him a dark look.

"During the hot summer," he told her, "the women of the People often go about in only their skirts. I have never understood why Witch Women refuse to do this. Come, let's run a little."

A little was three miles. When they slowed to a walk again, Phoenix was soaked with sweat. It trickled down her temples and dripped into her eyes. The waistband of her shorts had never dried after its dunking in the stream, and her light cotton blouse was drenched front and back. Moreover, the collar was chafing her neck.

Oblivious to the heat, Coconino was scouting the riverbank for tracks. The sweat trickled into his headband, not his eyes. Moisture gleamed on his chest and in the hollow of his back, but the occasional breeze that touched them speeded the evaporation and cooled his skin. Phoenix felt only clammy and rank. Finally she surrendered to logic, stripped off the shirt, and tore off one of the sleeves. This she knotted around her forehead. The rest of the shirt she tied to the belt that supported her canteen and a pouch of personal items. The deep canyon between the red bluffs was apt to be cool at night, and she would want the shirt then.

For his part, Coconino did not seem to notice. "Plenty of coyotes," he reported after inspecting a patch of soft sand on the bank, "and javelina and foxes and other small creatures. But no

mule deer and certainly no Tala. We must look farther north.''
So north they went, through the rolling, scrubby hills that seemed
to stretch forever until suddenly they were in the canyon.

There had been one or two buttes, like outposts of the red
rock, but they could not prepare Phoenix for the canyon. She had
seen it before, but only from the air. From there it had looked
simply like a red gouge in a black-green forest. Here, standing
deep within its shadow and gazing upward to cloudless sky, she
found herself wishing she knew one of Coconino's chants to the
Mother Earth. But she did not and could only stand in awe of the
striking red of the rock, the green of the trees, and the blue, blue
sky.

At points the fissure was narrow, only yards across; at other
places the forest on its floor spread well back from the stream
that tumbled, full and still icy cold, down its length. Phoenix
wandered awestruck, her eyes lifting to the soaring cliffs—

And tripped over Coconino's outstretched foot.

''Hey!'' she protested, picking herself up from the leaf-littered
ground, her left arm tingling unpleasantly from striking her elbow on a rock. ''That's not funny!''

But Coconino was not smiling. Instead his eyes watched her
critically, judgmentally, his foul morning mood having lasted all
day. ''Be glad I did not trip you on the rocks,'' he told her
sourly, ''or on the edge of the creek bed, so that you tumbled
down the bank. I am not a Healer who knows how to set broken
bones.''

''Then why did you try a stupid prank like that?'' she demanded.

''It was not a prank. You must watch the path, watch where
you put your feet.''

''You could have just said so!''

''You can tell a child not to put his hand in the flame or you
can let him do it—just once.''

''You're a cruel bas—''

''I am not cruel!'' he snapped. ''But the Mother Earth can be
if you ignore her ways, if you walk in ignorance and arrogance
as though you were the master and she the slave. She has put
many creatures within her bosom, and rocks and trees and
water—what makes you think you are more important to her
than they are?''

''I never said I was!''

''Then give them the respect they are due. Acknowledge their
existence, their right to be in your path from time to time. You

cannot walk through the world as though you were its only inhabitant or the Mother Earth will surely show you how weak and insignificant you really are.''

He turned and started back through the forest, walking carefully, noiselessly. Her dignity smarting, Phoenix followed him. Now she watched how he moved, trying to discern his techniques, separating that from the natural rhythm and grace that she found so distracting. But the magnificence of the landscape tugged at her. Cautiously she dropped back a pace, then two or three, so that she could let her gaze wander to the tops of the trees a hundred feet over her head or to the cleft of the riverbed now on their left.

And then Coconino was gone.

She stopped, knowing what he had done, fighting the urge to call out to him. Instead she looked around carefully. Where was he? Behind a tree? Which one? Or had he slipped behind a rock and down into the streambed? Wherever he was, he was surely mocking her, waiting for her to panic. Cautiously, thoroughly, she inspected the immediate vicinity and did not find him. Then she started for the creek.

Suddenly she stopped and squatted in the dirt. She peered at the ground as she had seen Coconino do a hundred times that day to study animal tracks. Carefully she brushed away loose pine needles, tracing with her eyes a path toward the creek, and squinted at the far bank. Half standing, half crouching, she took one noiseless step toward the near bank.

Coconino was beside her instantly. "What have you found?'' he asked, excitement crackling in his voice.

"Coconino,'' she said, a wicked grin on her face, "I wouldn't know Tala's tracks from a sidewinder's. What I found—'' She stooped to pick up the offensive object. "—was a plastic fork.''

In disgust Coconino seized the ugly remnant of the Before Times and ground it into the soil at his feet. "Tala's tracks are like those of an antelope,'' he growled, "with a split hoof. Here.'' He gouged the dirt with a twig to show her.

"Good,'' she said, feeling avenged. "Maybe if we both know what we're looking for—and how to go about looking for it— we'll find it faster.''

He growled and started off along the sloping, twisted ground again. Abruptly he stopped, motionless. Phoenix froze, too. "Do you see the squirrel?'' he asked quietly.

She followed his eyes. "Yes,'' she breathed. It was perched on a branch ahead and to their left.

He began walking again. "Let us see," he suggested, "who spots the next one."

For three days they crept through the dark and pine-scented canyon bottom, clambered inelegantly to its rim, stole upon watering sites in search of quarry—for Phoenix, any quarry. She saw newborn fawns, a proud bighorn ram, tiny nestlings, and skittering lizards. But for Coconino there was only one quarry, one prize, that he sought with absolute, unshakable confidence. Each day they set out, his objective was clearly in mind, and his every effort was bent on achieving it.

Not so Phoenix. For her, spending dawn to dusk toiling through the magnificent canyon was like being back on the Mountain, hiking with her father. As she had learned from him, so now she learned from Coconino. His restlessness of the first day soon gave way to an excitement that touched Phoenix as well. Over the rock, around the bend in the river, what would they find? A fox? A badger? Or would they actually see Coconino's Tala, the one-horned antelope? Well, why not? she found herself thinking on the third day. If not in this wonderland of nature, then where?

But the only large game they saw were bighorn and mule deer and an occasional whitetail. In her rapture, Phoenix did not notice as the restlessness began to seep back into her companion. Often he would stop at the creek's edge, motionless except for the flaring of his nostrils, as though the sound of its passage over smooth stones would tell him something; then, shaking his head in regret, he would go on.

On the fourth night Coconino came and squatted by the smokeless fire where Phoenix sat savoring the roasted meat of a bighorn kid. Coconino had shot it the day before, leaving it to roast in a pit while they searched. It had a gamy taste, and the tallow collected on the roof of her mouth, but it was tender and juicy, seasoned with herbs that grew in the canyon. To Phoenix, whose senses were clearer and more astute than she could ever remember, it seemed a sumptuous feast.

"Tala is not here."

She looked at him over the bone she was gnawing, a sudden knot beneath her breastbone. "It's a big place," she said. "He could be hiding anywhere. How would we know?"

But Coconino shook his head. "He is not here. I cannot feel him anywhere."

Phoenix stared sullenly into the fire, gnawing the bone once more. They had camped each night in this same spot, physically tired but mentally refreshed, the tall trees standing sentinel and a small fire warding off the chill. Her heart felt lighter than it had in three years. The thought of leaving so soon depressed her. And what did Coconino mean, he couldn't "feel" Tala? It seemed to her a poor reason to cut short their stay in the breath-taking canyon.

"I think he has returned to his home in the Black Lands," Coconino continued. "It may be that during the winter he came here, where it is warmer and the graze is better, or perhaps it was just his curiosity. But I think now he has gone home."

Phoenix drew back her arm and pitched the bone far down-wind of them, where any interested creature would not disturb them. Above her the whispering of the pines seemed to have increased to a mild roar. "What do we do now?" she asked.

"We follow the old Black Path," Coconino told her, "up-stream and out of the canyon by the northern rim. If we follow it, it will lead us north to the City That Was Buried, to the New Black Lands, where nothing grows. But we will need to turn off at some point and go east to find water. The Old Black Lands stretch far to the north and east. I think in that region we will find Tala."

Phoenix tried to worry a piece of meat from between her teeth with her tongue while her thoughts churned, the turbulence becoming visible on her face. She had not intended to go beyond the canyon. From here she knew she could make her own way back to the village by following the watercourses. But she was not ready to return. There were people there who expected things of her, specific and nonspecific. There were politics, a socio-logical structure, an image to maintain— Here there was only the rushing stream, the breeze in the pines, the quest, and Coconino. Coconino was no more political than the towering rocks and expected no more from her than did the rich loam of the forest floor.

"How long will it take to get there?" she asked.

He shrugged. "Two days, maybe three. I have never been to the Black Lands myself, so I don't know how far to the east we must go to find water."

If she went with him, she could not make her way back alone, not safely. Neither could she ask him to leave his quest and guide her back if she grew tired of traipsing around after a mythical beast. And there was no telling how long he would keep up the hunt. Weeks, of course. Perhaps months, through the summer or beyond . . .

Coconino noticed her deliberation. "You will turn back?" he asked in surprise. For some reason he no longer relished continuing alone. Once he would have preferred it to her company: she was sharp and rigid, and she made too much noise trying to stalk. He had to slow his pace to accommodate her—it was like hunting with his young halfbrother. But she learned quickly, like a child, and if she had begun as hard and rigid as the stone canyon walls, she had become more like the giant pine trees: Now and then the breeze stirred her.

Phoenix rose and stretched deliberately, all the ribs in her chest showing as the movement pulled her skin taut. "I'll come with you," she told him matter-of-factly. "Hell, if I went back to the village, I'd have to start wearing a shirt again."

He relaxed and reached for a joint of meat she had left on a flat stone just out of reach of the flames. "Why would you do that?" he asked. "It will be warmer there than here."

She laughed, pulling on the article in question against the night chill. "Unfortunately, that has nothing to do with it. I'd put a shirt on because Gonzales is there." With a sigh she sat back on the pile of leaves she'd collected for a bed and prepared to settle in for the night. "It's a shame, isn't it? To modify your behavior for the sake of of one person. Oh, well." She burrowed into the leaves, pulling three small pine boughs across her to help keep the warmth in. "When he leaves, I'll get rid of the shirt again, and by the time the next Teacher comes, I won't care anymore."

Coconino stopped chewing on the joint to stare at her. "When Gonzales leaves," he said, "you will go, too."

"Not me," she vowed. "I'm not ever going back."

"But the Men-on-the-Mountain are jealous of their women," he insisted. "They will not let you stay."

Her voice turned harsh. "They're jealous of their children," she snapped, "and that's just not a problem. I've got no reason to go back to that hill, and I don't intend to go."

Coconino looked down at the meat in his hands, his appetite gone. "The Mother will not let you stay," he said quietly.

"I'd like to see her stop me!"

"No," he replied somberly, "that is not something you would like to see. That is not something you would like to see at all."

A sudden chill seized Phoenix in her makeshift bed. The small fire seemed to quail noticeably, and she thought, Surely there is nothing that old woman can do to me.

Is there?

Climbing out of the canyon took most of the next day. Following the old road made it markedly easier, but it was still an exhausting uphill labor, and there were numerous places where the road had crumbled away and they had to pick a precarious path through the slippery rubble. Coconino wished that he had brought a coil of the strong yucca fiber rope to ensure the Witch Woman's safe passage over the most treacherous breaks. She slipped once and slid fifteen or twenty feet down the slope but landed on a firm section of the road just below and, cursing violently, hiked back to the same spot. Bruised and scratched, she started across again. This time she was victorious.

What troubled Coconino most was that he did not immediately know where to find water. The stream that cut the canyon had angled off to the northwest, away from the road. No doubt there would be others, for the land rose in that direction and would send other rivulets trickling down toward the ancient highway, but they had exhausted their canteens on the way to the rim, and he had little time to search. When they came across the ruins of a cabin, he did not avoid it, as he would have preferred, but searched through it in hopes of finding an old water source. Pumps and pipes had rusted long ago, but near an outbuilding he found a porcelain birdbath that still held water from a recent spring rain. They were able to drink and even pour some of the precious liquid into a canteen.

Other ruined dwellings along the way yielded other catch basins, and by nightfall they had replenished both canteens and selected a campsite close to more water. But Coconino adamantly refused to sleep in one of the buildings.

"It is an evil place," he said.

"Don't be silly!" she protested. "It's a house, like the houses on the cliff, like your wickiup. There's nothing evil about it."

"It is from the Before Times," he insisted. "There is a taint to it; the Mother Earth does not like it."

"There's a smell from the rotting wood," she told him. "And some dust and volcanic ash drifted inside. But it's not evil. Be reasonable. What if it rains? Besides, it's colder up here than it was down in the canyon."

Indeed, spring was only now arriving in this higher region, and the night promised to be quite cool. But Coconino was immovable. He slept in the forest, in the shelter of a fallen tree.

In the morning he was eager to push on. Floodwaters had not touched this part of the land, so there were numerous relics strewn about and the road had not deteriorated badly. Among the trees wind and erosion damage was minimal, but the wooden buildings had rotted severely and there was evidence that the area's last inhabitants had been given to looting and vandalism.

Where the trees ended abruptly, though, and they stepped out into the open, it was a different story. Almost directly north of them rose the cone of a volcano that had erupted over five hundred years before, burying the surrounding countryside, including a major city, in lava and ash. None of the lava flows had reached this far, but the ground was still black with volcanic particles, and the encroaching vegetation, though lush, consisted of piñon pines, low shrubs, and grasses. There were no buildings to be seen.

Coconino headed almost directly east. "There are lakes this way," he told Phoenix. "My stepfather told me about them."

They found the lakes without much difficulty, although the string of them ran east and south, away from their path. The travelers made their camp on the northern shore of the most westerly one, for Coconino was sure that a river ran more northerly not far from where they were. With fresh bodies and full canteens they could find it the following day.

That night Phoenix gave up on her unyielding shorts, her legs painfully chafed from yet another day of running. She fashioned a loincloth from the remains of her shirt. Earlier in the day she had braided her long hair to keep it off her neck. Coconino observed the effect with amusement. "You look like one of the People," he told her, and indeed she did. Her brown skin had grown even browner in the past week, and while her makeshift loincloth still looked like a shirt, at least it did not look like the garb of a Witch Woman or a Man-on-the-Mountain.

She smiled in the fading light. "That's what Dick always said," she told him. "I think that's why he married me."

Coconino's eyes widened. "You are married?" he asked in astonishment.

"Not anymore." Her voice was dark and cold.

"He died, then. I'm sorry."

"He's not dead; he divorced me," she replied.

Coconino blinked. "I do not know this word."

She turned and regarded him. "No, I suppose you don't," she said finally. "It's the breaking of a marriage contract."

"What is 'contract'?"

"*Contracto*," she translated, and when even that did not register, "an agreement."

He looked offended. "Marriage is not an agreement, a bargain."

"Sure it is," she said. "Even among the People. A man and a woman *agree* to marry. No agreement, no marriage."

"But it is not something that can be broken as you say."

"Don't look at me; it wasn't my idea."

He did look at her. Finally he began to comprehend. "He sent you away."

"They allow that on the Mountain," she told him. "Not often, but they allow it."

Despite the Witch Woman's obvious pain, Coconino's heart leapt suddenly: Corn Hair. If such a thing were possible . . . "The Mother would not permit it," he said aloud.

"You might be surprised."

He knew there was a veiled meaning, but he could not comprehend it. He studied her again. "Is it a disgrace among your people to be dee—, dee—"

"Divorced." She knelt and began arranging her bed of rushes. "Depends on the circumstances."

He caught her wrist. "And you?"

She lifted burning eyes to his. "I'd have been better off if I'd kicked him out when I found out he didn't want me." Her voice was hard and flinty with its bitterness. "Didn't do me a damn bit of good to hang on and fight him; only made a fool of myself. I just didn't want to make it easy for him, I wanted to—to strike back somehow, to make his life miserable, to make him pay for—" She broke off suddenly. "It was dumb. He just petitioned the Advisory Board, and they ratified it, and that was it. End of discussion."

Phoenix tumbled onto her bed feeling weak but still knotted inside. Fighting was useless. Pointless. It was over. But the anger remained.

Coconino was still trying to understand. "Why was it so easy? Did this Advisory Board not listen to your protests? Why should he be allowed to send you away without—"

"Because he had the very oldest and best of reasons!" she cut him off. "I can't have children."

Coconino was silent then. For a long time he sat watching her as she lay with her back toward him—a tense, unyielding back. Finally he stretched out on his own bed, pulled the rushes over him, and stared up at the stars, tiny hot pinpricks in the velvet black sky. She could not have children—even among the People this would be reason for a man to send his wife away, for children were the life and purpose of the People. It was the reason he, Coconino, would have to marry soon whether he wished to or not. It was the reason Nina would go to live in the Village of the Ancients and take any man who came to her. It was necessary for the survival of the People.

But he had never thought before, never had reason to think, of what it meant to a woman who could bear no children. To have the pain of knowing she must remained unfulfilled and then to have the pain of being sent away added to it. Sent away by someone she loved, for why else would she have fought so? It was not like the separation of a Man-on-the-Mountain from his Chosen Companion, for they knew from the start that their time would be brief and the maiden knew that another man would gladly take her to his wickiup. But if a woman bore no children, then no man would take her. She would be forever like Nina, rejected, unwanted, waiting alone in a house not her own.

But there is other worth for a woman, he argued. See my mother, who gives our village the finest clay pots and whose counsel is valued by the Mother.

And who gave the People three fine children, his mind replied.

Or Rosa, who weaves beautiful baskets and tends Corn Hair's children while their mother gathers the desert's bounty and their worthless father disappears for days at a time.

And who gave the People six children, four of whom lived to adulthood.

Or the Mother who, after her womb had closed, became the most honored and respected person in the village.

After, after, after . . .

But a Witch Woman was not expected to have children, only magic. Perhaps Phoenix was wise to wish to stay among the People, where no one would expect her to blossom with child. Here she could indeed have a separate worth— He would ask the Mother. Surely if she knew the circumstances, she would let Phoenix stay. And the Men-on-the-Mountain would not want her back.

Coconino turned and studied the woman across from him, her body now covered with rushes like his own but its tension still radiating like heat from a hearthstone. Why had this happened to her? Was it because her body was hard like a stone and so thin?

Or had she angered the Mother Earth, that her body bore no fruit? Or was it, perhaps, her own anger and rigidity that prevented any seed from taking root? Which had come first, the anger or the barrenness?

He turned his eyes back to the star-flung heavens. If she were not barren, she would never have come to the People. Then, Coconino thought, there might have been some other, a softer and gentler Witch Woman, for him. But the Mother Earth must have some design in all this that he simply could not see. Even the sand and the rocks had their place in her pattern, though nothing grew from them.

She must have some great magic, he decided finally. Some magic even she was not aware of. They must find it, that was all, and restore her to honor among her people.

Even after that he watched the stars a long time before sleep came.

Sleep eluded Phoenix as well in her bed of rushes. She had thought she had a handle on the bitterness, the anger; she had thought she'd put enough distance between herself and her trauma so that the hurting was over. She had brought up his name so easily, so casually, she'd thought it was all behind her at last—but with a rush it had flooded back, sweeping her away in a wave of pain as she remembered the whole bitter mess . . .

I was almost free, she thought. Here with the Mother Earth stretching away to the horizons, here with Father Sky vaulted overhead, here with the breeze and the grass and the cry of birds and a day of hard running, I thought I had stripped it off as I stripped off my clothes. And it almost worked. Almost.

If only Coconino had let the subject drop. If only he did not have to understand everything. If only his ideas were not so rigid and so simplistic. If only he were a bit more civilized—but then he would be like the people she had come here to escape, smiling to her face and pitying her behind her back. No. Thank God Coconino was not civilized.

But now he knew, and that would no doubt make some changes. He would look at her differently, maybe talk to her differently. How differently, she wondered, and for how long? She didn't know.

Well, at least she had said it, had gotten it out. It was no longer a dark secret festering inside her, so she should feel better. She should feel lighter and happier and freer.

But she didn't.

CHAPTER NINE

"You should be a hunter."

Phoenix looked at Coconino in surprise. They had reached a small creek and had begun to follow its channel north as it cut through the rolling hills that skirted the Black Lands. Phoenix had announced that morning that she wanted to learn a chant to the Mother Earth to use as she ran. Once taught, she had taken a mouthful of water and fallen into step beside Coconino. They had not spoken again till they had reached the stream.

She had no idea why Coconino had latched on to this notion, and her look said as much.

"You run well," Coconino continued. "You have self-discipline, singleness of purpose. You are learning to be quiet in stalking animals—yes, I think you would be a good hunter."

"You're forgetting one little detail, aren't you?" she asked. "I have no idea how to shoot a bow and arrow."

Coconino shrugged. "I could teach you that. You have a very strong will; you can learn anything you wish to."

Really? she thought. Then why can't I learn to put the past behind me?

"Why would I want to be a hunter?" she asked.

"I only said that you have the talent for it," he replied. "As for why, you would have to find that out yourself. Why does one want to be a farmer, another a basket maker, and another a potter? Each must search out his own desires."

"Well, I'll think about it," she growled. She had a vivid image of herself trying to bring down a bighorn and looking foolish to the point of hilarity.

"I only thought that if you discovered your magic, you would be . . . more content."

"I am content!" she snapped, and knew that she lied. "And what makes you think I have any magic at all?"

"You are a Witch Woman," he said simply.

"I'm a Witch Woman by choice, not because I had any 'magic' to offer!"

Coconino smiled. "You *think* it was your choice."

"It *was* my choice! I didn't present a proposal or fill out an application to be approved. I told them I was coming and they could either send me or I'd walk. I didn't get an argument."

But Coconino continued to smile infuriatingly, as though he knew something she did not, and trotted on toward the north.

By late afternoon they found themselves deep in a canyon whose limestone walls rose in eroded layers like steps to the blue sky. As in the Red Rock country, the trees included firs and oaks as well as the piñon pine and juniper of the southern region. The travelers had continued to climb in elevation, and in the deeply shaded canyon it promised to be a cold night.

When Phoenix first saw the houses in the cliff, she thought her eyes were playing tricks on her. Were those really walls, doorwayed chambers? Or only heaps of loose rock? But then Coconino spotted them, too—the ruins of mud-plastered homes not unlike those in the Village of the Ancients, except that these stretched horizontally in single-storied bands, scattered along the sides of the canyon.

"This is a great omen!" Coconino exclaimed excitedly. "The stories of the people say nothing of this place. We are the first of the People to find it!" In his exultation he forgot to distinguish Phoenix as not being one of the People. "It will be a great story to tell when we return, how Coconino and Phoenix found another Village of the Ancients in the far north, near the Black Lands. *Aiiee!* It will become one of the stories of the People."

She could not help but smile at his enthusiasm. He had an undisguised desire to be remembered among his tribe. "If we find Tala," she said, "it will be an even greater story."

"That is true. And we shall find him, now I am sure. This is a great omen!"

Farther into the canyon they found an "island" jutting up from the floor, its sides ringed with the ancient dwellings. When a fox broke cover on the lower slopes, Coconino brought it down with a single shot and decided this was yet another omen. They retrieved their prey and continued picking their way up the slope toward the ruins.

Here and there they came across the remnants of a paved path. "This must have been a tourist attraction once," Phoenix observed.

"What is 'tourist'?"

"People who travel looking for interesting sights."

"Ah," he said sagely. "We are tourists."

She laughed. "In a way, I guess. But we won't buy any souvenirs."

"What is—"

"Never mind!"

There had been no one to repair the ruins, and most of them were just that: ruins. But here and there a front wall remained intact with a doorway not too badly eroded. They were built into a cavelike shelf worn in the stone so that roof and floor were part of the cliff. Partitions divided the space into rooms approximately fifteen feet wide, reaching back into the cliff some ten or twelve feet. Eventually they found one chamber largely intact and started a fire in the fire pit before the open door.

A spark had just caught in the shredded juniper bark and Phoenix was nursing it into a flame when Coconino came in from outside with the skinned fox. He stood stooped in the chamber, which was scarcely over five feet high, and peered around. At the back the floor was stepped up into a low shelf or bench, the layers of adobe plaster still imprinted with the ancient fingers that had applied them. Here he seated himself while he stripped fibers from a handful of yucca leaves he had brought with him.

"I'm getting better at this," Phoenix announced as she fed more bark to the tender flame. "Didn't take me as long to get it started tonight." When she was sure of the blaze, she packed their spindle and hearth stick back into Coconino's leather pouch. She looked at him, grinning in triumph. But Coconino was casting wary glances around the empty room.

"I have never slept in a house of the Ancients before," he said quietly.

"You aren't claustrophobic, are you?" she laughed.

"What is 'claustro'—"

"Afraid of small, confined spaces. No, I guess you can't be if you grew up in a wickiup."

"Why would I be afraid of such a thing?" Coconino asked indignantly. "A place is a place. Why should its size make any difference in its danger?"

She shrugged. "To some people it does; I don't know why.

It's an irrational fear. Like some people are afraid of heights."

Coconino snorted contemptuously.

"Well, living in a stone house isn't so bad," she continued. "The floor's awful hard, but I saw plenty of ferns out there; they should make a decent bed. As long as the ventilation is okay, and—" She glanced up to observe a faint curl of smoke drifting toward the tiny smoke hole above the door. "I guess it is." When he was still silent, she looked back at him again. "What's the matter? Isn't this place *moh-ohnak*?"

He looked at her. "A place is not *moh-ohnak* of itself," he told her. "It may be *moh-ohnak* for a particular person to live in it."

"Oh." She added larger pieces of wood to her fire. "I thought it just meant 'appropriate.' "

"It is much more than that." He frowned as he trussed the fox onto a green stick with the yucca fibers. "*Moh-ohnak* is . . . a spiritual harmony, a rightness—it is very hard to explain. It is how we fit into the Way Things Are, and yet it is not something we must change to have, for *moh-ohnak* springs from within us. It is something we feel, but sometimes we have it without knowing it." He shook his head. "I am not saying it right, not at all. When you find what is *moh-ohnak* for you, you will know it. Until then it is only a word."

She thought about that as she fetched from outside several stones that had been the building blocks of another house. Stacking them on either side of her fire, she made pylons on which to rest their spit. Soon the fox was roasting. Turning to Coconino, she asked, "What's *moh-ohnak* for you?"

He glanced up quickly, an almost defensive look in his dark eyes and an underlying sadness evident in his face. Dropping his eyes to the fire, he shrugged. "Being of the People. Hunting and speaking with the Mother Earth. Having a name from the Before Times. Many things; some I know, some I have never thought about. Some I have yet to discover. Come. Let us gather some ferns for our beds, as you suggested." And he led the way out of the dark chamber into the brilliance of the spring dusk.

He was sure he had not fooled her, for she was quiet as they went about their task and he spoke too lightly. But how could he tell her what had been on his mind when she had asked her innocent question? What had been on his mind since he entered the stone house with its damp, dusty smell, its slightly pungent odor of limestone and former animal inhabitants?

Once he had thought it was *moh-ohnak* for him to marry a

Witch Woman. Once he had thought that the first, and only, time he would sleep in a stone house on a cliff was on his wedding night, in the arms of a beautiful fair-haired woman who was part myth and part warm flesh. The image had been so real to him, so certain.

This night he would sleep in a stone house, only it was a cold and lonely bed he would occupy. Across from him would rest a Witch Woman, but although he had grown to like her more, she would never be the love of his dreams. Warm flesh, yes, but hard; no myth but only brutal reality: the reality of an unexalted human being with private pains and sorrows, a body that did not function as she wished, a psyche bruised and battered by the trauma of her life. This was not someone to be worshiped or protected and provided for. She had no magic for the People and none for him.

And there would be no other. He kept coming back to the same fact, and still he could not believe it. He had lived with the dream too long to have it die so quickly and absolutely.

"I'll find you," the young boy had vowed. "I will come to the Mountain and find you."

"I have no doubt you will do whatever is in your heart to do," she had said gently. "You are not a Dream Chaser but a Dream Fulfiller. And perhaps one day you will find your way to our mountain. But do not expect to find me."

"Why not?" Panic. "Why not? Where will you be?"

"In your heart, Coconino. Oh, I may be on the Mountain as well, but I will not be the same. I will no longer be a Witch Woman."

Perhaps this is what she meant, Coconino thought as he watched the very real Phoenix beside him struggling with a reluctant fern, its fronds in her face, and smelled the odors of their unwashed bodies after a day's hard labor. Perhaps you need to be a child to see a Witch Woman.

But he did not believe it.

Phoenix picked up a chunk of lava, marveled again at its lightness, and tossed it aside. There were literally fields of it in this area, acres of the porous black rocks where as yet no vegetation had broken through.

But here among the tall pines were only pebbly cinders from old eruptions and occasional chunks that had broken loose from the flows and rolled or been floated here from their original resting places. The soil itself had a reddish tinge; the contrast between it and the black pebbles was pleasing—*ah-ahnta ah-ahn*, Coconino would call it. Phoenix had given up trying to translate such words.

She found what she had been seeking then among the sparse trees: a flint-tipped arrow. She pulled it from the loose cinders and examined the point for damage. Finding none, she wiped it clean on her loincloth and started to return it to its quiver. At the last minute she remembered she had not called it by name. What was this one? She examined the markings. "Faster Than the Fastest Antelope." The ritual complete, she put it away and started back for the stream.

You're going soft in the head, she told herself as she came out into the clearing. Talking to an arrow! And why? Because Coconino does it. So what? Coconino is an uneducated, superstitious, primitive young cub. And he's arrogant! He still thinks his way is always the best.

Turning back toward the forest, she nocked an arrow, pulled back on the bowstring, and drew a bead on her target: a large pine some fifty yards away. "Ouch! Damn!" she hissed as the string slapped her inner forearm. The arm was red and swollen now from numerous such accidents, and she decided she'd better quit for today. One didn't become an ace archer in ten days' time. So she retrieved the arrow, which had struck its mark after all, called it "Puma's Teeth," and headed back toward the wicki-up.

Actually, it was not a full-fledged wickiup they had built on the stream bank. It was a crude shelter of pine boughs and meadow grass thrown up to soften the chilly nights of this higher country. In front of its low opening a rabbit and a dozen yucca buds were cooking in a shallow stone-lined pit. When Coconino returned at nightfall, it would be to a hearty meal.

He had selected the spot nearly two weeks earlier as a base camp from which to search the surrounding countryside. Phoenix had been reluctant to leave their stone shelter in the canyon and climb up into the Black Lands themselves, but feeling Coconino's discomfort in the place, she had yielded. He had cried out with delight when he had spotted the black-crowned mountain tinged with red. "That is it!" he had shouted. "The fire mountain the legends speak of as Tala's home!"

Though they had searched diligently, they had as yet found no trace of the animal on the mountain. Still Coconino was undaunted. Game was plentiful in the area, especially browsers, and he felt confident that Tala must be near. At first Phoenix had insisted on coming with him as he searched the forests and glades for tracks, spoor, or any sign of their elusive quarry. As he ranged farther from camp, however, she knew she slowed him down. Lately she had been content to accompany him only in the mornings, returning to camp with the day's meal and Coconino's bow and quiver.

She had been amazed to see him bring down this hare; its incredible speed and frequent course changes made it a nearly impossible target. But Coconino had waited patiently, bow drawn, until the animal had stopped in a clump of sagebrush, sure it was safely hidden. Then the bowstring sang, the feathers whispered softly, and Puma's Teeth sank deeply into the furry pelt.

All of which would have been awesome if Coconino hadn't been so proud of himself. He grinned broadly at the Witch Woman. "Am I not the Mother Earth's favorite son?" he asked.

"Lucky shot," she chided. "And it's a stringy-looking rabbit, too. I'll bet it's tough."

"Yes. Tough and stringy. Like you."

She swung at him, but he caught her arm, laughing. "If your braids would stand up like ears, then you would look just like the rabbit."

She swung with the other hand, but he caught that just as easily. "If that matted mane you call hair stood up," she retorted, "you'd look like a porcupine! And if I had my way, you'd be just as extinct!" She threw her meager weight behind a lunge, trying to throw him off balance, but wrestling was not in her repertoire, whereas he had spent years practicing with Juan.

Phoenix smiled as she remembered just how quickly—and how carefully—he had pinned her, giving her just enough room to struggle and grinning wickedly as she did just that. "I'll make you pay, Coconino!" she had threatened.

"No doubt," he had replied, "for I shall have to eat your cooking again tonight."

Now she looked up as he trotted back into camp, skin shining with perspiration, the band that bound his unkempt hair dark with sweat. "You're back early," she said. "Did you find something?"

But he shook his head. "I have seen no sign of Tala," he said gravely. "I do not think he is here."

A heaviness filled Phoenix. Unexpectedly she discovered it

was important to her that he find what he sought, and not because he had made rash promises in front of witnesses. She had learned early in this journey that the task was not something he had undertaken out of pride, though no doubt he would be insufferably proud if he succeeded. Rather, it was the quest of a restless soul for fulfillment, for verification of all that he felt and was. He had described for her the encounter in the Red Rock country, how his eyes had met Tala's and there had been—what? *Moh-ohtay*, a communication of spirits, a touching of their essences.

"Where do we look next?" she asked, knowing there had to be a next.

"We will try farther east," he said, "for did you not say that is where the man kept his herd?"

"East and north."

"We will go back to the Black Path that runs east," he decided, "and follow it. In two or three days, if the Mother Earth does not speak to us, we will turn north."

The subject had troubled her for some time, and at last she asked, "What do you mean, speak to us?"

He looked at her in surprise. "Speak to us. Have you never heard the Mother Earth speak?"

"Not that I recall."

"But you are her daughter, you must—ah." He nodded sagely. "Stubborn children often do not hear their parents."

"Are you calling me a stubborn child?" she demanded.

He laughed. "I have never seen one more stubborn."

"And you're not, of course." She was glad his gloom had broken.

"I am her favorite son," he repeated.

"You are the most arrogant, conceited, spoiled, pigheaded—"

He snatched one of her braids and stuffed it in her mouth. She pulled it out, spitting, and he made another dive for it, but she dodged his grasp. Suddenly the game was on, he pursuing, she twisting and ducking like the hare till she reached the trees. There she bought more time for herself by endeavoring always to keep a sturdy trunk between herself and Coconino. Tired from his run back to the camp, he was hard pressed to catch her. She had grown strong these past weeks. But eventually he did and brought her ungently to ground on the pebbly forest floor. Then he stuffed both braids into her laughing mouth and rolled off onto his back, winded.

Phoenix pulled the braids from her mouth, still laughing, and lay there beside him, gasping for breath. Eventually she quieted and heard his breathing slow also.

"What is it like when She speaks?" Phoenix asked finally.

Though she could not see his smile, she could feel it. "Look up at these trees towering over us," he said. "Breathe deeply; smell the pine and the rotting leaves and the dust. Feel the ground beneath you, solid, rough. Hear the breeze as it moves through the leaves and the calls of the birds and insects. Feel the touch of the air on your skin." He paused, and she felt all the sensory stimuli wash over her, catch her up, suck her into their powerful grasp. "Now, what do you feel?"

"Contentment," she replied immediately.

"That," he said softly, "is the word of the Mother Earth. She says, 'All is well. It is good to be here, in this place, doing this thing. It is good that you built a wickiup and a fire and that you eat of my bounty. It is good that you do this together.' "

In the silence that was no silence but a clamor of birds and crickets and toads and leaves and branches and squirrels and tree lice, Phoenix breathed deeply. For a moment she had the vague sensation of the Earth breathing with her. Then she exhaled with a sigh. "It is *moh-ohnak*," she said at last.

Clayton Winthrop reviewed the manifest one more time, mostly to verify that it was indeed the one he had pored over for the last six weeks. Then he signed off on it, flashed a smile at Tony Hanson, and handed it back.

Hanson. Clayton watched the smug, thick-necked man move away and wondered once again why a man like that wanted to go to Earth. Perhaps, having retired from the Service, he sought some other roving life-style, but there were plenty of ships for a man with Hanson's experience. What secret dreams did the seemingly unimaginative man harbor that drew him back to the planet of his ancestors?

The thought of Earth sent a jolt of excitement through Clayton like an arrow. He drew a deep breath, quelled the thumping of his heart, and crossed to the holograph of Earth spinning in his quarters. Tomorrow morning they would all board the *Homeward Bound*, which would then leave its orbit around Argo and head for deep space. When enough distance had been put between them and major magnetic fields, they would make the warp jump to the Solar system and then coast on into Earth orbit.

Earth. What would it be like to see her from the porthole of the *Homeward Bound*, her image undoctored and unenhanced? How would he feel when he finally laid eyes on the birthplace of humanity, the once-beautiful world that had spawned and spurned the race of man? And what would they find there? A ghost planet, littered with empty cities and abandoned towns? A bare and ruined world with little trace of its former inhabitants?

Or would *Homo sapiens* somehow have survived?

There was more than just the one mountain installation, after all. Not everyone had escaped during the Evacuation. Some countries had intentionally abandoned certain elements of their populations: felons, dissidents, the poor. Even in the more humane countries, how did you sweep the ghettos clean? How scour the rural areas? Then of course there were those who had planted their feet and refused to leave, whether in protest or in ignorance. Had any of them survived?

"Begging the captain's pardon . . ."

Winthrop looked up sharply, wrested from his fascinated musings. Derek Lujan stood in the door Hanson had left open. "If you're busy," Lujan ventured, "I can come back."

"No, no," Clayton hastened, realizing he had been scowling at his first officer. "Come in, Derek."

Lujan stepped inside the doorway but no farther. "I thought you'd like to know," he told Clayton, "I've tested the navigational computer thoroughly. Works like a charm. I wish they had let me program it, though."

Clayton grinned wryly. "Don't worry, Derek. I know the programmer; she's an old pro. We're in good hands." That was typical of the young man, though: He wanted to do everything himself. The scary part was, he seemed perfectly qualified to do so. His degrees were from the finest schools, and he had proved himself under fire on the *Aladdin*. So why don't I trust him? Clayton asked himself.

Because of the *way* he proved himself on the *Aladdin*.

Lujan had taken command when the captain and her senior officers had been badly burned in an explosion at an asteroidal mining installation where they had been taking on cargo. The installation was entirely automated, so there were no medical facilities. The injured people were put on life-support systems in the *Aladdin*'s meager sick bay, but there was never any hope of their recovery.

The *Aladdin*, however, was in imminent danger. The explosion had set off a chain reaction that threatened to blow up the entire asteroid. The *Aladdin* had to get away and get away quickly. Derek Lujan had applied his extensive knowledge of physics and determined the exact amount of weight they needed to jettison in order to escape in time. He jettisoned the cargo, he jettisoned all unnecessary equipment and supplies, and then he jettisoned the three dying officers and their life-support equipment.

The desperate maneuver had worked; the *Aladdin* escaped with only minor damage. Had Lujan not acted so boldly and with such alacrity, the entire crew of twenty-eight would have been lost.

"Thanks for the report, Derek," he said. "And thanks for running the checks yourself. I appreciate your attention to detail."

Lujan smiled proudly and saluted his captain. "My pleasure, sir!"

Clayton wanted to feel compassion for the young man. He himself had once had to seal off a contaminated compartment, leaving one crew member inside. The decision still haunted him.

And that's the real problem, Clayton thought. It doesn't haunt you. I've looked in your file and in your eyes, and I've never seen any trace of your being haunted.

"Now, get some sleep," Clayton growled to cover his uncharitable thoughts. "We have a few things to do tomorrow."

Maybe he just hadn't seen Lujan at the right moments.

Derek shook his head slightly as he walked down the corridor away from the captain's quarters. Winthrop still didn't trust him. After months of impeccable performance, of building a strong rapport with the crew, of demonstrating his leadership abilities, Winthrop still did not trust him. But at least the captain had reached a point where he wrestled with those feelings. That was progress.

It wouldn't matter in the long run. Derek knew he had won over the crew, and those were the people he must command. When it came to a recommendation, Winthrop would give him the one he had earned through his performance, regardless of any personal misgivings. As long as he had no problems with the crew, as long as he did his job better than most people could, this Earth venture was going to jump his career ahead by years. And there would be all those collateral opportunities . . .

There were a few people in the crew, of course, who might prove difficult. Tony Hanson was one: his love of red tape, his insistence on procedure, ran against Derek's grain, but Derek grinned and bore it. The last thing he needed was Tony Hanson for an enemy. The man was small-minded, but there was no mistaking his authority. He was third in command, and Winthrop would tolerate no disrespect.

Neither would I, Derek thought. If I were captain, I would insist on respect for all my officers, because the captaincy is built on chain of command. The Tony Hansons of this world must be catered to, flattered as necessary, and assigned to the tasks they do best. Someday I may have the luxury of telling Tony Hanson what I think of him, but it won't be on this trip.

Then Derek drew near Karen's quarters, and he put Tony Hanson out of his thoughts.

Karen lay on her bunk, indulging one last time in an episode of *Twentieth-Century Valor*. It was silly, romantic fluff featuring impossibly beautiful women and artificially muscled men who were corporate executives by day and martial arts masters by night. But she still loved this series that had been her childhood favorite, even though she knew now that such dashing people had never existed. Her research into Earth history had revealed that the people of twentieth-century America had been overfed, underexercised, and ridden with all manner of diseases.

But how she loved the verbal fencing of the conference rooms, and she still thrilled at the sight of rippling biceps as shirtless men danced through the steps of the physical fights. Once she had dreamed such a man would come to her house and take her away, somewhere where she would never have to face her father's anger again, somewhere where he couldn't touch her, somewhere . . . like Earth . . .

Now she was going to Earth, and her heart beat an excited tattoo in her chest. Quickly she took a deep breath and forced herself to be calm. Earth was no escape, only a delay. They would go and find it black and ruined, its surface barren of vegetation, its atmosphere unbreathable, and then she would go back to Argo. Back to his anger. Maybe this time he would kill her; she wondered if she really cared.

A knock at the door startled her; she shut off her program but hesitated before answering. "Come in." She never asked who it was anymore; it was nice to know there was no one here she would like to keep out.

The door opened to reveal the tall, trim frame of Derek Lujan. He wore his customary tapered white uniform, a style that showed his narrow hips and flat stomach to their best advantage. Karen tensed immediately; visits from Derek were a disquieting experience.

"Good evening, Miss Reichert," he began as usual. "I hope I'm not disturbing you."

"No, that's fine," she lied. He was a disturbing man.

Derek waited until the door slid shut behind him. Then he removed a small device from his pocket. "I was just aboard the ship," he continued conversationally as he checked the room for monitoring equipment, "and I see from the log you've been using the communications station already. Getting a feel for it?" Having satisfied himself that there were no electronic ears, Derek set the device on a small table from where its high-frequency sonic emissions would garble any transmission.

"The captain asked me to send some messages," she replied, still sitting on the edge of her bunk and watching his fluid motions. "I sent yours, too," she added softly.

Derek smiled and sat beside her. "You're very good. I checked that log forward and backward; I couldn't find any trace of it." She shrugged. "Anything new come in on Tony Hanson?"

"Nothing," she replied. "He's clean as a whistle." That had been the favor Derek had come to ask her after the first self-defense class: to do some discreet checking on Tony Hanson. It was a simple task, and she had been glad enough to do it, but it had confused her when, having secured her assent, he had simply left. No suggestive comments, no casual touches, just that heart-wrenching smile—and then he left.

He sighed now and tugged at his mustache. "Well, maybe I was wrong," he said. "I was so sure if I scratched very far, I'd find some dirt."

"If all it took was a little scratching," Karen offered, "the Coalition would have found it."

"Ah, but I have connections even the TRC doesn't have," he replied, a twinkle in his blue eyes and a teasing smile on his lips. He held her eyes for several moments, as though daring her to look away; he did that often. Karen never looked away. She liked his eyes.

Then, after a time, his eyes changed from challenging to soft and Karen's stomach fluttered, as it always did when his eyes went soft like that. She could feel his desire, feel it like a warmth pressing against her, and she waited expectantly for him to make his move. Finally he did.

"Well, thanks for trying, Karen," he said, rising. "And let

me know, will you, if Tony sends any messages out.'' He smiled once more. ''See you in the morning.''

Karen watched him pack up his monitor-defeater and stride to the door. A wave of confusion washed over her again. How long would this go on? Was she wrong about what he wanted? No, men always wanted it. Had she discouraged him somehow? She wished she knew how.

But with his hand stretched out toward the latch, Derek stopped. ''Karen, are you all right?'' he asked, concern edging his voice.

''Fine.'' She wiped her hands nervously on her slacks. They were navy blue, like the captain's, with a separate white blouse.

''You look a little . . . perplexed,'' Derek pursued. ''You aren't worried about tomorrow, are you?''

''No.''

''Does it bother you, doing this sort of . . . shady checking around for me? Because if it does, I'll—''

''No, no,'' she said, ''it's not that. My boss at MotesOrg— well, let's say not everything in that company is run strictly aboveboard.''

Derek laughed. ''Show me a company where it is.'' He paused, studying her, then crossed to kneel on the floor in front of her. Taking both her hands in his, he gazed directly into her eyes. ''Tell me what it is. What's bothering you?''

Karen balked a moment. Then, ''I don't understand,'' she whispered plaintively.

''Don't understand what?'' he prompted.

''Why,'' she answered. ''Why you . . . don't . . .''

''Don't what?''

She tore her eyes away from his, looking down, concentrating on the strong, gentle hands that held hers. ''Men always want to stay the night,'' she whispered, ''and you don't, and I don't understand.''

Was he smiling? She dared not look. The touch of his hands betrayed nothing of his reaction to her words. Was he angry? Amused? Surprised?

''I'm an officer and a gentleman,'' he replied softly. ''I was waiting for an invitation.''

Now she looked up again, searching those blue eyes. Was he serious? No, Derek was not one to be bound by convention, let alone old-fashioned morals. No, this was some sort of game he was playing. What was her part? What was she expected to do? She knew nothing of the subtle games of men and women; she

only knew surrender. "I . . . I can't—I mean, I don't know how
. . . I've never . . . asked . . ."

Now his arms bore her gently backward onto the bed. "It's all
right," he whispered gently. "Your question is invitation
enough for me." Then his lips touched hers, and all the tension
drained from Karen's body.

Tony Hanson snapped off the electronic clipboard with a grimace of pure satisfaction. Tossing the unit down on top of his
duffel, he looked around his quarters. They were stripped bare;
everything was packed except his dress uniform, a change of
underwear, and his toothbrush. He was ready to move out; he
was ready to assume his kingdom.

Chuckling inwardly, he dropped his thick frame onto the edge
of his bunk. Up till now his role had been a lesser one; the supply
officer didn't have much contact with the crew during the pur-
chasing and receiving phase of his job. He had more contact with
the other officers, but that was mostly as a lackey: "Tony, we
need this" and "Tony, see if you can get us that." Then there
was inventory, loading, another inventory, getting signatures on
this and signatures on that.

But all that was due to change.

He could hear them now. "Mr. Hanson, may I have a whatz-
it?" "Where's your authorization?" Now *they* would be the
ones running around getting signatures. Now they must prove to
him that they needed something and why. Now the control was
all his. The captain wanted seismological readings? Not until the
geologists got the equipment from Tony. The mech techs needed
to repair the food synthesizer? They'd have to get a tool kit from
Tony first. Even Derek Lujan would have to see Tony if he
wanted a jet pack. Or a shiny new button for his fancy silk
uniform. Or a roll of toilet paper.

You've had your turn, Mr. Lujan, he thought. With your slick
smile and your wavy hair, turning the heads of the ladies as you
pass. You've had your golden day in the sun while you played
martial arts instructor and professor of five-dimensional physics
and group psychologist. Once the ship launches, I take over. By
the time we reach Earth, everyone will know. Mine is the kingdom and the power, if not the glory.

You will see, Mr. Lujan. I have waited patiently because I
know that soon, now, you will see. You, and the captain, and all
the others—like a star bursting before your eyes, you will see
just how much power over your lives Tony Hanson really has.

*   *   *

Coconino woke with a terrified start, sweat streaming form his forehead, his heart pounding in unspeakable panic. The star! The pain—!

Beside him Phoenix stirred. "What is it?" she asked in a whisper.

They were in their low shelter of brush, and he dug his fingers into the hard-packed dirt of Mother Earth. It was calm and unperturbed. There was no pain. It was only a dream.

"It's nothing," he told Phoenix softly. "A dream." He lay back down and forced his breathing into a regular pattern.

But the vestiges of the nightmare clung to him like cobwebs and would not let him sleep. He had been standing on a hillock in a green river valley, his heart lifted in song to the Mother Earth. Before him the land swept down to the flowing stream, then up into more hills and beyond to mountains purple with distance. Behind him, the land rose in sharp wooded folds and the cries of hawks filled the air. It was not a peaceful scene but one of active rapture.

Suddenly the ground beneath him seemed to gasp, though there was no movement, and cry out in agony. Away to his left in the valley a tiny light appeared like a star burning on the earth. As he watched, the land sent ripples through its skin, trying to flick off the light as an animal flicks off flies, but the light clung like a burr to the Earth's surface and began to grow. As it grew in size, its brilliance increased, a piercing brilliance that hurt not only his eyes but his skin as well. Coconino felt his insides churning in the same sour agony the Earth felt. In excruciating torment he flung himself down the hill toward the expanding light, screaming loudly, and leapt upon it with his knife. But the light swallowed him whole, like an enormous fire, and he felt himself being charred inside and out as he fell down, down, into the roaring terror of that light . . .

Now he struggled again to bring his breathing under control, fighting back the panic that still lingered. Mother Earth, why did you send me such a vision? he asked. And what was the devouring brilliance that so tormented you and consumed my very being?

CHAPTER TEN

They ran all morning, Phoenix exulting in her newly acquired strength and endurance. The old roadways here had been preserved by a covering of volcanic ash, only in the past century being laid bare again by the ever-present winds. They were cracked, and grass had taken root, with here and there a barberry or agave, but they still made for better traveling then the surrounding terrain that stretched away hilly and wooded on either side.

Around noon they crossed the small creek that, farther south, flowed through the canyon with the stone houses. Here they found a beehive whose occupants were not in residence, and they availed themselves of the honeycomb therein. Laughing and chewing the sweet, waxy substance, they continued east, the sun now at their backs.

"Today we find Tala, don't we," Phoenix said positively, licking her sticky fingers.

"You are the Witch Woman," he replied.

"That's right, and don't you forget it," she said, smearing a dab of honey on his nose. Coconino scowled and tried vainly to wipe it off with his own sticky hands. "I don't know if you can tell," she added, "but I'm having a good time."

"You were not so cheerful this morning," he reminded her, "when we took apart our wickiup."

"I'm not into home wrecking," she growled. "Call me sentimental."

He sucked one finger clean, rubbed at the spot on his nose once more, then gave it up. "We leave the Mother Earth as we found her," he said sternly. "So we break down our shelters and fill in our fire pits and bury our leavings. If the people of the

Before Times had done so, perhaps She would not have grown so angry.''

Phoenix thought to herself that it would be a little hard to tear down a fourth-floor apartment when one left, but she said nothing. Neither did she find the dead cities as offensive as Coconino obviously did. Her ancestors, the scientists and technicians who had stayed behind on the Mountain, had retained their technology largely by looting those cities, but that was not a subject to get into with Coconino. There were, she was discovering, a lot of subjects she didn't want to get into with Coconino. Not because she was afraid of his tirades but because it might cause him pain.

Often she thought about his story of the whiskey-dispensing Man-on-the-Mountain. After living with him the past few weeks, observing his religious devotion to the Mother Earth, she had no doubt that the story was true. Service to the Mother Earth was the Way of the People, and anything that endangered Her or Her creatures needlessly was Evil.

"Then how can you hunt?" she had demanded of him once.

"As we can harvest," he had replied. "We take only what we need; we do not waste or kill for the sport of it, as those of the Before Times did."

No, not for the sport of it, she thought. But for the protection of the People and the Mother Earth—she looked at the quiver of deadly arrows slung across his back and shuddered involuntarily. There was no doubt in her mind.

They were running well when they reached a dry streambed that sliced across the roadway. Phoenix was caught up in her chant to the Mother Earth and regretted having to break its rhythm while they picked their way across the breach. Immediately they picked up their pace again and had trotted several hundred yards when they began to slow involuntarily. In a moment they both came to a standstill and stared straight ahead at the landscape.

There were no trees.

As far as the eye could see stretched a vast grassland unbroken by hills or trees. Here and there was a yucca or a shrub of some kind, but for miles and miles under the cloudless sky there was only the great empty prairie with no living creature in sight. The hair rose on the back of Phoenix's neck, and she suppressed a shudder. It was only prairie, of course, this was the way prairie looked, only . . .

Coconino swallowed again and again, fighting off a queer nausea as he looked out across the land. In all his life he had never seen a place where no trees encroached on the open spaces, where no rocks or mountains erupted from the plain. But even in the far distance he could see no hills, no break in the featureless land.

For several moments they were silent. Then Phoenix spoke in a hoarse whisper. "Let's go back," she said. "To the island in the canyon. To the stone houses. Let's go back. Please."

Coconino swallowed one last time. "Yes," he said softly. "We will go back."

They turned their backs on the terrifying emptiness and trotted back toward the welcoming trees.

When they reached the small creek in its shallow channel, they slowed their pace. Coconino spit out the water in his mouth; he intended to run no more today. The feeling of a great monster at his back had disappeared when they had scrambled down into the ravine, and he felt the presence of the good Mother Earth on all sides of him again. Slowly, savoring the nearness of rocks and cactus and mesquite trees, they headed southward.

Before long Coconino realized that they would not reach the "island" until after nightfall, so he began to watch the surrounding landscape for a good campsite. Eventually he spotted a hollow in one bank that provided shelter on three sides. Here they stopped and built a fire.

"You will bring our supper tonight," he informed Phoenix, handing her his bow and quiver.

She looked at him dubiously. "Are you serious?"

"Yes. I will make a shelter here, and you will hunt."

"Coconino, you know I can't hit a moving target."

"Then find one that holds still."

"Nothing holds still in this country!"

He shrugged. "Then we shall be very hungry."

Phoenix glared at him and took up his weapons. All right, if he wanted to play that game, fine. She knew what he was doing. It was probably the same thing they did to teenage boys who were learning to hunt: succeed or starve. Well, Coconino, she thought, I hope you're prepared to be hungry for a while.

She flushed a hare and spent half an hour searching for an arrow that had not come close to its mark. Next she came upon a covey of quail and managed to collect a few feathers to prove that she had at least frightened them. When she encountered a rattlesnake sunning itself, she decided she wasn't that hungry, not yet. Snake meat was common in the diet of the People, but it still made her squeamish. So she went carefully on as the sun slipped closer to the western horizon.

At dusk she knew she needed to head back to camp or risk being lost in the unfamiliar terrain. Reluctantly she began to retrace her steps toward the creek and the taunting eyes she knew awaited her.

An insect buzzed at her ear, but she brushed it away. Sunlight danced in her eyes, and the animal was there.

At first she thought it was only a rock formation on the bank. But it moved, and she instinctively drew the bow and took a bead on the its broad side, thinking, "My God, it's as big as a house, how can I miss?"

Then she saw the one braided horn on its brow. Don't shoot! her brain screamed at her muscles. Don't shoot, for pity sake, don't shoot—!

Coconino heard her before he saw her, and relief washed through him. It was nearly full dark, and he had feared her lost or injured somewhere in the rough country. So at the sound of her feet in the brush, his heart lightened and a smile crept onto his lips. How I shall tease her, he thought, and moan that my stomach is empty and will keep me awake all night—

But her step as it approached was heavy, not fired by the anger he expected. By the time her tall form appeared among the shadows at the edge of the camp fire's flickering light, he had grown apprehensive. She stopped there, swayed a little, then came and squatted across from him. Her face was drawn and pale even in the reddish cast of the flames. He waited in silence for her to speak.

"I saw him," she said finally.

Coconino caught his breath. "Where?"

She waved vaguely toward the western bank. "Over there. My God, he's huge. And he's real. He's really real."

He reached out and laid a hand on her bony wrist. "We will go back in the morning," he said quietly, trying to cover his excitement. "You will show me the place."

She nodded dumbly. Then, after a moment, she crawled into the shelter he had constructed and stretched out to sleep. He banked the fire and crawled in beside her, but neither slept.

"Coconino?" she said after a time. He grunted. "He appeared to just me, by myself. Does that mean anything?"

"Without question."

"What?"

"I don't know."

The silence stretched between them again. Then, "Coconino?"

"Yes, Phoenix."

"I almost shot him, before I realized what it was. Does that mean something, too?"

It was a moment before he answered. "Without question," he repeated. "But I do not know that, either."

Phoenix stood towering over Coconino and dropped the plump little quail, still spitted on his arrow, in his lap. "Now," she said. "Can we eat?"

He grinned up at her. "Now we can eat." It had been almost three days since they had headed for the canyon with the stone houses, searching for Tala as they went, and although he had allowed her to present some cholla flowers and other foraged plants as a substitute, he had refused to take up his bow and bring in anything more substantial. "But of course," he added as he worked his arrow carefully out of the bird, "you must first clean your kill."

Phoenix wrinkled her nose but followed him down the steep slope of their island butte to where the messy chore would not offend their camp and took her lesson. It was half ritual: pouring out the blood as a libation to the Mother Earth, chanting a prayer that She would call the bird's spirit to Herself, then mixing the entrails with dirt as an offering of thanks for sustenance. This done, Phoenix plucked the bird and carried it down to the fast-flowing creek to wash the carcass and herself.

Denuded, it was a pitifully small bird. As she returned to the stone house, she was glad to see that Coconino had gathered flower stalks and some early currant berries from one of the sunny southern slopes in the canyon. She suspected he had been harboring them for some time, adding to the incentive of her empty stomach. Of course, she realized, they would now make this meager prize seem more a feast.

"How did your quest go today?" she asked as she spitted the quail and set it over the fire to roast. Since her sighting two days before they had found more tracks, but the tracks seemed always to end in some rocky soil or at the edge of a crumbling ravine where further detection was impossible. That morning he had gone alone while she turned her full attention to procuring a decent meal. He should not have been back this soon, she realized.

Coconino stroked his chin thoughtfully. "Have you noticed that both times Tala was seen, it was when he was not expected?"

"I hadn't thought about it," she said dryly.

"Perhaps he can only be found when he is not sought."

"Very deep, philosophically."

"I think," he said, ignoring her sarcasm, "that we must stop looking for him."

Phoenix tensed. "You mean leave here?"

"No, no," he assured her. "But we must do something other than look for Tala. We must focus on something else. Then perhaps he will show himself to us again."

Phoenix gave an exasperated sigh and sat back. "That's got to be one of the stupidest ideas I've ever heard." Drops of moisture from the roasting bird sizzled in the fire. "What did you have in mind?"

Coconino grinned at her, a flash of white teeth in a strong face that once again made her thoughts wander where they shouldn't. It's not fair, she thought. It isn't supposed to happen like this. Familiarity is supposed to breed contempt, but I've lived with him for three weeks, and his smile still starts my hormones dancing.

"We will make you a bow and arrows of your own," he announced. "I will teach you what woods to use and how to chip the flint heads. And you can make a quiver of yucca leaves. We do not have all the proper tools, but we will do the best we can. We will pretend we are Survivors."

"Did anyone ever tell you you're pigheaded?" she demanded.

"Only you."

"Well, you are. You're probably the second most stubborn, pigheaded person I know."

"Who is the first?" he asked.

"Me, of course!"

May ripened, and the edible flower stalks became laden with edible fruits. In this northern canyon the days grew warmer, though not as warm as they were to the south in the Valley of the People. Still the skies were a cloudless blue, the air was sweet with growing things, and the chatter of birds was sweet music all day long. The bow took shape, and four reasonably good arrows. Phoenix named them Coral Snake, Tarantula, Gila Monster, and Sudden Death; the bow she called I Think I Can.

Coconino had no weaving skills, however, and the quiver Phoenix managed to construct from the rough yucca leaves was not comfortable to carry on her bare back. She tied it to her waist instead. "When we go home," Coconino promised, "Corn Hair's mother will teach you basketry. She is the best in the whole village."

He was surprised to find that he had not thought of Corn Hair since the first week of their journey. He tried to picture her, her form growing thick now with child, her shirt discarded and her hair braided in the summer's heat. He wondered if she thought of him, worried at his long absence from the Village. Well, soon the clouds would begin to build in the southeast, heralding the summer rains, and Tala or no Tala, they would have to go back. He had no desire to be caught in unknown territory during the often violent thunderstorms.

As June dawned, however, Coconino grew increasingly restless. He had the dream again, the one with the Mother Earth crying out in agony, and it wrested him violently from sleep. This time he thought he recognized the valley. It lay to the south of the Valley of the People, not here in the north. How many days would it take to get there? Five? Four? The following morning they stumbled across Tala's tracks as they washed in the river; if they had not, Coconino believed he would have abandoned his quest.

As it was, he insisted they break their camp before leaving, in case they did not return. "For if we find Tala today, we may not return," he told Phoenix as he pitched their fern beds out the door and over the steep cliffside.

Phoenix swept cold ashes from the fire pit with green leaves, feeling as cold and gray as the ashes herself. She, too, had dreamed, but not in allegories. Her dream had been of Dick, of being married once more, of his smile, his laugh—and finally his cutting logic regarding propagation. Oh, yes, she thought bitterly, propagation had everything to do with it. The fact that Tina was young and pretty and had breasts like cantaloupes had no bearing at all.

So she also was peevish this morning. They had snarled and snapped at each other before finding the tracks, and she knew as well as he that the time had come to leave this place. But she was possessed of a contrary spirit, especially in her darker moods. Resentment bubbled within her now, as though it were his fault that change had overtaken them, his fault that they must throw out their beds, his fault that the stones they had used as hammers and chipping tools must now be tossed aside, never more to shape her weapons.

"I thought we weren't going to look for Tala," she groused as they started back toward the river.

"When we did not find tracks, we did not look," Coconino growled back. "But when he places his tracks under our noses, only a fool would ignore them."

"Well, let's not get into name-calling," she suggested darkly. "I'd win."

"No doubt," he agreed. "You always use words I have never heard before."

The tracks led downstream, then cut up toward the eastern bank when the gorge grew shallower. Coconino followed them doggedly, ignoring the woman who trailed behind. He felt separated from her that day, separated from the fine weather and the clear sky and everything except the haunting dream.

Phoenix's anger brewed as she watched his back, scrambling up the steep bank behind him. Do you know why I hate you, Coconino? she thought. Because you're beautiful. Because you move with a hunter's grace and your body is carved with the same rugged beauty as these canyon walls. Because your eyes are dark and I can always feel them on me; because they are windows to your soul and because your soul is even more beautiful than your body. That is why I hate you. I hate you because I want you, oh, yes! I want you. Though you're as much younger than me as Dick was older, though you're arrogant and vain beyond belief, though you're naive to the point of foolishness, I want you. But I'll stuff any proposals, any propositions down your throat because you still want her: the blond-haired, blue-eyed Witch Woman I can never be. I will not take leftovers anymore.

How much alike they were, Coconino and Dick. Both were striking, proud, egocentric men. Both were sought after, both respected by their peers—how lucky she had thought herself when Dick had first turned his attentions on her. For what was she? Too tall, too thin, too flat, too plain. "A perfect mechanic," her father had told her. "Small hands and big feet." It was her only redemption.

But Dick had seen something else in her. A professor of history and now administrator of the Archives, he had as a young man spent nearly three years among the People. He had been deeply in love with his Chosen Companion, or so she was told; Dick would never discuss her. Kevin Mendoza intimated that the young woman had died, he surmised in childbirth, and upon his return to the Mountain Dick had lived alone nearly ten years.

Then Phoenix had caught his eye, a dark-haired, dark-skinned, dark-eyed girl not much older than his Chosen Companion had been. Their first encounter had ended in bed, with Phoenix astounded at his passion. After a month of such lust-filled meetings he had married her, and although she had suspected at the time it was not really her he was marrying, she had asked no questions.

Still, in the end he had left her. Whatever she had represented to him had faded, and he had moved on to the next shining illusion.

And so it is, Coconino, that I will never have you. Even if, some chilly night as we huddle for warmth, your blood should begin to burn and you desire me—even me, the too-tall, too-thin Witch Woman—I will reject you. For when it was over in one night or one month or one year, your heart would yearn for someone else while I would have grown so deeply in love with you. Then the pain would begin again, and I won't let that happen, Coconino. Not for all the tea in ancient China. Not even if it meant a child would grow in my womb.

Suddenly he reached back to motion her quiet, and she nearly ran into his outstretched arm. She almost snarled at him, but his bearing of caution stopped her. She crouched as he crouched, and together they crept silently forward.

Some fifty yards away the unicorn was calmly cropping leaves from a barberry bush. They dropped to their knees and crept into the cover of a large stone.

Coconino had felt Tala almost before he had seen him. Like the Voice in the Red Rock Country that had whispered to him once so many weeks before, he felt the presence of the great beast. Brother, he thought, reaching out with his mind. Brother, can you hear me? Can you feel me now as I felt you then, before I saw you?

Tala raised his head and looked around, his slightly telescoped eyes shifting eerily. Seeing nothing, catching no scent on the breeze, he dropped his head and went back to browsing.

Phoenix felt her heart thundering in her chest, her throat suddenly gone dry. In broad daylight the animal was even more magnificent than it had been at dusk. The single horn was bone-white and gleamed in the sun. Its sleek, sturdy hindquarters were well muscled and covered with tawny, almost golden fur. Golden—hadn't Coconino said red? Regardless of the color, the most astounding thing about the beast was its deep, powerful chest, the rippling strength in the bulky ridged neck and withers. Coconino was right. There was a confidence to the creature that said, What have I to fear? I am a kachina; I am Tala.

In fascination they studied him, horn to tail and back again. "Ah, see his chest," Coconino murmured, "how deep it is; what strength of wind he must have! And his neck is so thick—perhaps for the same purpose."

"It's not really that thick," Phoenix whispered back, pleased to know more about the animal than the know-it-all hunter. "A lot of the bulk is just the wing sock."

He stared at her. "The *what*?"

Again Tala lifted his head, and they both held their breath until he went back to grazing. "Wing sock," Phoenix repeated. "All that dark hide on his neck and withers—inside there are vestigial wings."

"Tala can *fly*?" Coconino demanded in astonishment.

"No, no, not anymore." She wondered how he would feel about evolutionary theory. "Eons ago, when the breed was on its home planet, they probably could. Glide, at least, if not fly. But the species got larger, and the wings weren't strong enough to lift the heavier bodies. They came to depend more on running, and the wings became leftovers, decorations." Phoenix snorted. "They probably use them in mating rituals. Some females are impressed by wing flapping."

Coconino shot her a sharp look, sure he had been insulted but not sure how.

"Well," Phoenix asked, settling herself more comfortably behind the rock, "now that we've found it, what do we do with it?"

At that moment the wind carried some sound or alien scent to Tala, and he jerked his head up, testing the breeze. His flaplike tail flicked into the air, and suddenly his color changed from the golden tan of his surroundings to a deep, intimidating brown.

All is well, my brother, Coconino thought. All is well; it is only I, Coconino, another son of the Mother Earth. You have nothing to fear. You know me.

But nearby a coyote pup caught their scent and yipped in excitement.

With a loud trumpeting Tala reared back, and two magnificent wings snapped open. They were easily forty feet from tip to tip, bones and cartilage covered with dark hide. Tala took half a dozen running steps into the wind, launched with his powerful hind legs, and was airborne.

Coconino and Phoenix rose involuntarily from their hiding place and stared at the animal as it climbed aloft, leathern wings beating the air. After a moment Coconino turned smugly to Phoenix. ''Perhaps Tala does not *know* he cannot fly,'' he suggested.

Phoenix was too amazed to take exception to his remark. They'd never believe this back on the Mountain. A unicorn, a celux, alive, five hundred years after they were thought to have been killed off. That was miracle enough. But one that could fly—! Not just glide, mind you, but actually fly!

Coconino's heart soared with the flight of Tala. Such a creature! Such a magnificent creature! Surely the Mother Earth has made me for this moment, to behold Tala and bring his story back to the People! There are legends, oh, yes, but none that tell of this wondrous thing, that Tala can fly like the raven, the hawk, or the ancient eagle! Unable to contain his rapture, Coconino broke into song:

> ''Wondrous is the Mother Earth
> And wondrous Her gifts to me!
> For my eyes have gazed upon
> The noblest of creatures,
> The greatest of miracles,
> And my heart soars with Tala!''

Phoenix found she was holding her breath. Coconino was transformed, his countenance ablaze with rapture. The sun shone around his form like his personal corona; his deep baritone voice reverberated through her chest and loins. Who are you? she wondered, awestruck. What is this thing I witness? This is just an adventure, a great story to tell the People—isn't it?

Above them Tala seemed to hesitate. Slowly he banked and began to circle around. Coconino felt the animal's curiosity like an unvoiced question in his mind, but he was too caught up in his song to think about it.

> ''Tala! Tala!
> Magnificent child of the Mother Earth.
> Tala! Tala!
> Adopted son of my Mother.
> We are brothers, you and I.
> We are one in our love for our Mother.''

Gradually Tala glided earthward, his wings no longer beating. As he neared the ground, he fanned the air again in a backwash and settled lightly on his feet. Then he folded his wings gently, drew them back inside their protective sac, and stood there, ears twitching, watching Coconino. *What are you, Brother?* the beast seemed to ask. *And what is that sound you make?*

Like a man in a daze, Coconino stepped out from behind the rock. "Sweet is the bosom of the Mother Earth," he sang. "Strong are the creatures She nurtures." Slowly his feet carried him closer and closer to the animal. "Those that should have died live; those whom She has chosen cannot perish. Blessed are we of Her choosing! What should we fear?"

Phoenix watched him as though from a distance. *You're crazy,* part of her objected. *You can't just walk up to that animal. That horn may look blunt, but don't doubt that it is lethal. And those hooves—they could rip you to shreds.*

No, they could rip me *to shreds,* she realized. *But not you. He won't touch you, will he? He won't harm you or fear you, will he?* She stood transfixed, watching them both.

Tala waited cautiously, but indeed there was no fear in his eyes, and his color had returned to that of the landscape. "Peace, Brother," Coconino sang, extending his hand toward the creature. "We are one, you and I. Peace, Tala. Let there by *mohohtay* between us. We are sons of Mother Earth. Her enemies shall flee before us. Together we are invincible."

He stopped a yard away from the animal. Tala blinked his protruding eyes once, twice, then carefully extended his neck and sniffed the outstretched hand. *What an odd smell! Not like anything he knew.* Now he took one small step, then another, and sniffed the man's hair. *Strange stuff. A stronger smell here, and not mixed with so many other smells.*

Carefully, gently, Coconino laid his hand on Tala's neck. A small tremor ran through the beast, then it relaxed as Coconino began to stroke its fur. "Peace, Brother," Coconino whispered. "We are meant for one another, you and I. The Mother Earth has given us this gift, and I will not question Her." Tala laid his surprisingly soft black muzzle against the man's neck and sighed deeply. "Ah," Coconino sighed in return. "It is good that you do not, either."

Still Phoenix watched, her amazement dulled by the barrage of impossible events. Tala, alive. Tala, flying. Coconino singing to the animal, and Tala returning. Man and beast coming together as equals, friends who had never met but knew each other nonetheless. This was not just an adventure; no, there was something more here . . . Why should she be surprised, then, when Coconino's arms gripped the beast's wing sock and he vaulted lightly to its back? This is not real, none of it is real, Phoenix thought numbly, and yet of course it is real. It is not even unusual. Coconino is going to ride Tala—what else should he do?

His friend in place, Tala stretched his wings once more. Coconino clung to the loose skin of the empty wing sock as Tala ran, bunched his muscles, and then leapt. Wings beat furiously; Coconino squeezed his eyes shut and prayed, and then they were sailing, the man's body finding the rhythm of the powerful wing strokes and relaxing, straightening, glorying in the thrill of flight.

On the ground, a strange sadness crept over Phoenix as she watched the pair in flight. She had called him a cub, a fool, an arrogant man-boy, but it seemed now that the names had all been sword strokes designed to protect her from the truth of her own inadequacy. You are so far above me, Coconino, she thought, and a knot tightened in her throat. You are indeed a most favored son of the Mother Earth; and I—I am Her querulous daughter who will not listen to Her voice. You are the Believer who can do miracles, but I am the Doubter who will never do better than walk one step behind.

Yet that much will I do, she thought, her despair shifting to resolve as the lesson of this journey came home to her. That much I will do, Coconino, and not resent it. For me, it is *mohohnak*.

CHAPTER ELEVEN

In the years that followed many stories were told of the day Coconino returned to the People riding on the back of Tala, the flying antelope. It was said that where their shadow passed, the corn grew six inches and rabbits who endangered the tender plants dropped dead in their tracks. It was also said that as they landed, the Witch Woman, who rode behind Coconino, fell from Tala's back and her words scorched the grass for ten paces. Still another story had it that as they approached, the Mother, who had guided the People so wisely for so long, clutched her chest in pain, and that from that moment on her force abated, though her wisdom continued.

Some said that after the feast that night, Castle Rock seduced Coconino and that the child she bore the following spring was his and not the Man-on-the-Mountain's. But the Witch Woman never believed that and bitterly contested anyone who repeated the rumor. Others said that half the maidens in the village threw themselves at Coconino's feet and offered lavish gifts if he would take them as bride but that he declined them all to sleep alone on the flat hill just northeast of the village, with Tala beside him.

What was true was that the whole of the village dropped what they were doing when Tala appeared in their skies and that old and young alike began to chant praises to the Mother Earth. As the trio landed on the flat hill, the People feared to come too close, for they did not in truth know what it was or who the riders were.

It was also true that the Witch Woman fell, and if her words did not scorch the grass, it was only because the Mother Earth was laughing so hard that she did not take offense.

Juan was the first to clamber up the steep slope. "Coconino!" he cried excitedly. "And—and—" He stared at her a moment.

"Witch Woman." With a bow slung across her back and only the makeshift loincloth for covering, he could hardly believe it was she. "It is true!" he exclaimed over and over. "It is true, you've done it! You've found Tala!"

"No, my friend," Coconino replied. "Tala and I found each other."

Tala pawed the ground and eyed this newcomer suspiciously. For Coconino's sake he had come here, to this place of humans, and for Coconino's sake he stayed now, although the smell of them was overpowering. But if any of them made a threatening gesture, they would find that Tala had more weapons than fast hooves and a sharp horn. Reluctantly Juan dragged his eyes from the awesome creature. "The Mother will want to see you," he told Coconino. "*Aiiee!* What a story you will have to tell! We will feast for two days!"

But Coconino shook his head. "It is a bad time of year for feasting. The People must not neglect the fields or it will be a long, bitter winter." He surprised himself; he was always eager to feast.

Juan was undaunted. "I will go myself to hunt," he insisted. "Surely the Mother Earth will send me an enormous prize to honor you!" Again his gaze slid to the unicorn with blatant awe. "See what you have brought the People!"

It was then that Coconino had his first inkling that he might not like notoriety.

They found the Mother seated at her great loom, weaving the intricate pattern of the Man in the Maze. As always, her hands flew back and forth with the shuttles, black, white, black, white, but her face had changed. It was pinched and drawn, and Coconino frowned as he seated himself at her feet. "Mother," he said, "you do not look well."

Phoenix hesitated a moment, then sat beside him. Up on the hill, where the village had greeted them, she had stared belligerently at one and all, daring them to comment on the change in her. She had chosen, and none would daunt her. But here, before an old woman who would not even look at her, she felt suddenly naked.

The Mother's gnarled hands never ceased their constant motion, drawing up the right colors in the right place, never off by a string. "I grow old, Coconino," she said softly. "I dream strange dreams."

Disquieted, he reached out and touched the loom. "I have dreamed, too, Mother," he told her gravely.

At this she looked at him and smiled sadly. She knows, Coconino thought. She knows what I have dreamed even before I tell her. Truly she is the greatest, wisest leader the People have ever had. She will tell me the meaning of this dream.

"We will speak of dreams another time," the Mother said, turning back to her work. "For now, let us speak of this kachina, this legend you have brought to us. Let us speak of Tala."

He told her as briefly as he could of how they had chosen their path, of Phoenix's sighting, and of the tracks that led them at last to the momentous encounter. He told of his first flight, the exhilarating, terrifying sensation of sweeping down over trees and cactus, startling quail and rabbits, nearly falling off as Tala banked to turn. They had flown briefly over the prairie, which was not so frightening from the air, and he'd seen a large herd of a kind of antelope he did not recognize, with graceful curving horns. "The hunting there would be very good," he told her.

Throughout his account she only nodded, as though he were a schoolboy reciting a lesson she had learned long ago. "You are greatly blessed, Coconino," she said when he had finished. "Blessed is the Mother Earth, and blessed is Her favored son, Coconino . . ." Her voice trailed away, breathless, and her eyes drooped for a moment. Then, "Go to Two Moons now," she commanded. "Let her embrace her son who has done this wondrous thing in the sight of the People. Only remember this, Coconino: To whom much is given, of him is much required."

Hair raised on the back of his neck. But having been dismissed, he bobbed his head and rose to leave. Phoenix started to follow.

Abruptly the Mother held up a hand. "Stay, Witch Woman."

Apprehensive, Phoenix sat back down. When Coconino was out of earshot, the Mother spoke again. "You were alone many weeks with Coconino."

Phoenix's cheeks burned. "Don't worry, your prize stud is still pure; I haven't touched him."

"It is of no concern to me where you make your bed," the Mother replied sharply. "Take him or a dozen other men, I do not care. You are Witch Woman; it is your right. I know you will not bear away any child of the People."

Phoenix's mouth flew open, but the Mother pushed on. "But do not fetter him, Witch Woman. Do not bind his heart. Coconino is rare among the People, among *all* people. He is something beyond us, something more, and we must have his seed. I would give him six wives, were it the Way of the People, in hopes that one of his children, just one, would inherit his gift. But he will take no wife not of his choosing, and the Way of the People does not permit taking a maiden in disgrace. His heart must remain free to love one who will bear him children."

Phoenix rose slowly to her feet, trembling with bottled rage. The Mother glanced up at her, never losing track of the shuttle. "You think me unfeeling because I seek to guide his choice."

"You're treating him like a goddamn piece of livestock!" Phoenix retorted.

"Am I?" The Mother's eyes became suddenly cold and mocking. "You do not know whereof you speak. I know what it is to be treated so. Many years ago I made a bargain with the Mother Earth. I traded everything I had and was—my home, my family, my purpose, my very body—for a life of service to the People. A life of service, and Great Heart as my husband. At that time the Shaman ruled the People, and he was neither kind nor just, but he spoke with the Mother Earth, and the People followed him. My bargain with the Mother Earth could only be sealed by him. What he said was law in those days, and I had no other choice.

"To procure his blessing I became as his slave for a great ceremony, one he made up especially for me, and to his own liking. I will not tell you of his deeds, of my humiliation, of the pain—pain!—but I endured it all because the prize was great. So do not speak to me of livestock! I love Coconino as my own son, and I force nothing upon him. I only warn you—do not bind him with your love or your bitterness. He, too, must do what the Mother Earth requires of him."

"Fine," Phoenix said, her voice shaking. "You don't want him to have me, I don't want him to have me, *he* doesn't want him to have me. We're all agreed. As for him ever loving me, the idea's preposterous. But I'll be sure not to turn my charms, abundant as they are, on him. God knows how dangerous that would be."

"Do not underestimate your magic," the old woman said quietly.

Phoenix wanted to cry, to scream, to lash out at the old woman whose warning mocked her frustration. Instead she drew herself up, body stretching proudly in its newfound hunter's bearing, and turned to go. At the last minute she stopped and faced the old woman again. "There is one maiden for whom disgrace would be no disgrace," she said. "Send Nina to the houses on the cliff."

The Mother said nothing as Phoenix walked away.

But that night after the feast Nina took her sleeping mat and climbed the ladders to the Village of the Ancients.

Coconino watched her go and knew that it was no accident she had chosen this night to begin her Plea for a Husband. By custom he had to wait six nights for any man seriously interested in her as wife to visit the chamber and make known his intention without fear of rejection. After that any man spurred by desire, or pity, or whatever emotion could come to her by night to give her a child and leave without ever speaking his name. One week, and he could satisfy his lust any night it pleased him without having to take the girl as bride. It seemed to him horribly unfair to Nina, but in terms of his own need . . .

He turned back to the fire, to Elvira, whose flames were dying down now. His retelling of their adventures had gone on for hours and hours, with eager faces all around absorbing every word that fell from his lips. Now, exhilarated by th ttention and fueled by the high spirits of his tale, his longing for a woman was huge. He saw Lame Rabbit asleep by the fire with his oldest son and knew that Corn Hair was alone with only the two-year-old in the wickiup. Soon the drums would begin . . .

He remembered as well the hungry look in Castle Rock's eyes as she listened to his story. And Brook, and Too Pretty, and all the others—how easy to tempt them from their mothers' wickiups this night! It would not be the first time he had walked outside the Way of the People.

And now Nina waited in the Village of the Ancients . . .

Well, why not? he asked himself. You will never have the Witch Woman you want, but you have Tala and there is *mohohtay*, communion of spirits, between you—that is enough for your soul. So why not take Nina as wife? She is modest, at least, and well behaved, and she would be so grateful. Ha! How that would torment Castle Rock, to see you take Nina as bride! And with Tala to carry you swiftly away, you need not look at her more often than you wish. No doubt the children she bore you would all be handsome, anyway, like their father.

But he knew that the reasons were all wrong. Then it would be a marriage like Corn Hair's, with more sadness than joy. He could not do that to himself; he could not do it to Nina.

Beside him Phoenix rose and stretched in the fading firelight. Her appearance had caused many whispers, but she had stalked belligerently through the village with her bow and her braids,

challenging anyone to speak of it. Finally a woman had brought
her a cotton loincloth to replace the makeshift one she wore. "A
hunter should have a proper covering," the woman had said,
"especially when she is a Witch Woman." After that nothing
more had been said, and by the end of the evening even Ben
Gonzales had stopped casting covert glances her way.

Now, in the firelight, Coconino admired her new look. Her
legs and arms had grown more muscular, and her torso seemed
complemented by nakedness. She no longer looked thin, only
lean—but that is your eye, Coconino, he told himself. You have
come to like the Witch Woman, and so she seems to you better
proportioned. No doubt others still think her thin and ungainly.

But there was a new air about her, one of self-confidence and
self-worth. She had accomplished much on this journey, and it
showed in her swagger, her voice, and her eye. Oh, she was still
hard and cold, and the anger had not gone, but mixed with it now
was a sense of pride.

And unexpectedly, something inside him stirred.

Coconino was totally taken aback to realize that the Witch
Woman had kindled a fire in his blood. It is the night, he told
himself, and the celebration. It is because the longing is so keen
in me, I would burn for anything tonight. It is because she is my
friend now and I know her so well . . . or not so well . . . At any
rate, I would offend her to speak of it.

But as their eyes met, he saw a startled look on her face, and
he knew she had read his desire. Immediately a cold mask
slipped into place across her features, and she studied him critically for a long moment. Finally she turned and started off
toward her cliff house.

Coconino watched her disappear into the darkness, his eyes
lingering over the sinewy movements of her legs. It seemed
strange that he should go now to his mother's wickiup and lie
down—outside, for it was a warm night—but not have Phoenix
nearby. Perhaps, he thought, I should go to her house of stone.
Not to sleep with her but only to sleep near her, so that it would
feel right—

Fool, Coconino, he told himself. Your eyes have seen a new
thing in her this night, and it will never be as before. To lie
beside her tonight and not touch her would be torture, but to
reach for her—

Value your life and your manhood, Coconino, he thought
wryly. Seek solace elsewhere.

*   *   *

The People did not linger at the feast, for Coconino was right; it was the wrong time of year to leave the fields untended, the tender shoots of a second crop open to the ravages of rabbits, mice, and other creatures. But even as they returned to their dusty beds, the People knew that a great and wondrous thing had happened to them and to Coconino.

They had always known him to be a good hunter, taught by the great Made of Stone, and an expert storyteller, having learned at his mother's knee; certainly his birthright as the child of a Man-on-the-Mountain gave him not only physical stature but societal stature as well. But this association with Tala put Coconino in a class by himself. Now the Mother's description of him, grown dull with overuse, came home to them: favored son of the Mother Earth.

So they felt themselves twice blessed. Not only did Tala stand on the hill above the village, his single horn silhouetted in pale moonlight, but Coconino, Favored Son of the Mother Earth, trod the paths of the People.

The oldest among them, however, feared the curse that might come with such blessing. Why were these two given to them at this time? What evil approached that the People needed such gifts from the Mother Earth?

Firekeeper began to beat on his drum: long-short-LONG, long-short-LONG. Immediately the other drummers picked it up. Long-short-LONG, long-short-LONG . . . It was perhaps the most ancient song of the People, used to call up the wisdom and strength of the Survivors. Those remaining at the ceremonial fire began to chant the words whose meaning was lost in antiquity, words that were sung only in the presence of Elvira's flames:

"*Giddy-up, um-bappa um-boppa, mau mau . . .*"

Tala was gone.

In panic Coconino searched the rise above the village where the kachina had been the previous night. What did you expect? he demanded angrily of himself. Tala is Tala; he goes where he wills. You have learned to guide his flight cleverly by leaning your body one way or another. But you cannot tell him where to stay or for how long. He has probably returned to his home in the Black Lands.

Just then there was a soft trumpeting from a gully that cut

away to the west, and Tala's now-familiar head appeared among the jojoba, horn gleaming in the sun. Coconino scrambled down to greet his friend.

"Good morning, Tala," he called. "I see you are having breakfast." The animal chewed contentedly on jojoba leaves. "If it is not too much trouble, when you are through, I would like you to take me hunting."

"And how will you carry back your kill?" asked a voice behind him. "I doubt the smell of blood will sit well with Tala."

Coconino turned to see the Witch Woman standing on the rise. Tall and bronzed, with the sun behind her, she was a striking figure. Her long black hair hung loose, stirred by an occasional breeze, and her arms were folded across her chest. Coconino felt his blood surge.

"I will walk back if I must," he replied. "I do not intend to go far."

She laughed, a cold laugh. "You will grow lazy, Coconino," she told him, "asking Tala to carry you where your own feet should." Her smile was wicked.

He came back up the slope and stood before her. His height advantage was slight, but he made the most of it, looking down into her glittering dark eyes. "Come with me," he said. "You must bring back your first kill to show the village that you do more than look the part of the hunter."

She felt the difference in the way his eyes rested on her. Damn you, Coconino, play fair, she thought. Don't do this to me. "Maybe I should hunt alone, then," she suggested, "and you can take Juan with you."

"I will take Juan another day. Today I will show you the best places to hunt so that your kill will be a fine one. So my step-father did for me, and so I will do for you."

She shifted her weight and broke their eye contact—only for a moment but long enough to pull herself back from the brink of a precipice. "You're a little young to be my father," she teased.

His smile revealed surprisingly white teeth. "Then I shall be your brother."

Slowly a smile crept onto her face as well. "My *younger* brother," she insisted.

"But I am still your teacher, Older Brother."

Phoenix laughed dryly. "I can't be your older brother. I know it's easy to forget, but I *am* female. I'll have to be your sister."

Coconino made a face. "I have a sister. You are nothing like her."

"Too bad!"

"You shall be my sister-brother," he decided, "for you are woman but our friendship is like that of brothers." He extended his arm.

Phoenix hesitated, then clasped his forearm firmly. "Yes," she said with feeling. "Our friendship is like that of brothers." And she thought, Dreamer! Even in this touching there is an electricity that gives lie to our fraternity—

"Coconino!"

She turned in relief to see Juan scrambling up from the village to join them. "Coconino, I was afraid you had—*aiiee!* He is still here, then!" Juan gazed with undisguised wonder at Tala.

"Would my brother leave me?" Coconino boasted unabashedly. "Of course he is still here. He may decide to stay for many days. We are good friends, you know."

"Would he let me ride him?" Juan asked.

"That is up to him, of course," Coconino replied, "but he does not trust people he does not know. As the Witch Woman can tell you."

Phoenix scowled, remembering how each time she had tried to approach Tala, the beast had skittered away. When Coconino held his head, he did suffer her touch and let her climb on his back. But as soon as Coconino let her go, Tala would take one disgusted glance at the woman and casually dump her on the ground. She still had bruises.

As though reading his friend's mind, Juan grinned. "I will wait," he said. "Maybe in time he will come to trust me. Until then his pride and mine shall both remain intact. Shall we go hunting today?"

Involuntarily Coconino glanced back at the Witch Woman. "I was—we were going hunting, yes, the Witch Woman and I. She wants to bring back a kill to share with the village."

Juan caught the look, and his eyebrows shot up. "Oh. Another day, then, when—"

"Please, come with us," Phoenix interrupted. "I would be honored to have two such able hunters show me the best places to hunt." Please, Juan, I can't be alone with him just now; it would be too easy. "Besides, Coconino spends so much time singing his own praise, he'll scare away all the game. I'll come back to the village looking like a fool with no kill. You must save me from this fate."

"*I* scare away the game!" Coconino protested even as he felt a burden lift. Perhaps it would be better to have Juan and his crooked grin between them. "Your step is so heavy, it leaves prints in the rock!"

"You see what abuse I put up with, Juan?" Phoenix cackled, relieved as the seductive tension flagged. "You must save me from the snapping jaws of this mud turtle!"

"Let us get our weapons. Then we will see if we can tip him on his back," Juan suggested. "Whoever sights your kill first will share in the choice portion." And he thought, What strange transformation is this? Even her speech has taken on the patterns of the People. What happened to them on their journey through the northern lands?

The great heat of summer baked the Valley of the People and the surrounding lands. As he had for so many summers before, Coconino flung himself into hunting and stalking and tried to ignore the surges of his body. Following the Witch Woman's precedent, he always invited Juan or Falling Star or others of the young men of the village to accompany them. It was gratifying to see them come to accept her, to respect her growing skill as a hunter, to laugh and joke with her as they did with each other. And it was good to see more of the bitterness drain from her soul. Yet even as he rejoiced, his desire for her grew.

From time to time he would look wistfully at the trail that led to the Village of the Ancients. There Nina waited with relief for his very acute distress, but he could not make himself climb the ladders. To reach her he would have to pass the Witch Woman's door.

You have magic, indeed, Witch Woman, he thought, but it is a dark magic. Every way I turn, you forbid me the fulfillment of desire. Are you indeed a daughter of the Mother Earth? Then you are drought as well as stone. Or worse yet, you are all-consuming fire . . .

When it grew unbearable, he would call to his friend Tala and escape in exhilarating flight above the ridged and rippled surface of the Mother Earth. One day he flew alone to the Red Rock Country and landed on the very butte where he had first encountered Tala. The creature, too, seemed to recognize the place. He pawed the ground and turned his near eye to give Coconino what could only be called a sly look. "I knew who *you* were," it seemed to say. "Why did it take you so long to find me? We have a destiny, you and I, but you are so slow to see it!"

And that feeling of his impending destiny continued to nag at

Coconino as the monsoon rains of summer reawakened sleeping rivers and brought oppressive humidity to the Valley of the People. He had felt it that spring as he had waited for the Witch Woman he was sure would come. He had read it in the calm and curious eyes of Tala at that first clifftop meeting. And he had known it in his dream, the dream of pain and violation and the burning thing that consumed him . . .

Clayton Winthrop rounded on the navigator. "Off course!" he barked. "How the hell can we be off course?"

The navigator flinched under Winthrop's fiery gaze. "There—there must have been an error—in the computer," the navigator stammered. "In the programming. I swear I checked and re-checked."

An image of the programmer flashed in Winthrop's mind; she would not make such an error. She had been programming more years than this young navigator had been alive. But for the moment that was a moot point. "How far off course?" he demanded, crossing to stand at the navigator's shoulder, the lines in his face deepening minutely.

"Days, sir," the navigator replied. "We're in the right plane, but we're—" He checked his panel again. "—ahead of Earth, not behind it as planned. And too far out, away from Sol."

"High and outside," Winthrop muttered.

"I'll reverse course—"

"Belay that!" Clayton snapped. "We haven't enough fuel to reverse course and still be able to warp back to Argo when the mission's over."

At the communications station, Karen Reichert swallowed once. "Does this mean . . . we'll have to abort, sir?"

Winthrop turned to look at her. In a crew of distinct personalities, this woman with the porcelain features and clear blue eyes was strangely unremarkable. Had he imagined a tinge of fear in her voice just now? And was it fear of danger—or fear of failure?

One puzzle too many just now. He turned his attention to the problem at hand. "High and outside—ha!" The answer flashed in his mind. "If we slow our speed just enough to decay our orbit into the proper range, will we still be traveling faster than Earth?"

The navigator brightened immediately and ran the calculations. "No, sir," he sang out. "If we slow down by . . . point

three, we'll drop dead into Earth's orbit and she'll overtake us in
. . . sixteen days.''

"Good!" Winthrop rubbed his hands together in genuine glee.
"That will take little enough fuel. Ms. Reichert, send a dispatch
to TRC headquarters, advising them of our new plan. Instead of
going to Earth, we'll let Earth come to us.''

Camilla was pale and beautiful in the soft turquoise gown
Dillon had bought her. She moved through the portico like a
ghost floating among the white alabaster statues, her hair stirred
occasionally by the breeze. Dillon was charmed.

"Sir.'' Ah, yes, pale and ashen! No doubt she had news of the
Earth venture. "I've . . . overheard . . . some messages coming
into the Terran Research Coalition's offices. Captain Winthrop
has reported that the *Homeward Bound* came out of warp off
course.'' She swallowed. "He's taken measures to correct their
course without overconsumption of their fuel, but he suspects
sabotage.''

Dillon smiled faintly. "Winthrop is a very astute man.''

"Will he find your operative?''

"Eventually.'' Dillon sipped his wine and waited for the rest.
Camilla crossed to a pillar and gazed up at the deep blue line of
mountains that towered over his estate. "Wine, my dear?'' Dillon asked.

"Please.'' She waited in silence until he brought her a glass.
Then, "They called for the programmer, the one who laid in the
course for Earth,'' she told him. "She was dead. Overdose of
medication. They're calling it suicide.'' Camilla sipped at the
dry beverage, then turned searching eyes on Dillon. "Was it?''

"I'm sure I don't know,'' he replied mildly.

Camilla took a longer drink now, and Dillon frowned. Such
inelegance was unbecoming.

"Will they all die?'' Camilla asked in anguish.

"No, no, my dear!'' Dillon laughed, taking the glass carefully
from her hand and setting it aside. Wine ought not to be gulped.
"As I told you before, my operative in the crew has a very
strong sense of self-preservation. Why accept large sums of
money if you don't live to spend them? Rest assured that the
crew of the *Homeward Bound* will return; they will simply return
unvictorious.'' He brought Camilla's hand to his lips with a deep
appreciation for the softness of her skin, for the subtle scent of
rosewater. Her wrist was bare of jewelry, though. He would
have to correct that.

*   *   *

"Probe away, sir," Lujan reported.

"Very good, Mr. Lujan," the captain replied. He had made Lujan program the probe himself. Cost constraints had precluded duplication of any major equipment. This probe was their only one, and Clayton wanted no screwups. He wanted that probe dead on target at the foot of the mountain installation.

"It should touch down in less than three days," Lujan promised. "I'll let you know how it's progressing, sir."

Clayton recognized the subtle reminder that it was time to turn the bridge over to his first officer. He might as well do so; if he didn't, Jacqueline would be up here reminding him in less subtle terms that there was nothing more he could do just now and nothing to be gained by hovering over the technicians, watching them do their jobs.

"Thank you, Mr. Lujan," Clayton replied. "I'll be in my ready room if I'm needed." But I won't be needed, he thought as he turned and started for the door. Perhaps Jacqueline is right; perhaps it is time to retire for good. When I start being distrustful of junior officers simply because they do their jobs so well, it's time to retire.

Only I want to see Earth first. I want this to be *my* mission, with my name in the history books. I've never hungered for glory before, but I want this. Don't try to take that away from me, Derek. Whatever else you do, don't try to take that away.

CHAPTER TWELVE

This was the place.

Circling above it, astride Tala's powerful shoulders, Coconino looked down on the valley and knew this was the place of his dream. Seeing it, he felt again the wound on his soul, as he had the night he had awakened in a cold sweat, heart pounding, body shot through with the tension of fighting great pain. It was here that he had felt the agony of the Mother Earth, hurled himself desperately into the blinding light . . .

The land was lush with the summer rains. A docile band of silver slipped through the green, a river that now belied the strength that had once swept a town from its banks. Only a mound here and there indicated that men of the Before Times had recognized the richness of this valley and built upon it. Sycamores grew along the water's edge, and the grass on the richly silted valley floor vied for dominion with the bur sage and the devil's claw.

But this was the place. Tala, too, was skittish. Coconino stroked the ridges of the unicorn's wing sock as much to comfort himself as the creature. Did Tala dream also? A quiver rippled through them both, as though they were one body.

"What do you think, my brother?" Coconino asked him. "If we touch the soil, will we feel its pain?"

The animal made a soft trumpeting noise that sounded like a bleat and, with no signal from his rider, began to drift down toward the valley floor.

Coconino did not try to stop him, knew it would have done no good. It was as though the Mother Earth called them both, drew them closer to the deceptively peaceful valley . . . They landed on a hillock near a mesquite bosque, and Coconino slid gingerly to the ground.

There was no shock, no gut-wrenching agony. Whatever he had felt in his dream was not here now. There was only the hot, humid breeze of the monsoon season and the afternoon sun blazing without mercy in the west.

But to the southeast, billowy dark clouds were scudding ever closer. Lightning played among them, and in the distance their contents could be seen tumbling earthward as blue streaks against the straw-gold of the parched hills. A distant rumble made Tala flinch; he did not like the electrical storms that accompanied the rains.

"Peace, my brother," Coconino crooned with a reassurance he did not feel. "It is only the pleasure groaning of the Father Sky. Soon he will release his waters upon the Mother Earth, and Her joy will be manifold. Then the corn and the cotton will thrive and the People shall prosper. So be at peace, my brother. This is well, this season of storms." He managed a laugh. "You have lived through many such seasons; no doubt you will survive another."

But Tala was not comforted by the man's voice or the *moh-ohtay* between them. He rolled his eyes and sniffed the breeze nervously, as he did at each approaching storm. Yet this time it was more than the storm his senses sought. Something was wrong here, a disturbance in the rhythm of things. Brother, do you not feel it? Not just a great wind is brewing, not just the cracking of sky and the fire that tears the air. Something more powerful than these things makes its way toward us.

Cautiously Coconino took a step or two away from his mount, testing the ground. Unlike the animal, his senses were not turned toward what was coming; instead he tried vainly to feel what was wrong here and now. What do you feel, Mother Earth? he wondered. What is wrong with this place that haunts you and thus me?

All he could sense was joy, a well-being that pervaded the soil and the air. All was *moh-ohnak* about this place: the hawks circling above, the roadrunners scurrying across the grass, the lizards darting up and down the paloverde trees. A good place to live, Coconino felt, a place to start a second village with rich, fertile fields and a river to water them.

Tala followed his friend, rubbing his soft nose against the man. Let us go, Coconino. This is a good place but a bad time. Let us go now . . .

But Coconino was distracted by the paradox. This was the place of pain, he was certain. Where was it?

You cannot rush your destiny, Coconino. It is time to go . . .

Coconino knelt, putting his palms flat on the ground. A tiny garter snake slithered away. Speak to me, Mother, he prayed; whisper the import of my dream. I lay my cheek upon your bosom—

The jolt sent him sprawling unceremoniously forward. He whipped around in panic, for it had not come from any point in contact with the ground but from his awkwardly exposed posterior.

Now! Tala stood over him, his dark eyes impatient.

"I know the storm is coming, my friend," Coconino said soothingly. "And we will leave soon, but—did *you* do that?" he asked suddenly.

As though in reply Tala leaned forward and touched his long horn to Coconino's knee. The young man jumped back as an electrical shock pulsed through his leg. "Aiiee! Stop!" he protested. "Don't do that!" Tala came at him again, and he rolled away, but this time the animal merely pointed the twisting horn and a crackling spark arced the distance between them. *"Aiiee!"* Coconino cried again. "Don't! All right, we will go, we will go!"

He scrambled quickly to his feet, startled at the attack from friendly quarters. "Only this is a poor way to treat your brother, the only man who believed in you," he grumbled, reaching for the ridged wing sock. "Who else sings to you of the Mother Earth, your mother, and your own beauty? Who brushes you with grass when you are hot and sweaty? Who—"

Suddenly the Thing passed by Coconino's head so close that he felt the heat of its wash as well as the wind. Its whistling whine trailed seconds behind its passage. Tala bolted, trumpeting loudly, and with a crack of his wings was airborne. Caught off balance, Coconino tumbled to the ground, his ears ringing. An acrid smell pervaded the air.

Cautiously he raised himself and peered after the smoking Thing. It had buried itself in the earth just down the hill from him, a cloud of dust still lingering over the site of impact. A low buzzing came from it. Coconino crept slowly closer.

In fascinated horror he watched as the Thing shivered, jiggled, and finally raised itself on spindly legs. Its smell told Coconino it was a machine of some kind, but what kind he had no idea. He had no use for the foul relics of the Before Times. This one whirred, clicked, and chirped, then slowly began to walk out of its burrow.

Coconino followed it as it tottered down the hill on its spidery appendages, lenses peering, shutters clicking, antennae vibrating. It was shaped like a slightly flattened sphere two feet in diameter with countless bumps and depressions on its dull surface. Coconino kept his distance but watched it closely, trying to open himself to any word from the Mother Earth regarding the device. It seemed only to make noise and move jerkily across the soil.

Suddenly it stopped. It was near the edge of what had been a concrete foundation. There the legs braced and a small drill dropped from its belly. With a high-pitched whine it began to bore into the earth, sending plant shreds and small stones flying.

"Aiiee!" Coconino jumped back. Then, with a terrible cry of rage, he picked up a chunk of concrete from the rubble and hurled it at the Thing.

One of the appendages snapped at a joint. The Thing lurched to one side, and the drilling stopped. Savagely pleased, Coconino found another chunk of the stuff, larger, and hurled it as well. Another leg snapped, and the Thing squealed, began limping away. But Coconino was riding the crest of his blood lust. He found more and more missiles to launch, forcing the Thing back into the rubble. Lenses cracked, antennae broke, until at last the Thing lay smoking and whimpering among its battered members, hemmed in by pieces of debris. Helplessly it rocked back and forth like a wounded child, vapors seeping from a tiny crack along one of its seams. Coconino stood over it and knew that it was dying.

Silently he found the largest rock he could carry and lugged it to where the Thing lay imprisoned. Then he hoisted the rock high over his head and killed it.

"I suppose that was an accident, too!" Clayton snarled, his face flushed red. "Like the 'error' in the navigational computer."

"It passed through some electrical storms on the way down, sir," his duty officer said. "It was already two hundred miles off course by the time it landed; it could very well have sustained major damage which caused the malfunction."

A frown creased the captain's forehead, and he ran his hand absently through his dark hair. "How long till Earth catches up with us?" he asked.

"Thirteen days, four hours," the navigator replied.

"Barring further 'errors,' " Winthrop growled. "Well, then. I guess Earth will be as much a surprise to us as we are to it."

Phoenix found Coconino on the stream bank below the village, seated on sandy ground still wet from the day's rain shower. "What happened to you this afternoon?" she asked.

Coconino was throwing small stones viciously into the water. "Tala left me. I had to walk back." He did not look at her but continued his missile assault on the muddy creek.

"Aw, poor thing! In the rain, too, I bet," she mocked. "Juan and I brought down a mule deer. A nice doe. Cactus Flower is roasting a haunch; you should join us."

Phoenix had come to enjoy hunting with Juan. She found him a pleasant companion, in many ways more comfortable to be with than Coconino. Her feelings toward Coconino were disquieting enough, but since their return she was all too conscious of his growing fascination with her. His eyes would follow her as she moved, only to be quickly averted when she turned to him.

Yes, turn them away, Coconino, she thought. Don't let me see the hunger there as I saw it in Elvira's light the night we returned from the north. I could not understand the Mother's concern; I thought she mocked me, but she has proved herself astute once again. How impossible it seemed—and in that moment of firelight, how exhilarating, how terrifying! The wanting of you is dangerous enough without knowing I am wanted as well. For to act on this want would only lead to pain—for me.

Yet Phoenix returned to him always, like a moth to a flame. The brilliance of him dazzled her, and she would not trade it for the cold darkness that was safety. The trick was to hover, to circle, without being consumed. So she came to him carefully, pulling her boisterous taunts around her as a defense.

But his anger was the shield between them now. "I am not hungry," he growled in answer to her invitation.

Phoenix hesitated, then dropped to the ground beside him, disarmed by the cloud of emotions that engulfed him. "What's the matter?" she asked.

He clawed at the ground, searching for more pebbles to throw, every line of his face set in ferocity. As he drew back an arm to launch yet another stone, she seized his wrist. "Hey! Are you building a dam?"

He glared at her a moment, then wrested his hand free. "Tala hurt me," he said bluntly.

Surprise filled her face. "Hurt you? How? Where?"

There was a brief hesitation; then he indicated his knee. "Here. He touched it with his horn, and it felt as if I had been struck by a rock. A large rock. A burning rock. I felt it all the way to my head."

She puzzled over that. "A burning sensation?" She frowned. "Topical poison, maybe. Or—did the sensation travel? Up your leg, into your body?"

"All the way to my head!" he repeated.

"Like an electrical shock?"

"What is 'electric'?"

"Oh . . . like when your clothing rubs against you and you touch another person and you get a shock—although you probably don't wear enough clothes to have that problem. But in the winter, with furs and—"

"I know what you mean," he snapped. "We call it *tkah-kha-ahn*: little love lightning. This was much stronger, much. But yes, it was like that."

"Let's check it out," she suggested, jumping to her feet. "Where is Tala?"

"I do not know. Right now I do not care."

"Well, don't take it personally," she prodded. "Fish gotta swim, eels gotta shock—so does Tala, apparently. Call him; we'll run a little test. I'll even volunteer to be the guinea pig."

But Coconino only leaned back and stared up at the gray sky, which was streaked here and there with the gold of a sun that was rapidly setting. Phoenix sighed and plopped back down beside him. Abruptly he said, "I want to marry."

Phoenix barked a short laugh, startled. "Well, this is a new tune."

"I want to marry and leave children. I do not want to disappear from this place with no trace. I want to leave my seed for the People. Finding Tala is nothing; children are the greatest gift I can give to the People."

There was a tense silence. "Then go bring Nina down from the cliff," Phoenix said harshly. "Or leave your gifts at Too Pretty's door."

At the pain in her voice Coconino looked up, saw her dark and stormy face. Only then did he remember why the subject of children should be so sore with her. "I'm sorry," he said. "I had forgotten . . ."

She laughed a laugh dangerously close to tears. "Forgotten!" she echoed. "Only you could forget."

"I know. I am clumsy and stupid." He got to his knees beside her and bowed his head apologetically.

"Clumsy, sure," she laughed bitterly. "You make a swan look awkward."

The wash of her pain had cleared his own dark mood, drawn him out of his suffering and into hers. He took her hand, and she tried to pull it away, but he held on. Slowly, with her contesting him for every inch, he drew the hand closer and closer to his mouth—and bit her.

"Ouch!" she howled, finally breaking free. "*Estúpido,* why did you—" She struck out at him, but he caught her hand, laughing. "Damn it, Coconino, you play so rough all the time!" She struck with her other fist and found herself, as always, powerless in his grasp. But this time she threw her body weight and knocked him off balance so that they both tumbled down the bank to the water's edge. There she grabbed a handful of soft mud and smeared him lavishly while he laughed, clinging to her waist. Then she collapsed on top of him, feeling somewhat vindicated, though she herself was nearly as filthy as he.

They lay there in the fading light, acutely aware of how their bodies were tangled together yet neither willing to move or call attention to their closeness. Phoenix was afraid that if she so much as shifted a finger he would respond, so she lay with her head on his chest, listening to his heart, feeling the rise and fall of his chest with each breath.

The gently flowing water trickled across Coconino's feet and legs, sucking at the mud beneath them, forming mini-channels around these new obstacles. He could feel the mud drying on his skin, the tickle of her hair fanned across his chest. If only he could lead her into the stream, wash the mud from her body, feel it smooth and wet beneath his hands . . . but she would never allow that. So he lay with his desire only a pleasant ache within him, fed by the touch of her thighs and breasts naked as his own, stymied by the knowledge that one caress would rob him of even that.

Finally the sun dropped below the bank of gray clouds and shot a beam of bright light through to the earth. Phoenix inhaled deeply as though she would hold the sunlight in her lungs, then exhaled slowly, collapsing even tighter against him. "Tell me about the Witch Woman who never went back to the Mountain," she asked softly.

Now he drew in a deep breath, his rising chest pressing her almost imperceptibly closer into his encircling arms. The rush of breath from his nostrils stirred her hair, and she smiled a little, a movement he felt against his skin. "She died," he said softly.

"Did she?"

Now he sighed audibly. "There is no other way to say it. Her people wanted her to return to the Mountain, but she begged to stay. 'One more year,' she said, 'only one.' For she loved a man of the People and could not bear to leave him. So the Men-on-the-Mountain said, 'One year, but then you must return.' So she promised, and they went away."

Phoenix could feel the rumbling of his voice in his chest. She could feel the shift of his thoughts to the story and hoped it was a long one so she could lie this way a very long time.

"The next year she still did not want to leave," Coconino continued, "for she had borne her beloved's child and would not take away the wealth of the People. Nor could she leave the child behind. And her love for the man burned even stronger so that she wished even more to stay and become one of the People."

"Then why do you say she died?"

"It is not easy to become one of the People," he said sadly, "if you have not been born to it. There is as much to forget as there is to learn. For the Witch Woman it was a great ordeal. The Shaman—for this was before the time of the Mother—the Shaman required a great ritual before all the People. I do not know just what, for it is not spoken of in the stories of the People. But there was a great fire, and something was burned, and the people were ashamed of their Shaman, and the Witch Woman died."

"Truly?" Small tears trickled down her face onto his chest.

"Truly." He sighed, feeling again the lovely weight of her on his chest. "But that day a new woman was born, a woman of the People. She was a timid and cowering thing, and some thought that she would not live. But the People prayed to the Mother Earth, who sustained her. The Men-on-the-Mountain came and were angry to find that their Witch Woman was no more. They did not send any Teachers for many years, and no Witch Women came for even longer."

"But she lived," Phoenix whispered happily, clinging to him unconsciously. "She lived, and she was of the People."

"Someone lived," he modified.

"What was her name?"

"The Witch Woman?" he asked. "Or the woman who lived?"

"The one who lived."

"Then she was called Trembling Leaf, for so she was. That is the Way of the People, to call each by what they are. Today she has another name, though, for she no longer trembles." Carefully, thoughtfully, he stroked her hair. "Today we call her Mother."

That night Coconino went at last to Nina's house on the cliff. But he did not bring her down. He went quietly, in the dead of night when none could see him, and spoke no word to her to betray his identity. Even his necklace, the blue-green bird set in silver, he left behind so that it would not give him away.

"I could not bring her back with me," he whispered to Phoenix, who had insisted that he go. "I loved her as tenderly as I could, but it was from pity and from guilt. It would be wrong to marry her, Phoenix. I cannot do this thing."

They were sitting in Phoenix's cliff house, savoring the coolness of the morning. Phoenix nodded and handed back his necklace, for she had kept it for him during the night. But Coconino pressed it back into her hand. "You keep it," he said. "I will forget it one night, and it will betray me."

Phoenix snorted. "You think she doesn't know who it was?"

He suppressed a smile. "I whispered 'Cactus Flower' once, just to confuse her."

Phoenix laughed, but a tear glistened in her eye. "How clever. Now the whole village will say you've been sleeping with Juan's wife."

She held the necklace out again.

Still he shook his head. "It is a phoenix. You should keep it."

Her voice was anguished. "Coconino, I can't. The Mother will be angry."

Anger flashed through his dark eyes. He stood up and pulled her roughly to her feet. "Come with me," he snapped, and climbed out the door.

He led her down the ladders and into the village, to the great loom under the ramada where the Mother sat weaving, always weaving. She seemed to have grown thinner, and her breathing was shallow. Phoenix trembled a little to see her.

But Coconino stood erect, a challenge in his bearing. "I would ask a favor, Mother."

She did not look up but sent the shuttle back and forth, back and forth. "Speak, my child."

He took the necklace that Phoenix still clutched in her hand. "This necklace is mine. But it is a symbol for the name of my sister-brother, Phoenix. I would give it to her because it is her name and because she is my sister-brother, but she will not accept it."

"I cannot make her do so," the old woman replied tightly. "She thinks you will be angry."

Finally the Mother lifted her eyes, and there was indeed anger in them. Phoenix noticed now that they were not black but brown. "What is your favor, Coconino?"

Brazenly he handed her the necklace. "You give it to her. She will take it from your hand."

"Coconino, don't!" Phoenix whispered desperately. For the first time she saw the Mother not as a superstitious old woman with too much power but as a woman who had given up everything to gain everything. A husband, yes, and a child, but there was more to it than that. What was it the Mother had said? "A life of service to the Mother Earth." Yes. It was not just the man or the People but what they represented. This was what the Witch Woman had died for the Mother to obtain.

"You don't need to," Phoenix said quietly to the old woman. "Let him keep it to give to his wife someday."

"It is not a thing I would give to a wife," he snapped. "It is a phoenix. It is for Phoenix, my sister-brother."

Drifting down from the houses on the cliff came Nina's voice, a prayer of thanks to the Mother Earth. Coconino tried to turn his face to stone, but for a brief moment it betrayed him.

The Mother sighed deeply and handed the necklace to Phoenix. "The giving of a token is only an outward sign," she said. "What's done is done. Take the phoenix, sister-brother of Coconino, for he is right. It is your name."

CHAPTER THIRTEEN

The morning was hot, but the air was dry, first promise of the coming fall. The sky was a rich blue, and below it the land was uncommonly green from the rains and from the river that curled through it. Already the hot, sticky sleepless nights grew distant in Phoenix's mind. Here aloft, the steady beat of Tala's wings thrummed with her lightened heart and the wind blew her long black hair out behind her.

Every night this week Coconino had gone to Nina's house, but each dawn had found him at Phoenix's door, wanting her to fly with him. His restlessness, his moodiness she put down to the obvious cause: He spent all his days with her, watching her, wanting her, but at night had to lie with another. There are worse fates, she thought wickedly. And it's not necessarily forever. Maybe, when Nina is finally pregnant . . .

Her left arm circled his waist, the other rested on his back; he was warm and slightly sweaty to her touch. His phoenix medallion was a tangible weight against her breastbone. Phoenix, she thought. Sign of my rebirth. Contentedly she breathed in the scent of him and clung to the moment as though she wanted to know no other moment in all of time.

Tala alighted bumpily in the river valley. She had given up excusing his rough landings as being caused by the extra weight of two riders. He tries to tumble me off, Phoenix thought. He thinks it's a great joke. But Coconino's hand on her thigh kept her from slipping while Tala folded his great wings. Then they both slid down.

The heat rose from the ground in shimmering waves, and the sun beat relentlessly on Phoenix's bare skin, but they could not drag down her spirit. You're jealous, Tala, she decided. Jealous because I, too, am his friend and companion, jealous because I, too, am a child of the Mother Earth.

It is good, so good, to know at last who I am! Phoenix, sister-brother of Coconino, daughter of the Mother Earth. There is only one thing left to complete my identity. I must be of the People. I will ask the Mother what I must do, and whatever it is, even if it's everything she was required to do, I'll do it. But she won't be as cruel as the Shaman. Harsh, yes, but not like the Shaman. And I am as strong as she, maybe stronger. Whatever it takes to become one of the People, I will do it.

A breeze touched her, and she breathed deeply of her new resolve.

But Coconino did not share her contentment. Restless, he paced the valley floor, trying to feel any trace of the pain from his dream. Still the Mother Earth was calm and breathed gently. Lizards scuttled through the undergrowth; a sidewinder "walked" on its coils away from them. A bevy of quail scurried off, but neither hunter drew a bow. Neither wished to disturb the rhythm of life here.

Phoenix watched her moody friend. What was wrong? Something had happened last week, something more than Tala leaving him in the storm, more than a mild jolt of electricity from Tala's horn. She had tested the horn herself and knew its voltage to be low. So what was it? And why did he prowl this valley like a coyote searching for scorpions in its den? What did he expect to find?

Forget the scorpions, she thought, feeling the coursing of blood through her veins. Forget the scorpions and look at me. Turn and look at me the way you did after the feast. Tempt me again, Coconino, you may be surprised. At any rate look at me, see my body, see whatever it is in me that stirs you now, for I crave your eyes resting on me as tangibly as a caress. I crave the feelings you stir up in me, the blatant flattery in a young, attractive man desiring this hard and barren body. You were right, Coconino, I am a rock—but when you look at me, I am the most magnificent rock in all creation.

Just then the sun glinted off something in a nearby pile of rubble. Her heart leapt—there had been a town here once; what relic might she find in the debris? She remembered scavenging with her father among the ruined cities farther south, the excitement of finding some useful tool, some glass container or piece of metal that had escaped oxidation. "Hey, Coconino, let's take a look over here," she called.

Coconino glanced up and saw where she was headed. "Do not go there."

She shot him a puzzled look. "Why not?"

His eyes were dark and glowering in his craggy face. "There was an evil Thing in this valley, and I killed it and buried it there."

An inexplicable chill crept along Phoenix's spine, an icy foreboding. She started involuntarily toward the mound. "What was it?" she asked.

"I do not know," he admitted grudgingly, "but it was evil." Reluctantly he followed her, feeling suddenly obliged to defend his actions. "It stank," he told her. "It defiled the Mother Earth. Something from the Before Times which had forgotten to die." A bitter smile twisted his lips. "I helped it remember."

The chill Phoenix had felt was now a knot between her shoulder blades. "Defiled the Mother Earth, what do you mean?"

"It fell from the sky," he said harshly, "and tore a hole in the ground. Then it crept like a spider to another place and started to tear at Her again—"

Phoenix was scrambling swiftly through the chunks of concrete and other debris. "What did you do to it?" she demanded. "How could you—oh, my God—!"

She dropped to her knees beside the wreckage of the Thing, clearing more stones away. "What have you done?" she moaned, recognizing the carbon fiber they could not manufacture on the Mountain. "It was a space probe, look at it—oh, God!" The moan became a cry of despair as she touched the lettering etched in its battered surface. " '*Homeward Bound.*' They were coming back for us! They were looking for us, they sent a probe, and you—"

Suddenly her life wrenched back to its old focus, and she turned on him with fists flailing. "Damn you, Coconino!" she said, pummeling his chest. "You've destroyed it! They tried to make contact, and you— Why do you hate everything you don't understand?"

He tried to stave off her blows, to catch at her wrists, but the unexpected ferocity of her attack had caught him off guard. Tears edged her voice. "Just because you don't like the smell of machines— Oh, God," she cried, collapsing against him, "what do I do now?"

Coconino was baffled both by her violence and now by the fact that she wept. What had he done? He had destroyed the evil Thing—or was it evil? In truth, he did not know what it was. Men-on-the-Mountain always said that machines were only tools, that good or evil was in how they were used. He had thought its purpose evil, but now—

Abruptly she straightened up. "I've got to get back to the Mountain."

He shook his head. "The Flying Machine will not come till after the harvest. There is no way—"

"I've *got* to get back!" she screamed at him. "They've got to know about this! If that came from a ship, we can signal her from the Mountain. There's a beacon; it hasn't been used in a while because of the power drain, but if it still works— They've come back, don't you understand? They've come back to look for us!"

Coconino did not understand, but he got up and pulled her to her feet. "We will go to the Council," he said. "If it is so important—"

"It's the most important thing to happen on this planet in five centuries!"

"If the Council wishes," he told her, "Tala and I will take you back to the Mountain."

The chamber was dark and dank, its coolness rapidly being displaced by the bodies gathered inside. Ben Gonzales was there, sunburned and sweaty, pulled from his day's labor in the fields to honor this most solemn assembly. Two Moons, Coconino's mother, was also there, graying hair impeccably braided, billowy cotton dress embroidered with the emblems of the Council. Large Oak sat near the door, for he was Gatekeeper, his lean face a mass of wrinkles, teeth gone, eyes clouded by cataracts. The two youngest members of the Council, Many Waters and Cactus Wren, sat beside him. Across from them were Gray Fox, father of Falling Star, and Ernestina, a plump woman of twenty-eight whose faith was nearly as legendary as that of her Survivor namesake.

Coconino sat beside Gonzales, his face set in sullen lines. Across from him Phoenix's eyes burned with the intensity of her demands.

At the head of the room sat the Mother, her head bent, her breathing still labored from the effort of climbing all the way to the Council Chamber. Beads of sweat stood out on her forehead and cheeks, though she shivered occasionally and pulled the shawl of her office tighter around her. She had listened impassively to Coconino's account of the Thing that fell from the sky, and now she was hearing Phoenix's explanation of its significance.

"It's a messenger," the younger woman said urgently, "from other people. Descendants of Those Who Left. It may come from a larger vessel, the *Homeward Bound*. It may mean that somewhere in the heavens above the Earth this great vessel hovers carrying these Others, and they want to know what the Earth is like now, whether or not she is still angry. But Coconino killed the messenger, and it can't send information back. So I must go to the Men-on-the-Mountain, who can signal the vessel and let it know that the Earth was merciful and her children have survived."

"Those Who Left," Large Oak pointed out, "were those who wronged the Mother Earth. Should we allow them to come back?"

"But these Others are their children," Phoenix urged. "Are children responsible for the deeds of their parents? If so, we are all guilty, for in the Before Times all wronged Her. Even the People died in great numbers during the Bad Times. Don't you teach that it was not the worth of the People that was their salvation but the mercy of the Mother Earth?"

"That is true," Two Moons agreed. Her face told so little, unlike her son's. "But by Her mercy the People came to see their error and live now in harmony with Her. Do these Others live so?"

"The Others need never have anything to do with the People," Phoenix said, trying to miss her point. "They will traffic only with the Men-on-the-Mountain. We can make sure they leave you alone."

"But will they respect the Mother Earth?" Gray Fox asked. He had a long face, as did his son, and a habit of stroking his chin. "Or will they bring the evil of the Before Times back with them." It was not a question but a statement of their one collective concern.

Many Waters and Cactus Wren exchanged glances but said nothing.

"They will bring much good with them," Phoenix insisted. "Medicines and knowledge that will make life easier—"

"Life should be a challenge," Large Oak interrupted. "We

need hard times to keep the People strong and alive. Only a fool wants a life that is easy.''

"Only a fool wants to die young!" Phoenix shot back. "They have skills and equipment, vaccines that can save lives! Mother, you know what their medicine can do for—''

With a sharp gesture the Mother cut her off. "I know what it can do for *you*," she hissed. "You have weighed their good against their evil on *your* scales—as you weigh everything! These Others must come for *your* benefit. You must be a hunter because it gives *you* worth. You would be of the People not for the good of the People but for *your* good.''

Phoenix drew back in surprise. She had said nothing to the Mother of her desire. Had Coconino? Or was it just another of those things the old woman seemed to know without having to be told?

Breath rasped from her lungs as the Mother continued. "We cannot deny the Others the Earth, not for any reason you have said but because they, too, are children of the Mother Earth. If she rejects them again, then she rejects them. It is not for us to do so. As for you, sister-brother of Coconino, Witch Woman you are and Witch Woman you will always be. Go back to your Mountain, tell them of your messenger and your *Homeward Bound*. But come no more to the Valley of the People. You are no longer welcome here.''

For a shocked moment Phoenix only sat, her chin quivering. Then she bolted for the Council door.

Coconino stepped into the small upper room of the stone house the Witch Woman had used. He waited a moment for his eyes to accustom themselves to the darkness, then he spoke. "The Mother spoke in anger," he said softly. "She will recant.''

"Ask me if I care.''

She was dressed once more in the heavy cotton trousers and sleeveless leather shirt of a Witch Woman. Her long arms snapped back and forth as she stuffed her belongings into a duffel. Coconino watched her a moment. "I care.''

She spun on him. "Don't you understand?" she barked. "She's right. I'm not one of you; I never will be. It suited my purpose for a while, but now I've got to go back. Now I know how to go back. And I know what to do when I get there.'' She strapped the bag shut, hoisted it to her shoulder, and stood facing him.

Slowly he reached out to the leather thong around her neck and drew the bird stone from beneath her shirt. She started to take it off, but he stopped her. "It is a Phoenix," he said. "It is yours. Wear it always to remind you that once you were of the People."

"I've never been of the People, don't you understand?" she hissed. "I've only been of me. She's right. Damn her to hell, she's right. My only thought my whole life has been for me. I married Dick because *I* wanted him, with no thought of his needs. I clung to him when I should have let him go. And I came here to escape because *I* didn't want to deal with it. I have no place among the People. I'm like that island in the northern canyon where we stayed—I may look like the canyon walls, but I'll never be part of them."

He wanted to reach out and hold her, to tell her that she was a part of him and always would be, but she had made herself untouchable. All the anger, the hate and self-loathing, had flooded back into her, and she had separated herself from all around her. So instead he said, "It is starting to rain, and Tala will not carry us in this weather. In the morning I will take you to the Mountain."

There was a moment, then she let her pack slip back to the ground. "Better than walking," she said, and turned away from him.

Still he did not leave. She tried to ignore him, but his presence in the room, his nearness, was something that pressed on every fiber of her consciousness. Finally she faced him again. "What do you want?"

In the shadowy chamber he whispered, "You."

Phoenix staggered back with an exasperated cry, one hand flying to cover her tortured face. With words he tried again to reach for her. "This is your last night among the People. I would stay in your stone house and—"

"*No!*" she fairly shrieked. "Go sleep with Nina, sleep with Castle Rock, sleep with Corn Hair—sleep with your mother for all I care, but—"

He struck her a blow that knocked her up against the wall of the house. "Do not say such an evil thing again!" he roared, trembling with rage in every muscle. "Filth, filth, that's all that comes from your mouth! I will not hear such defamation, even from you. No wonder the Mother Earth makes you barren!'' And he ducked out the doorway into the gentle drizzle of the late August rain.

Phoenix sank slowly to the floor, her head reeling with the pain of his blow. The sweet taste of blood was in her mouth, and she felt a trickling sensation on her upper lip. Stupid! she raged at herself. Stupid, stupid, stupid! Always shooting your mouth off— How could you say that to him? What did you expect him to do? How much abuse do you think people will take?

Outside there was a great crack of thunder that rumbled on and on and on . . .

"Oh, God, I want him back!'' she sobbed. "I want him back, I want him back, I want him back . . .'' Great wrenching sobs choked off her voice, and she wept until, exhausted, she slept.

Phoenix slipped out of the village before dawn, her duffel in one hand, her bow and quiver in the other. She would carry the bag out of the village, beyond a hill or two, then bury it with its contents save those few things she would need for her journey. She would change into her loincloth, keeping one shirt for her arrival on the Mountain, and set off southward along the rivercourses. She knew they would take her from here to the Dead Cities, and below that, if she found the right wash—well, she'd worry about that when she had to make the choice.

At the stream she stopped to wash the crusted blood from her nose and lip and to fill her mouth with water for running. Her stomach rumbled and threatened to give back the bile that churned in it, but she declined to squander time finding food. All she wanted was to get out of the village quickly, to put behind her every hurt and every hope she had known there. She would take nothing more from the People.

Just below the village she angled away from the stream, trying to hide her trail on rocky ground. She kept to the gullies as much as possible—not that anyone will try to follow me, she thought bitterly. I've sealed every door with my own stupidity, but maybe it's better that way. Better to end it here, now, before I contaminate anything else.

The bag was heavy, and she thought, The first stretch of soft ground I come to, this thing goes. The one shirt, maybe my hairbrush—Mother Earth can reclaim the rest.

When finally she thought she had put enough distance between herself and the village, she slowed her pace to conserve her energy. The jeans she wore were restrictive, but at least they protected her legs from the thistled vines that seemed to reach out and clutch at her every step of the way. You should be glad to get rid of me, she thought, reaching down to brush away a tenacious creeper as she struggled out of a small ravine. But I guess you can't resist one last chance to complicate my life—

Ahead of her a soft trumpeting sounded, and her heart stopped. Slowly she looked up the steeply sloping embankment.

Coconino stood above her on the uneven ground near the crest. One knee was bent for balance on the slope, his hand resting casually on it, and the muscles in his bare chest were shadowed in the gray half-light of dawn. His face was set but not in anger; his dark hair framed it, falling loosely just past his shoulders. Behind him Tala cropped thistles quietly. They had been waiting for her.

Coconino tried not to wince when he saw the angry bruise on the side of the Witch Woman's face, the swollen lip. He had never struck anyone like that. To think that of all people he had hit Phoenix—but, he told himself resolutely, it had to be done. If she said such a thing here and now, he would do it again.

"If you stayed near the stream," he told her, "the walking would be easier."

She climbed the last few steps to stand just below him. "Life should be a challenge," she replied.

"Would you carry that bag all the way to the Mountain?"

"I was going to get rid of it somewhere away from the village. Where it wouldn't offend the People." He nodded but said nothing, so she asked, "Think I can make the Dead City by nightfall?"

He shifted his weight deliberately, crossed his arms over his chest, and studied her. Oh, Coconino, don't move, she thought. You are so beautiful when you move.

"I have seldom been south of the river where the Thing fell from the sky," he told her. "But I do not think so."

Well, it didn't matter. Today or tomorrow she would arrive when her strength carried her there. Then beyond, heading southeast toward the other Dead City, but not all the way. There was a wash that went more directly south—but where? And would it still be flowing with water from the monsoons, which would surely stop any day now? She was carrying two canteens. Would that be enough?

"Give a lady a ride?" she asked finally.

He cleared his throat. "There is something that needs to be said first."

Again she nodded, and this time her head dropped. She was not accustomed to apologies. Words always seemed inadequate to the point of uselessness at such times. But she had to make this one. She wanted to. "Coconino, I'm sorry." Her voice was too soft; she cleared her throat and tried again. "I was angry and—I say things I don't mean." Then her voice died to a whisper. "I never meant to hurt you."

"That is exactly what you meant to do."

Surprised, she lifted her eyes to meet his. They were stern but not angry. *Like my father,* she thought. *God knows how many times I hurt him, striking out at anything and wounding him because he was so close. You should have worn a flak jacket, Dad, for all the shrapnel you caught . . . but you always knew. You always knew it wasn't meant for you, and you were always there. I still miss you . . .*

She swallowed hard and took a deep breath. "Yes, I did," she confessed. "I do that. When I'm hurt I—lash out at people—anyone—and . . . I'm sorry." Wasn't there something more she could say? "If I could call the words back, I would. Please believe me." *I'm sorry, Coconino. I'm sorry, Dad.*

Gently he touched the dark bruise, and she winced. "I'm sorry, too."

She tried to force a smile, but it hurt too much, so she only grimaced. "Oh, this?" she croaked. "I'll live."

"Perhaps," he suggested, "these Others will have a way to cure it."

She laughed then and wished she hadn't, for the shaking jarred her tender jaw and she winced again. "I'm sure they have bigger worries than this."

He took the bag from her hand, let her sling the bow and quiver across her own back, and they started toward the grazing Tala. "Can they truly make you able to have children?" he asked.

She broke stride, glanced at him, then continued. "Depends how big a ship it is, what kind of medical facilities they have aboard. It was a fairly simple operation at the time of the Evacuation; it's probably even simpler now. We just don't have the equipment or the proper anesthetics on the Mountain."

Tala came toward them now, trumpeting softly to the man. Phoenix he ignored, but he sniffed at the bag Coconino carried with obvious distaste. "Perhaps," Coconino conceded, "I was too hasty when I killed your Messenger."

"Perhaps nothing, you big ox," Phoenix groused, standing back while he swung up onto the unicorn's back. "But then, you always were pigheaded."

"I've been meaning to ask you," he said, shifting far forward to allow her room to climb up behind him. "What is a pig?"

They camped that night on the bank of a great river channel that cut southward from the Dead City. The land was lower here than the Valley of the People, and the general climate warmer. The night air was heavy with unspent rain.

Lying on her back, clad only in her loincloth, Phoenix felt remarkably light and unencumbered. Her cheek throbbed slightly, but the kiss of the warm blackness on her naked flesh was a balm to her spirit. It was like being on their quest again: no walls around her, Coconino close at hand. Above them the stars seemed larger and more liquid than she remembered.

Was the *Homeward Bound* already in orbit, she wondered as she watched those gleaming lights, or had they launched the probe from a greater distance? How many were aboard her, and what was their purpose? Did they indeed have the facilities for the surgical procedure she needed? Perhaps techniques had developed far beyond conventional surgery; perhaps there was some other treatment. After all, it had been over five hundred years.

And the vaccines they would bring, the complex antibiotics lost generations before. The children would not die now from Reye syndrome, or the elderly from pneumonia. The People would grow stronger, healthier . . . they would all prosper . . .

She woke to the sound of Coconino's voice chanting in the gray dawn. Not far from where they'd slept, a low range of hills sprouted from the otherwise flat plain; these Coconino faced, his hands lifted in invocation. Nearby Tala pawed the earth, then began to move closer to Coconino, drawn as always by the sound of his chanting.

> "Ancient as the mountains,
> Tall and towering,
> Green with life yet gray with age.

Grandfather! You are near.
Grandfather! I have seen you.
I will come and pay homage
To that which was
And will never come again.
Grandfather, hear me!
Grandfather, call out
So that I may find you
And know your glory once
Before it vanishes forever.''

When Coconino turned back to Phoenix, there was an odd
glitter in his eyes. "I dreamed," he explained. "The Grandfather is somewhere near. To find him—would be a great omen."

"Who's the Grandfather?" Phoenix asked.

Coconino turned to stroke Tala's neck. "He that was and is no
more. You will know him when you see him."

Phoenix stiffened. "How near is near?" she asked, not wanting to lose time on another of Coconino's tracking sessions.

He shrugged, scanning the line of hills parading away toward
the south. "Down there, somewhere, I think. We will fly," he
assured her, swinging deftly up onto Tala's broad back. "I have
seen the place; it will be easy to find from above."

The tension drained from Phoenix's shoulders. At least they
would be going in the right direction and at the right speed. She
mounted behind him, and Tala launched into the first streaks of
golden dawn.

Riding the air currents, Coconino felt a kinship with the hawk.
Below him in the half-light the hills looked like an old blanket
that had been cast aside and had fallen in ridges, covered in the
mosslike green of cholla and prickly pear and paloverde trees.
Then he saw it.

Phoenix heard his intake of breath. "What is it?" she asked.

"There!" he cried, pointing to a mountain that seemed to
stand alone, flatland stretching away on all sides of it. Like a
tower it raised steep walls from a sloping base, and the top was
notched in the semblance of a crown. "It is the place I saw in my
dream," he told her. "We will find the Grandfather there."

As they drew closer, the notched top of the mountain revealed
itself as twin peaks, one slightly behind the other. Smaller hills
were attached to it, but it remained isolated from other escarp-
ments in the area. Soon they were close enough to see the vegetation on its slopes.

"I do not see him," Coconino said in puzzlement as they approached the northern face. "I was sure . . ."

Tala banked lazily and began to glide around the mountain to the west. He's going for water, Phoenix thought. I don't blame the animal; I'm getting thirsty, too, and he's doing all the work. The river should be just—

"There!" Coconino cried excitedly. "On the side. The Grandfather! He lives!"

Phoenix peered over his shoulder, trying to see what had caught his eye, but Tala's great wings were blocking it now as they beat the air mightily, breaking their descent to earth. In a swift and practiced gesture Coconino swung his leg over the beast's neck and slid down, clambering farther up the rocky incline. Phoenix climbed awkwardly down and followed him.

Then she, too, caught her breath. "My God," she whispered. "It's a saguaro."

Towering over them, clutching the hillside tenaciously, was the hulk of a giant cactus. It rose some forty feet into the air, its girth that of two men. But it was a lonely and timeworn sentinel, the last of its species. Once they had covered these hills and the arid flats for a hundred miles, monarchs of the desert, their peculiar armlike limbs not sprouting until they were seventy-five to a hundred years old.

But development of the land had thrown the great forest of saguaro into decline. Floods had cleared the lowlands of them; great winds had overpowered others. Eventually the slow-growing, shallow-rooted plants had been unable to replenish themselves.

The Grandfather had stood on that hillside for 239 years, and he was tired. Brown wartlike blemishes covered half his trunk. Woodpecker holes had cut through two of his five arms. The stumps were gnarled; even his good arms had been bent into odd shapes by their own water-soaked weight during countless rainy seasons. The trunk was banded by a frost line acquired in its youth, and more woodpecker holes had left ragged openings in the soft, pithy flesh of the trunk and remaining arms. It had been so for decades.

Soon he would die. But as Coconino lifted his voice and his eyes, the young man saw the reason the Grandfather had clung to life so long. High atop the gentle giant were small red fruits.

The chant died abruptly on Coconino's lips. A quick search

of the ground produced a stout stick; he snatched it up and strode toward Tala. Then man and beast were airborne. "Watch closely," he called to Phoenix as they circled closer to the cactus. "See where the fruit lands!" Swooping as close as he dared to the ancient plant, he leaned down and knocked the fruit free with the stick.

When he landed, Phoenix picked up the fruit and cradled it in a scrap of leather. "You know, people used to eat these," she said. "Your people. They were a staple part of the diet, like the mesquite bean."

"We will not eat this," he told her. The fruit had split open, revealing a myriad of tiny seeds inside. "This is the reason the Grandfather stood alone for so many ages, though he longed to rest. He waited to give this gift to the People. He waited to give us his seed." And he tucked the precious fruit into the leather pouch at his waist.

His seed. Phoenix stood gazing up at the grizzled monarch, dwarfed by its age and its size and the incredible fact of its survival. First Tala, now the saguaro—what was it in her companion that made such legends reality? Slowly she turned to the young hunter, no different in looks from others of the People— yet there he sat at ease on the back of a unicorn. A unicorn that flew. "How did you know?" she asked him. "How did you know the Grandfather was here?"

Coconino looked down into her face. "I told you," he said. "I dreamed."

"But you believed the dream. You don't believe all your dreams."

He looked away, off toward the west, where stretched a land he had never seen, a country as unknown to him as the Sisters of the Mother Earth. For a moment he allowed himself to slip back into the mists of his dream, the mists through which he had walked and seen the Grandfather, even as the Grandfather stood before them now. Finally he shrugged. "The Mother Earth speaks to whom She will and how She will. Sometimes it is in the cry of a hawk, sometimes in the voice of a brook—this time it was a dream."

"But how did you know this dream was the voice of the Mother Earth?" Phoenix persisted.

Again he shrugged. "A son must know his mother's voice." Then a small smile played at his mouth. "And I am her favorite son."

But Phoenix did not rise to his taunt. Instead she turned for one last look at the ancient cactus. " 'That which was and will never come again,' " she chanted softly. "Grandfather, hear me—let me be as fruitful as you." Then she climbed up behind Coconino and was silent for a long time.

CHAPTER FOURTEEN

"Will you try to find your father?" Phoenix asked.

Coconino looked up, startled. He had never thought about it.

They had spotted the Mountain in the distance around noon, the gleaming white roofs of its domed towers catching the sun. With the first of it her thoughts had turned to her homecoming. Whom should she see first? Dr. Martin, of course. The beacon came under his authority. But how much should she tell those persons she ran into first? As little as possible, she decided. No sense in starting wild rumors, touching off false hopes. She'd see Dr. Martin first and let him take over.

Beyond the mission of her return, however, she began to grow uneasy about her reception. What would it be like to be back on the Mountain? What questions would her friends in the shop ask her, what kind of remarks would they make? They could be insensitive beyond belief. What would they say about Coconino?

Already she could feel the stares as she walked into the compound with the grimy, half-naked youth at her side. Everyone there had heard the stories brought back about the People, but few had actually seen one. What would they think? And what would they be foolish enough to say in his hearing? She'd have to stay close to him, run interference—

Ha! Me, a diplomat! she scoffed. I'll probably bury an arrow in some offender's chest myself. Who's going to watch out for me?

I've changed, she thought suddenly. Changed beyond any changing back, ever. I've acquired some of your pride, Coconino, and it feels so good . . . Let its mark be forever on my soul, for I am of the People.

I am not of the People.

Oh, God, what am I? she wondered. She understood something of how Dick had felt, why he had stayed alone for so long after he had come back. She understood that haunted look he would sometimes get . . . For the first time since he'd left her, Phoenix could not muster any hatred for him. How would she face him without any hatred?

But I can hate that saccharine young twit he married, Phoenix thought. I can hate her without any problem whatsoever. And if I look at him and remember that he left me for her—left me, left what he saw in me, the black hair and eyes—how could he surrender it? How could he surrender his longing for the People?

Will I ever come to that? Forbidden to return, will I finally reach the point where I don't ache every moment of every day to be back among them, to run with Coconino or Juan, to stalk the mule deer and the hare— I wish Daddy were still alive, she thought for the hundredth time. I wish he could see me. He wouldn't understand at first, but he would be proud of me anyway. He'd be proud to know that I was strong enough to survive, to take up Coconino's challenge and grow with it—

It was then she had remembered that Coconino had a father somewhere on the Mountain, one he had never met. So she had posed her question.

"Will my father be there?" he responded.

"Where else would he be?" she laughed. "He was a Man-on-the-Mountain, wasn't he? What was his name?"

Coconino shrugged. "If it was ever mentioned, I do not recall. The People do not use names for the Men-on-the-Mountain very much. One is like another."

In truth, Coconino had never been curious about the man who was his biological father, had never thought of him as a man. To Coconino he had been some demigod who had graced the village briefly and favored his mother because she was so favorable. And that made him, Coconino, special indeed.

Was there truly a man living on the Mountain who was his father? As Phoenix had pointed out, there must be—unless he was dead. A man with a face and a name, a man with all the faults and foibles that men possessed . . . A shiver ran through Coconino. He did not think he would look for this father.

But there was someone on the Mountain he wished to find. Someone he wished very much to find.

"Do you know the Witch Woman that was before you?" he asked Phoenix.

Her heart sank; she could not help it. "Probably."

"She had blond hair and blue eyes and was very beautiful."

Phoenix sighed and shifted; Coconino urged Tala downward. A short ridge of ground just north and east of their destination blocked their view of the tall domed towers. Soon they would have to decide whether to go around it or over it. "I never paid attention to who was in the program," she confessed listlessly, "even when I was in the program. It didn't interest me. But Kevin Mendoza will know; he's the coordinator."

They slid from Tala's back and studied the lay of the land. To go over the ridge would mean much climbing or calling on the weary Tala to fly them across. Going around to the east would bring them up on the side of the mountain with the clearest view. If they went to the west, only someone on the observation deck of the Mayall Tower could spot them coming. "We'd better let Tala be a surprise," Phoenix cautioned. The course thus decided, they took water in their mouths and began to run, with Tala loping easily beside them.

But for once Coconino did not chant; his thoughts were busy elsewhere. To see his Witch Woman again! Since they had first sighted the Mountain hours before, he had been unable to think of anything else. How old would she be? Would her hair have turned gray? Would her face be lined? Did she now have children of her own, and what were they like? Did they have her golden hair, her shimmering laugh?

Only eight years. It seemed a lifetime, and for Coconino it was. He had grown to manhood in those eight years. But if the Witch Woman had a daughter—as he hoped she did—she would be only seven at most. Another seven years before she could marry.

There were many men and women on the Mountain, though—more than five times the number of the People, Phoenix had told him. Among them there must be at least one Witch Woman with blond hair who was the right age . . .

He glanced over at Phoenix, her muscles flexing rhythmically, a slight sheen of perspiration glistening on her lean brown body. He had come to admire and respect her, to care for her feelings and now even to desire her. But her rebuke was final: she would have none of him, in pain or in splendor, and he could not go unfulfilled. Perhaps here was the good, then, the only good in this journey to the Mountain. Perhaps here at long last he would find a Witch Woman for a bride.

Her face was set in a mask of concentration. She is wiser than

I, he thought. She is a Witch Woman. I will not press her again for her favor, will not cause her such anger and distress. Though this foolish heart of mine desires her above all other women, I will keep silent. Instead I will seek among the women on the Mountain.

Then Phoenix will be pleased.

"Why is he stopping?" Phoenix asked.

They had remounted only after crossing out of sight of the towers, hidden by the Mountain's jutting folds. Now Coconino's answer was lost in the wash of the great wings as Tala fanned the air to cushion his landing on the northwestern slope.

"He can't be that tired," Phoenix protested as the unicorn folded his wings and tucked them inside their protective sock.

"I do not think he is tired," Coconino replied. "He has just decided he will not carry us any farther up the Mountain."

"Well, can't you tell him to—hey!" she squawked as the great beast buckled his rear legs and dumped them both unceremoniously on the ground.

"One does not 'tell' Tala anything," Coconino reminded her. "One makes requests, and if Tala is willing, he will cooperate. But it would seem that he is not willing to carry us farther."

"Great." Phoenix rolled to her feet and dusted herself off. "I was hoping not to be too dirty when we got to the top. So much for that idea." She eyed the slope above them. "At least he dumped us in a saddle of sorts—climbing shouldn't be too bad up this way. We'll catch the road farther up and take that on in.

But Coconino was watching his four-footed friend. Tala sniffed the air carefully, then snorted in disgust. Coconino sniffed the air, too.

"What is it?" Phoenix asked. She could smell nothing.

Abruptly Tala shook himself and pawed the ground viciously. He waved his head from side to side, then gave a loud trumpet, turned, and ran back down the slope.

"What is it?" Phoenix asked again. "What's wrong with him?"

"There is nothing wrong with him," Coconino told her, "but he will not go with us to the top of the Mountain. It smells of too many men."

"And you can smell that, too?"

"No," he admitted. "My nose is not quite so keen. I only smell Machines."

*   *   *

Krista Peterson strolled away from the Archives and along the paved road that led to the northernmost towers of the installation before spiraling away to the valley floor below. The bulk of the compound was behind her, but on a ridge to her left was a string of buildings, the tallest of which was the Steward Tower. Once it had housed a ninety-inch telescope; now the ancient equipment was idle, and much of the space had been converted to a storehouse for the grain that was grown on the plains north and west of the Mountain.

Twilight thickened, and Krista pulled her shawl closer around her bare arms. The shawl was not a product of the textile mill they had activated sixty miles to the east. She'd made it herself, every step of the way from spinning the cotton fibers, to twisting the threads into yarn, to carefully hand knitting the garment. Not bad for a Level Four Health Technician! Here on the top of the mountain, even in early September the nights were chilly.

The approaching autumn seemed to have a tangible scent. It was a time of expectation, of closing one door but opening another. Krista felt strangely invigorated and anxious for the days ahead.

Sam Cordoba was coming down from the hill. She smiled at him as he passed. "Evening, Sam."

"Is that Krista?" The compound lights had switched on half an hour ago, but these farthest towers were not lit. Sam squinted at her in the darkness. "Well, Krista, I keep forgetting you're so tall. Nice night for a walk, isn't it?"

"Sure is." Krista was not really tall, only five foot four, but Sam remembered her as a little girl when she used to help him empty the wastebaskets in her classroom at the Education Center. She had been ten years old, skinny, with long, dirty-blond braids and a crush on Sam's son Gary.

She was not skinny anymore. In a society where races had blended beyond distinction, Krista had blossomed with strong Scandinavian traits from goodness knew what ancestor, becoming a buxom, rosy-cheeked young woman. With the help of a few lemons, her dirty-blond hair had been transformed into glossy tresses of the palest shade. That and her laughing blue eyes had made short work of Gary. The pair had dated heavily in high school, had thought they would marry, then had broken up when sheer passion had run its course and they realized they'd be better friends than mates. Gary had married Sandra Dorcett a year ago.

And me, Krista thought as she hiked contentedly down the road, I'm still sampling the cuisine. After all, I'm only eighteen. Time enough to think of a family after I've made Level Three. Or even Level Two.

Just below the Steward Tower she turned left onto a side road that sloped steeply upward to the base of that tower and, beyond it, in corkscrew fashion to the base of the Mayall Tower, the northernmost building on the mountain. She intended to go all the way to that building, perhaps up to the observation deck that encircled it, but the view from the edge of the mountain transfixed her. Here the rock fell away sharply, giving her the feeling of standing on the edge of the world. Somewhere below, hidden from view by the trees, the road spiraled around this rock promontory, having zigzagged far to the east before turning back on itself and approaching the peak from the west.

Once a guardrail had protected the unwary on this great height, but now there was nothing but the evening breeze between her and disaster. Krista crouched down, drawing her knees under the shawl, and gazed out at the host of stars winking into being in the darkness just beyond her.

She had been sitting for some time, lulled by the night birds and the comforting texture of her shawl, when her ears detected movement on the slope below her. Who in the world? she wondered, peering into the blackness. Even if someone's vehicle had broken down—as vehicles were prone to do in this day and age—why would they come climbing up this slope instead of following the road around?

Probably Luis and one of his friends—they were always up to some kind of prank, sneaking around playing tricks on each other, each trying to top the last. Well, she'd just go and wait for him in the shadows. Wouldn't he be surprised when she popped up!

The paved path where she stood had been notched into the side of the mountain, and Krista slipped back into the deeper darkness of a nearby rock face. As she watched, two climbers came into view. To her surprise, both had long, dark hair caught in white muslin headbands. Not Luis, then—his hair was curly, and he sported a dashing mustache. The one on the left could be a woman, Krista decided, in a white shirt and trousers, but the one on the right was a man, shirtless, wearing some sort of white shorts or—

The skin on her arms and shoulders turned to gooseflesh in spite of the shawl. Her eighth-grade teacher, Mrs. Martin, had taught a unit on the Indians, the People, as she called them, who lived to the north. Far to the north, Krista thought, and although this man looked like the men her teacher had described, how could one possibly have traveled to the mountain?

Why not? It was a long distance, but the Indians were accustomed to running miles at a time, either hunting or out to tend distant fields. Mrs. Martin had even said something about that. "Don't be surprised," she'd told the class, who had thought the customs of the tribe terribly backward and unenlightened, "if one day one of these 'primitives' comes climbing up our mountain to knock at our door. They have keen minds for all their lack of classical education, and ambitions as lofty as ours. Don't be surprised if they come here and teach *us* a thing or two. For there are in any civilization at any given time one or more dreamers, and among those, at least one dream fulfiller."

Perhaps this was he, Krista thought excitedly. Perhaps this was the dream fulfiller. But who was with him? That was no Indian, not by speech or dress.

She could hear their voices now. "Fat lot of good it did me to put on clean clothes after that rain shower," the one on the left said. The register of the voice gave her away as a woman. "I'm all sweaty and dirty again from climbing this stupid hill."

"If we had taken your road," the man grumbled back, "we would still be climbing."

"It would have been easier climbing," she complained. "I don't know why that stupid animal wouldn't just bring us up here. Save me all this grief."

"Tala does not exist for your convenience."

The moon had risen, a large white moon drifting slowly through the skies behind the strangers. Its light gave everything a ghostly quality. Krista watched in fascination as the two figures stood panting on the crest, getting their wind and their bearings. The woman stripped off her headband, mopped her face and neck with it, then tied her hair at the nape of the neck. She looked familiar now. The Infirmary, Krista thought. I've seen her at the Infirmary . . .

The man stood quietly, chest working from the climb, looking around him. The features of his face were veiled in shadow, but his body was well proportioned and muscular with trunklike thighs and bulging biceps. He gazed up the length of the tower that loomed over them, obviously impressed, and reached for a gourd canteen that hung at his waist. Taking a quick mouthful, he handed the canteen to the woman.

Then he froze, and Krista knew she had been seen. She stepped forward into the moonlight, heard his intake of breath. "Hi," she gulped.

The woman nearly choked on the water and swore emphatically. "A blond," she muttered. "And not two minutes in the compound. Do they smell you?" Then she stepped closer to Krista. "Hi, yourself. Who is that?"

"Krista Peterson." She tried not to let her voice tremble.

"Krista—you work in the Infirmary, right? I remember you." The woman seemed to relax. "Look, it's real important. I have to see Dr. Martin."

"It must be important," Krista acknowledged, looking at Coconino. How old is he? she wondered. I can't tell at all. "Did you come all the way from the Indian village?"

"I've been away for six months," the woman said, and suddenly it all made sense to Krista. This was Debbie McKay, of course, Dick McKay's ex-wife. Krista had been taking her first health tech course at the Infirmary when Debbie had gotten the infertility test results—poor woman! And then the scandal that had followed . . .

"I have something very important to tell Dr. Martin," Debbie was saying.

"Well, he's probably at home," Krista said, stirring herself. "You know where he lives?"

"Yeah, I haven't forgotten. Long as he didn't die or anything. Come on, Coconino."

The man was slow in following. Krista studied him openly as she fell into step beside them. "Coco what?" she asked.

"Coconino," he told her. His eyes drifted over her appraisingly.

Krista felt his gaze on her, knew that he liked what he saw. She herself felt the tingling attraction of something she had never before encountered—a stranger. Here was a man she truly knew nothing about. What was he like? How would he act? And what did he think of her?

He's young, she thought. Not too young—in his twenties, maybe. It's hard to tell. I know they don't live as long as we do, and living under such primitive conditions ages them faster, but he's probably—

"What time is it?" Debbie asked abruptly.

She looks different, Krista thought, turning her attention reluctantly to the woman. Not older but—healthier. Still as cross and cold as always, though. It's just there's nothing spindly about her now. "About eight," she said aloud. "I can't see my watch, but it should be eight or a little after."

"Not that it matters," Phoenix muttered almost to herself. "If it were two in the morning, I'd still have to pound on his door."

It should have piqued Krista's curiosity, but she was more interested in the man at her side. The smell of dust and sweat clung to him, but it seemed only to tantalize Krista, making him seem more intensely real. Here was a legend enfleshed, a man of the proud and noble People. Here was a man whose survival depended upon his physical strength and a storehouse of skills that people on the mountain had forgotten. Here was a man who lived in rhythm with the seasons and the pulse of the earth . . .

At the bottom of the short slope they rejoined the main road and climbed it up to the main section of the compound. There Coconino stopped. The electric lights baffled him. "Are those stars?" he asked.

"No," Phoenix snapped, intent upon her mission. "Come on."

"Are there fires inside?"

"No!"

"What is that?" he asked, pointing to a pedal car parked on the side of the road.

"A machine."

"What does it do?"

"It moves. People ride in it."

"Is this the kind of machine you fix with spit?" he asked. "Why does that help? Doesn't the machine grow angry?"

She turned on him with an exasperated noise. "I'll explain everything tomorrow, okay? I haven't got time tonight. Come on, it's this way."

But Coconino planted his feet and glared at her. Seeing the set of his jaw, she rounded on him, eyes blazing, prepared for battle. Quickly Krista intervened. "Maybe you'd let me do that," she suggested. "Tomorrow. Or later tonight, after you've seen Dr. Martin. Whenever. I'd be glad to play tour guide."

Phoenix drew back as though slapped, and Krista felt a pang. Why do I always get myself in the middle? she wondered. I've done something wrong now; she's going to yell at me, and I remember her invectives well. Oh, Coconino is smiling and his eyes are warm, but she—

The woman's burning eyes turned back on Coconino, though, and the fire went out. She regarded him coldly, dispassionately. Krista shivered. "Fine," Debbie told the primitive in a flat voice. "Tag along if you like; I don't know how long this will take. If you get tired—" A touch of sarcasm colored her voice. "She'll still be blond in the morning." Then she turned and stalked across the compound.

Jim Martin was at his desk in the small study of his bungalow. He had an office in the Administration Building, but it was cold and sterile; he preferred to work here, at the handcrafted wood desk surrounded by earth-toned weavings, worn furniture, and children's artwork. As he glanced up at the clock, he smiled. Just below it were two of his favorite charcoal sketches: one a landscape done by his youngest daughter, Karen, at age seven; the other also a landscape done by Karen, but at age twenty-three. *Promise* and *Fulfillment*, he called them.

"Jim?" Kate was at the door. His wife was a tall woman, gray hair curled to soften the squareness of her face. There was an odd quality to her voice now, and she looked drawn.

"What is it?" he asked, alarmed. Something unexpected, to ruffle Kate's composure.

"Oh, it's all right,"she assured him quickly. "It's just—you remember Debbie McKay?"

His mind raced quickly to put a face and an identity with the name. "Oh, yes. She's with the primitives this summer, isn't she?"

"Well . . . she was . . ." Kate stood aside and glanced apprehensively back at the visitors in her living room. "Why don't you come in and explain to him yourself?" she invited them.

Jim recognized the dark-haired woman at once. Dick McKay's wife. Ex-wife. Jim had abstained from the Advisory Board vote granting Dick the divorce. It was justified, of course, perhaps even necessary, and because of the peculiar circumstances it would not start a trend. But the poison that ate the woman from the inside because of her rejection—

The poison was there still, almost tangible beneath her high cheekbones and behind the coal-black eyes. Yet she looked different: still tall and thin but stronger. Not so brittle. He wondered what had caused that effect.

Then the primitive stepped into the room at her elbow, and Jim caught his breath. He had met primitives only once, when Gail Mendoza had invited him to accompany her to the village. She had just been made chief administrator and had asked her key staff to join in a brief meeting of the minds with the primitives regarding policy. It had been a wasted trip; the Mother had met them at the landing field and told them bluntly that no change in policy was needed or desired.

He recalled looking down from that rise on the busy village, the squat women with their naked children, the ragged-looking men with their bone hoes and their throwing sticks, and wondering, What would you do if we refused? If we decided to change the Program, open trade, bring modern technology— what would you do? How would you fight us?

Looking at the young man in his study now, Jim had a different reaction. The body veiled only by a loincloth conveyed strength and purpose. The eyes demanded respect; the thrust of the chin, honesty. This was no ignorant savage but a man of great dignity and stature. Unconsciously Jim rose to his feet.

"Debbie," he greeted the woman firmly. "I'm surprised, to say the least. What's going on?" He turned his questioning look on the primitive.

The woman cleared her throat. "This is Coconino. He's—he brought me here. He also found something I think you'll find of great interest. A space probe."

Silence. Jim stared at her while the message crept home through his numbed brain. A space probe. Contact. At last.

"When?" he asked brusquely.

"About a week ago," she told him. "He was there when it landed. But he—he didn't know what it was, and—"

"I killed it," Coconino said bluntly.

"He damaged it," she modified. "It's not transmitting."

Jim turned away and paced to the window, where the compound lights washed his side yard in silvery hues. The trees sighed slightly, and their shadows stirred the silver gently. "A week." Too late? Too soon? "You're sure it's not just an old satellite that—no, the orbits on those things decayed decades ago," he answered himself. "What kind of probe?"

"The inscription was in English," she said. "*Homeward Bound.* It had tentacles, looked like some camera lenses; I couldn't tell what else—"

"It walked," Coconino put in. "Like an insect, on many legs. And it chewed the Mother Earth, spitting dirt and plants from its foul mouth."

The other two stared at him, then exchanged a look. "Taking samples," Jim guessed. "Then they're serious."

"They'd have to launch it from a ship, wouldn't they?" Debbie asked hopefully.

But Dr. Martin shrugged. "Who knows how they do it nowadays? Our knowledge at best is five centuries old. Presumably they've been advancing all this time while we've been losing ground. Can they warp without ships? Who knows? Maybe they don't warp at all; maybe they've found something better.'' He turned back to his guests. ''Well, we can do one of two things. We can sit like a lump and wait for them to stumble across us, or we can activate the old beacon and try to flag them down. Doesn't sound like much of a choice to me.'' He threw the woman a crooked smile. ''What do you say?''

But she did not smile back, and in that moment he saw in her face what he would not, could not, let himself feel: fear. For they were not going back to what had been but on to something that was probably as far beyond them as they were beyond this young primitive.

Coconino spoke up, ''Is there not a third choice?'' he asked. ''Can we not tell them to go away and leave the Mother Earth in peace?''

Peace. Phoenix sagged back against the doorjamb of the Administration Building, suddenly overcome by weariness. She had forgotten that part of humanity's heritage: the constant bickering, the squabbling, and the insane wars. What were they letting themselves in for? What if their ''saviors'' brought back to Earth the one disease that had faded from memory here—war?

That and a hundred other ills that had dogged the heels of humankind across the millennia. Well, there was no retreating from it, she told herself. As Dr. Martin had pointed out, they could seek or they could wait to be found, but the outcome was the same. One could not run away from the future, only forward to embrace it.

The people here on the mountain had chosen to embrace. It was nearly midnight, but few were sleeping; they were all rushing to and fro, ecstatic with anticipation. The word had spread like wildfire, and there was no want of hands to prepare a welcome for interstellar visitors.

Halfway across the compound a flock of technicians was at work in the Mayall Tower trying to get the ancient beacon started. It was virtually impossible: program disks had oxidized, optical fibers had worked loose, circuits had disintegrated. The skills to repair some of the installation's equipment had survived, and much more could be dug out of the Archives. But the delicate manufacture of spare parts was seldom possible. Repeated attempts to make use of facilities four hundred miles to the west had only reaped frustration. Everywhere one turned on the mountain, strange appendages grew from machines where a microchip had been replaced by a circuit board. Adaptation had become the mountain dweller's byword.

So even as he ordered the attempt to reactivate the existing beacon, Dr. Martin had started other willing personnel on an alternative: constructing a new beacon from equipment they did have. The design was under way, the main computer humming happily with the project. Tomorrow machinists, including Phoenix, would be handed plans for the pieces that needed to be tooled, and there would be days of intense, nerve-stressing work as they employed skills seldom brushed off to construct those parts.

Just as well, Phoenix thought. I won't have time to think about what I've lost in the process . . .

Involuntarily her eyes sought out Coconino in the courtyard. He had left the Administration Building and the hubbub hours earlier. "These buildings do not like me, nor I them," he had said. "I will wait outside." She saw him now, curled up asleep on the stony soil beneath a tree, Krista's shawl draped over him. It was no surprise to her that Krista sat beside him, rubbing her arms and shivering against the night chill.

They're a sight—and one I'd better get used to, she thought grimly. The electricity between the two of them was tangible. Not an odd match when one thought about it: both young, beautiful, sensuous. Where does an old lady like me fit into the picture? Nowhere. Not anymore. He's found his Witch Woman finally, the kind he always dreamed of—for all the good it will do him! She'll never go back to that village with him, live out her life in a wickiup with the lizards and the scorpions.

Why not? I would.

But she's accustomed to the niceties—look at her. All brainwork for her here and a family to fuss over her, young men making eyes at her. Lots of men, I'll bet. Besides, the Advisory Board would never let her go, not a health tech and a fertile, intelligent female—

Or would they? If contact was made with the rest of humanity, then there would be no need to covet childbearing women. An expanding population could be imported. Why should the Council begrudge the People one teenage girl and her offspring? No doubt adventurers and developers would return to Earth now in droves . . . droves . . .

How long will you last, Coconino, in your wickiup with your

blond Witch Woman and your dark-skinned children? How long before someone breaks the pact, brings foreign ideas, strange tools, new desires? How long before someone sells whiskey to the Indians?

Slowly she walked toward the sleeping youth. Krista looked up. "I offered him a bed in the Infirmary," she said softly, "but he insisted on sleeping out here."

Phoenix nodded dully. "It's all right. He'll be more comfortable."

"But it's so cold!"

Phoenix knelt on the ground beside him, watching the strong and craggy face expressionless in slumber. Like a sleeping volcano, she thought: docile, dormant, but never without its latent strength and innate beauty.

"Find us a couple of blankets, then," she told Krista. "I'll stay with him. Just for tonight," she added, catching the girl's eyes. Tomorrow night he's yours, and the night after that, and the night after that—as long as he chooses to stay.

She watched Krista leave, then stretched out on the hard, lumpy ground beside Coconino. As for me, she thought, I have to stay. Have to switch gears from proud hunter to cocky mechanic. Will it be easier now? Harder? Whichever, I know a part of me will always run with you, Coconino, holding water in my mouth, chanting to the Mother Earth . . . But tomorrow I have to try finding that kind of fulfillment here, in this concrete and computerized world, a world about to be wracked by change. Up from the ashes once more . . .

Coconino stirred, and she reached out, brushed a strand of hair away from his face.

Tomorrow.

CHAPTER FIFTEEN

Coconino studied the antique binoculars curiously, then chalked it up to magic and lifted them again to his eyes. Far below them in fields that spread from the base of the Mountain, large machines harvested a crop whose dimensions awed him. The produce from one harvest would supply the People for ten years if it did not spoil, yet these machines would gather it all in within a few weeks' time. To him it seemed wealth beyond belief.

"Of course, we have a lot more people to feed and clothe than you do," Jim Martin pointed out. The two of them stood on the glassed-in observation deck of the Mayall Tower, looking down over a tall shoulder of the mountain toward the western plain. "But I'm glad we've been able to keep the machines running. Had to simplify them, revert to more primitive mechanics, but they run. Only because we've been able to keep recycling metal. We have a plastics factory just a day's flight north of here, but raw materials are a problem." He leaned a sturdy shoulder against the glass panel. "So's energy. Thank God for solar and wind power. If we had to go back to hand harvesting as you do, we'd be hard pressed, I'm afraid." He grinned at the young man. "You'd have to send *us* Teachers."

Coconino lowered the binoculars and smiled back. He liked Dr. Martin. There was an honesty, a warmth to the man that charmed him. "Have you been a Teacher among the People?" he asked.

"Your people? No," Martin replied. "I taught here for a good many years, but I've never had the privilege of serving your people like your friend Debbie."

Coconino raised the glasses again, but this time he scanned the lower reaches of the Mountain itself, wondering if Tala was still there. "Her name is Phoenix," he corrected Dr. Martin.

"Phoenix." The older man considered it a moment. "A strong-sounding name. For a strong woman." Then he glanced at the young man. "You two are—close friends?" he probed cautiously.

"She is my sister-brother," Coconino replied, handing back the glasses. "She should not have come here; she does not belong on the Mountain. She belongs with the People."

"I'd say that's for her to decide, wouldn't you?" Jim suggested as they turned and headed for the stairway.

"She is a Witch Woman," Coconino agreed. "She will do what she will do. Only it is not always good for her."

Descending the enclosed stairway to the ground disturbed Coconino, but it was better than the elevator Dr. Martin had wanted to take up. Coconino had flatly refused that ride. Walls and floors, walls and floors—why did these people try to block themselves off from the Mother Earth? There was no need for shelter on this beautiful late summer day—why did they not set up their work out of doors? As they passed technicians who were stripping the old beacon for usable parts, Coconino asked, "Is my sister-brother in one of these towers?"

"Yes, she's in the Burrell Tower," Dr. Martin told him. "All our precision instruments are there for tooling the relays and connectors we need for our new beacon. Some facilities we've salvaged we simply fly to, but we discovered long ago that we needed tools such as she uses close at hand." His voice echoed slightly off the plaster walls of the narrow stairwell.

"My sister-brother is—restricted—among her people?" Coconino asked.

Martin hesitated a moment before he picked up the sense of Coconino's question. "Respected," he corrected the boy. "Yes. She is a fine mechanic like her father, and a better machinist, I think. It's difficult work, and she does it well."

"That is good." Ah, Phoenix, trapped away from the light and the fresh air and the touch of the Mother Earth! "She is respected among the People as well."

Dr. Martin hauled on the heavy door that opened at last to the outside. Sunlight streamed in, and a strong breeze caught them. "I'm glad they like her," Dr. Martin said.

"I did not say they like her," Coconino murmured.

Krista was waiting outside, out of breath from the steep climb up the knoll. Her cheeks glowed, and she radiated excitement. "Here you are!" she exclaimed, and Coconino could only beam back at her. "I've been looking for you. It's a slow day in the Infirmary, but I know Dr. Martin has plenty to do, so I thought I'd offer to take over showing you around."

Martin watched them, the look that passed between them. Some things never change, he thought. Technology, civilization, government are all ephemeral, but young men and women will always look at each other like that. And as long as they do, there is hope for humanity. "Much as I'd love to spend my time this way," he sighed, "I'm afraid you're right. Take good care of him, Krista."

"Oh, but Coconino," he called back as he started down the hill. "Will you have supper with my wife and me tonight? You and Debbie—uh, Phoenix. I'd like to hear more about your village."

"I will come," Coconino replied. "But the Witch Woman is the Witch Woman; I cannot answer for her."

Krista heard the sadness in his voice and took hold of his arm. It worked; he smiled down at her, his features melting from their hard lines into a softer expression. "What have you seen so far?" she asked.

"Machines," he replied, wrinkling his nose in distaste. "Lots and lots of machines. How do you live with so many smelly, noisy machines around?"

She laughed, the light, silvery laugh he expected of her, then led the way down the road toward the main campus. "How do *you* live," she asked, "with the smell of curing hides and the noise of lizards running through the thatch? It's all what you're used to, Coconino."

She beamed up at him, and he drank it in. Here was perfection, a ray of sunshine caught upon a cholla flower. "How is it that you have no husband?" he asked.

"Oh, I could have," she replied lightly, "but I'm in no rush. We don't marry so young here—we don't have to. We live longer, you see, because we have better medical care and—"

His hand on her arm stopped her short, and she gazed up into his suddenly anxious face. "Your medicine—can it do nothing for Phoenix? She thinks it requires the magic of the Others to open her womb . . ."

Krista's heart sagged. "She's right. We've lost so many skills here, skills to make the surgical tools, the anesthetics, skills to perform the operation—but all that will change now. Just as soon as we make contact with the spaceship. The Others, as you call them. I know they can help her."

That did not relieve him, however. Instead he scowled at the silhouette of the Mayall Tower looming huge against the brilliant blue sky. "Then they may come," he said finally. "And bring their medicine. But after that I think they should go away again."

Phoenix stood in the gaping maw of the shop door, feeling as hollow and empty as the cavernous building. It reeked of burnt wiring and rancid lubricants, a smell fraught with memories for her: learning her trade at her father's elbow, finally making use of her gangly arms and legs, carving her niche as "one of the guys." It was a smell of childhood, a smell of home—a smell of another existence. She felt alien here now.

"Debbie, that you?" Reed Johnson slid out from under a harvester, wiping his grimy hands on a grimier rag. His grin showed oddly spaced teeth in a swarthy, stubble-shadowed face. "Don't just stand there, girl, get your tail over here. There's a hopper I can't find the worm in for the life of me."

Phoenix grinned in spite of herself and sauntered over to her comrade. "Hell, Reed, you couldn't fix a leaky radiator if it were more than three feet off the ground. Put a balloon in the cab of that harvester, you couldn't fix that, either."

Reed scrambled to his feet, beaming. He was fifty-three, barely her height, with a small beer belly sagging over his belt. "You and your daddy," he chuckled. "Climb clear out on the wing to listen to the engines in flight if that's what it took."

"Not me!" she protested. "I always stayed in the cabin. Dad was the crazy one. Kept saying, 'That's what parachutes are *for*.'"

They laughed heartily, then stood awkwardly looking at each other. Finally Reed extended his hand. "How you been, girl?"

She smiled and slapped his palm. "I've been pretty good, Reed. All things considered, I've been pretty damn good."

"You look good," he told her. "Different but—better. It was good for you, I think, living with those Indians."

Were those drums she heard? No, of course not. Just the throb of a compressor somewhere, perhaps a hopper coming back from scavenging. "Where is everyone?" she asked.

"Lunch." Reed twirled his crescent wrench idly. "One of those wasteful habits I never developed."

"That and teetotaling," she quipped.

The silence stretched between them, and Reed's smile faded. "Think there's really a ship up there?" he asked softly.

It was the question on everyone's mind. "I don't know, Reed. If they can send a probe, they can send a ship. Did they? Speculation."

He turned back to the harvester, rubbing at a rust spot with his greasy rag. "Like to see that probe. If it was mechanical, maybe—maybe they still need good mechanics."

"It was mechanical, all right," she assured him. "Don't worry, you and I will always have a job." But they both knew she had lied. The sudden availability of improved technology would make the wrench and the lube gun obsolete. Their only hope was that the change would take a generation to complete.

And what hope did the People have?

"I hear you brought an Indian back with you," Reed said, facing her again. "I've never seen one. Maybe you'll bring him by sometime."

Phoenix balked. "If he sticks around that long. If I finish up this work for Dr. Martin." Sure, trot him around for all your friends to stare at. "Look, I gotta grab some lunch and get back to the work. We'll catch up later, okay?"

"Sure." Reed knew he had been brushed off. "Sure, Debbie." He stretched out on his dolly and disappeared under the harvester.

As she climbed the hill toward the dining hall, Phoenix wondered if this place would ever feel right to her again. The trees were tinged now with yellow, tight-packed despite the stony soil . . . Birds. Why had she never noticed all the bird calls before? She felt she had lived here all her life and never seen it, never heard its voice or felt its—

What? Spirit, you were going to say, weren't you? she demanded. The spirit of the Mother Earth in this place. Leave spirits behind or you will never be able to survive here in a walled room, a ceiling always blocking the sky, your tools and your schematics and your diagnostic printouts hemming you in on every side. Let spirits stay in the desert with the People. Here you have to live with reality.

As though to mock her, Coconino sat on the dirt in front of the dining hall, lounging on one elbow beside Krista, carelessly unaware of the grace of his body or how different he was from the men and women passing by. The latter gaped in open amazement at the dark-skinned, half-dressed stranger. You would park yourself there for all the world to see, Phoenix thought in disgust. Well, don't blame other people for gawking when you flaunt your—

Just then a woman her own age detached herself from a group of schoolchildren and approached the couple on the grass. Honey-colored hair swept in soft waves around her face, and her middle swelled with a child due in early winter. Even before Coconino rose, Phoenix knew who she was . . .

"Witch Woman," Coconino breathed.

Lois Martin smiled and held out her hands to the young man. "I knew it would be you," she said, her voice as mellow and clear as he remembered. "When they said a young primitive had brought Debbie McKay back, I knew it would be Coconino."

Tears gleamed in her eyes, and he grasped her outstretched hands fervently. His own eyes moistened, and a knot twisted his throat. After eight years she was still sunshine and summer and all the things she had ever been to him. His jaw worked, but no words would come.

"Who else but my Dream Fulfiller would journey all the way to the Mountain?" she continued, her voice husky with emotion. Looking down into her eyes, he thought she seemed smaller than he remembered, but it was he who'd grown nearly a foot in the intervening years. Still, it did not diminish her beauty or his awe of her. She glowed with health and happiness, and the child . . .

"You have many children?" he asked, touching her protruding stomach with reverence.

"Three," she laughed. "This will be the fourth, if you can believe that. And you? Have you children of your own?"

Just behind her he saw Phoenix crossing quickly toward the dining hall door. "Not yet," he answered. "But I will. Phoenix, wait!"

On the threshold Phoenix stopped and turned, her face frozen in a mask of stone. Don't do this to me, Coconino, she raged inwardly. Don't make me stand next to her where you can compare us point by point by point. "I'm in a hurry, Coconino," she told him. "Can it wait?"

He drew back from the coldness in her tone. "Yes," he said. "It can wait." I only wanted you to know her, this other Witch Woman who was so much to me. And for her to know you, who are my sister-brother. I want to share the excitement of each of you with the other—but I can see it is not important to you.

"I'll talk to you later, then." Phoenix ducked into the noisy dining hall and lost herself in the crowded lunch line. She remembered little of Lois Martin from their student days—they had moved in different circles. But she knew her by reputation:

Jim Martin's niece by marriage, a favorite with her students, an easy person to like. If only she weren't beautiful. And sweet. And pregnant.

Outside, Lois Martin looked after the brusque McKay woman. In Coconino's face she read the hurt, and she wanted uncharacteristically to kick the rude woman who had caused it. How dare you hurt him? How dare you hurt the sensitive boy who grew up with too great a burden, too large a reputation to live up to? If you had only seen him as I did: struggling with his letters, fighting back tears of frustration because he thought the son of a Man-on-the-Mountain ought to be able to master this easily and he could not. Practicing with his bow hour after tedious hour because Coconino could not be the second best shot among the young boys. Losing himself in prayers to the Mother Earth because only there did he find respite and reward for all his efforts.

Now she let her eyes travel his frame and saw the man he had become. His relentless driving of himself had apparently paid off. There was a confidence, a pride to his bearing, that said he had achieved his goals. He had earned the respect of the People. Yet under that polished sense of accomplishment was the sensitive boy who could be hurt by a word, a look, a tone of voice.

It made him magnetic. No wonder she had heard about him from the women first. "Have you seen that primitive that brought Debbie McKay back? What muscles!" "And his eyes. You'd swear he was drinking your soul with those eyes." "I got chills just watching him. He set every hormone in my body on edge." You are a heart stealer, Coconino, she thought, and always were.

She noticed Krista sitting on the ground where he had been, looking up at them uncertainly. Ah, Krista, you would find him, Lois thought. That the homely little girl with the sharp mind should grow into such a beauty did, I admit, surprise me, but not your unerring sense of quality. That was always there. "Have you been showing Coconino around, Krista?" Lois asked.

"Yes, I have, Mrs. Martin." Krista rose and brushed off her trousers. Beside Coconino she looked petite and dainty and golden. "He was especially interested in the livestock pens. I didn't realize they don't have domesticated animals."

What preconceptions and prejudices we have, Lois thought. There is much about this boy—man—that will surprise you. "But," Lois asked with a sly smile, "did you show him the library?"

"Library?" Krista was confused, her eyes darting back and

forth between the earthy primitive and the schoolteacher. "No, I—I thought— Can you read, Coconino?"

"In your language *and* mine," he boasted, then backed off. "Though it has been a long time." Apologetically he added, "I had only the same books to read over and over."

"Then you will find our library fascinating," Lois assured him. For a moment she hesitated as she looked at the young people. She should leave them to each other's company—but they would have time together. They'd make time. This was something she really wanted to do. "Krista," she said, "would you mind if I stole Coconino for a little while? You can have him back in twenty minutes, I promise."

"It's all right, I have to check back at the Infirmary, anyway," Krista replied, glancing reluctantly at her watch. "I'll see you later, Coconino," she promised. "Bye, Mrs. Martin."

They watched her leave, hiking up the hill toward the west.

Then Lois took Coconino's arm and guided him along the pathway toward the Education Center. "You've grown tall," she told him, enjoying the feel of his well-muscled arm, the strength of his closeness.

"The tallest man in the village," he asserted. "And the best hunter."

Her eyes twinkled as she recognized the swaggering tone. "Better even than Made of Stone?" she asked.

"That we will never know," he sighed, "for he has gone to the bosom of the Mother Earth."

How ephemeral life is among the People! she thought. Coconino's stepfather had been a man in the prime of life when she knew him. He'd been shorter than his stepson was now, and more stockily built, but with the same strongly muscled legs and thighs. That was only eight years ago. "I'm sorry," she said, but knew it was more because of the way life whirled away from her than because of any grief for the man himself.

She looked up at the face of the youth walking beside her, but there was no pain in his expression. Death was part of the rhythm of life for the People. There was grief and mourning, but there were births and weddings as well, all part of the Way of the People. They danced the steps, felt their sorrow intensely in its time, then went on to another dance. Soon enough it would be time to dance Grief once again. She thought of her mother-in-law, suffering still from the loss of her husband two years before. "Two Moons," Lois asked. "Is she well?"

"Well and happy, praise Mother Earth."

"That's good." She brushed a sweat-dampened lock of hair back from her forehead as the road continued to climb toward the Education Center. "She was always so kind to me and so willing for you to learn reading, though it was a mystery to her."

Coconino noticed that her face was flushed with exertion and slowed his pace. "She thought it well that I learn the magic of the Men-on-the-Mountain," he explained, "since my father was one." How she glowed, his Witch Woman! How dainty and feminine she was—like Krista, he thought. Except her years had added a richness to her face and manner that Krista still lacked.

"I hope the Mother wasn't too hard on her for that," Lois was saying. Then, after a moment, "How is the Mother?"

Coconino frowned. "This summer, not well," he admitted, glad to voice his concern for what he had seen since his return with Tala. "I don't know what has happened. Her strength slips away."

Lois sighed, and Coconino wondered at her pensive expression. "We seemed always to disagree, the Mother and I," she said. "Yet one day a Teacher will return to tell me that the Mother is no more, and on that day I shall be very sad. She is a great lady."

"On that day the People will be sad," Coconino replied. "There is none to take her place."

But here all sorrow melted from the Witch Woman's face. Her eyes danced with a thought that was not new to her. "There is Coconino."

He jumped, genuinely startled at the notion. "I am a hunter," he protested, "and a storyteller. Nothing more. I do not have the wisdom to lead the People."

"But you have the love, Coconino," she told him, stopping to gaze fully into those dark and innocent eyes. "And a sharp mind. Both will serve you well."

He started to turn away, shaking his head at the absurdity of the idea, but Lois caught his arms and held him fast. "You have the love," she repeated, drawing his eyes back to hers with the utter confidence in her voice. "And now," she added knowingly, "you, too, have been to the Mountain."

Cyd Ryan looked up from her instruments on the bridge of the *Homeward Bound.* "Your call, Captain," she said to Clayton, who stood at her shoulder.

Only a slight frown betrayed the strain he felt, the accumulation of days of schedule adjustments and equipment checks. He rubbed his chin as he considered what the meteorologist had told him. Computers could provide all the facts, even recommend courses of action, but the final decision had to be a human one. Till now he had always thanked God for that.

Even before their probe had stopped transmitting, it had missed its target by some two hundred miles. He was still not satisfied that either of those occurrences had been due entirely to the violent electrical storms in the area, but the danger from such storms was very real. Now Ryan had informed him that the storms appeared to be seasonal, occurring in the target region on an almost daily basis. Getting the shuttle to the surface could be risky.

But the shuttle was their only option. They had no more probes—it was a manned vehicle or orbital observation. Observation from this distance would not satisfy Clayton.

He wiped his mouth. "Keep tracking the weather patterns. See if there's a regular occurrence of a decent window anywhere in that general area. Once the shuttle is down and the warp terminus installed, we can take down some land vehicles and get to the mountain."

"Sir, perhaps another loca—"

"Ms. Ryan!" Ryan flinched as the captain continued. "Searching for human life on a planet this size could be like finding the proverbial needle in a haystack. We'll start with our best shot; we'll start with that mountain."

"Yes, sir."

Clayton took a careful breath. "I'll man the shuttle myself."

Her eyes widened. "Sir, do you think—"

A new voice joined the conversation. "Begging the captain's pardon . . ."

Clayton knew his first officer would object. He turned and faced the young man, biting back a reprimand. Lujan was only doing his job.

"It's unwise for the captain to put himself at risk," Lujan continued sincerely. "The plan was for me to take the shuttle down."

"I can't order you to—"

"I'm volunteering, sir."

Clayton surveyed the young officer: physically fit, mentally sharp, eager—

"Very good, Mr. Lujan," he relented. "As soon as we're within range, take the shuttle as close to the mountain as you can and establish a warp terminus there. If conditions permit, we'll send a small landing party and some ATVs by the first available window. But I'll go with you to that mountain. If there are still people there, I'll be the first to shake their hands.''

As Winthrop stalked away, Lujan returned to his instruments. Not until the captain was off the bridge did the young officer permit himself a small smile.

Jim Martin twirled his spoon idly. ''In the early years we did a lot of searching for other survivors,'' he was telling Coconino. ''Never stumbled across any, but that doesn't mean they're not out there somewhere. Maybe in China or Africa. Most of our searching was confined to North and Central America, even when we still had the capacity for long-distance flight.'' Supper dishes littered the table in the Martins' close, congenial dining room. ''In those days we—our ancestors, that is—scavenged from Vancouver to Mexico City. But we could never make the solar batteries practical for that range, so when the fossil fuel was gone, that was it. We couldn't activate the equipment to drill and refine very large quantities. It's like nuclear energy; it's just too big an operation to . . .''

He saw then that he was losing the young primitive, indeed had lost him at the mention of cities unknown to him. It wasn't that the boy wasn't bright—the concept of solar batteries had been quickly accepted if not totally understood. But the rest of it was empty speech with no reference point in legend or experience. ''Well, let's just say,'' Jim concluded, laying the spoon back on the colorfully striped tablecloth, ''that while the People have grown wiser and more productive than their ancestors, we are steadily losing many of the gifts of ours.''

Across the table from Coconino, Phoenix finally stirred. ''Perhaps we need to do as the People have done,'' she said. ''Go back to the wisdom of our ancestors, the older ways of doing things.''

''To what purpose?'' Jim asked.

She raised haunted eyes to his. ''Finding our peace.''

''Well, it won't matter soon, will it?'' Kate Martin put in. ''Soon we'll make contact with the other planets and our technology will be restored, won't it, Jim?''

''One would think so.''

Coconino watched Phoenix as she dropped her eyes again to her plate, the food barely touched. *She has gone into her stone* house again, he thought, and pulled the ladder up after her. I must take her off this Mountain soon to see life in her eyes again.

"Do the Men-on-the-Mountain hunt?" he asked suddenly.

"Not as you think of hunting, Coconino," Jim replied. "As you've seen, we have herds of animals—javelina, mountain goats, and so forth—fenced or penned in where we can get at them any time we need to. Any 'hunting' we do for wild game is to catch it alive and add it to our herd as breeding stock."

"Breeding stock?"

"Linaje nuevo." Phoenix translated. "Fresh blood."

"Ah. That is a wise thing to do," Coconino agreed. He was familiar with the concept not from animal husbandry but from the mating practices of the People. The traditions guarding against inbreeding were old and deep. "But as for me, I would not like to kill an animal that had no place to run. How, then, would you know that it was a gift of the Mother Earth? Tell me, Dr. Martin, do your people not sometimes forget who it is that truly provides for them? Do they not get puffed up and think they provide for themselves?"

Jim held his eyes for a long moment. "Yes, Coconino, they do," he said finally. "I have never thought of it in those terms."

"That is a dangerous thing to let happen," Coconino admonished. "The Mother Earth may grow angry with their arrogance and withdraw her blessing. What good will your harvesting machines do if the crops do not grow? What good are your pens if all the animals in them sicken?" He reached for the cup of steaming beverage Kate had handed him. "I plan to hunt tomorrow morning. Perhaps one of your men would like to come with me. It would be good for all of you."

"I will give that some thought, Coconino," Jim promised. "Thank you for offering."

"Will you join me, Phoenix?" Coconino asked.

Phoenix stared at her coffee cup, her hand wrapped around its warm shell. "I won't have time. I have work to do."

There was a moment of silence. "That is too bad," Coconino said sadly. "The Mother Earth will miss your presence."

Clint Patrone watched the Indian leave Dr. Martin's bungalow and start across the compound. It was Clint's turn to make the security check, and he was half-through with his circuit. Just don't be going to the women's dorm, he thought darkly. You sleep out here if you want, or in the Infirmary or anywhere else, but you sleep alone.

Clint moved awkwardly, trying to keep his stocky frame in the shadows as he followed Coconino westward past the dining hall. He'd seen the primitive with Krista Peterson earlier in the day, seen the look that had passed between them, and it turned his stomach. Not that he himself had any designs on the girl, but hell! The ignorant savage walked around half-naked, dirty—and he smelled. Why didn't he take a bath? And put on some clothes? And the way he strutted around, as though *he* were the superior being—!

Why did Krista hang around him? Clint rubbed his thick neck in puzzlement. Krista wasn't the only one, either. Clint had seen other women looking the savage up and down—what was it about him? Didn't they have any sense? Well, he'd better just keep his hands to himself, that one. The very thought of him touching Krista or one of the others . . . Let the primitives give their own women away to strangers; that sort of thing didn't happen on the mountain.

But where the road broadened, the Indian angled right and not left, toward the Administration Building. He slipped inside— what devilment was he up to?—then reappeared with a blanket. Well. Fine. Let him sleep on the ground like an animal.

I'm going to check on you, though, Clint thought as he pulled up the collar on his rough jacket and continued his circuit. Just to make sure. And if anything goes wrong tonight, I'll know who to look for.

Coconino's hunting trip was fruitless.

At first it was only irritating, because he found no tracks, no sign of game on the upper slopes of the Mountain. Reasoning that animals had enough sense to stay away from this place with its machines and odd noises, Coconino traveled farther down.

There he found Tala waiting. The beast trumpeted softly and pranced forward to meet him but stopped several yards off and sniffed the air suspiciously. "Do I smell bad?" Coconino asked. "Has the foul odor of their village clung to me?" He dropped to his knees and rubbed his skin with dirt and grass. "There, is that better?"

Tala approached gingerly then, sniffing and snorting, until Coconino rose and slid his arms around the sturdy neck and gently scratched the ridges of the wind sock. With a great sigh Tala leaned against his friend, nearly forcing him off his feet. "Careful, my brother," Coconino laughed. "You're bigger than I."

The noise Tala made in reply was almost a whine. With an impatient pawing of his front hooves, the unicorn danced off a few steps and looked back at Coconino. But the man shook his head.

"No, Tala," Coconino said sadly. "We cannot leave this place yet. My sister-brother is still here. She is caught in this place like a beetle in a black widow's web. The fibers which bind her are so fine, she cannot see them, yet they cling to her and wrap around her, and soon she will not be able to move . . ." He sighed and brushed stray grass blades from his skin. "I do not yet know how to cut her free," he confessed. "Until I do, I must stay. She must come with us, Tala. She must come with us when we leave this place, or—" Or what? he wondered. What will happen if I have to leave the Witch Woman in this place?

Mother Earth, hear me, he prayed as he turned his footsteps away from the unicorn. I do not even want to think of life without her.

A hare jumped up in front of him. Coconino loosed an arrow reflexively—and missed. Using one of Phoenix's favorite words, he retrieved the arrow and found the shaft had been damaged when it had glanced off a stone and skidded into a tree root. His mood darkening, Coconino prowled westward, searching for some quarry on which to vent his anger and redeem himself. In the distance harvesters paddled their way through golden grain fields, storing up the wealth of the Mountain.

A pigeon took flight, and Coconino's spirits soared with the arrow he sent to intercept it. But the pigeon kept flying, and the arrow tumbled uselessly to earth. Then Coconino could not find it. He spent nearly an hour searching the thickets where he thought it had fallen and finally gave up. Empty-handed, he toiled his way back up the steep slopes to the bustling compound at the top of the Mountain.

People came and went with obvious purpose as he wandered across past the Education Center. Even the children who came charging out to play radiated a tension, an excitement linked to the building of the beacon and the Sky Ship it would call to them. Coconino watched them a moment, feeling somehow empty because he did not share their high spirits.

"Children are children, aren't they, Coconino?" a warm voice lilted behind him, and Coconino turned into the radiant presence of Lois Martin.

One hand rested on the small of her back, the other on her

protruding stomach. She was small and bright and calming to his troubled spirit. "One could almost imagine," she continued, "that they were children in the Village of the People, rushing out to play after a rainstorm."

"Do they truly read books all day?" he asked her.

Lois laughed. "Not all day. And we study many things beside reading. But yes, they spend a lot of their time reading books. It's one of the ways they learn the wisdom of their ancestors."

"It is best to learn by doing," Coconino observed. "I would rather hunt to learn about hunting than read about hunting."

"But you would like to read about a great hunt, wouldn't you?" she countered.

"Yes, to read the story of a hunt," he agreed. "But that is the story of the hunter and the prey, not how to shoot an arrow or string a bow."

Again she laughed, and Coconino thought it the most musical sound he had ever heard. "Your perceptions amaze me, Coconino," she said. "They always have. Come." She led him next door into the Archives. "I will find you some stories of hunters and their prey. But the shooting of arrows and stringing of bows will be yours to teach to your children. And maybe mine."

Coconino rolled his head from side to side to ease the crick in his neck. He had been seated at the reading table all afternoon, and now his stomach rumbled to tell him what the artificial lights could not, that afternoon had become evening. The books that the Witch Woman Lois had found for him were interesting but difficult. Therefore, although he would have preferred to take them out into the bright September sunlight, it was more convenient to stay in here by the Lexicon, which she had adjusted to define unknown words at his reading level. The afternoon had disappeared in a fantasy world of ancient civilizations and the conquest of the New World.

As he sat back to rest his shoulders a moment, his neck began to prickle. Someone was watching him. That in itself was not unusual; people stared at him everywhere he went on the Mountain. He told himself that they had never seen a true Child of the Mother Earth before and were in awe, so he squared his shoulders proudly and walked with the regal dignity befitting one of the People.

But this was different somehow, and he turned to see who it was.

The man was perhaps six feet tall, straight of limb and car-

riage, although a little fleshy in the face and stomach, as though
life had been soft in recent years. He was much older than
Coconino though not as old as Dr. Martin. A young old man,
Coconino thought, noting the age lines in his forehead and
around his eyes. Those eyes were blue and clear behind gold-
rimmed glasses, and the look in them was—what? Envy? No.
Regret.

Slowly Coconino rose to his feet and faced the man, for he
knew who it had to be.

It neither surprised nor chagrined the man to be so confronted.
Indeed, that was why he had come. But to see the vision realized, to give face and form to an idea forced away but never
really forgotten . . . He licked his lips. "You are Coconino," he
said.

Coconino tried to see the man as a man, to see the gray streaks
in the light brown hair as distinguished, to see the bearing as that
of a man at peace with his choices. But in some part of him a
voice nagged, Why did you come, young old man? Why did you
trade immortality for a body, any body? You should have stayed
what you were, an emblem of my pride, my honor. Now you are
human, and I must deal with you. "Yes," he replied finally. "I
am Coconino."

The man did not try to explain himself. The look in the boy's
eyes told him it was unnecessary. Suddenly words failed him;
with so many questions, so much to say, he could not find a
way to start. Finally he forced himself forward. "How is your
mother?"

His mother; an obvious starting point. The boy had been only
months old when he'd left. "She is well," Coconino answered.
"And at peace. She has her own honor among the People."

"Good. I'm glad." The man nodded, though he did not smile.
The silence stretched between them once more. Then, "Did she
marry, then?"

Coconino was puzzled by the question. "Several men brought
gifts to her mother's door. There is much honor for the Chosen
Companion of a Man-on-the-Mountain. She accepted Made of
Stone."

"Ah." There was strain in the man's voice. Did he object to
Made of Stone? "I remember him; he was a good man, a good
hunter. I'm sure she was happy with him." The man cleared his
throat. "Did she—what did she tell you . . . about me?"

So that was it. It was not the quality of the man who had
replaced him that bothered this man—it was the fact that he had

been replaced. He was hurt. Coconino had never thought of his father as having feelings. Of the Men-on-the-Mountain Coconino had known while growing up, none had shown much regret at having to leave his Chosen Companion behind. Guilt, perhaps, but not regret. The concept was new to him, and he considered for a moment how to answer his father. "It is not the Way of the People to dwell on their sorrows," he hedged. "But she insisted that I learn to speak your language and to read books. Surely that says something."

Finally a smile played on the man's lips, bittersweet though it was. "I used to read to her," he said softly. "Browning and Yeats—and Burns. There was one poem about summer coming . . ." Suddenly the smile faded, and a haunted look glazed his eyes. "I never told anyone here about her. Or you. Not even my wife. As though I could keep you only as secrets . . ." He shook himself, then flashed a quick smile. "I have another son now. Finally. My wife—"

But Coconino held up his hand. "The People have a saying: The fox seeks to know everything, the owl only what he needs. The owl lives longer."

The man sighed deeply, sadly, knowing it was over now. He took one last look at the son he'd lost. "I told people she died," he said, "because they couldn't understand why I . . . But sometimes I think it was me who died."

Neither had heard the woman approach, and the sight of her over Coconino's shoulder startled the man. Coconino saw the surprise, the pain on his father's face, and wondered at it until the woman spoke.

"Hello, Dick," Phoenix said.

And suddenly Coconino knew more truth about his father than he thought he could bear.

CHAPTER SIXTEEN

Dick McKay read the shock in his son's eyes and opened his mouth to speak, but Coconino cut him off. "The owl," Coconino hissed, "lives longer." Then he reached for his book that his face might not betray him.

"Catching up on village gossip?" Phoenix continued, her voice rough with old bitterness that had nothing to do with the question. "A bit late, aren't you? What's it been, fifteen years?"

Dick shot a quick glance at Coconino, whose face was carefully averted as he marked his place in the book and turned off the Lexicon. "More like twenty," Dick said evenly. "How are you, Debbie?"

"Lousy. Yourself?"

He didn't bother to answer. Instead he looked at her, tried to see past the hostility to know what her time among the People had done to her. She had a wild look to her even in her customary trousers and vest, the look of a hawk recovered from the desert that would never thrive in captivity again.

"Are you back for good?" he asked.

"Not my good," she snapped. "But I wasn't given a choice; the Mother threw me out. That should please you."

Here Coconino looked up. "The Mother will change her mind," he said quickly. "She may have done so already. You will live among the People again."

The look that passed between his son and his ex-wife unnerved McKay. He was more than just her guide, it seemed. How much more? "I should get back to work," he said quickly. "Coconino, if I can be of any assistance—I'm the director of the Library and Archives, you see—just let me know." Then he turned back to the woman.

It was clear that she saw nothing of him in the boy; as always, her own pain engulfed her, blinded her to any similarity of build, of brown, of thin-lipped mouth . . . I'm sorry, he wanted to say. I'm sorry it hurt you so badly. But I was dying. When you found you couldn't have children, you grew so cold, got so caught up in your own misery that you couldn't see how I felt. Me. I hurt, too, damn it. I'd left one son behind in the village, and now were there to be no more? None? Only your coldness and your hurt for the rest of my life? No, by God! I will have children! And a wife who is warm and sweet, who can laugh. You stopped laughing, Debbie, when you found out. I kept hoping that would change, but it never did. I haven't heard you laugh since.

But I am sorry. Sorry for your pain. Sorry I had to add to it to protect myself. Sorry you never learned how to laugh again.

"Good-bye, Debbie," was all he said, and walked away.

Coconino did not watch his father go. Nor did he try to hold the haunted eyes of the Witch Woman. Instead he turned back to his books, gathering up those he had not finished. But his thoughts roiled and eddied like a flood-swollen stream, clouded and overburdened. The woman he prized above all others was his father's wife; the father he had venerated was the man who had caused her such pain. You should have stayed a legend, he cursed silently. You should have been only a Man-on-the-Mountain without name, without soul—I would never have known. How can I look at her and not remember I am of the blood of the man who betrayed her? I cannot see her without longing, cannot long without remembering that it was my father who touched her as I would, and she touched him . . .

"I'm hungry," Phoenix said, her voice shaking in spite of her efforts to control it. "Want to get something to eat?" She flicked her long black hair over her shoulder with a bony hand.

It exposed a graceful neck. Like a young doe, Coconino thought. It is a neck whose curve I would trace with my lips. It is a neck which has pillowed my father's head.

Slowly he straightened up. "I am not hungry," he lied. "You go ahead. I think I will find this place called Infirmary."

Phoenix tensed reflexively. "Suit yourself," she said. "Out this door, down the hill to the Administration Building, and go right." Then she turned on her heel and strode out, eyes smarting with unwept tears.

Krista dashed down the hallway of the Infirmary tearing off her white coat but stopped before she rounded the corner to retuck her thin shirt and slow her breathing. Then she stepped out to greet Coconino.

"Hi, I'm glad you found the place," she said brightly, tossing the coat into a laundry basket.

He wrinkled his nose. "It stinks," he said.

Krista laughed. "It does, doesn't it? Well, look, let's go outside where there's fresh air. Have you eaten yet?"

"Not yet."

Her luck was running. She snatched up the knapsack and jacket she'd brought from her room in the dorm. "Well, let's pick up a few things from the dining hall and walk over to the western slope," she suggested casually. "We can watch the sunset."

Coconino studied her a moment, feeling some of his depression drain away. She was a meadow indeed, this one, full of bright sunshine and warm earth, blue skies laughing in her eyes. Yes, here was his answer: to bask in a meadow, forgetting the awesome rocks that stirred his soul but threatened his peace. He flashed a smile at her. "The People are fond of sunsets."

She grinned. "So am I. Come on."

The western sky was ablaze with the brilliant hues of sunset. A bank of dark blue clouds just above the horizon caught the reds and golds and flung them back dramatically. Circling in the vivid fire, the ominous shapes of two hawks were dark and beautiful against the spectacular sky.

Nestled against the mountainside, Coconino and Krista inhaled the almost tangible glory of the sunset. Its fire burned inside them, and they spoke in breathless whispers of the majesty of the Mother Earth, the splendor of the Father Sky. "Night comes," Coconino said, "when Father Sky would lie with the Mother Earth; so he dresses himself in his finest colors to dazzle her and fill her with desire."

"And she?" Krista asked, drinking in his words, his voice, his smell. "Does she dress herself for him?"

"Oh, yes. See"—he pointed—"how she spreads light and shadow upon her breasts and thighs to lure him." Krista wondered at his frank imagery, unabashed and beautiful, feeding her arousal. "Feel the heat she radiates, smell the fragrance of her soil that entices him, filling his senses and drawing him closer and closer to her outstretched body."

Krista could almost feel the racing pulse of the Mother Earth beneath them but knew that it was her own pulse racing. Coconino's voice was fraught with sensuality; his face glowed with an inner fire that reveled in the sunset. Touch me, she willed. I don't know your customs or your ways, but please touch me. I burn as the Mother Earth burns with heat that warms the night.

"I would like to visit your village," she ventured.

"I would like for you to come." She could taste his craving as his eyes searched her deeply, lingeringly. "You would be Witch Woman indeed."

"What is a Witch Woman?" she asked.

"One who brings her magic among the People and dazzles them."

She giggled softly. "You think I would dazzle the People?"

"You have dazzled me." His dark eyes sparkled, and a smile lit his face. They led each other artfully through the steps of the dance. "All the men would bring gifts to your door and beg to be your Chosen Companion."

"What is that?" she asked, her blue eyes sparkling as well.

"It is the custom of the People that when a stranger comes among them, he—or she—may choose one of the People for a Companion to join with as the Father Sky now joins the Mother Earth. The fruit of such a union is considered a special blessing to the People."

The sun had slipped below the graceful curve of the horizon, and shadows deepened around them. The chill of the settling darkness was lost on their flushed skin as eyes locked and they fed greedily on their mutual desire.

Hesitantly Krista reached out to stroke Coconino's chest, savoring its warmth beneath her fingers. "You are a stranger here," she said quietly. "If this were your village, then you could . . ."

"Claim the right of the Chosen Companion?" he filled in. "That is the Way of the People. It is how we honor a guest and how he honors us."

"I think," she whispered huskily as the twilight seeped away, "that we on the Mountain should honor you, a guest in our midst."

"It is a good custom," he replied.

So they honored each other slowly, intensely, far into the night.

"Hey! You with the loincloth!"

The very tone of the voice knotted Coconino's stomach. He

turned to glare at the group of men lounging in the shade of a dormitory.

They were young men, about his own age, with the nondescript coloring and build that characterized most of the Men-on-the-Mountain. Here and there a trace of African ancestry could be seen, or Latino, but largely the races had blended through generations of intermarriage to a stock that was slightly paler than he, slightly taller, with even features and a hair color somewhere between blond and brown.

"What's-your-name," the speaker continued. "Come on over here."

"My name is Coconino," he replied, taking only two judicious steps closer to the group.

"Lay off, will you, Clint?" another man said. Then he stepped forward. "Sorry. He's always like that. My name is Jeff." He held out his hand.

Jeff was leanly built, clean-shaven, with an open face dominated by dark brown eyes. His brown hair was a bit unruly, standing up where he had run his fingers through it to lift it away from his forehead. Coconino clasped the outstretched arm and found Jeff's grip firm. The height difference between them was not remarkable.

"What's that you have?" Jeff asked, indicating the carcasses in Coconino's left hand.

Coconino held up the brace of quail. A fine catch, he thought. Things had gone much better for him this morning. The Mother Earth must be pleased that he had taken a Chosen Companion. "They are the fruit of the Mother Earth," he replied. "I have been hunting." If Phoenix had come with him, no doubt there would have been more.

"You got those with an *arrow*?" chimed another man.

"With two arrows," Coconino corrected. "One for each."

"Not bad," the man murmured approvingly.

"Whatcha going to do with them, Hiawatha?" Clint sneered.

Coconino squinted at him. Clint was somewhat heavier of build than the others, his brownish hair curly and closely cropped, adding to the roundness of his face.

"It is not enough to share in the dining hall," he answered. "So I will give them to Dr. Martin's wife, a gift, because she prepared food for my sister-brother and me."

Jeff choked back a smile as he tried to picture that woman, who was his grandmother, plucking and dressing the two small birds. "I'm sure she'll be delighted," he lied. "We're just having a brew in the shade. Would you like to join us?"

Coconino had no idea what a "brew" was, nor was he overly anxious to join any group containing the loudmouth called Clint. But Jeff was a pleasant fellow, and Coconino did not want to offend him. So he followed Jeff back to the shade.

"This is Eddie, Rene, Clint, and Paul," he indicated, introducing each in turn. "You guys see the quail Coconino shot?"

"Kinda small, aren't they?" was Clint's comment.

"Shut up," Jeff reprimanded. "You think it's easy to hit something that small?"

"The size of a thing does not determine its worth," Coconino replied. "Which would you rather eat, an ear of corn or the branch of a tree?"

Jeff gave a short laugh, but Clint stiffened, not at all pleased by the barb. "Yeah, well, if I were in a fight," he growled, "I'd rather have the tree branch than the corn."

"But I am not going to fight with the quail," Coconino pointed out. "And neither is Mrs. Martin."

"Give it up, Clint," Jeff laughed, trying to curb the exchange gracefully.

"How long have you been practicing with that bow?" Rene asked.

"This bow I made for my manhood ceremony," Coconino explained, "but I was given my first bow when I was four."

"You're pretty good, huh?"

"I am the best in my village," Coconino told him proudly.

"Oh, yeah? Well, let's see you hit this," Clint challenged. He drained his beer bottle and held it out. "Ready? Here you go, hotshot." He lofted the bottle.

Coconino watched the bottle go up and fall again nearby, but he made no move for his bow. "Why would I shoot at that?" he asked, puzzled.

"As a target, just to show how good you are."

But Coconino shook his head. "It is a bad target. I could chip an arrowhead on it. I am not a child; I do not risk good arrows on such games."

"Well, excuse me," Clint snarled.

"Hey, have a cold one," Jeff intervened, handing Coconino a bottle.

"What is it?" Coconino squinted at the handwritten label, then glanced around at the group of men tipping such bottles to their lips. " 'Parsons, summer batch,' " he read. "How does it open?"

Jeff peeled off the sealer for him. "It's good stuff," he assured Coconino. "Jack Parsons is the best brewmaster on the mountain."

Coconino sniffed at the liquid; it was pungent and not particularly appealing. But the others seemed to be enjoying it. Perhaps, like _tai-ayoh_, one had to develop a taste for it. Cautiously he lifted the bottle to his lips.

A bony hand on his wrist stopped him abruptly, and he looked into the fiery eyes of Phoenix. "You don't want that," she said evenly. Then she turned to the others. "Any of you jokers stop to think what this might do to a system that has no experience with alcohol?"

"Christ, McKay, it's only beer!" Clint groused.

"I didn't even think of it," Jeff apologized. "Sorry. We didn't mean any harm."

"Let him try it; maybe he'll like it," Clint badgered.

Phoenix turned back to Coconino. "It's a spirit water," she told him.

The bottle dropped from his hand and thudded on the soft ground, its contents spilling and foaming in the grass. Coconino stared with horror at the damning liquid. "It could have killed me," he whispered.

"Not likely," Phoenix grumbled, letting go of him. She picked up the bottle. "That much probably wouldn't even make you sick. But it is what it is, and you had a right to know before you drank it."

"We didn't know," Jeff repeated, taken aback by Coconino's sudden pallor. "Honest, we didn't."

"It's all right, fellows," she said, saluting them with the bottle. "Thanks for the beer." She took a deep draught and, bottle in hand, walked away.

The beer was strong and good. Staring out over the plains to the southeast, Phoenix wished she had another bottle. Another six bottles. It seemed like a good time to get rip-roaring drunk.

She hadn't slept well since her first night back, curled up beside Coconino on the dirt in front of the Administration Building. Her room in the dorm seemed smaller and more sterile than ever. The close, stale air bothered her, and not even an open window could freshen it. At first she had felt an alien in her own bed, as she did everywhere else on the Mountain, but slowly, gradually, she was being sucked back into it. The machine shop became familiar, the smell from the dining hall more natural, the brick of the buildings less harsh.

But she dreamed incessantly. Night after night she flew with Coconino over the island canyon—*their* canyon—landing on the bank of its winding river to make love in the afternoon sun. Other times they ran side by side along ancient roadbeds with feet, hearts, thoughts pounding in unison and the song of the Mother Earth pulsing in their veins. She would awaken with heart aching, the smell of mesquite still in her nostrils, to discover only the close walls of her darkened room. Then the despair would sweep over her like an ocean tide. Help me, Coconino, she would cry silently. Help me. I'm drowning, I'm slipping away, I'm losing myself . . .

Angrily Phoenix hurled the bottle out over the stony edge of the mountain. It sailed down the slope and landed with an audible thud in the vegetation below. Jack Parsons would be upset; he liked to get all his bottles back. Coconino would be even more upset. She had despoiled the Mother Earth.

Damn the Mother Earth, Phoenix thought. What has she ever done for me? And damn Coconino. Why doesn't he take his blond conquest and get out of here? And damn Dr. Martin for sending me home today to rest when I *can't* rest . . .

Above her the sun was harsh as it made its way westward through an impossibly blue sky. Phoenix raised her eyes toward what orbit she knew not. And damn you, too, she cursed silently. I was doing all right for a while there; I was really doing all right until that probe showed up. Now I've staked everything on you, and I don't even know who you are.

You'd better be worth it.

Jeff caught up with the young primitive just below the basketball court. "Trying to find my grandma's—uh, Mrs. Martin's house?"

"Good hunters do not lose their way," Coconino told him sourly.

"You know, I almost applied for the Program last year," Jeff forged on, falling into step beside him. "Only I couldn't think of anything I could teach your people that they'd need to know; all I could think of was how much they could teach me."

"The People have never tried to teach the Men-on-the-

Mountain," Coconino growled. "We have always respected their ways. The ones who came to the village respected ours as well. I did not know it was otherwise on your mountain."

"It isn't," Jeff pleaded. "It's just that we didn't know it was against your laws. We wouldn't have offered it if we had."

Coconino nailed him with a look. "Clint would have."

"Okay, maybe you're right," Jeff admitted. "But he's the only one. Probably the only one on the whole mountain. Will you condemn us all for one man?"

Coconino stopped in the road and faced the other man. "I do not condemn you," he said flatly. "But I see now I must not trust you, either."

Jeff was genuinely pained. "None of us?"

"You are the one who handed me the spirit water," Coconino pointed out.

"Because I didn't know," Jeff repeated. "I had no idea or I wouldn't have. Believe me."

"Oh, I believe you," Coconino assured him bitterly. "I believe you are a good person and have great respect for all people and probably all the creatures of the Mother Earth. But if you, who have such good intentions, can make such a mistake, how can I trust anyone on this mountain?"

Can I trust even you? Coconino wondered that night as he brushed Krista's golden hair away from her sleeping face. They lay twined beneath a blanket where they had agreed to meet, beyond the reach of the compound lights. Once again she had tried to entice him to sleep inside one of the buildings; adamantly, he had refused.

She stirred now; she didn't seem to sleep well, he noticed, although he had brought soft ferns and other plants to cushion their place. Why are the people of the Mountain so uncomfortable sleeping under the stars? he wondered. And you, my golden-haired, silver-voiced beauty, how can you be so out of touch with the Mother Earth? You are a Witch Woman . . .

Or are you? You claim healing is your magic, but you cannot heal my sister-brother. If you could, I—

Coconino sighed deeply. If you could, I would take Phoenix and return to the village and lead them all far away from the place of my dream. Or if the Mother still rejected Phoenix, I would go away with her and we two would find another place to live, perhaps in the northern canyon in that other Village of the Ancients. There, at last, my wedding would be consummated in a chamber of the Ancients. There I would sow the seeds of many children within her, and we would see them all grow and flourish like sunflowers . . .

Krista woke, sensing his tension. "What's wrong?" she asked.

"The Others are wrong," he grumbled. "Your mountain is wrong. The Mother is wrong. Everything is wrong."

Her silence was soft on his ear. Then, "Am I wrong?" she asked.

He looked at her, pale hair tumbling around her shoulders. Witch Woman, he thought. Witch Woman, Witch Woman— how could I have doubted it? Who could have hair like moonlight, a voice like a breeze in summer, except a true Daughter of the Mother Earth? "No," he whispered, taking her in his arms once more. "Not now."

They made love unhurriedly, with great tenderness and deep passion. In the aftermath they lay satisfied, looking up at the star-jeweled sky. A soft breeze chilled their sweat-slick bodies.

Coconino laid a gentle hand on her flat stomach. "How wondrous are the ways of the Mother Earth," he murmured. "To think that a seed so planted may catch the spark of life and grow to be a child, safely cradled here—" He felt her tense. "What is wrong?" Surely she was not also barren.

"Children mean a great deal to your people, don't they?" she asked.

"Do they not to yours?"

"Yes. Yes, they do," she assured him. "But it is important to have them at the right time."

He tried to think what she meant. "It is not good to have them during the winter rains," he agreed. "There is much sickness at that time, and babies often die. But we take what the Mother Earth gives us and when, for is She not wiser than we?"

There was a silence; he could almost hear her thinking, knew she wanted to say something. Finally she ventured, "Do you— do you think then that Debbie—Phoenix, that is—can't have children because—the Mother Earth doesn't want her to?"

"I don't know," he admitted. "It is possible. She sometimes withholds her bounty deliberately. But it is also true that the Mother Earth does not always get Her own way. Her children interfere. Or sometimes She asks Her children to help her, to use the gifts She has given them to accomplish what She wants." He sighed. "I do not know which way it is."

Krista had relaxed now. He watched her face as she gazed up into the heavens. With his thumb he gently stroked the curve of her cheek. "I hope She will give you the gift of a child," he whispered. "A child from my seed. I would like you to have that gift."

A sardonic smile twitched on her lips. "A gift from you," she mused. "You have a way of saying things, Coconino, that . . . but surely there are other gifts. In case," she added, "the Mother Earth does not favor me."

He sat up suddenly. "Indeed, I have another gift," he told her. "It is here in my pouch."

"Oh, no, Coconino," she protested. "I only meant—"

"No, it is *moh-ohnak* for you to have this," he insisted, unfolding a piece of leather. "Because, you see, these also are seeds. Very special seeds." Carefully he removed one red fruit and wrapped it in his headband. "They are the seeds of the Grandfather, the last seeds. You will have some, and I will have some, and no other."

"The Grandfather?" she asked. "What is the Grandfather?"

"He that was and is no more—or so it was believed. A gentle giant of the Before Times whose race has vanished, and he alone remains." He pressed the fruit into her hand. "Phoenix calls him 'sahuaro.' "

Clayton had always thought the white clouds swirling around Earth's blue form were beautiful. Now, gazing out the thick plexi of his ready room at the planet they circled, he realized just how problematic those graceful wisps were.

Cyd Ryan had found that the storms seemed confined to the afternoons in the target area; they should be able to fly the shuttle down with little danger. If only they had known this when they had launched the probe! But the idea of warping in and out of that environment disturbed him. Erratic electricity did strange things to spatial warps. Nasty things. People came out of them at the wrong place, the wrong time. Lujan's image of a person arriving with his feet six inches below ground level was only a minor grotesquerie. If the warp shifted, he could arrive inside a tree or in the path of a falling stone. Even with a terminal waiting at the other end.

The door chime sounded, startling Clayton from his morbid reflections. "Come in, Derek," he called, knowing it would be his first officer.

He was not disappointed. "Everything's set, Captain," Lujan reported crisply, his face glowing with excitement. "I'll be launching in three hours, equivalent to six hundred hours target site time. Even if entry time is double what it needs to be, I'll be in long before the storms hit that area."

Clayton nodded absently. "Good, good." He hesitated. "You've checked the navigational programming yourself?"

"Yes, sir, no problem there." Now it was the younger man's turn to hesitate. "Captain Winthrop . . ."

"Yes?"

"I think we should reconsider the landing site. I think we should check on our probe first."

Clayton arched an eyebrow. "Check on a dead probe? Why?"

"Well, I, for one, sir, would like very much to know why it died."

Clayton rubbed at his chin and found it was scratchy already. When he retired, he was going to quit shaving altogether, grow his beard to three feet if that was its inclination. Jacqueline would have fits. "You think the probe was tampered with before it left here?" he asked quietly.

Lujan shook his head slightly. "I don't see how, sir. I checked it over myself, every inch. Unless someone got to it after I did."

"Which is not impossible."

"No, sir."

"But you think something might have happened to it on the ground."

"It was largely carbon fiber, sir," Lujan pointed out. "Not a prime target for a lightning strike."

Clayton sighed deeply and turned back to the porthole. "I'll go with you on this one, Derek," he said. "Check it out and let me know what you find. But once you've assessed the situation, take the shuttle atmospherically to the plains at the foot of that mountain. That's where I want the warp terminus set up; we'll warp down a helicraft ASAP and go to the top."

Karen was still checking the communications equipment in the shuttle when Derek returned to the launching bay. She was hunched over a panel in the fifteen-by-fifteen control/passenger compartment. Six feet away another tech was going over the guidance system. Derek slid up to Karen, his arms circling her from behind, and kissed her cheek. "Everything A-okay?" he asked.

"Fine," she said, hardly responding to his caress. "Just finishing up. I need to send the daily dispatches next." Then under her breath she asked, "Any you need to see?"

"I've seen them," he whispered back. "But listen, I'm counting on you to screen everything while I'm on the surface."

"Done," she replied. He gave her a quick hug and was gratified when she responded by squeezing his arm. It was not easy to get a response from Karen. He liked to think he was one of the few men who ever could.

Whistling brightly, he sauntered back to the cargo bay doors and touched a panel. With a soft *whish* the doors slid back, and he stepped through into the crowded bay. A squat treaded landcrawler was bolted at one side, taking up over half of the twenty-by fifteen-foot space. The warp equipment, broken down and carefully cushioned on sturdy cases, took up another quarter. In the remaining space was lashed an assortment of tools and equipment that might prove valuable in his initial assessment of Earth.

Derek opened one of the cases of warp equipment, satisfying himself that everything was secure. Slender plexi tubes of electrolytic solution shimmered up at him, each one four feet long and three inches in diameter. They exhibited an assortment of pastel hues owing to the various types of tiny crystal suspended in each. They would be placed in carefully angled sockets in the cargo bay walls to create the complex crisscrossed pattern that sent and received three-dimensional objects via the fifth dimension.

Satisfied, he sealed the case once more. Everything was under control. Everything was very much under control. Now, if he could only keep it there.

Krista looked down at the key in her hand. Tiny little silver key, cheap little piece of metal—a nail file would probably work as well. But she had the key. She had always had access to the key, even before she had made Level Four. They had always trusted her with the meds.

Dr. White knew, of course, that she occasionally used one of the "morning after" pills. Dr. White had prescribed them the first time. He didn't want a young health tech burdened with a child; that would interfere with her studies. Time enough for children later, when she had a husband and a home. So when the inventory came up short, she would simply tell him, "I needed one," and he would shake his head and sign the report.

They why was she hesitating? It might not be, of course, that she really needed one; it might not be the time in her cycle when she was in danger. But she would hate to be wrong.

Would she hate to be wrong?

She had taken the fruit Coconino had given her to Dick McKay. From books in the Archives he had verified that it was, indeed, from a saguaro, a plant supposedly extinct for at least two centuries. Krista had stared in awe at pictures of the giant cacti soaring to heights of forty feet and tried to imagine how they could grow from the small black grains that bristled in the red fruit pulp.

Willingly she turned the fruit over to Mr. McKay for safekeeping. The rarity of Coconino's gift frightened her—why had he given it to her? Why not to Dr. Martin, or Mrs. Mendoza, or even Debbie McKay? She didn't want the responsibility for it. What if she lost it? What if she planted all the seeds and none of them grew? What if she did it all wrong?

Mr. McKay had studied her with penetrating eyes, as though reading all the questions in her mind. "Coconino trusted you with a very great treasure," he had observed, and Krista had only nodded dumbly, afraid he was not talking about the saguaro seeds at all. Then he had plucked one seed from the fruit with a pair of tweezers, folded it into a square of paper, and handed it to her.

"The gift was given to you," Mr. McKay told her. "Plant at least one seed, see how it grows." Krista had taken the square of paper, afraid to meet his eyes. "You'll have to take care of it, nurture it—I'll help you," he had offered. "But this one should be yours, something to remind you always of Coconino, of the remarkable young man he was."

Krista shivered now. Why had Mr. McKay used the past tense? Because Coconino would leave, of course. He'd go back to his People, and she'd never see him again. That was all Mr. McKay had meant.

Slowly Krista unlocked the meds cabinet. She took out the analgesic for Maria Gonzales, the diuretic for her cousin Rodney, and penicillin for little Shari Anderson. Then she closed the cabinet and locked it securely.

There was not much chance the saguaro seed would grow, anyway.

Coconino closed the book, stretched, and eased the pain in his back. He should have gone hunting today. He had seen the tracks of white-tailed deer yesterday before he'd brought the quail back to Mrs. Martin. And his fine words about the unimportance of the size of a kill had been largely bluff; he would dearly love to walk into the dining hall with a five-point buck slung over his shoulders.

He had even gone looking for Phoenix. "She went to the library looking for Dr. Martin," a hurried engineer had told him. "We're almost ready to try the beacon."

In the library he found neither Phoenix nor Dr. Martin but the dainty Witch Woman Lois. She beamed her sunshine smile at him. "Oh, Coconino, I'm so glad you're here. Look, I've found some more books for you." In the warmth of her eyes he could not refuse but sat down at the reading table while she laid them out for him.

And indeed, among the volumes on the table were two that captivated him. One was on the early tribes of the American Southwest: Tohono O'odam, Apache, Hopi, Navaho, and others more ancient. The second told of the Plains Indians: Comanche, Arapaho, Sioux. Here were the stories of the ancestors of the People. Their art, their religion, their legends were here—all that was good about the ancestors who were only a vague memory to the Survivors who had established his own culture.

He had devoured every word, feeling his blood pulse in sympathy with his forbears. Their ways of war were strange to him; he could not understand killing as a sport. But he understood the need of athletic competition, of pitting oneself against another to measure one's strength and cunning. He smiled briefly as he remembered stalking the puma in the Red Rock country. And he felt the fierce joy of being part of the Cycle of Life. With Black Elk he rejoiced: "It is a good day to die! Have courage, boy! The Earth is all that lasts!" How wise were these ancestors of his, who knew that death was only another event in life. Long before the Wrath of the Mother Earth had consumed nearly all her creatures, they knew that She was the only constant.

His appetite whetted by those marvelous volumes, he now looked around the library for the technician on duty. At the desk was a thin, mousy man engrossed in research of some kind. A half dozen books were open around him, two monitors were active to his left, and he was making notes furiously on a keyboard to his right. Coconino approached with his book and coughed to get the man's attention.

The technician glanced up, did a double take, and stared at Coconino a moment. "Can I help you?" he asked.

"Yes," Coconino replied in his best richly accented English. "I would like more books like this."

The man blinked several times. "More?"

''Yes,'' Coconino said patiently, ''more. Are there more like this?''

Finally the man looked at the book. ''On American Indians? Yes, we have several. Over here.'' He slid out from behind his desk and led Coconino to a section of shelves. ''Here,'' he said, patting a group of volumes. ''These are all on American Indians. Help yourself.''

The technician went back to his desk, and Coconino knelt by the shelf. The Mother was wrong, he decided. Reading was good. It was well to know about the ancestors of the People, how they had lived, the spirits they had worshiped, the stories they had told. The Men-on-the-Mountain had been wise to preserve all this knowledge in books, and the People should do the same.

Coconino selected two volumes at random and returned to the reading table. He opened the first and read the title: *Bury My Heart at Wounded Knee.*

CHAPTER SEVENTEEN

Lujan opened the hatch of the shuttle and gazed out onto paradise. Slowly he reached up and pulled down the useless face mask he had donned when he had still hoped the instrument readings on the shuttle might have been wrong. But the scene before him confirmed everything the instruments had told him: clean air, plenty of oxygen for plants and animals, and more sunshine than he'd seen in three years. His stomach knotted; his chest grew tight.

Dillon wasn't going to like this.

Dillon had shown him a library of reports on the projected fate of Earth. None of them had admitted the possibility that life—animal or vegetable—could have survived the natural disasters in progress during the Evacuation. Lujan had expected a wasteland of volcanic rock, a place devoid of vegetation. He had expected either a dust-clouded atmosphere and freezing temperatures or a surface so hot that molten magma oozed for years without solidifying. Only when the probe's initial readings hinted at breathable air and vegetation had he begun to question his information.

But this—how in the universe could he keep this quiet?

Dazedly Lujan stepped out into the wonderland of verdant green. Grass, trees, birds—there! That was a rabbit! And over there something else moved in the grass. A snake? A lizard? Look at that sky! Clear and blue and beautiful, and the air sweet—damn!

Dillon wasn't going to like this at all.

For although Dillon was a man of many talents with his fingers in many pies, most of those pies were related to Terran art and artifacts. The high value of his collections rested largely on the fact that there was a finite quantity. An expedition to Earth could bring back new treasures in quantities to compete with his. Worse, it could prove that future expeditions were viable and create the potential of flooding the market. Dillon's instructions to Lujan had been very clear: See that the Earth venture failed. *If* reports came back from Earth at all, they were to be negative. Extremely negative.

Of course, if contact with Earth could not be avoided, Dillon wanted to know if it was possible to retrieve artifacts himself. In a few years, when interest in the expedition subsided, discreet trips could be made to recover only what was needed, only what the market would bear. Perhaps the legal details could be worked out so that Dillon's various companies obtained a monopoly on the traffic and it could be brought aboveground. If not . . .

Lujan had his own private irons in the fire, too. Together with his courageous handling of the *Aladdin,* this Earth venture was sure to earn him a command of his own. That would put him in a position to take additional assignments from Dillon, a very lucrative arrangement.

But how did you keep thirty-seven people from telling the universe about a picturesque river valley that flourished in the sunshine? He could seal the lips of at least six with money. But what about the rest? What about squeaky-clean bureaucratic Tony Hanson?

It was very simple. Anyone who came to this valley would have to stay.

His initial shock past, Lujan scanned the area quickly for any sign of the probe. With all the clutter, however, vision was ineffective, so he picked up an instrument that would register the crystals powering the probe. Soon it homed in on the foundation of an ancient building. There, battered and abused, the shell of the probe lay among the rubble. It hadn't wormed its own way under that pile of rock. Someone, or something, had attacked it. Given the species native to this area, only one conclusion was possible: something of human descent.

Damn. Dillon wasn't going to like that, either.

Jim Martin gazed up the central shaft of the Mayall Tower. All that machinery, all that equipment, rigged together like an elaborate mousetrap and ready to go when he gave the command. There ought to be more to it, he thought suddenly—a ribbon cutting, an assembled crowd, a speech. But he only nodded to a technician, who entered the proper command in a computer terminal, and the mighty beacon came to life.

"It works!" someone whooped. "She's transmitting!" Jim looked up again, past the wires and the conduits and the relays to a patch of blue sky visible through the open dome. That was it, then. Either they heard the signal or they didn't.

He turned to Phoenix, who gazed numbly at the computer screen, its symbols a blur to her. "Thanks for your help," he said. "Couldn't have done it without you."

"Couldn't have done it as fast," she replied dully. "You've got other machinists."

Her eyes were red and sunken, her face sallow beneath its tan. God, will this woman get no peace? he wondered. Now, even if she could have her infertility corrected, she had lost her husband. And if, as he speculated from time to time, it was Coconino she wanted now—well, that young man's preference for Krista was obvious.

"Still not sleeping well?" he asked kindly.

"That's an understatement."

"Why don't you get something from the Infirmary?" he suggested. "You're not doing yourself any favors."

"I'll think about it."

It's your own bitterness, Debbie, he thought. You make everything worse than it needs to be, he wanted to say. But she'd heard the lecture before. Dick had given it to her, Dr. Delacourt had given it to her—in fact, he was sure he'd given it himself at least once, in some variation. No point in giving it again.

"Well, no reason to hang around here," he said, stirring himself. "Can't dance, as they say."

Something flickered in Phoenix's eyes. He could not know the drums she heard in her head at that moment.

She followed him outside, and a gust of autumn wind caught them, and on it was the pungent scent of cypress. For Phoenix it was as though it had suddenly slapped her, stealing her breath and rousing her muted senses. It cleared the smells of metals and machines from her lungs, blew the sleep haze from her eyes, sucked the echoing emptiness from her ears. Almost she could hear a voice calling her, but it was the cry of a hawk soaring just off the edge of the mountain, casting its shadow on the ridges and rocks below.

Phoenix looked down on the hawk—strange to look *down* at a bird in flight. Then her chin came up; she planted her feet and gave the sky a critical survey. "Good weather for hunting," she said finally.

"So it is." Jim watched, amazed, at the transformation in her. A moment before she had been a defeated woman, bruised, listless. Suddenly she was taller, straighter, stronger.

Now she shaded her eyes and looked down toward the winding road that led off the mountain. "Coconino said there might be deer of some sort on the lower slopes," she observed. "If we could get two, maybe three—ever taste fresh venison, Dr. Martin?"

"No, I haven't," he admitted.

Her eyes glittered. "We could make a feast, like they do in the village," she went on. "To celebrate the beacon." Then her voice dropped slightly. "And to honor the Mother Earth."

"I think it's a fine idea," Jim said.

"I have my bow cached just down the slope here," she told him, remembering how Coconino had sneered when she'd hidden it, unable to understand why she was ashamed to walk into the compound with a bow and quiver slung across her back. "I'm pretty good with large targets," she continued with some pride, "and Coconino—" The eyes warmed. "Coconino's the best." She flexed her shoulders once, as though to free them. "We can do it." With that simple statement, she strode off toward the library, purpose in her every move.

Phoenix knew Coconino would be in the library, although she didn't ask herself why. He could have been out hunting already, or with Krista, or exploring some other part of the compound, but he wasn't. He was in the library, and it didn't occur to her to look anywhere else. She didn't know whose voice had spoken to her or even that she had heard a voice at all.

His back was to her as he sat at the reading table. Suddenly she saw him as a young boy, sitting outside his wickiup, knees drawn up as he pored over his precious books. That's who you were, she realized, and who you are still, the boy with the book, with the love of stories—yet you are more now. You are also the hunter, the best hunter, a man whom the People respect. And you are the storyteller, who can weave tradition and adventure and the love that is in your soul and pass it as a gift to young and old alike. The Mother is right: The People need you, need your children—

Oh, God, Coconino. If they can do this operation for me, if I can be made whole— Your child, Coconino. That would justify the rest. That would be payback for all the pain in my life . . .

She stopped just behind him, swallowed twice before she trusted her voice. "Coconino." He turned slowly toward her.

Suddenly she froze. Coconino's face was twisted and drawn, mouth tight, eyes burning like a madman's. His whole body quivered with pent-up rage.

"What is it?" she asked, her voice small. She had never seen fury like this, unmasked hatred that contorted his whole body into that of a demon, an evil kachina. Unleashed, he could destroy this mountain, she thought wildly. Mother Earth help us. What is wrong?

Slowly Coconino extended the book to her. His jaw clenched around his words. "Are these stories true?"

Phoenix took the book from his hand, stared stupidly at the writing.

"They must be," Coconino continued. "No one could make up such filth, such—desecration. This is a true accounting, isn't it?"

Blinking, Phoenix forced herself to focus on the book's title, and her heart stopped. "Oh, God," she moaned weakly. It was an account of the atrocities perpetrated on the American Indians by their white conquerors.

"Is it true?" he demanded again, his voice raw with emotion.

"It was long ago," she pleaded. "No one would do that again, no one would—"

"Children!" The outrage burst forth at last. "Even children! Women with babes in their bellies, old men, widows—butchery!" he howled. "Desecration!" The words rolled off his lips like an ancient prophecy, words used only in the Mother Earth's Lament. "Abomination! Mutilation—" The strain broke off, and a new one surfaced like a groan. "Humiliation."

"Long ago," she insisted, rising now to the defense of her generation. "All that was long ago, by men long dead—ignorant, fearful men. It changed, even in the Before Times. We have learned from their stupidity."

"Is this your 'civilization'?" he roared. "Is this what awaits the People at the hand of your Others? 'Take this piece of land, it is no good for us,' " he mimicked. " 'Change your ways, they do not please us. Do not hunt but take what drops from our hands after we have gorged ourselves—or better yet, take the excrement we leave behind.' " He raised his hands in wrathful invocation. "Fire and Ash! Lightning and Wind and Quakings of the Ground! *Aiiee*, Mother Earth, send forth your destruction once more, tear the Others from the sky and grind them to dust before they touch your People, before they bring their spirit of evil.''

''And that makes you better than them!'' Phoenix shouted. ''Sure, tear 'em out of the sky, wipe 'em out. How many lives? Thirty? A hundred and thirty? Four hundred and thirty? Does it matter? Maybe they've got pregnant women on board, too. Maybe children; maybe they're colonists. You call for their destruction; are you any better than the villains in this book?'' She threw the offending volume at him. ''That's what your ancestors did, you know. Whites were cruel to them—they turned around and killed whites in return. Yes, even children! Mutilation and butchery, just like they got. Only they didn't stop to ask if the people they retaliated against were the same ones who'd hurt them.'' She stood with her face inches from his, stealing the brunt of his blaze with her backfire. ''People are people, Coconino, some good and some bad. I can't promise these Others will all be sympathetic. I can't promise there won't be a Shaman among them.''

Coconino drew back. The People were not proud of their Shaman.

''But I can't promise there won't be a Mother, either,'' Phoenix continued. ''You don't even know them, you've never met them; how can you pass judgment on them?''

At this his head came up; he straightened his shoulders, and a look of grim resolution settled over his features. ''It is not my judgment,'' he told her, ''but that of the Mother Earth. That was the dream; that was what she tried to tell me.''

''Dream? What dream?'' Phoenix asked, but Coconino was headed for the door. ''Hey! Where do you think you're going?''

''Back to the People.''

Oh, no, not yet! And not like this. Please, no— ''Wait! Coconino, wait, let's talk about this, let's talk about the dream . . .''

Coconino flung the door open to the blinding sun of midafternoon. He'd been in these cursed buildings too long. He needed the sun to purge him.

Phoenix was right behind him, catching at his arm. ''Okay, maybe the Others are not good. Maybe we have to deal with that,'' she said. ''But not with mindless destruction. That is not the Way of the People.''

He looked down at her as though she were some troublesome

thorn he would pluck from his flesh. "I will protect the People," he vowed. "However I must." Snatching his arm away from her, he pushed through into the daylight.

"It didn't do your ancestors any good," she shouted after him. "They tried with violence; it nearly got them exterminated."

"They tried peaceful acceptance as well," he called back to her. "The result was the same."

"Damn it, Coconino, just don't start anything, all right?" It was half plea, half command. "Just don't *you* start it all!"

Coconino hauled himself up short, the image of himself in the dream slamming suddenly home. He had attacked the shining evil, and it had consumed him . . . A shiver ran through him. Now he must go to the Mother, tell her all he had learned on the Mountain. She would help him see what was right.

But as his foot touched the grass-tufted earth beside the walkway, pain shot up his leg and exploded in his chest. "*Aiiee!*" he cried out, staggering from its shock.

"What is it?" Phoenix asked anxiously, crossing the short distance between them. As her foot left the sidewalk and touched the ground, she, too, felt a shock, as though ice had rushed from her toes to her scalp. But she thought that it was only his pain she felt and that he was leaving, leaving in blind anger that could only destroy him.

Pain! Coconino gasped with it. *Mother Earth, they are here! They have touched your soil once more!*

He staggered, drew himself straight, steeled his body against the onslaught of pain. His muscles knotted; he forced them under control. Then, with a howl of rage that echoed from the rocks and towers of that place, wrenching the heavens with its utter despair, Coconino fled from the Mountain.

Dozing at her loom, the Mother also cried out. Two Moons rushed up anxiously. "What is it, Mother?" she asked. The old woman was panting, sweating heavily. Her skin felt cold and clammy to the touch. "Mother, come and lie down," Two Moons bade her. "Talia, bring water, cool water!"

But the Mother held up a gnarled hand. "We are not lost yet," she croaked. "Not . . . yet. But we must . . . act quickly. Summon the People together. We must call Coconino home."

Then she slumped forward across the intricate weaving.

*   *   *

Clayton peered anxiously over his comm tech's shoulder. "Are you sure, Karen?"

Karen looked up at him, felt the tension, the crackling excitement, and carefully forced her own excitement back. "Captain, there's no doubt," she told him simply. "That is a radio signal, and it is coming from your mountain." Whatever it was, it would prove to be a disappointment in the end.

"What are they saying?" he demanded, incredulity edging his voice.

"It's not a voice transmission," she explained. "It's just— noise. But consistent noise. *Boop-boop-boop*. Like a beacon." That had been her first thought. But of course it wasn't possible. Derek was right; Earth was dead.

Winthrop turned away from her, his thoughts churning visibly. "Might be automated," he suggested.

Part of her wanted to agree, but— "It wasn't there twenty minutes ago," she pointed out. "Someone just turned it on."

"Or something." She saw him struggle inwardly; he wanted so badly to believe it, but the rational man in him balked. "It might be on a timer," he suggested. "Or it might have been triggered by our presence in orbit."

"Yes, sir, it might," she replied flatly. She had liked the captain at first, but he was full of such powerful emotions. Noble emotions. She was more comfortable with Derek.

"Have we heard from Lujan at the shuttle?" Winthrop asked.

"There was too much interference earlier," she lied smoothly. "Now he is apparently outside the craft because I get no response. I left a call message for him to report as soon as he returns."

Winthrop straightened. "Well, I'm not going to wait," he announced. "Tell Rita to prep the mini-shuttle; I'm going down there."

Karen's heart jumped. "But sir!"

"When Lujan calls in, tell him to get his ass over to the mini-shuttle landing site at the foot of the mountain and get that warp terminal set up as ordered. Now it's imperative to have a fast access route between the ship and that mountain. Besides—" Winthrop gave the lopsided grin that heralded his dry wit. "—the mini-shuttle's a one-way craft. I need him to get back."

Karen knew she shouldn't let him go, but what could she do? "Sir, how are you going to get up the mountain?" she asked. "You can't pack a helicraft in that mini-shuttle."

"Jet pack," he replied, heading for the hatch. "Or if I have to, I'll climb the damn thing. But I'm going to find out who or what is making that noise.'' Then he stopped, sent one severe look around the bridge. ''And no one—no one—mentions this to the good doctor until I'm gone.''

Winthrop ducked through the hatch into the companionway and began whistling.

Karen waited till he was gone and the crew had turned back to their duties. Then quietly she opened a comm channel. ''Derek, this is Karen. We have a problem.''

''Clay, you're too damn old to go playing Johnny Space Cadet and the Unknown Planet.'' Dr. Jacqueline Winthrop handed her husband a jet pack, which he stowed deftly in the cargo bay of the mini-shuttle. ''Send one of the geological team. Or a mech tech. One of the line people—not yourself.''

''A captain shouldn't send anyone where he wouldn't go himself,'' Winthrop lied.

Jacqueline called it what it was. ''You just can't bear to let anyone else have all the fun,'' she said.

He grinned up at her as she stood in her favorite authoritative pose: hands on hips, feet planted firmly. ''Okay, I admit it,'' he said, giving in cheerfully. ''This is why I signed aboard. I want to be the first man to shake hands with a native-born Terran. I damn near let Lujan cheat me out of it, but ha! The Fates are on my side. He's at an uninhabited probe site, and I am going to that mountain.''

''You have no idea what's down there, Clay. Oh, I heard Lujan's cryptic first report: breathable atmosphere and the rest he'd rather report to you personally in due time. I'd watch that boy, Clayton; there's something very suspicious about him. And I don't like you going down there on his information. His tight-lipped *lack* of information, that is.'' She handed him another jet pack.

''I only need one of these, Jackie,'' he told her. ''It's only one mountain I intend to scale, and not a very tall one at that.''

''Well, I've never known a single jet pack to carry two people,'' she snapped. ''You don't think I'm going to let you go down there alone?''

Phoenix paced the conference room in agitation. ''What's the big deal?'' Eric Jackson was saying. Eric was head of Security for the compound as well as an electrical engineer who had worked closely with Dr. Martin on the beacon. At thirty-eight, his rapidly balding pate made him look older than he was. "So the Indian took off, so what? We didn't really want him to stick around, did we?"

She rounded on the thickly built man, his eyes small and snakelike in his square face. "The big deal is," she hissed, "that he left here with a gutful of hatred for the 'Others,' as he calls them, and an intense fear of what they might do to his people. He could do something very rash."

Jackson guffawed. "What's he going to do, shoot arrows at their ship? Get serious, McKay. How much trouble can he be?"

Disgusted, Phoenix turned away from him. Is that what they all thought? One Indian with a bow?

Behind her, Jim Martin cleared his throat. "I think there's a little more to it than that, Eric," he said calmly. "Maybe Dick could shed some light for us."

It had been Martin's idea to invite Dick McKay to the Advisory Board meeting. Chancy, having him and Debbie in the same room; their verbal battles were legendary. But McKay probably knew more about the primitives than anyone else on the mountain, including Kevin Mendoza, who ran the Facilitation Program. He'd lived with them for three years and carried them in his heart longer.

Dick shifted uneasily in his chair. "Debbie's right; the boy can be dangerous," he said. My son, my son! his heart cried. Somewhere you are bleeding, and I can't even talk to you. "The People have a set of values that—that will be more deeply offended than you can imagine if he tells them the contents of the book."

"Who the hell gave him that book, anyway?" Phoenix exploded. "That's like giving a butcher knife to a baby!"

"The technician is not to blame," Gail Mendoza intervened. As Chief Administrator of the installation she sat at the head of the conference table, a small woman accustomed to filling a large chair. Her gray hair was pulled back from her face and plaited in neat braids that coiled on the back of her head, adding strength and dignity to her sharply featured face. "The library is an open facility; no restrictions were placed on Coconino's access to the books."

"What happened to common sense?" Phoenix demanded. "And don't tell me he found that book without any help. I don't buy that."

"How he found it is not at issue," Gail reminded her. "The

results of his reading it are. Dick, why do you feel he—or the whole tribe—could be dangerous?"

Phoenix bit her tongue and waited for his answer. Go on, tell them, she thought. Tell them what's at the back of your mind and mine. *You* get them to believe it. *You* explain that somewhere inside me something is quaking because I'm afraid he really *can* call up the wrath of the Mother Earth. There really might be volcanoes and earthquakes and maybe even a meteor strike—who knows? I'd like to see you explain that to them.

But Dick McKay swallowed twice and began in a rational tone. "Remember that we're dealing with a people that is uneducated but not unintelligent. Their experience is limited to what they encounter in that village and the surrounding area. If they meet a poisonous snake in the wild, they call it brother and give it a wide berth. But if that snake comes into their camp, they deal with it more harshly. If they feel that a landing party, for instance, represents a threat to them, that it has in essence 'come into their camp,' they are apt to try to remove it by any means possible."

"Remove it?" Jackson was not impressed. "You mean a physical attack? They'd be annihilated."

"That," Phoenix snarled, "is exactly the point!"

"For four hundred years," Dick continued, "we've protected that community, nurtured it as an anthropological treasure. Contact with the rest of humanity makes it even more imperative that we continue to do so. But they've never seen a weapon stronger than their bows. They don't know how easily their attack could be repelled and the attackers destroyed. That ignorance makes them dangerous to themselves and, yes, to the Others."

"So haul a few of them up here," Jackson suggested, "and I'll give them an object lesson in the power of disrupters. If they're as bright as you say, they'll think twice about attacking anybody."

Suddenly Dick McKay was on his feet, brown eyes flashing behind his glasses. "You ignorant son of a bitch!" he hissed, powerful hands slamming against the tabletop. "Fear won't solve the problem. Fear *is* the problem, fear that their way of life, the Way of the People, is threatened! If something threatened to destroy you and all you held dear, would you rest until you'd done something about it? At least *tried* to do something about it? Even if it cost you your own life? What we have to do is not scare them but reassure them."

"The trouble is," Gail Mendoza said quietly, "their way of

life *is* going to change. With contact restored, how can we keep them isolated? They will be touched as profoundly—as profoundly, my friends, as we ourselves.''

For a moment they all stared at each other as the parallel became clear to them. Then suddenly the awkward silence was broken by a sharp rap at the door. It opened immediately, and Ruth Anderson, Gail's assistant, stood in the doorway, flushed and flustered. ''Gail!'' she exclaimed, out of breath. ''They're here!''

''Who is?'' Gail asked.

''From the spaceship! The captain and the ship's doctor of the *Homeward Bound*!''

CHAPTER EIGHTEEN

"Thanks, Karen, I'll be in touch." Lujan snapped off his transmitter and swore eloquently. Then he picked up a stone and hurled it at the wretched life-bearing soil. A lizard scampered away, startled. If only Winthrop had waited for him!

Well, at least Karen would keep any reports hushed up till he decided what to do about this new wrinkle. A beacon! Who would have thought?

Assuming the worst, that there really were survivors on that mountain, Winthrop would have to be marooned. The beacon could be explained away, but no eyewitnesses could return to tear the fabric of the lie Lujan must weave. No one could know that there was life on Earth.

If only Winthrop had aborted the mission when the navigational error was discovered! They'd all be safely back on Argo now, and it would be years, maybe decades, before funds could be raised for another attempt. But the veteran space commander had been smarter than Lujan; his use of minimal fuel to slow them down, allowing Earth to catch up, had been brilliant in its simplicity.

Shifting to his alternative plan, Lujan had programmed reports of a poisonous atmosphere and extreme temperatures, all set to kick in when the first air and soil samples were taken. But the probe had quit transmitting before it could send much of anything. Fortunately, he and Dillon's money had arranged for the "first officer" to be in charge of landing the shuttle. This provided him the opportunity to send back manufactured reports from the surface, but before he could program all the false readings to coincide with what the ship was picking up at a distance, Winthrop had fouled him up again.

Well, Plan D would take care of that. Winthrop was not going home.

But what to do right now? The captain's orders to him, relayed through Karen, had been specific and had been given in front of the crew on the bridge: He had to take the shuttle to the mountain and set up a warp terminal there. But damn! If there *were* people on that mountain . . .

He jabbed a button that activated a microphone and began his log entry. "First Officer Derek Lujan, from the landing site of the shuttle on Earth. I don't know what damage was incurred by the navigation equipment during landing, but until it has been checked out by a mech tech, I dare not fly the shuttle to the captain's landing site as ordered. I have no choice but to set up the terminal here and request personnel warp down to check for possible malfunctions." As on the *Aladdin*, a little discreet tampering would prove his decision had been correct.

"In the meantime, I will take the landcrawler and report to Captain Winthrop at his landing site in person. There is information about this planet not immediately visible and which I feel requires his screening before it is made accessible to the crew at large." He stopped a moment to glare at the ungainly landcrawler. Of course he could request a helicraft from the *Homeward Bound*, but Hanson or some other yo-yo would be all over his back wanting to come along to the mountain. Best to leave before they knew what he was up to.

One good thing about all this, he thought as he turned back to his report. There was plenty of profit to be made exploiting this world, and a piece of it was his. That and a ship of his own—as long as he remained useful to Dillon.

Of course, there were those letters detailing Dillon's connection with the *Aladdin* disaster, letters Lujan had left in sundry undisclosed locations. They were to be opened should he precede Dillon in death. So far Dillon had found and destroyed only one. But staying useful was better insurance. Yes, he and Dillon should have a long and profitable association. Then perhaps one day Dillon would cease to be useful to *him*.

Lujan smiled, warmed by the thought.

Thunderheads built in the southeast, dark and ominous as they scudded ruthlessly closer to the Mountain. Brilliant sunlight from the west still illuminated the white towers on the crest, making them seem to burn with an inner fire. Tala sniffed the breeze that had sprung up and trumpeted uneasily.

With a critical eye the animal watched Coconino worry a pipe out of the ground. In the Before Times a gate had shut off this road at night, a metal gate with crossbars of two-inch steel sleeving. The fence was long gone and most of the gate, but this one crossbar had survived, buried in the stony earth.

Now it made a formidable weapon. Coconino brandished it, hearing the rush of its passage as it sliced the air. It felt strong and sure in his hands, like a channel for the pain that coursed through his body still. He had separated the pain from himself so that it did not jab him with every step he took. He could think now, function, plan—but it ached in every fiber. And in his head was a throbbing, the strong rhythmic pulse of the drums . . .

Tala shook his head and pawed the ground impatiently. He had been waiting as the man, racked by the pain of the Mother Earth, had rushed headlong down the mountain. With his great strength he had succored the youth, comforted him, and borne him gently away beyond the shielding ridge of low hills just northeast of the Mountain. There they had waited until Coconino's panic was replaced with purpose, his rage with resolve.

The sun burned its way relentlessly toward the western horizon, and none too soon for the great unicorn. He wanted this day to pass, as he wanted the impending storm to break and be over. Let the violence be done; let their purpose here be fulfilled. He would be glad enough to return to his home in the Black Lands, though the idea of leaving the man behind troubled him somewhat. Yet there was no alternative; the man had his place in the Mother Earth's scheme, and Tala had his. Only for this brief time would they walk together.

Again Coconino swung the pipe, this time crashing it into a dead mesquite. The tree exploded, sending splinters flying.

The noise startled Tala, and he shied away, trumpeting and spewing sparks from his horn, but he held his ground. Why did men relish such things, the making of sudden noises, of unexpected movement? Perhaps it was best that their ways part.

As the sparks scorched the dry grass, Coconino called soothing words to his friend. His tough bare feet stamped quickly on the ground where a wisp of smoke began to curl up, snuffing the small ember. Then Coconino began to laugh darkly. "*Aiiee,*

Tala, my brother," he crooned as he squatted to rub the ash of those blades of grass between his fingers. "Between us we shall confound these Others, as the Mother Earth confounded their evil fathers. For here I have the thunder," he said, standing and hefting the pipe. "And you, my friend—" Here he rubbed the animal's nose and gazed with glittering eyes at the ivory length of twisting horn. "You have the lightning."

Jacqueline Winthrop took the X-ray films handed to her but did not look at them; instead, she looked long and hard at the face across from her. Dark, haunted eyes, hollow cheeks, a bitter set to the mouth. "Good God, woman, don't you sleep?" she demanded.

Phoenix gave a wry smile and shrugged. "It's not a question of sleep," she replied, "it's a question of rest." There was something about the brusque older woman that she liked. Honesty, she decided. And a total absence of prejudice.

Jacqueline gave her one more critical look, then held the films up to the light. "Mmm," she grunted. "Simple enough to correct." She handed the films back and studied the face again. "On Argo."

Phoenix's heart crashed against her ribs, and she almost staggered before she pulled back, took a deep breath, and spoke. "You mean you can't do it on the *Homeward Bound*?"

Jacqueline gave a short laugh. "Your Infirmary here is better equipped than my sick bay. Well, not entirely, but in terms of surgery. I could handle an emergency—severed limbs or compound fractures, even a disrupter wound. But this kind of delicate work—I don't have the right instruments. I could do more damage than good." She saw the sinking of the gaunt woman's heart. "But we could bring you back to Argo, where it's outpatient surgery. There are bound to be any number of research flights now. We'll take you back; you come home again with the next ship."

Phoenix nodded dully. "I'll think about that."

Jacqueline watched as the woman turned and started away again. "What happened to your husband?" she asked suddenly.

Startled, Phoenix spun around. It was a moment before she could reply. "Oh, he's around. Married someone else."

"This won't bring him back, you know."

"Don't want him back," Phoenix said curtly. "I want *me* back."

"And those films are what you're all about?"

The pain deepened in Phoenix's face, but some of the bitterness drained away. "They're in the way," she whispered. "They're just in the way."

Jacqueline sighed. "If that's the way you feel."

"It's more than just a feeling," Phoenix snapped, "it's a way of life here."

"Seems to me your way of life is going to change," Jacqueline observed.

"People keep saying that!" Phoenix flared. "And the truth is—the truth is, some of it can't. It mustn't. There are things we want to preserve . . ."

"Terra for Terrans?" Jacqueline guessed. "I wish I could hold out some hope for you, but the one thing that hasn't changed much in five hundred years is the nature of the human race. When something new—or old—is discovered, people want to know how it can benefit them. They bring their own myopic attitudes and ideas to every situation. We can't build a fence around you. Sorry."

For a long moment Phoenix just stared at her, and Jacqueline wondered what it was she wanted to protect. Then the young woman stirred. "I have to talk to the captain," Phoenix said with decision. "We have to get some things straight, and we have to do it now, before any more of your people come down."

"I'm sorry, Captain, there's no way our people can fix this," Jim Martin apologized. He and Clayton Winthrop were examining Winthrop's opened radio. "I've never even seen crystals like this. You have to remember, we were still using microchips at the time of the Evacuation."

Clayton snapped the casing closed in irritation. He'd smelled sabotage from the beginning, and this was just one more noxious odor from what must be a plot to doom this mission. But who? Who was doing this? Someone on the ship? Had to be. Hanson? He wasn't creative enough. Lujan? Clayton shook his head. As satisfying as that would be to believe, Derek Lujan had been on the planet's surface when someone had tampered with this transmitter.

Well, Lujan had better show up soon, he thought. And he'd better have some good explanations for his tardiness. Where is the boy? He should have been here by the time our jet packs brought us up to the top of this amazing mountain.

"Captain Winthrop."

Clayton looked up sharply, unaccustomed to being addressed

in so sour a tone. He saw a tall, spindly woman with jet-black hair dressed in worn trousers and a white cotton shirt. Her eyes were hard and dark, her movements crisp and controlled. Jacqueline stood at her elbow.

"Captain Winthrop, I need to talk to you," the woman said. "We are not the only people on this planet."

Her words cut off the clipped remark he wanted to make about her tone of voice. Her words and the even gaze Jacqueline was sending his way. He knew that look all too well: This is a wounded creature, and don't you dare hurt it.

"What do you mean?" Clayton asked.

"We were not the only ones to survive the—" Phoenix faltered; she had almost said the wrath of the Mother Earth. "The natural calamities on Earth," she continued. "A group of Native Americans survived, but in a primitive state. They've built themselves up from nothing, Captain. They've built up a culture and a way of life that are unique, and we've gone to great pains to see that it wasn't overwhelmed by the rest of us, by our technology. Captain—" Suddenly the command slipped from her voice. "Captain, I'm begging you. You must see that it doesn't change. You must protect the People."

Clayton exchanged a startled glance with his wife, who shrugged openly, as bewildered as he. Then he looked back at Jim Martin.

Martin took a deep breath and nodded. "There are so many things to talk about, so many plans to be made—but she's right. It's something we'd better make clear before any of your crew stumble across them accidentally."

A prickling sensation crept up Clayton's neck. "Where are these people?" he asked.

"North of here," Jim told him. "About two hundred miles. They've inhabited an old cliff dwelling in the Verde Valley."

Clayton's mind was racing. Two hundred miles north—the probe site. My God, do you suppose Lujan—

"Are they hostile?" he demanded.

"No," Phoenix jumped in. "They're a peaceful people who respect the land and all the creatures of the Mother Earth. But they—they know you're coming, and they—they aren't exactly—"

Just then a young boy pounded up to them. "Dr. Martin, Dr. Martin. Mrs. Mendoza says come quick! There's a machine crawling up the mountain, and it's not one of ours!"

*   *   *

"What are you doing in that thing?" Clayton demanded as Lujan climbed out of the landcrawler, hiding his relief at seeing his first officer alive and well. Lightning flashed all through the eastern sky, where ominous thunderclouds had engulfed every star. The wind was picking up, and the smell of rain pervaded the air.

"Problem with the shuttle, Captain," Lujan reported as he climbed out. He had stopped the vehicle on what was obviously a landing pad of some sort, perhaps two hundred yards along the roadway from the northernmost tower. With the captain stood four other people, and beyond them lay a well-lit compound. His suspicion had been right; fertile Earth had not destroyed her spawn.

"I've got Terry and Mike Johanneson checking it out," Lujan continued as he secured the landcrawler's door against the coming rain, "but I wanted to meet with you. My God, it's true." He turned to the other figures standing behind Winthrop in the deep shadows of tall trees. His arrival must have been quite a surprise to them, but then, they wouldn't have an electronic security system. Not anymore. "Gentlemen—ladies—let me shake your hand. I never in a million years thought I'd meet a native Terran."

Clayton was put off, disarmed by Lujan's apparently heartfelt emotion on meeting the Survivors. More equipment failure— more sabotage, that was. Couldn't the boy see something was wrong? But even if he did, he was canny enough not to talk about it in front of strangers. They needed a private talk, and they needed it soon. Maybe that was why Lujan's reports had been so tight-lipped. "How long till we can get the warp terminal set up here?" Clayton asked, postponing the subject for a more discreet time.

"Twenty-four hours," Lujan assured him. "Thirty-six at the most. I can't believe this," he repeated as a deep rumbling of thunder crept up, seemingly from the bowels of the earth, and rattled the air around them. "You've kept it all running, haven't you? This whole compound—streetlights! Incredible. And the paving on that road I came up—how did you manage? You are indeed a tribute to the quality of the task force left behind, to—*what in God's name is that?*"

In the illumination of a lightning bolt a dark shape swooped toward the Mayall Tower behind them. Wings spread, its bulk backlit against the menacing thunderclouds, it seemed a nightmare apparition from hell itself.

"Tala!" Phoenix breathed, pushing forward from behind Jim Martin and Gail Mendoza.

"Debbie, do you know something about that?" Jim asked incredulously.

"Yeah, I know something," she growled. "It's Coconino. Coconino and a celux—oh, you crazy fool, what do you think you're going to— *No-o-o!*" Her rebuke turned to panic as she saw a security guard step out of the shadows and take aim with a disrupter rifle.

Like a bolt from a crossbow she launched herself at the guard. On his nightly patrol, Clint Patrone had spotted the intruder also, but this time he was prepared for trouble. The disrupter fit snugly against his shoulder, comfortable and deadly.

Phoenix hit him at the waist, knocking him down and sending the shot wild. Clint swore roundly, struggling to bring the weapon to bear.

But Jim Martin was not far behind Phoenix. He snatched the weapon away from the young man. "What in God's name are you doing with a rifle, Clint?"

"I knew there'd be trouble," Clint panted, gaining his feet. "I knew when that Indian lit out of here this afternoon, there'd be trouble."

"You butcher!" Phoenix hissed, rolling to a crouch and ready to tackle him again, heedless of the blood that trickled from a badly scraped arm. "You're everything he accused us of being!"

"Settle down, both of you!" Martin roared. "Clint, you're on restriction as of right now! Report to your room till you're sent for. And Debbie, will you kindly tell us how that apparition—"

A mighty crack of thunder rent the air, cutting off all speech. In the simultaneous flash of lightning they saw the circling Coconino dive for the tower, a slender shaft in his hand. In the open dome the beacon still chattered, forgotten by all but him.

The pipe bit deep into the apparatus of the transmitter, sending shock waves back up Coconino's arm. The sudden impact nearly tore him from Tala's back, but the creature sensed his peril and countered to keep him from falling. Then, with an angry trumpeting, Tala himself turned on the beacon. Thunder and war cry exacerbated the animal's hatred for this Thing in the tower, and he discharged his horn.

The electrical charge struck the beacon and overloaded the circuits, frying connections and sending sparks jumping among the relays. There was a crackling, a hissing, and then the acrid smell of burnt wiring. In a moment small flames licked at the equipment.

Phoenix charged up the road toward the tower. "Coconino, you stupid, pigheaded son of a—" The beating of wings drowned out her voice as Tala landed, fiery-eyed and trumpeting, on the roadway. Behind him loomed the Mayall and Seward towers, and sheet lightning lit up the space between them where she and Coconino had first climbed to this place. Was it only a week ago? Less than that—five days. Five days that had consumed an eternity for her, an eternity of sinking in an ocean where she lost everything she'd come to love.

Now Coconino looked down at her from the back of the unicorn. "Damn it, Coconino, that was a worthless gesture," she shouted. "You're too late! They're already here."

"I know," he said simply.

"Then do you mind telling me what this is all about?" she demanded, infuriated by his calm when he had so nearly been killed.

Coconino looked up the sloping roadway toward the group of figures staring in amazement. "Tell them not to speak to the sky anymore," he said. "Tell the Others they must go away and not come back. Tell them the Earth is no longer their home and they must leave her alone. She does not want them here."

"Coconino, you can't just send them away. It doesn't work like that." Phoenix was nearly weeping with frustration. "Besides, you're not the only people on this planet. There are some of us who've been waiting a long time for these Others to show up, and we don't intend to kick them out, even if we could. Damn, look what you've done!"

Flames were visible now in the Mayall Tower. Jim Martin and Gail Mendoza were running back toward the compound, calling for fire fighters as they went. But Coconino only gazed down at the Witch Woman, her sweat- and tear-stained face gleaming in the occasional flashes of lightning. "Come with me," he said gently. "You do not belong here."

"I don't belong with the People, either!"

"You are Phoenix, my sister-brother," he told her. "You belong with me."

"I'm not your goddamn sister!" she shrieked. "Or your brother! And till they fix what's wrong with my body I can't be anything else!"

Behind them alarms sounded and voices clamored as men and women rushed for fire-fighting equipment. But Phoenix heard only the roaring in her own brain, the vociferous silence that followed unintentional confession. There was no chance he had not understood what she meant. She waited, naked before his pain-masked eyes.

Suddenly Coconino bent low from Tala's back and seized her roughly in one arm. For a moment Phoenix thought he would drag her up with him, carry her far from the tumult on the mountain and back to the Valley of the People. But he only clutched her to him, his cheek pressed to hers, his lips at her ear. "Seek your fulfillment where you will, Witch Woman," he said. "Mine lies with the Mother Earth." Then, as the first of the Men-on-the-Mountain pounded down the hill toward them, he released her. One last cry tore from his chest, and as one, man and beast hurled themselves into the sky.

"I say we find the bloody savage and string him up by the balls!" Jackson raged, his face flushed from his thick neck to his balding pate. "And I want Clint off restriction. He's the only one who responded with any sense. If you hadn't stopped him, that red bastard would be history and the Mayall Tower would still be standing!"

"Violence won't solve anything," Gail Mendoza replied, her voice edged with uncharacteristic impatience. "Your nephew was out of line, and he stays on restriction pending a hearing."

"Out of line?" Jackson shrieked. "He's not the one who incinerated the tower. I've got four of my people in the Infirmary still, I don't know how many treated and released."

"Twenty-three!" Gail snapped. "And they are not 'your people.' In fact, only three of those injured work a security shift, one of whom is indeed in the Infirmary—my grandson Lyle. Now, I'm not saying we don't need to deal with Coconino, but we will not fly off the handle in righteous retribution and jeopardize our relationship with the primitives!" She turned to Jim Martin, summarily ending the conversation. "Jim, any idea on the damages?"

Jim glanced up. He had been watching the thin woman beside him, trying to penetrate the veil of pain that had nothing to do with her bandaged forearm. "Doesn't matter," he said softly, turning his gaze once more to her drawn face. "The fire's contained; nothing in the tower was needed for daily survival. As for the equipment lost—antiquated. Unnecessary. For now we have our link to the stars."

There was a moment of silence. Though they had spoken of it

before, none of the people seated around the table had quite grasped the reality of their new situation. It was still hard to shift their minds from old patterns of thought.

"Well, then," Gail said finally. "Loss of property irrelevant. No loss of life but considerable jeopardy to the fire fighters. And the idea of an assault on our equipment. Not something to be dismissed, I'm afraid." Her voice became gentle. "Debbie? We need your input. We need your . . . perspective on this."

Phoenix did not raise her eyes. Something nagged at her consciousness, something she still didn't recognize. Instead she stared at her bandaged arm, concentrating on the pain, clinging to the pain like a tree in a sandstorm. If she let go, if she let go for even a second— "He said," she told them, "not to talk to the sky anymore." Pain is real. Pain is familiar. Hope is a stranger and ephemeral. "He said, tell the Others to go away and not come back." You can leave the Earth, go to where they can heal you, go to a new life and leave all of this behind—but not pain. No, never pain. Pain is always with you. Pain is on the mountain, pain is with the People, pain is out there among the stars. "He said this is not their home anymore; the Mother Earth does not want them here."

"How do you suggest we deal with him?" Gail asked.

Finally Phoenix looked up blankly into the older woman's inquiring eyes. "Send them away," she echoed.

Silence. Beside her Jim Martin cleared his throat. "I think, Gail, we need to go out to their village and speak with the Mother. She'll understand that we can't let this incident go. Perhaps her tribe has a way of dealing with the boy or perhaps he'll be turned over to us and—"

"You'll never get Coconino." Phoenix's voice was quiet, but they all turned to her. "He's a god to those people. He rides Tala, the one-horned kachina. He's the finest of the People, the wisest, the best. He speaks to the Mother Earth. If She told him to do this, you'll never touch him." Still she fought not to recognize the nagging at her consciousness.

"The hell we won't!" Jackson growled. "No savage with a bow and arrow is gonna stop me from—"

"*From what?*" Phoenix demanded, suddenly vicious. "From acting on your ignorant and self-centered ideas of right and wrong? From taking what you want, regardless of its impact? From forcing your narrow-minded views on others?"

"Listen here, lady," he warned.

"No, you listen!" she snarled. Jim's hand rested on her good arm, tightening slowly, but she ignored it. "All of you listen. How can you presume to judge him for what he did? How do you know he wasn't right?"

"That's why we need to talk to him, Debbie," Gail soothed. "We need him to explain to us, and we can explain to him—"

"So *you* can decide who's right and who's wrong. But who made you the authority? Any of you? How do you know *he* isn't the authority? How do you know we shouldn't all be listening to what *he* decides?"

Jackson snorted. "That backward brave? The sum total of his intelligence is in his loincloth."

"And it's twice yours on both counts!"

"Enough!" Gail snapped. "Eric, you will refrain from such comments or I will have you removed from this meeting. And as for you, young woman . . ." She took a deep breath. "It is late and we are all tired, and I suggest we continue in the morning."

"Late! You're damn right it's late." Phoenix forced her weary body to its feet. "Maybe too late. But I never learned how to roll over and die."

"Where are you going?" Jim asked.

She hadn't known until he asked. "The only place left to me—no-man's-land," she replied. "You know, that place between two opposing forces that gets shelled by them both."

He was on his feet beside her. "Where you can see both sides," he countered. "It's a unique position. We need your help. You're his friend, Debbie; you can—"

"My name is not Debbie!" she shouted, shaking off his arm and the last vestiges of rational thought. "It's Phoenix! And I am not just his friend, I am his sister-brother. And if he is a child of the Mother Earth, then so am I." She lifted her face, her arms outstretched, as the nagging finally came into focus. "Do you hear me, Mother? So am I!"

In the startled silence she fled the room.

Coconino was waiting for her at the foot of the mountain. Mounted on Tala, he was a darker shape in the shadows just before dawn. To her sleepless eyes he was strength personified as she staggered to a halt some five feet away.

"The People call us," he said simply. "We must go home quickly."

She nodded, shifted her bow and quiver to her good shoulder. She had picked them up from their cache just below the rim of the mountain. "The Men-on-the-Mountain may come looking for us," she told him. "I don't know. We'd better stay close to cover."

Tala whistled softly, and Coconino rubbed the great beast's neck ridges. Gray light filtered to them from the east, gleamed on the white bandages of her arm. "What is that?" he asked, pointing at them.

She waved the arm carelessly. "Nothing. Minor. I tried to take out a security guard—did, too, the bastard. Scraped up my arm a little."

For a moment she thought he smiled, but of course it was a trick of the light. Such a statue, so magnificently silhouetted in the dawn, would never smile. Damn fool, she thought, you don't know how hopeless it is, do you? But I'm the bigger fool, because I do and here I am anyway.

Somehow she crossed the last few feet separating them and struggled up behind him. "I'm tired," she whispered, sagging against his back. "Let's go home."

CHAPTER NINETEEN

Lujan lounged in the open door of the landcrawler, eyeing the ancient aircraft with obvious skepticism. He had driven the landcrawler off to one side, turning the landing pad over to the "hopper," as the natives called it. It would, they said, take off vertically, then fly horizontally at speeds up to two hundred miles per hour.

Clayton Winthrop was grinning like an idiot. "This is great!" the captain kept saying, circling the hopper and patting its metal sides, a gesture that amused his pragmatic wife. She, like Lujan, watched from a distance, indulging the child in her man. "This is unbelievable!" he went on. "And you've kept them in service all these years?"

"Like Ben Franklin's ax," Jim Martin told him. "Of course, it's had three new handles and two new heads since then."

"But the fact that you've managed to maintain flight capability under these conditions—Jacqueline, look at this! Flaps! Can you believe that?"

Lujan hauled himself upright and approached the craft. "Sir, I want to go on record as objecting to this flight," he said. "I can't believe it's safe."

"Come on, Lujan, you checked it out yourself," Clayton rejoined. "Don't be a party pooper! Just because you're stuck with that landcrawler . . ."

Lujan scowled. "I checked it all right, sir, but I'm no expert on these museum pieces."

"I am," said the pilot, a woman in her mid-thirties. Her mousy brown hair was sun-bleached, and a spattering of freckles decorated her face. There was an easy confidence about her that made Lujan believe what she said. "I've logged plenty of hours on this baby and two others just like her," she told him.

"She's safer in the air than you are going down that mountain road."

Lujan walked around the hopper, pretending to give it another skeptical examination, but his thoughts were elsewhere. Two cultures! Not just one group of Terran survivors but two, and in this one area. Who knew how many others there might be on other parts of the planet?

Well, if they were all as primitive as the village to the north he'd been told about, that was no problem. Such cultures were easy to control and could actually be used to great advantage. It was this technological one that presented the problem. The beacon was out now, at least, thanks to that flying phenomenon who'd caused such an uproar last night. But flight capability could bring them to the probe site and the landing party that was inevitable . . .

Lujan came back to the captain. "Well, since you're set on bringing the shuttle back yourself, I'll head down the mountain and retrieve the mini-shuttle." The mechanical arms on the landcrawler could easily lift the mini-shuttle and secure it for trucking back up the mountain. "Dr. Martin, be sure this landing area is well cleared for the shuttle landing. It'll be tricky enough with the trees this close. Captain, I'll see you back here in a few hours. Dr. Winthrop, enjoy your flight." With one more wary look at the aircraft, Lujan climbed into the landcrawler and started down the mountain.

The aircraft had been a real blow to him. The Winthrops could reach the shuttle and the mech techs working on it long before Lujan had a chance to intervene. Once the word about this mountain culture was out, it was all over. He must at all costs keep any landing party from making contact with either the mountain dwellers or the Indians.

Judging from what he'd learned via a transmitter discreetly planted on Gail Mendoza, the Indians were as anxious to avoid contact as he. At least, the one who had attacked the tower wanted nothing to do with the *Homeward Bound*. That could definitely be used to his advantage. But before he decided what to do about the mountain, he needed to know how much of Winthrop's report had gotten past Karen.

As he hailed the ship, he saw the ancient aircraft rise and head almost due north. He'd tried his best to get the captain to wait on the mountain while he fetched the shuttle, but Mendoza's offer to fly him there was too appealing to Winthrop for any hope of dissuasion. The best Lujan could do was see to it that Dr. Winthrop was included in the expedition.

Karen responded immediately to his call. "Derek, I've been trying to reach you. Tony Hanson is at the shuttle site, and he's getting awfully antsy. I, uh, altered the captain's radio before he left, but Tony has a hard time buying that both the captain's and your communications equipment are out."

"None of Winthrop's reports got through, then?" Lujan asked.

"Just the one from the mini-shuttle: safe touchdown and start up the mountain. I told Tony the thunderstorms last night were probably preventing you from transmitting, but that doesn't hold water this morning."

"You're doing great," he told her. "I'll have a report to transmit in a couple minutes. But I'll talk to Hanson first. Patch me through to the shuttle, will you."

"Derek, are you sure—"

"Patch me through," he snapped. "I know exactly how to deal with Tony Hanson."

A moment later the ship's second officer came on. "Mr. Lujan, this is Anthony Hanson. Is the captain with you?"

That stiff, petty little supply officer. Lujan was looking forward to this. "Mr. Hanson, where are you?" he demanded.

"I'm at the shuttle site, sir. I—"

"And who is in command of the *Homeward Bound*? Mister, you are the second officer, and while Captain Winthrop and I are ashore on an unexplored and possibly hostile planet, I don't find it in the best interest of the ship or her crew that you take it upon yourself to leave your post and place yourself at risk as well! Now, get yourself back to the ship immediately and report back to me when you're safely aboard. I'll be standing by for your call."

In less than ten minutes Hanson was back on the line. "Anthony Hanson reporting from the deck of the *Homeward Bound* as ordered, *sir*."

"Good," Lujan said, and waited a short beat. Then he continued in a milder tone. "Look, Tony, I'm sorry I jumped on you, but the captain had a near accident here last night, and the idea of having all three of us off the *Homeward Bound*—I keep remembering the *Aladdin* . . ."

"Where is the captain, Mr. Lujan?" Hanson pressed.

"He is attempting to fly the mini-shuttle to the probe site," Lujan told him. "The doctor is with him."

The disbelief in the following silence was almost palpable. "What's he using for fuel?" Hanson demanded. The mini-shuttle normally used all its fuel in the landing process.

"I guess it was a smooth landing," Lujan lied. "It's the only thing on this mission so far that *has* been smooth. But he and I both checked the gauges; it looked like enough to make the trip. And after last night no one wanted to stay on that mountain any longer than necessary."

"Why?" Hanson asked, hooked. "What did you find?"

"First of all, " Lujan began, deliberately digressing to annoy the man, "the outpost up there was a shambles. I don't know what went through there, a fire or a hurricane or the wrath of God himself, but it is a total ruin. Why that ancient beacon cranked up and let out a signal is beyond me—maybe a thunderstorm touched it off. The captain was awfully disappointed that so little remained of the place."

"And?" Hanson prompted when Lujan paused.

"Well, you know the captain," Lujan continued. "He went inside what was left of the tower where this beacon was, and—well, I suppose the thing just shorted out. Anyway, a fire started. And the structure was so rotten, it didn't take much—a wall fell, trapped him inside. We managed to get him out, but it was a pretty harrowing ten minutes, let me tell you."

Lujan was enjoying the fiction, embellishing it as he went along. "Then this tower was right above the roadway we needed to go down, and I was afraid the whole thing would topple over on us. So we just holed up in the landcrawler till morning. The tower was still smoldering, but it finally cooled down enough for the captain and I to inspect it and determine we could pass below it in relative safety. We came back down the mountain as fast as we could. By then we saw how late it was, and he wanted to get back to the probe site the fastest way possible, so he decided to take the mini-shuttle while I called in a report."

Lujan could picture the supply officer's face as he tried to digest this yarn. "Why doesn't the captain call in from the mini-shuttle?" Hanson asked.

"For chrissake, Tony," Lujan snapped, "he'll be there in twenty minutes—" Lujan took an audible breath. "—if things go smoothly. I'm the one stuck in this landcrawler for five hours. Doesn't it make sense I should call in the report?"

He was down the mountain now, approaching the grounded mini-shuttle. "You're in charge for now, Tony. If you don't hear from the captain in twenty minutes, let me know. I'm counting on you.'' He loved the English language; so much could be said without being said. ''Tell Karen to stand by for my report now. See you later.'' He cut off the channel and switched over to a high-speed transmission mode before Hanson could object.

As his fabricated report whirred over the communication equipment, Lujan pulled the landcrawler up beside the mini-shuttle. Loading it onto the crawler would be the cleanest part of his work today. At least Hanson was out of his hair temporarily. That would leave only Terry and Mike at the shuttle site, and they'd believe whatever he told them.

He glanced at his chronometer as he opened the hatch and started to climb out of the landcrawler. The Winthrops had been airborne for some twenty minutes now.

Almost as an afterthought he reached back inside the cab, touched a detonator, and blew them out of the sky.

Coconino had seen the Flying Machine pass over their heads early in the day. ''They'll be waiting for us at the village,'' Phoenix assumed. ''They'll tell the Mother you destroyed their tower.''

Coconino only grunted and rolled onto his back in the shade of a rock outcropping where they had taken cover as the Flying Machine passed. The late summer sky was so blue that it seemed unreal, and the temperature was so comfortable that he felt he could just close his eyes and sleep forever. If only there were no pain and no drums.

Beside him Phoenix forced herself to her feet. Her limbs felt like weights, and she knew if she did not keep moving, she would soon be dead asleep herself. Stepping into the sunlight, she stretched herself luxuriously, then paused with her arms flung high, trying to draw in strength from the pure air and the sweet-smelling soil.

Coconino watched her, dark skin glistening in the light, naked except for the shirt that once again served her as a loincloth. Framed against the azure sky, her outstretched body filled him with a longing that drove back the pain, quieted the pounding drums. She is your father's wife, he told himself sternly, but he had ceased to think of that Man-on-the-Mountain. Dick McKay and all the others were part of some other existence. This was Phoenix again, his sister-brother, a Witch Woman. His Witch Woman. He remembered what she had said in the light of the burning tower.

She felt his gaze on her and turned toward him. Lack of sleep had darkened her eyes, but even now the frustration of the Mountain had begun to drain away. "You have spoken with the Others?" he asked.

"They're good people, Coconino," she told him. "The ones I met, anyway. But you're right—they don't belong here."

"And were they able to do for you, with their medicine, what the Men-on-the-Mountain could not?"

For a moment she held his gaze; then, turning away, she answered softly. "No. I would have to go back with them or wait for other doctors to come. I can't do either one."

Slowly he rose and crossed to where she stood. His own intimate knowledge of pain now deepened his understanding of what she felt, what she had lived with for so long and must now bear for the rest of her life. Kneeling before her, he touched the smooth, flat skin of her belly, where no child had ever ripened. "My seed is strong," he said stubbornly. "Like the Grandfather. I could give you a child."

Her cry was half laugh, half sob, but she did not rage at him. Instead she buried her hands in his matted hair and clutched him to her. "You arrogant son of a . . ." Her voice choked off, and she was silent, only holding him. Coconino drank in the feel of her body pressed against his cheek, his chest, his arms, washing away the pain. "What would I do with a child, anyway?" she asked. "Can you see me hunting with a baby strapped to my back? I am what I am, Coconino, and a baby just doesn't fit into the picture."

"And I am Coconino," he replied, "and I will marry a Witch Woman. I have always known it."

At this she drew his head back and gazed down into his eyes. "No, Coconino," she said gently, knowing finally what she had refused to admit before. "You must marry Castle Rock; she will give you the children you must have. A wise man does not scatter his seed on barren rock."

Regret was all too clear in her face and voice. Stubbornly he thought, That is what you say now. Perhaps it is what you will say next time. But it is not what you will always say, and I will wait. I will marry the Witch Woman. And the Mother Earth will bless us, for we are both Her children.

It is the least She can do for the service we must perform now.

Lujan recoiled from the gory corpse, his skin suddenly cold and clammy in the ninety-degree heat. His already unsettled stomach rebelled, and he retched violently, but even that could not clear the stink of blood and putrefying flesh from his throat and nostrils. Damn Dillon. And damn the lady doctor. And damn this sweltering heat!

But cursing would not change the features on this third corpse, would not clean away the mess of this carnage, would not untangle the situation he now found himself in. His options were gone. There was only one course of action for him now . . .

He'd had no trouble locating the wreckage of the downed aircraft; a small transmitter in the cargo bay had survived the crash. His plan had been simply to remove the bodies of the Winthrops, place them in the mini-shuttle, and crash it somewhere near the probe site. Thus their unfortunate demise could be verified in a place and under conditions that Tony Hanson could inspect for himself. There might be suspicion, speculation, but those he could deal with.

It wouldn't have solved all his problems, but it would have been a start. He could no longer keep the verdant condition of Earth quiet, but he could probably prevent contact with human life-forms. There remained two major challenges: arranging for the expedition to be cut short and finding some reason why return expeditions would be hazardous or, better yet, costly.

But all that was academic now. In the nauseating process of removing the bodies from the aircraft his neatly laid plans had curdled with the contents of his stomach. He had identified the pilot first and the grizzly remains of Captain Winthrop. But mutilated as it was, the third body was not that of Jacqueline Winthrop. It was a man, and though there was no face left to recognize, he guessed it might be Jim Martin.

Damn the good doctor! He could almost hear her: "You go ahead, Clay, I want to observe their techniques in burn treatment. I'll catch up with you later." And Martin—he was a high-ranking official, from what Lujan could gather. His disappearance would not be lightly dismissed on the mountain. There would be search parties. At least, he thought grimly, there will be no air search.

But Tony Hanson would not be persuaded to leave Earth with Jacqueline Winthrop still unaccounted for. If her body were not found in the wreckage of the mini-shuttle, they would believe her alive, and Lujan had no time to execute a kidnapping and rectify that. Briefly he considered trying to pass off the pilot as Dr. Winthrop, but even after a second crash too many identifiers would likely remain intact.

The crash site was a flat, shrubby area of desert where winds and tumbleweed would soon obscure the debris. Lujan decided to leave it and the bodies for the coyotes and vultures. Thank God no flammable fuels were used in the aircraft so no smoke or scorching would aid searchers. Considering the amount of territory that had to be covered, it would not be quickly found.

As for the mini-shuttle, he'd have to disconnect its sounders and ditch it somewhere else. He needed to buy time, time to set up his only remaining option. Staggering weakly back to the landcrawler, he crawled inside and turned on the environment controls. After several deep breaths, with the cool air blowing gently across his face and chest, he opened a comm channel. "Karen? This is Derek. Have landing parties stand by. As soon as the captain and Dr. Winthrop are safely back at the shuttle site, I think we can authorize the research teams to warp down. That site should make a good temporary HQ; there's plenty of water, and—well, it's kind of pretty, actually, in its own way."

Lucky for the landing parties, he thought. They won't be leaving.

Karen delivered the message to Tony Hanson, then turned calmly back to her communication panel. Outwardly, she was an island of quiet on a bridge now jumping with excitement and activity. Inwardly, her heart beat just a little faster and her breathing was shallow. Would Derek want her to come down with one of the landing parties? Would she at last see the planet of her fantasies?

For days now she had worked to quell her despair as it became clear to her that Derek's plans did not include having other members of the crew visit the planet's surface. To have come all this way—but then, it was what she had expected. The favorable readings from the probe before it had ceased to transmit, the sudden sounding of a beacon, had kindled brief hope in her, but she had choked it back, knowing Derek wanted no one but himself to set foot on Earth's surface. Now, though . . . Should she tell him how much she wanted to see Earth? To set foot on its legendary surface, to gaze at the horizon for some glimpse of a man on a horse—

Karen forced herself to breathe deeply, to control her rapid pulse. Of course not. She would never tell Derek. He might not laugh, but— She just didn't want him to know. Not about that part of her. It had always been secret. Besides, what she wanted wouldn't matter, only what Derek wanted. Derek would decide.

Under control once more, Karen returned to her work.

"It's my fault," Lujan muttered, his face suitably ashen thanks to a little pill from the medical stores. "I take full responsibility. I should have known better than to trust the fuel gauge. Everything else has gone wrong on this mission; why should that be an exception?"

Tony Hanson sat across from him in the ready room of the *Homeward Bound*, his pale blue eyes glittering. "Sir, to deny the possibility of sabotage at this point would show blatant disregard for the facts," Hanson said, "and my report—"

"Of course it's sabotage!" Lujan roared. "The navigational error, the communications failures, the fuel gauge—I'm not stupid, Tony!" Hanson retreated, unaccustomed to such an outburst from the slick, controlled first officer. "The question is who, and why, and what are we going to do about it several hundred light-years from home?"

"When my report reaches Argo—" Hanson began, but Lujan waved him off. His report, of course, had been squelched by Karen at the comm controls.

"We can't continue to risk lives on this planet," Lujan protested.

"With all due respect, sir," Hanson replied, no respect in his voice, "we have no assurance that attempting to warp back to Argo will be any less hazardous than remaining here."

Lujan sighed and slumped back in his chair. "You're right, of course. We'll mount search parties and look for the captain and Dr. Winthrop. Wait till our messages get through to Argo, wait till we get a response back. The planet is habitable, at least; we can set up camp down there and make use of native plants and animals to extend our supplies. Take care of that, will you, Tony? Take down whatever tools and equipment are needed to establish a base. I'll coordinate the search teams. The captain's a damn good pilot; he may have been able to bring the mini-shuttle down with a minimum of damage."

What a story, he thought as Hanson left the room. It won't hold up for too long. I'll have to come up with something better for the folks back on Argo. Let's see, now, how many crew will I need to get back safely? I can probably do it on six. Myself, Mike Johanneson—no, he won't go without his wife, and I can't trust her to keep her mouth shut. Nigel, then. Nigel and Randy and Mark—oh, yes, Karen . . .

Tala stood high on a ridge, clothed in darkness, nostrils quivering. A breeze wafted up from the valley floor, a breeze of death and putrefaction, for a dead city lay there in the darkness being reclaimed but slowly by wind, water, and dust. There was a greater evil, Tala knew, taking root beyond it somewhere, though even his excellent night vision could not spy it. Tomorrow they would pass close to it.

The unicorn did not know why it was evil, only that it was to be feared. And he feared it, not with trembling, like the hare or the quail, but with anger. It was not to be avoided but dealt with. He and Coconino would deal with it.

Behind him the man slept deeply, drawing needed strength from this gift of the Mother Earth. His woman slept also, exhausted, but she had never known how to receive a gift. Why does he keep her, Tala wondered, this useless female? He does not mate with her, she does not bring him other females, she does not lead the herd in his absence. Instead, when he leaves his herd, as it is proper to do in the summer, she goes with him. Why does he allow this? It only slows him down.

But the ways of Men were strange, even the ways of Coconino. It was not for Tala to judge, and so he suffered the woman's presence. For now.

An owl called from across the valley. "Mine," it said. "Mine." Some distance away another owl replied. "Mine. Mine." They could hear each other's voices, and they knew where they were not welcome. Not so this evil that spread even now upon the bosom of the Mother Earth. In the time Tala had stood here, the evil had grown and strengthened, nourishing itself on the unwilling Earth.

Wake, Coconino! Tala commanded. Wake! Dawn comes, and we must make haste. Soon it will be too strong even for us.

CHAPTER TWENTY

"Sabotaged?" Gail Mendoza's face was ashen, as drained of color as her body was of strength. They had waited till nightfall for either the shuttle or the hopper to return, thinking they might have taken a side trip to the primitive village or to one of the impressive natural wonders in the area. But the hoppers had no night-flying capabilities, and when darkness settled finally over the mountain, they knew their craft was in trouble somewhere.

On top of that, Derek Lujan had not come back up the mountain with the mini-shuttle. Instead, his landcrawler had been seen heading east, over broken highways, toward one of the dead cities. Or perhaps he would head north before he got there, along one of the washes, where his vehicle could churn its way through the dry riverbed and back toward the shuttle that had brought him, the shuttle that Captain Winthrop had apparently never reached.

By morning Eric Jackson, with Gail's approval, had search teams organized. Only two aircraft were left, but there were numerous land vehicles to join in the effort. Solar-powered trucks started down the mountain at daybreak, each equipped with a radio and a map of the quadrant it was to search. In the mountain hangar nervous pilots made thorough checks of their hoppers—and found they would not fly.

It had taken mechanics little time to find out what the problem was. The power units had been tampered with. Ruth Anderson had brought the news to Gail and Eric.

"That primitive!" Jackson howled, slamming his fist on Mendoza's desk. "I knew he was—"

"Oh, shut up, Eric!" Gail snapped, her restraint gone, her control eviscerated by the untoward news. "Coconino couldn't begin to sabotage our hoppers; he hadn't the knowledge. Ruth, you're sure?''

Ruth was as pale as her superior, her mind overwhelmed by the implications of the treachery. ''Bob checked them both out himself, Gail. The solar units are completely fused. So is the one spare we had.''

Reeling, Gail tried to assign consequences to the information, to make deductions, draw conclusions. Repairing the units was impossible; they would have to be replaced. That meant new ones needed to be constructed—who could do that? Debbie McKay was good with hoppers, but Debbie was gone. Solar units might be out of her league, anyway. Who else? Jim . . .

She stared dumbly at the maps spread on her desk, at the quadrants drawn for the search. No air search was possible now, not for weeks at best, months, more likely. And the usefulness of a ground search—

''It was one of those people from the *Homeward Bound*,'' Eric charged. ''Had to be. Get the Winthrop woman in here; we'll get to the bottom of this.''

''Eric!'' Gail Mendoza rose shakily to her feet, trying to exert a will she no longer possessed. ''You don't give the orders here. Do you think if Jackie had anything to do with this, she'd be waltzing blithely around our Infirmary, waiting for us to come after her?''

''Jesus, she's probably sabotaged half the equipment in there! I'll send two of my boys.''

Overcome by stress and lack of sleep, Gail sank weakly into her chair. The absurdity of his logic was too much for her; laughter spilled uncontrolled from her lips. She laughed till tears streamed down her face, and then she was crying, weeping for all that had been lost, that would never come again. Willful sabotage in a community that for five hundred years had depended on cooperation for survival. The loss of their flight capability, a cherished link with their technological forebears. And Jim Martin's hopper lost—

Lost? She stared stupidly at the maps once more. If the other hoppers had been sabotaged, then his . . . Oh, Jim, my good, strong right arm. You always backed my authority even if you thought my decision was wrong. It was your calm, rational perspective that balanced this board and made it possible for me to lead us forward. I relied on you so much . . .

Wearily she lifted her head, straightened herself in her chair. ''Eric, call in the ground search teams.''

He was stunned. "But the search—"

"It is obvious that someone does not want that hopper found," she snapped. "If they sabotaged the hoppers, they may have sabotaged the trucks as well. Call them all back and have them checked out. Thoroughly. And Ruth, please ask Dr. Winthrop to come here. I want to know everything she knows about this Derek Lujan."

Phoenix looked down into the Valley of the People as Tala made his circling approach. Where was the Flying Machine? Where were the angry Men-on-the-Mountain who should be waiting for Coconino, waiting to take him to task for destroying their tower? She had not seen the Machine go back toward the Mountain. Perhaps it had not come here at all, then. Perhaps it had gone to some place where the Others were.

Then she saw the People gathered around Elvira. "What is it? What's happened?" she asked Coconino in trepidation as Tala landed in the center of the village.

"They have been calling us," Coconino told her. "They will go back to the fields now. We have answered."

"What do you mean, calling us?" she persisted as she slid wearily from the unicorn's back, stiff and sore in body and spirit.

Coconino hesitated a moment before he dropped carefully to the ground. The drums had ceased, but the pain continued as he looked at the People—his People. Suddenly he felt a fierce loyalty such as he had only known for individuals: the Witch Woman Lois, his friend Juan, Phoenix. And coupled with it was a compassion that was new to him. His People, the children of the Mother Earth . . . They were so innocent of their enemy—or were they? "For two days they have been here," he told Phoenix. "The drums have sounded, and the People have chanted and danced, calling for Coconino to come home."

"How do you know that?" she demanded.

He looked at her, incredulous that she did not know, never knew, that communion which had been his from childhood. How will you help my People, he thought, when I am . . . With a sudden sagging of spirit he turned toward the fortress on the cliff face. "I heard them," was all he said.

"My son." Two Moons waited for them at the foot of the cliff. As her eyes met those of her son, the silent communion, the *moh-ohtay* between them, made Phoenix feel even more the alien. Two Moons said nothing, but a sudden despair wrote itself on Coconino's face, and his eyes lifted to a chamber in the fortress above. Quietly he and Phoenix followed his mother up the shelves and ladders to the Gatehouse of the Village of the Ancients.

The Mother had been carefully lifted up on the cliff face on a pallet and installed in the cool shelter of the first house of the Village. Here the air was sweet and fresh and the shade plentiful, but there was a roof to shield her from the rain. And here the spirits of the Ancients watched over her while the People executed their summons in the valley below.

Phoenix was surprised to see Ben Gonzales in the darkened room, watching over the wheezing woman. Ben looked up now as the three entered. "Thank God you're here," he whispered. "Listen, you must go back to the mountain right away. Tell them to send a Flying Machine and—"

"No."

The Mother's voice was no more than a hoarse whisper, yet it stopped Gonzales. He turned back to her. "Mother, we have doctors there who can help you, medicines and equipment."

Phoenix thought at first the Mother was choking; then she realized it was laughter. "I have no need of your doctors and your medicine. The Mother Earth calls me, and I go gladly. I have carried the weight of Her service too long. Yet there is one more thing to do before I leave."

"Don't talk, you'll tire yourself." Ben Gonzales fought back a personal despair. The others could not know that he had sat at his own mother's bedside as her life had quietly ebbed. He could hardly bear to watch this good and wise woman, so much like her, slip away unnecessarily.

But she waved him off weakly. "Coconino," she called, and the young man knelt at her side, taking the gnarled brown hand in his.

"I have brought you a gift, Mother," he began, loosing the leather pouch at his waist. "See what I have brought you: the fruit of the Grandfather."

There was a small gasp from Two Moons. She took the pouch and opened it, gazing in wonder at the red saguaro fruit inside. "The seeds," she breathed. "Mother, see all the seeds Coconino has brought us!"

But the Mother seemed unimpressed with the rare offering. She kept her attention on Coconino. "Tell me what happened on the Mountain."

Coconino hesitated, a pause that earned him a sharp glare from the Mother's ancient eyes. "They have much magic,

Mother," he said carefully. "Some of it is very good. But they built a Machine that could speak to the Sky, and it has called down a great curse upon us."

Her cough carried an unmistakable note of derision. "They called nothing down," she wheezed. "The Others would have come with or without their Machine."

"But the Men-on-the-Mountain called out to the Others," Coconino said. "Called out in greeting, invited them to set their poisoned feet upon the Mother Earth. Did you not feel it, Mother? Did you not feel the searing pain in the ground when this—this abomination, this disease touched our Mother Earth?"

Phoenix stared at him, at his face twisted with revulsion, and her stomach knotted. Was this what she had committed herself to, a madman who hated a people he had never met, who claimed to feel their malevolence in the soil of the earth? Then she remembered his cry of pain when he left the library, the cry just as his bare foot touched the sod—

"I felt it," the Mother whispered. "It rent my heart."

"I could not send them back," Coconino moaned, his anguish great. "I could not banish them from the Mother Earth. But I took a stick, a strong stick, and Tala and I flew to the Machine of the Men-on-the-Mountain, the Machine That Speaks to the Sky, and we smashed it. Together we destroyed the Machine that called to the Others, and I told the Men-on-the-Mountain that they must speak no more to the Sky. No Others may come here. None."

There was a long pause; the only sound was the Mother's labored breathing. "That is well," she said finally. "It was rash, but I think it is well that you did it. Because the Way of the People is one of harmony with the Mother Earth and her creatures, the Men-on-the-Mountain sometimes forget how jealously we guard that Way."

"The Men-on-the-Mountain forget much!" Coconino spat.

Suddenly the Mother squinted at him in the gloom, reading his face. Coconino felt oddly naked as her eyes pierced him, as though his heart were open to her and contained some foulness. "You learned too much on the Mountain," she said sharply. "It has poisoned you." He was silent. "What did you learn?"

Coconino lowered his eyes and could not answer.

Phoenix had watched all this through eyes that cried for sleep, dimly aware of the throbbing in her injured arm. But she knew now what the Mother saw, knew she was right. "He read books from the Before Times," she said. "Things the Whites did to the ancestors of the People."

For a moment the Mother shifted her penetrating gaze to Phoenix, but the younger woman met her eyes. She was expunged; she had nothing to hide. Finally the old woman turned back to Coconino. "Put this poison away from you," she said sternly. "It is for you to deal with the Others, and you must not deal from hatred. Clear your mind. Cleanse it. How can you hear the voice of the Mother Earth through the noise of hatred?"

Coconino drew a deep breath but said nothing. Again the Mother turned to Phoenix. The tall woman sat proudly, like a hunter; she had made her choice and was committed to it. But still her eyes were haunted, dark circles of pain sinking them into her face. "How can you be his guardian," the Mother asked, "you who are full of poison yourself? Yet you must be. You are his sister-brother, and yes, you are Witch Woman, though once I doubted it. Stay with him, Bird that Rises from the Ashes of Its Nest. He will need you."

She closed her eyes then, and her head lolled back. A look of panic flickered across Gonzales's face, but as he checked her pulse he relaxed. "She's resting," he said. "But it's only a matter of time. Please. Go to the Mountain. She doesn't have to die."

Coconino rose to the stooped position that was all the low ceiling would allow him. "Yes, she does," he replied. "But we must act first to deal with the Others. Then will her rest be complete."

The bright sunlight seemed unusually harsh as Coconino and the Witch Woman stepped out of the stone building and started back down toward the village. "You cannot kill those people," Phoenix told him bluntly. "They are good, decent people, and you cannot kill them for what they *might* do if they're allowed to stay."

Carelessly descending the ladder, his back to the cliff, Coconino looked down on the collection of mud and stick wickiups and thought how much he would like to do just that. He wondered that the wickiups did not quake from the pain in the soil, pain he must consciously control to keep it from overwhelming him. What grim pleasure in wiping out the source of that pain! But the Mother's admonition was clear and, he knew, correct. "I do not intend to kill them," he assured Phoenix. "I intend to send them away."

Even Phoenix had grown confident in descending the ladders facing out, and she scuttled down behind him despite her fatigue. "They'll go, but they'll only send more back," she told him. "That's not the answer. We have to give them some reason why they shouldn't come back. And don't tell them the Mother Earth doesn't want them; they won't care."

"We will find some way," he said with a confidence he didn't feel. "The Mother Earth will speak to us, and we will find a way."

"Where are you going?" she demanded as he started toward the creek.

"Hunting," he replied.

Her bones protested with weariness. "Hunting? Now?"

"If a gila monster is in my wickiup," he explained patiently, "I cannot put it out unless I know what a gila monster is, how it is dangerous, what parts of it can be touched and which parts must be avoided. So I must learn of these Others. Then I will know how to send them away."

She was confused. "So you're going hunting until they show up in your wickiup?"

"No," he replied. "I am going hunting in a river valley to the south of here, the valley where the Thing fell from the sky. It is not mule deer that I expect to find."

Pain throbbed unexpectedly in Coconino's chest, and his stomach threatened to give back its contents. He sucked in his breath sharply, then forced himself to exhale slowly and take his next breaths with greater care. In a moment he was able to push the pain back, back to its controlled level, back to where it did not interfere with his thinking.

Below them in the lush river valley a plastic city had sprung up. At the center sat the shuttle, a ponderous white behemoth some sixty feet in length with stubby wings jutting from its fuselage. Around it the native grasses and shrubs had been battered in a roughly spherical pattern for several yards, victims of the powerful jets that had slowed the shuttle's final vertical descent. Lujan had spun the craft slowly during the landing as pressure readings from the jets told the shuttle's computer which angle presented the smoothest surface and how far each of the nearly two thousand hollow rods on her underside should protrude to provide a solid, level footing.

Now it was attaching to the earth like a caterpillar to a leaf, its many rods hugging the landscape. A ramp extended from the gaping maw of the cargo bay, its twin doors locked in their tracks on either side. Inside a rainbow of tubes glittered and gleamed, jutting out from two opposing walls at odd angles. Now and again a boxlike vehicle would materialize between the pastel protrusions and trundle down the ramp to churn and tear its way across the helpless foliage.

Clustered about the shuttle were geodesic domes, their slick windowless surfaces like angled, artificial versions of the wicki-ups Coconino knew so well. They seemed small in comparison with the mothering shuttle craft, with the exception of two that were still being assembled. These larger ones would rival the shuttle in size, but their form was the same misshapen wickiup style of the smaller buildings.

Human beings in drab coveralls danced back and forth be-tween the shuttle, the buildings, and the ugly turf-tearing vehi-cles. Their movements seemed to have no purpose, but after fifteen or twenty minutes the vehicles set off, some bouncing and whining across the valley floor, others screaming up into the cloudless sky.

Coconino turned from the abomination to Phoenix, who crouched in the brush beside him. She was entranced, watching the Flying Machines lift off and streak away. "How do they do that?" she breathed. "No rotors, no jets—what gives them lift?"

Feeling his eyes on her, she bristled. "Scientific curiosity," she said. "I'm checking out the gila monster in my wickiup."

"Do not be dazzled by his colors," Coconino retorted.

"Okay, okay. Let's go down and have a look," she said, rising and brushing at her bare thighs. She'd be glad when cooler weather arrived and she could wear leggings of some sort to protect her still-sensitive skin. How Coconino could sit or lie in the prickly foliage was beyond her.

"We will not go into its burrow just yet," Coconino told her, turning to start back down the other side of the rise to where Tala waited testily. The sound of the engines had halted the beast's incessant cropping of thistles, and he trumpeted softly as though accusing Coconino of taking too much time.

"Then what are we doing here?" Phoenix demanded, follow-ing Coconino. "I thought we were 'hunting' Others."

"We are," he replied. "But not in their burrow. We will follow one of their Machines."

"We can't keep up with them," she pointed out.

"We won't have to," he said. "They will stop for us. There."

He pointed to a landcrawler that was veering away to the north.
"That is the one. Quickly!" With a practiced leap he was on
Tala's back, reaching back to help Phoenix up.

Lujan had waited until he was out of visual contact with other
members of the search team before he changed course sharply
and headed north. Karen's voice sounded on the intercom almost
immediately. "Derek, what are you doing?"

"Taking a little side trip," he replied. "There's something
north of here I want to check out."

There was a pause. "What shall I record officially?" she
asked.

He smiled. "That I'm checking out sector HJ, of course." He
had debated whether to leave Karen on the ship, monitoring
reports back to Argo, or bring her down to anchor the search
efforts. In the balmy night air with the smell of earth and growing things around them, he'd been afraid his judgment might
have been based more on his own desires than on the logic of his
planning. But now, with his faculties focused once more on his
scheme, he knew it had been the right choice. She would be
valuable to him in carrying off the marooning.

Odd, he thought, that he should still find her so intriguing.
There was not much challenge anymore in manipulating her.
Perhaps the challenge lay in their physical relationship; Karen
was not easy to excite. She was content enough to give him what
he wanted, but it took his most artful lovemaking to rouse a
genuine response from her. Last night had been a high point.
The raw, unprocessed air of Earth had put new vigor in them
both, and Karen's air of detachment had been easier to overcome. Perhaps tonight—

A blip on his instruments pulled Lujan back from his reflections. He was traveling the relatively flat surface of an ancient
roadbed, and precious little registered on the instruments; hills
rose rapidly on either side of him, forested with cacti and scrubby
pines. He wondered whether it was heat or movement or texture
that alerted the computer in his vehicle that something unusual
was ahead.

When he saw it, he gasped involuntarily. Waiting on the road
were two people and a large animal. His heart pounded, wondering if his luck could be so good as to have put in his path the
perpetrator of the disturbance on the mountain.

As he slowed the vehicle to a halt, he was sure of it. The
primitives had been described as "Indians," and the dark hair

and skin of the man before him fit the image attached to that word. And the animal was obviously a *Celux nobilis,* a unicorn; he'd seen others on their home world, though they were fleshier and more indolent. The woman took him aback, for he was unaccustomed to exposed breasts, but when he trained his eyes on her face, he was sure she was the same woman who had defended the primitive on the mountain. Yes; her arm was still bandaged.

Slowly he climbed out of the landcrawler and faced the pair. They were imposing, less for the sharp features of their unreadable faces than for the authority of their stance. Every muscle in their lean, athletic bodies told him that he was an intruder and must explain himself to them.

So he drew himself up and planted his feet in a manner that, he hoped, told them that he was a leader of his people. He met the man's jet-black eyes first, then the woman's, before he spoke. "I'm Derek Lujan," he said, "of the *Homeward Bound.* You must be Coconino."

Coconino nodded gravely.

"I saw your attack on the tower two nights ago," Lujan continued. "I was hoping we would meet."

Coconino took a few steps laterally, coming no closer to Lujan. "Why is that?" the young primitive asked.

Lujan held the compelling eyes. "I respect a man who acts on his convictions." Peripherally he saw Phoenix shift uneasily, but he did not take his gaze from the man. "And I suspect that you and I have the same purpose in mind."

Now he could see the mental shifting of gears behind the young man's impassive face. "What purpose is that?" Coconino asked evenly.

"You don't want us here," Lujan replied. "You made that very clear. You'd like us to go back where we came from and never set foot on this planet again." His mouth twisted in a wry smile. "That's exactly what I have in mind."

"Exactly?" There was a sarcastic edge to Phoenix's voice as she joined the conversation.

Lujan took his time; he would rather have dealt with only one of them. At the very least, he wished they stood as one unit, but the uneducated primitive had pulled a very crafty psychological maneuver. Lujan had to shift his attention between the two of them, putting himself at a disadvantage in this confrontation. "Not exactly," he told her honestly, then returned his focus to Coconino. "You don't want people disturbing your way of life, bringing new ideas, new ways of doing things. That's what would happen if my people were allowed to come here without restriction.

"As for me, I would like nothing better than to convince my people that there is nothing here they want or need. If they thought there was, they would come and take it. What I want is to be able to find what is of value to them—and not to you—and take it to them."

"Why, you scamming lowlife—" Phoenix began, but Coconino cut her off.

Encouraged, Lujan forged on, focusing now on the woman. "It's no scam," he told her. "I intend to make people pay for what they get instead of letting them steal it from you, destroying what is yours in the process. I'll be glad to compensate you, if you feel that's necessary, for the privilege of taking a few objects back with me. I should think my efforts to keep others away would be compensation enough."

The woman spoke in another language, and though her words were unknown to him, the venom in her tone spoke volumes. Coconino spoke back sharply, and they glared at each other momentarily. Lujan repressed a smile; a house divided was to his advantage.

"This weasel stinks to the mountaintops," Phoenix told Coconino in the tongue of the People.

"And his stench is clear to me," Coconino snapped back. "Unfortunately, you are making our scent clear to him as well. A hunter stands downwind of his prey."

At that she drew back, fighting the logic of it temporarily, then gave in. She turned cold eyes back to Lujan.

Lujan saw the gap between them narrow but knew it was not closed. For now, Coconino was still in charge, though, and he turned his attention back to the man.

"How would you keep the Others from coming?" Coconino asked.

"I haven't solved that problem yet," Lujan told him frankly. "I thought perhaps you and I together could find a solution."

Slowly a smile tugged at the corners of Coconino's mouth. "This is good," he said finally. "You will come to our village and speak with the Council. We would know more about your plans. Many herbs season a stew." Summarily he turned and started back toward Tala.

"It's a saying," Phoenix explained to Lujan. "Sort of like 'Two heads are better than one.' "

Coconino was mounted. "Follow the Old Way," he told Lujan, indicating the roadbed. "We will go ahead and tell the People of your arrival. They will make a feast for you. I will send runners to greet you and guide you to the village."

"Take your time," Phoenix called dryly as she clambered up behind the young primitive. "This beast doesn't break any speed records."

In truth, there was no problem in arriving well ahead of Lujan. The old roadway would take him far to the north before the runners would intercept him and lead him back around by another old road to approach the village from the east. That would give Coconino the time he needed to meet with the Council and prepare the People for the advent of this Other.

The Mother still hovered between life and death, and Gonzales had given up his watch. There was nothing he could do. He returned to the fields, where the second crop of cotton and corn was ripening. There he sweated out his frustrations under the broiling sun, bending his back to a labor that comforted him somehow. Perhaps it was the productivity it represented; perhaps it was the mindless nature of the work. Or perhaps it was the closeness, the very smell, of Earth . . .

It was decided to greet the Other as a Man-on-the-Mountain was greeted, with great hospitality and festivity. Yet they would deal with him as they would with any Man-on-the-Mountain. Should he defile the Mother Earth or her People, he would be punished appropriately.

At Coconino's request, the Council also decided to advise extreme caution in the presence of the Other. Though he would be given a chance to prove himself, his evil nature was assumed. They would keep him ignorant of all they could and place no trust in his words.

The message was quickly passed to all members of the village. Children whispered among themselves as they gathered fuel for the Elvira. What sort of kachina could this man of the Others be? Did he have burning coals for eyes or hair growing from his ears? Did he sport feathers and beak, or would his face shine like the sun?

Bringing back water from the river, the maidens of the People speculated, too. Would he be handsome, like Coconino? Exotic, like the Men-on-the-Mountain? Would he be offered the Right of the Chosen Companion? What would it be like to bear a child of the Others?

The maidens were quickly distracted, though, as Coconino strode through the village, his moody, purposeful visage even more striking than they remembered. Ah, to be wife to such a man! There were whispers that when the Mother died, Coconino might be their new leader. If not he, surely his mother would be, for Two Moons was greatly respected. Either way it could only add to the stature of a man who was already becoming a legend among them.

Only one maiden said nothing. Nina knew she could never hope that a man like Coconino would take her to wife. Season after season she had watched the eligible men of the village turn their eyes elsewhere, take their gifts to some other maiden's door. She knew the look now when she saw it; Coconino was in love with the Witch Woman. By the time she had realized it, she was beyond tears for him or any other man.

There was a certain peace in knowing she would never have a husband. The absence of hope meant an absence of strife as well. But in the past few weeks she had come to know still another kind of peace, one that sprang from other knowledge. It had crept upon her during her nights along, had been whispered on the breeze and sighed in the branches of the great sycamores, and she knew its source.

On a clear, fresh dawn before Coconino returned, Nina had risen and made her Prayer of Thanks for Fulfillment to the Mother Earth. Then she had collected her things and come down from the Village of the Ancients of her own accord. She would make her Plea no more.

Castle Rock slipped away from the group of chattering women grinding fresh corn in the shade and started quickly down the ladder. She hated their solicitous inquiries about the Man-on-the-Mountain, their sly winks and knowing smiles as they chatted about morning sickness, food cravings, and soft kicks from within. Nina had come down from the Village of the Ancients radiant with inner joy, while Castle Rock had endured the Man-on-the-Mountain for months with no sign of life in her womb.

Nina was too hasty, Castle Rock thought tartly as she headed for the creek. She is only late with her bleeding time and wishes herself pregnant. Soon she will be proved wrong, and what a fool she will look then! Then she will have to go back up to the Village of the Ancients, and who will take pity on such a foolish girl?

I wonder who took pity on her in the first place, she's so ugly.

Probably old Purple Thistle or that worthless Lame Rabbit. I'll bet that's why she won't tell anyone, because she's ashamed to admit who it was. Oh, I know it's a tradition that no one is to know, not even the maiden herself, but she usually does. And she usually finds ways to let others know without exactly saying it, but I couldn't get a word out of her.

Just then Castle Rock stopped, for Coconino was coming up the bank from the creek.

His eyes caught hers, and they held a moment; then he would have gone on, but Castle Rock called his name.

"What?" he asked, eyeing her suspiciously over the intervening ground.

He's looking at my stomach, she thought, looking to see if I carry a child yet. "The People are favored that Coconino walks their paths once more," she said.

He shrugged off her greeting impatiently. "Castle Rock, I have no time for your coy games today. A man of the Others comes to our village, and I have many things to do before he arrives."

She bridled at his tone, his dismissal of her purpose without knowing what it was. "I only wished to ask what I might do to help prepare for his arrival," she improvised imperiously. "But if the great Coconino does not want the assistance of a lowly Chosen Maiden, that is a great relief to me. No doubt you will ask Corn Hair's help instead, though she is as close to the end of her time as I am to the beginning of mine."

Coconino stopped then and looked at her with different eyes. "So the Chosen Maiden has her fulfillment," he said softly. "May the child prosper in you, and both of you in the Mother Earth."

Castle Rock had only meant that she hoped she was nearing the beginning of her pregnancy as Corn Hair neared the end of hers but the change in Coconino at his misunderstanding was a surprise. Castle Rock decided not to correct him. The softness in his voice, the poignancy in his eyes, she took to be regret that it was not his child. So that is the key, she thought hopefully. When he sees what a fine mother I can be, then his resistance will dissolve and he will bring his gifts to my door.

"Shall I have the children decorate the village?" she asked. "Or find Fire Keeper to ready Elvira for a celebration?"

For a moment he only looked at her with something she interpreted as longing. "Both have been done," he said then. "But Two Moons needs help to prepare the feast. I am sending hunters for meat. Will the Man-on-the-Mountain honor us with his presence?''

''He prefers to sleep in the fields, to keep the rabbits from his vegetables and cotton,'' she told him. ''Gophers have been very bad this year, too.''

''Then we shall be content with his Chosen Maiden,'' Coconino replied, and turned toward Falling Star's wickiup, where several young men had gathered.

Yes, you will be content, Castle Rock thought to herself as she hurried toward the center of the village, where Two Moons presided over the digging of a cooking pit. And you will be content with his child being raised alongside yours.

But I must lure the Man-on-the-Mountain in from the fields soon so that the child may be started. Coconino will be angry if he thinks I lied.

The encounter with Castle Rock had leached some of the anger from Coconino and left in its place a strange hollowness. Her news of new life reminded him that the Witch Woman could never bear his child. The sons of Coconino could be only the sons of his spirit. Perhaps it was better that way. Perhaps all the children of the People should be his children.

As he glanced back at the towering cliff with its ancient fortress, he noticed one of the women leave the group that ground corn diligently in the shade. When she saw him, she stopped, however, and Coconino looked quickly away. Framed against the limestone wall, Nina seemed somehow forsaken, a dark and isolated figure on the edge of her sun-baked world. A few strides farther down the path, though, he could not resist. He turned to look back at the solitary woman, but Nina had gone.

Just ahead of him Phoenix lounged with the other hunters outside Falling Star's wickiup. Her voice crackled with tension as she laughed at some ribald joke Juan had made. Then, following the looks of the others, she turned and met Coconino's eyes.

Phoenix hadn't been happy with his decision. ''You're putting a rattlesnake among children!'' she had told him furiously when they had left Derek Lujan on the road.

''I am putting the rattlesnake in a glass jar, as you do on the Mountain,'' he replied. ''There he may fix his beady eyes on one and all and wave his hypnotizing tongue, but his fangs cannot reach us. We, on the other hand, can observe him in his jar. We can even keep him prisoner. Or we can let him loose exactly where and when we like.''

"Or you'll make him good and angry," she grumbled.

"We will feed him good food, make music, and show him honor," Coconino told her. "How can he be angry? Did not a wise man from the Before Times say that was how to trick your enemy? By pretending to be his friend?"

"He said that's how you get *rid* of your enemies," she corrected in exasperation, "by making friends of them. It's not the same thing!"

"Good," Coconino snapped. "Then generations from now on will quote wise Coconino, who said, 'Trick your enemy by pretending to be his friend.' "

"Does it occur to you that that's what Lujan is trying to do?"

"Of course," Coconino replied loftily. "But I will be better at it than he is."

I have to be better at it, Coconino thought grimly as he crossed the remaining ground to the band of hunters that awaited his direction. If I am not, we shall become like our ancestors in the Before Times. We shall lose our dignity and freedom and who will honor the Mother Earth then?

CHAPTER TWENTY-ONE

Lujan's heart pounded at the sight of the adobe fortress carved, it seemed, from the very stone of the towering cliff. For a moment he imagined their warp dispatcher had malfunctioned and transported him into the middle of the fifteenth century. There was a lookout high on the rampart, and several figures scurried up and down ladders with amazing speed.

But the ancient roadbed that his landcrawler bounced along belied any such notion. The pavement had long since eroded as spring runoff had rushed through the winding gullies between small hills, but here and there chunks of asphalt protruded, and the broadness of the cut through the landscape attested to human intervention. The marvels of twentieth-century man had broken and decayed, but the houses on the cliff flaunted their existence.

Lujan wished the runners leading the way would accept his invitation to ride inside the crawler. He was impatient now to see this people that had survived, seemingly out of time. But they were adamant; they would not ride in the Machine. Even the youngest, a boy of about fourteen, refused, though Lujan could tell from the look of longing in his eyes that the refusal was not easy.

It was not until they bade him leave his vehicle in a cleared area northeast of the cliff that Lujan realized there was more to the settlement than the cliff dwellings. Almost entirely concealed by surrounding hills and thick riparian vegetation, a collection of domelike brush structures nestled among the sycamores and walnut trees. Here he could see even more activity: women crouched at small cook fires, children dancing impatiently. A group of some dozen men and women in highly decorated cotton garb stood facing the eastern slope, waiting for him.

They descended a set of steps that had been roughed out in the rocky slope and reinforced here and there with sticks. One of his

guides preceded him, a stocky man with deep lines in his face
and not an ounce of fat on his body. Behind him came the youth
and a broad-shouldered, hook-nosed man who kept his polished,
painted throwing club ever in hand. The hair on Lujan's neck
prickled as he realized that with proper force the club could
damage much larger prey than rabbits. He touched the innocuous
T-shaped device hooked on his belt and was comforted.

Coconino stood with the group at the bottom of the hill, but to
Lujan's surprise, it was a woman who stepped forward to greet
him. She was short and plump, but there was an air of great
dignity about her. Even had she not worn the highly embroidered
dress, he would have known she was a leader here. Her posture
and her tone of voice left no doubt.

"The People welcome you," Two Moons said carefully. "It
is the Way of the People that all who . . ." She paused, and
Coconino leaned toward her to supply the correct word. ". . .
honor the Mother Earth be greeted in peace." She inclined her
head solemnly.

Lujan clicked his heels and made a grave, albeit short, bow.
He had not missed the warning implicit in her words. Infractions
of their code would not be taken lightly; he must mind his p's
and q's.

But Lujan was a master in the art of diplomacy. "The People
do me great honor to receive me in peace," he replied. "It is my
greatest wish that there be only peace and friendship between
your people and mine."

The woman conferred with Coconino momentarily; Lujan assumed that she was getting a translation. The runners had greeted
him in a language that sounded vaguely like Spanish, and Coconino's speech had been marked by oddities of grammar and
syntax. Lujan gathered that English, which had been almost
universally understood at the time of the Evacuation, had not
retained that status here.

Two Moons turned back to him now. "Please, come," she
bade him. "The Council meets."

As he joined the solemn procession toward the cliff, Lujan
took in the faces of the people around him. The young ones
gaped openly; they were not accustomed to strangers. He winked
slyly at one as he passed. There seemed to be a great number of
them in relation to the adults; either these natives had very large
families, which was not likely under such primitive health conditions, or there were more adults somewhere else. Where? he
wondered. And how many?

The women at the cook fires were mostly old or gave the appearance of age with lined and toothless faces. This enforced his suspicion that the active population of the village was somewhere else. He turned to Coconino, who marched half a pace in front and to his right. "Where are the rest of your people?" he asked.

Had he surprised the primitive? Yes, he thought so. "They are not *my* people," Coconino objected, "they are *the* People. The children of the Mother Earth. Many are in the fields, tending the crops. Others are gathering food for our feast."

"A feast!" Lujan exclaimed. "I'm flattered. And where is Phoenix?"

Coconino darted a quick look at the innocent face of the Other. "She is hunting," he replied, "with some others. We would have fresh meat for you."

Phoenix had protested loudly at being sent out of the village. "Excuse me, but you don't speak the language well enough to translate for Lujan at a Council meeting," she had snarled.

"Excuse me, but you don't hide your opinions well enough to translate for him," Coconino had fired back.

Phoenix had muttered a string of obscenities that Coconino had long since grown numb to, then taken up her bow and followed Juan and Falling Star out of the village.

Passing between the wickiups, Lujan tried to take a quick count of their number, but they were scattered about with no discernible pattern, and it was impossible to tell how many others might lie in the trees near the stream or beyond a rocky point in the cliff wall. From the perspective of the cliff houses he was sure to get a better idea. He was about to ask Coconino if that was their destination when he was distracted by a group of young girls standing bashfully beside the path, whispering and giggling together.

Lujan smiled at them, amused that some things were the same in every culture. Seeing his smile, they giggled all the more, poking each other and chattering so that Coconino looked up and scowled at them. Lujan made a subtle show of seeing this and trying to look sober, but when Coconino's head was turned, he smiled at them again and cocked an eyebrow. The girls smothered their laughter in each other's shoulders.

They had reached the cliff face now, and Lujan was filled with trepidation as he saw how high and steep it truly was. It was obvious now that the primitives intended to climb to the elevated fortress. High places were not a favorite of his, and the rough ladders did not increase his confidence. But seeing them bear up under the weight of his stocky hosts, he swallowed his misgiving and seized the rungs firmly.

Coconino stood at the bottom, waiting for Lujan to clear before following him up. He had seen the fear flash through the short-haired man's eyes, and Coconino was sorely tempted to shake the ladder. But he had also seen the determination with which Lujan had forced his fear away and grasped his foe without hesitation. You are a strong man, Derek Lujan, Coconino thought. And a clever one. You are not like the men of the Before Times who thoughtlessly trampled the ways of my ancestors. Oh, no. You are much more dangerous.

Ignoring the ache in her bandaged arm, Phoenix drew a deadly bead on the fat javelina sow. She had been sorely tempted to mark an old, scrawny animal as being all that Lujan was worth, but her pride as a hunter outweighed her desire to insult Lujan. Feeling the hunters on either side of her in place, their bows also drawn, she darted a quick plea toward the Mother Earth and let fly her shaft.

Three of the bristly, piglike animals went down. Startled, the others stopped chewing prickly pear pads, then bolted toward the west.

Swiftly nocking another arrow, Phoenix got off another shot, glad that the javelina had charged away from them rather than toward them. The mean-tempered, nearsighted creatures were far smaller than the legendary wild boars they resembled, but they were just as vicious. That they were of a different genus made little difference.

Her second shot missed, and a third would have been imprudent, but Juan on her left brought down a fourth animal, and Falling Star's arrow protruded from the flank of yet another as it dashed madly after its comrades. He would trail the herd to see if it lagged back while she and Juan retrieved their collective kill.

"*Aiee*, what a feast we will make!" Juan crowed as they scuttled down the steep hill to approach the fallen pigs. "Coconino will be proud of us, no?"

Phoenix stopped short as she realized the change that had occurred. Not "The Mother will be proud of us," as it used to be, but "Coconino will be proud of us." What was more, the change had occurred so gradually that she could not say when it had begun.

"What's the matter with you?" Juan called back up the hill to her. "Don't you want to see how cleanly your arrow struck her? Or—" He grinned wickedly. "—are you afraid your kill is smaller than mine?"

"I'm afraid yours isn't quite dead," she shot back, "and if it's going to jump up and slash at someone, I'd rather that someone was you." Juan laughed, but he approached the javelina with a bit more caution, his knife ready in his hand.

As she approached, Phoenix wrinkled up her nose at the strong natural musk of the javelina. Juan, seemingly inured to the smell, was methodically slicing the throats of their prizes; she noted with a smile that he cut them all before returning to the first and ritually spilling its blood as a libation to the Mother Earth. She fell to helping him, and with practiced hands they had dressed and trussed all four animals before Falling Star trotted back into view, a fifth pig slung across his shoulder. "*Aiee*, but she was a stubborn one," he sang out. "I had to explain to her three times that she was going to honor a feast of the People before she would lie down before my knife."

"Your knife?" Juan quipped. "I think you talked her to death."

But at the mention of honor Phoenix's stomach turned. She had disliked Lujan as instinctively as she had liked Jacqueline Winthrop. Is that your prompting, Mother Earth? she wondered. Or am I just suspicious of slick, handsome men?

She glanced at the hunters who trudged on either side of her, steps turned back toward the village. Juan was not handsome, not even by the standards of the People, yet she loved him as she had loved Reed, as a friend and comrade. Falling Star, on the other hand, was considered quite a catch. Broad-shouldered and heavily muscled, at seventeen he showed none of the squatness that characterized older men of the People. His bright eyes shone from a face still sharp with youth, and even white teeth added sparkle to his appeal. Yet Phoenix felt no more attracted to him than she did to Juan. They were *compadres*.

They were not Coconino.

Phoenix sighed heavily, knowing that the man-boy she had found so attractive when she had first come to the People was not the same man-boy who rode Tala restlessly through the Season of Storms. And neither of them was the man-god who had called down the curse of the Mother Earth on the Others and who now strode about the village giving orders to hunters and cooks and having them obeyed without question. Why hadn't someone said, "Wait! Is this not Coconino, who has not yet taken a wife? Didn't we laugh at him when the Witch Woman rejected him? And didn't we scoff at his boast to find Tala? Why now do we respect him as though he were the Mother's son?"

Why did they respect him? Because he had found Tala and brought him back to the People. Because he went to the Mountain, and because he returned. Because in his every movement now, in his very visage, was the spirit of the Mother Earth.

Why can I see it in him, Phoenix lamented, and not anywhere else? Why can't I hear Her message in the wind, in the creek, in the call of insects? Mother Earth, I pray to you, but I never know if you hear me. Am I blessed? Am I cursed? Will I never hear your voice?

From somewhere within her came the answer. You are blessed; you are beloved of my son Coconino.

After the heat of the late summer day, the velvety perfection of the night was almost surreal. Comfortably full of succulent roast javelina and cornbread seasoned with green chilies, Lujan leaned back against a ridge of dirt that seemed to have been heaped up exactly for that purpose. Overhead crisp stars bejeweled the cloudless black sky, and no breeze stirred the branches of the trees that framed his view. He longed to strip off his shirt like the men around him and feel the kiss of the night air on his bare skin.

Now a maiden came forward with yet another dish, a wooden bowl etched with antlered figures and filled with a dark liquid. Lujan let his gaze linger on her, on the softness of her somewhat plump body beneath the loose cotton clothing. Accepting the bowl from her hand, he fastened her eyes with his and let a slow smile spread across his face. The response in her was gratifying. Controlling men was exciting, but controlling women was the headiest sensation he knew.

He held her transfixed as he lifted the bowl to his lips and tasted the liquid within. It was sweet, almost syrupy, and he let it linger on his tongue before he swallowed it. He savored the aftertaste, tried to detect any trace of alcohol, but found none. Just as well, he thought. This evening is intoxicating enough.

"*Gracias*," he said to the young woman, having badgered that simple word out of Coconino. Had the light been better, he knew he would have seen the color rise to her cheeks as she tore her eyes away, bobbed her head, and hurried back to a young hunter. Ah, you're married, he thought. A plus in my book.

Single women are too easy to seduce; they don't have the inner conflict or the repressed desires. Married women are much more interesting.

Then he turned his attention to the bowl in his hand. Worth a hundred thousand, easily, on Argo. As long as no one tested it and found it had been made in this century. Artifacts of natural fibers would be a problem to pass. Better to stick with the ceramic ware or things these natives had picked up that dated back to pre-Evacuation.

He smiled to himself, remembering his meeting with the Council. They had sat in the dark, cool chamber high on the cliff while he told them his story. Coconino's translation had been halting, but he was sure the message had come through.

"As I told you," he had begun, "I wish only peace between your people and mine. However, there are many among my people who think that peace is to be achieved by changing your ways to fit ours. There are others who think that peace means taking what they want even if it does not belong to them and still others who do not care about peace at all. It is a sad thing, but among my people it is true."

At that the Council members had nodded their heads and spoken together. Lujan had looked to Coconino for translation but had gotten none, so he had continued. "I do not want to see this happen. If I have my way, only people that I know will respect you and your ways will ever come to Earth again. Earth is your home; it should remain so."

He watched them carefully as Coconino relayed this; then, sure he had their sympathy, he broached his next topic. "Soon I will return to my home in the stars," he said. "I will tell my people there is no one here, there is nothing they desire on the Earth. That way they will not come to disturb you, to disturb your peace. Instead, I will come myself. I will bring you many gifts to demonstrate my friendship. I will bring you jewelry, and fine cloth, and rich foods. Should drought come to you, I will bring food in abundance so that your people will not starve. All this I will do because you are my friends and because I want peace between us."

"And how," Coconino asked curtly, "will you keep others from coming here? One coyote cannot speak for his cousins."

The challenge was clear in his eyes. Lujan did not try to deceive him. "I don't know yet," he admitted. "But I will find a way. Believe me, I will find a way."

And I will, he thought now as he lounged in his place of honor just beyond the heat of the ceremonial fire. Nearby a small group of men and women were putting on feathered wristbands and strings of beads. Ah, but not tonight, he decided as he settled back to enjoy the entertainment. Tonight is a time for relaxation, for resting the mind from its labors. Then tomorrow I can give the matter my undivided attention, and the solution will come to me.

Across from his nemesis, Coconino stared at the man with barely concealed contempt. Lujan spoke to the Council as if they were children, he thought angrily. Only with me was he direct, and who knows how much of that was truth? He seeks to use us all, as he and his kind seek to use the Mother Earth, without regard for the consequences.

Where is their weakness? he wondered. What is the fear that I can use as an arrow to their soft spot? Ah, Mother Earth, speak to me this night that I may know how to drive this evil from your breast!

So deep in his thought was he that Castle Rock caught him by surprise. "I saw that you had no *tai-ayoh*," she said gently. "Will you not partake of its sweetness?"

Her tone was so guileless, her bearing so modest, that before he knew what he had done, Coconino had taken the bowl she offered and sipped at its contents. "Thank you," he said. Then, to cover the fact that she had served him his favorite drink in front of all his friends, Coconino turned to Phoenix. "Here, my sister-brother," he called to her. "Have you tasted of *tai-ayoh*? It is much prized among the People."

Phoenix had been watching them from the corner of her eye. What the particular significance of *tai-ayoh* was, Phoenix did not know, but she knew that unmarried women did not serve unmarried men unless they were offering more than food or drink. She took the bowl from his hand. "No, I haven't," she replied while thinking, Pay attention, *bobo*. How many times do you think I'm going to bail you out?

Lujan had watched the exchange as well. Interesting, he thought, that she is the only young girl here who has approached Coconino. Is she his sister? Not from the cow eyes she was making. And was his passing off the drink a rebuff?

Then Castle Rock turned, and he saw the unmistakable look of victory on her face. Match point, he thought. Only what game are you two playing? And how can I use it against him?

Just then the drums began.

*   *   *

The dances were mesmerizing. Lujan reveled in the smell of
wood smoke, the color of the dancers, and the women— The
women had covered their bodies with ornate clothing, but as
they danced and grew warmer, they began to shed unnecessary
articles. To them it was only practical; to Lujan it was erotic.

The moon had risen and climbed past its zenith to hang briefly
over the cliff when, drawn by the infectious spirit of the People
and the throbbing of the drums, Lujan found himself dancing
with them to the hypnotic rhythms of their music. At the song's
conclusion they cheered him, the men pounding his back, the
women reaching out to touch his arm. Coconino, however, kept
his distance, and Phoenix watched his every move with hawklike
eyes.

Sweating freely, his chest heaving from his exertions, Lujan
flopped down on the ground next to the tall woman. She had
disdained to put on her finery; she wore only a loincloth and
headband. A turquoise medallion hung from her neck. "Nice
piece of jewelry," he commented.

She nailed him with a look that dared him to focus his eyes to
either side of the stone.

"They make those here?" Lujan asked her.

"No."

"On the mountain, then."

"Maybe. We do some jewelry."

"And you find some, is that right?"

"Lot of stuff got left behind," she conceded.

"That's all I want," he told her. "Just a few of the things that
were left behind. That's not much to ask, is it? For being left
alone? For seeing that hordes of treasure hunters and con artists
and other enterprising felons don't pollute this place, these people?"

It was a moment before she answered, but her eyes never left
his. Then a mirthless smile twisted her lips. "A horde of one?"

Just then Two Moons rose to leave the fire, and there was a
sudden collective murmur from the young girls who had been
waiting impatiently all evening. The older woman stopped,
looked at them, then shot an inquiring look at her son.

Lujan saw the alarm on Coconino's face, heard the tight caution in his tone as he spoke to Two Moons. She hesitated, looked
back at the girls, then made up her mind. Signaling Coconino to
follow, she approached Lujan.

"The People have . . ."

"A custom," Coconino filled in darkly.

"A custom. A stranger in the village . . ." Again she stopped, but this time she spoke to Coconino and did not try to continue.

"Two Moons wishes me to say," Coconino told Lujan, "that a stranger in our village may exercise the Right of the Chosen Companion."

Lujan drew in his breath sharply. "Right of the Chosen Companion?" he echoed.

"You may choose a companion from among the maidens of the village," Coconino growled.

Still Lujan hesitated, not wanting to misconstrue. He turned to Phoenix. "Companion?" he asked, knowing that Coconino's English was not always accurate.

"They're offering you a woman for the night," she told him bluntly.

Lujan swallowed carefully, cleared his throat, and tried to ignore the messages his body was sending him. "Do I have to worry about VD or anything?" he asked her.

Phoenix looked blankly at him. "VD?"

"Yeah, VD," he repeated. "You know—syphilis, herpes, AIDS . . ."

"Oh," she exclaimed as the light dawned, "you mean sexually transmitted diseases." She shook her head. "With the small population base, those were eradicated centuries ago."

Coconino had been listening intently. "Please explain this to me," he interjected. "What are 'section lee trans—trans—' "

"I'll explain it to you later," she growled. "If you're worried, Mr. Lujan—"

"No, no, I'll take your word for it," he answered too quickly. The tantalizing array of female flesh glistening in the firelight and the insistent beat of the drums had stirred his blood early in the evening. "I don't want to insult their hospitality."

"I'm sure that's uppermost in your mind," she said dryly.

"I get to choose, eh?" He turned slowly, looking at them all. The giggling girls did not interest him much, being scarcely past puberty. Most of the young married ones seemed attached to a child, however; he did not want to contend with youngsters. Besides, it was best not to risk offending a husband. He studied the gigglers again. Now, there was a pretty one, and well formed for all she was young—

"It is not necessary to choose," Coconino spoke up. "It is your right, but it is not required."

His tone brought Lujan back. So you don't want me to choose, he thought. You've rolled out this red carpet, feasted and entertained me, but the truth is you hate my guts, and the thought of me sleeping with one of your women . . .

Suddenly Lujan turned and pointed across the circle to Castle Rock. "I choose her," he said loudly.

"No!" Coconino cried involuntarily, stepping between him and the girl. "It is not allowed; she is already Chosen."

There was a general stir through the crowd, and Castle Rock herself seemed angry at Coconino's intervention. I was right, Lujan thought. That one's his. Will they override his objection in favor of their custom? Or does he have so much power over them that they won't cross him? Either way, I've pushed his button. I know how to get at him.

Raising his voice, Coconino overrode the murmuring. "She cannot be Chosen," he repeated. "She carries a child already. Only women who do not carry children can be Chosen Companions."

Surprised, Lujan deferred politely. "Forgive me, I did not know your customs. I withdraw my choice." Carrying a child? Whose? Is that why he rebuffed her earlier?

Startled at his own response, Coconino took a deep breath and regained some composure. "You may choose another," he told Lujan.

"Thank your people for me," Lujan said, "and thank the young ladies, but I will not choose."

"I can tell you which ones are available," Phoenix jumped in.

"No, thank you. I will not choose." It was an imprudent thing to do, anyway. But his refusal now would, he hoped, make Coconino lose face. "I am tired, and I will go sleep in the landcrawler. Ladies. Gentlemen." He made a smiling bow and left the circle of flames.

"So what did you learn, hotshot, from your snake in the jar?" Phoenix demanded of her friend as they sat alone by the dwindling flames of Elvira.

"What are 'six shally trans immed—' "

"Sexually transmitted diseases," she filled in. "You're dodging the question."

"How can I answer the question when I do not know all that he said?" Coconino demanded irritably. He had held the pain at bay all day, but his control was wearing thin.

Phoenix laughed unkindly. "You're clutching at straws, *amigo*. All right. Sexually transmitted diseases are those that can only be contracted when two people make love."

Coconino's eyebrows furrowed. "You can get sick from this?"

"In the Before Times," she told him, "People not only got sick from such diseases, they died horrible, debilitating deaths. And every time a treatment was found for one, a new one would crop up that they didn't know how to cure."

Still Coconino was confused. "But if a man has only one wife, and she only one husband, then how—"

"Do you keep to one wife?" she asked.

Coconino bridled. "A man should not exercise the Right of the Chosen Companion if he knows he is sick," he retorted.

"Fine in theory," Phoenix said. "But then you're counting on him knowing he's sick—or her knowing she's sick—and you're counting on them giving a damn. Not a fair assumption for the Before Times."

Coconino brooded, poking at a charred log with a stick. "Then the Others are like the people of the Before Times if they still fear such sickness," he announced.

At that moment it clicked, and Coconino sat up suddenly, grabbing Phoenix's arm. "This Other was afraid that the People might give him a sickness!"

"Ironic, isn't it?" she observed. "We should be worried about what sickness he and his kind might give *us*. Our people have been living under rarefied conditions for so long, we probably have no immunity to the sorts of diseases the Others could bring."

"Please explain that in words I know," he asked impatiently.

"I'm just saying that because we've lived by ourselves for so long, there are certain diseases that have been stamped out. However, the Others probably still have them and a dozen new ones besides. Ones that even the doctors on the Mountain don't know how to treat."

"Yes, but we might have diseases that the Others don't," he pursued.

"I suppose it's possible," she admitted, "though it's not very likely. New diseases are usually mutations of— Yes, we could!" she exclaimed suddenly as she realized what he was thinking. "Different conditions here on Earth could have given rise to different mutations—I mean, new diseases, ones that the Others don't know about, ones they don't know how to cure."

"And the Others fear such diseases." For the first time in days Coconino felt a measure of hope. "But do they fear them enough to stay away from the Mother Earth?"

"They might, Coconino," she answered. "They just might."

Crouched in the moon shadow of her wickiup, Castle Rock stared glumly at the silver crescent that was rapidly slipping behind the cliff. In his righteous indignation Coconino had published the fallacy of her pregnancy to the entire village. If she did not conceive soon, she would appear even more foolish than Nina.

She had been flattered that the Other had been so attracted to her when she hadn't paid him the slightest attention. He was a young man, tall and muscular, with the light hair and skin she associated with the Men-on-the-Mountain—unlike the present Teacher in every respect. The Other was a man whose Chosen Companion she could have been without any difficulty.

But Coconino had pointed out that the honor shown to a stranger was to offer him a companion who could bear his child, and the honor to the Chosen Companion was that her child would have "new blood." That carnal pleasure might be involved was to the People a pleasant but inconsequential fringe benefit. The Council had agreed: A pregnant woman could not be Chosen.

I'm not pregnant, though! Castle Rock wailed to herself. And if I want to be, I'll have to go out to the field and lie in the dust, sweating among the cornstalks with that fat old Teacher grunting over me. And on a feast night!

Reluctantly she gathered herself up and started away from her wickiup, toward the path to the creek. Unpleasant as it was, it was better than being caught in a lie.

But I didn't lie, she told herself firmly as the shadows of the wickiups blended with the darker black of night. Coconino made a false assumption, but that's his own fault for being so stupid. And then he got angry with the Other, which he told all of us not to do, and spread this falsehood about me. So now *I* must pay for his stupidity and quick temper! Instead of lying in the exciting arms of this stranger, I must go the fields and—

Suddenly she stopped, almost laughing out loud. If what she sought was a child, there was no need to go to the fields. One man could start a child as easily as another, couldn't he? With a cautious look around to see she was not observed, Castle Rock turned her steps away from the path to the fields, away from the ugly Man-on-the-Mountain and toward the shiny, strange Machine of the Other.

Only one pair of eyes watched the girl slip quietly toward her tryst. Coming back from relieving herself in the foliage by the creek, Phoenix had stopped by an ancient tree to wrestle with her own problems. Standing motionless in the dark pool of its shadow, the huntress was invisible.

Go ahead, little fool, she thought. Go waste yourself on that piece of carrion. Tonight I'm going to have the man you really want.

Watching Castle Rock sneak off had finally convinced Phoenix. Why should I be noble? she asked herself. If she's not above seeking a little excitement where she can, why should I be? In the end Castle Rock may have his children, but for tonight I have his love.

Two Moons was just returning to the dying fire as Phoenix approached. She had been up on the cliff, relaying the events of the evening to the Mother. Coconino rose to meet his mother. "What did she say?"

"She says nothing," Two Moons told him. "Says nothing, sees nothing, but who can say what she hears and knows? Her life lingers, as though waiting permission to depart, but she can give us no answers. It is for us to decide now, my son. What shall we do?"

"I will go to the camp of the Others," he said. "My sister-brother and I will see how their messages are sent to the Sisters of the Mother Earth. It seems to me this Lujan will send the messages for us; they serve his purpose. Then we will see how to stop his Sky Ship from leaving."

"It is a simple plan, my son," Two Moons replied. "Perhaps too simple. Let us think long upon it."

"There is no time!" he cried impatiently. "The Others will not await our pleasure."

"That is true." She looked around at the Council members beginning to reassemble now that the Other had gone to his bed. "We will sing the song of Elvira, the fire, and know the will of the Mother Earth in these things."

Slowly the leaders of the People moved into place around the fire as Fire Keeper heaped more wood upon the embers and the flames leapt once more to life. Coconino turned away; this was Council business, and when all was said and done, he was only a hunter and a storyteller. Morning would be soon enough to know what they had decided.

"Coconino," Phoenix called softly, following him away from the Elvira.

The eyes he turned to her surprised her. The spirit of the Mother Earth seemed a tangible fire within him, only tonight it was a dark and menacing fire. "Yes?" he prompted.

He will consume me, Phoenix thought in panic. If I lie with him tonight, that spirit inside him will consume me, engulf me, take me over. I want to be consumed. No, I don't. I want to stay who I am, I want to be in control. He is not the beautiful, spoiled son tonight; there is too much power in him. There is more to the loving of such a man than simple carnal pleasure.

"Nothing," Phoenix said. "See you in the morning." Then she fled into the protective darkness and to the ladders that were her escape.

"The People are generous, and I will not forget them," Lujan told Coconino and Phoenix, wondering privately why none of the Council had come to see him off. "When I come again, I will bring many gifts."

And expect many in return, Coconino thought. "We will show you the way back on Tala," he offered.

"Oh, that's not necessary. The guidance system on this thing will get me home. I think it would be better if none of my people saw you."

Coconino smiled and waved as Lujan started for his Machine. Better for you, he thought. But your people, as you call them, have already seen too much, and we both know they will not return to their home. What you don't know is that neither will you.

And what is better for the People is if Phoenix and I come to your camp and learn more about your ways and how to deal with you. So I bid you farewell for now, Derek Lujan. Soon enough I shall be *your* guest.

Lujan put his hand on the door of the landcrawler. But before he could open it, a rattling sound froze him in his tracks. Just beside him on a flat stone, a six-foot rattlesnake had coiled to sun itself in the early morning light. Lujan did not know what it was, but its attitude was hostile. He didn't move.

From behind him came a soft *whizzzz*, and suddenly the snake jerked, impaled on the point of an arrow that dragged its muscular body four feet through the air before pinning it to the soft earth beyond the stone. Lujan turned to see Coconino poised, bow in hand. Beside him Phoenix had drawn her bow as well should his shot have failed.

"Thank you," Lujan said, keeping the shake from his voice. "I assume that thing was dangerous." He backed cautiously away from the flailing body of the reptile.

"They don't always kill you," Phoenix reassured him as she and Coconino approached. "We have antitoxin on the Mountain, but that's a fair hike from here."

"You're very good with that bow," Lujan observed as Coconino retrieved his arrow.

"I am the best," he said simply.

"Very impressive." The snake was no more than an inch and a half in diameter where the arrow had pierced it. It still twitched and spasmed on the shaft. "Is it still alive?"

"It is dead," Coconino assured him. "It just does not know that yet."

"What are you going to do with it?"

Phoenix grinned at him. "Lunch!"

Lujan swallowed back hard, wondering if such creatures had been on the menu the night before.

"I didn't realize those weapons could be so accurate," Lujan admitted grudgingly. "Can you do that, too?" he asked Phoenix.

She shrugged. "Don't know. Never tried." Then she added, "He really is the best."

Well, at least I know he needs me alive, Lujan thought. But do I need him? Questionable at this point. Still— He looked at the twitching snake and the young hunter wiping blood from his arrow. Best not to make an enemy of him, not just yet. Friends are more useful than enemies.

Overhead a hawk cried, and Lujan flinched, but the bird dived downward at some prey a hundred yards west of them. It rose again with a rabbit dangling from its talons and beat furiously toward the east.

Almost without thinking Lujan drew his own weapon and fired. There was a crackling sound, the smell of burned feathers, and the blackened remains of both bird and rabbit plummeted to earth almost at their feet.

Coconino was stunned. The blackened lump bore no resemblance to either creature. "Why did you do that?" he gasped.

"They cannot be used for food like this; the feathers and fur are gone. Why?"

Lujan noted his host's horror with satisfaction. It was a shot well spent if it impressed the young man with his firepower. As he flung open the door to the crawler, an icy smile flashed on his face. "Target practice," he replied. Then he climbed into the crawler, pleased with himself, and drove away.

CHAPTER TWENTY-TWO

Jacqueline Winthrop focused on the taste of the fresh coffee: fresh-grown, fresh-ground, fresh-brewed. She savored it, marveled at it, indulged her senses in it. Anything not to think about Clay.

Across from her, Gail Mendoza sat at her wooden desk watching the doctor, wondering at her composure. Her white hair was neatly combed, her borrowed clothing crisp and clean. Only the reddened eyes gave her away.

"If they made a soft landing," Gail began, "Jim is well versed in desert lore. He knows where to find water."

Jacqueline took one more sip of the pungent brew, closed her eyes as she let it slip down her throat. "They didn't make a soft landing," she said quietly.

"Leslie is a crack pilot—"

"He didn't want this mission to succeed," Jacqueline said firmly, unable to speak Lujan's name. "I don't know what his motive was, but he didn't want us to know what was here. He didn't want us to know *you* were here. And when we found you, he made sure we would never tell."

"Jacqueline—"

"He made sure," she repeated. "I've seen his profile, I've seen how he works. He leaves nothing to chance."

Gail pushed at the maps on the desk in front of her. The searchers had wanted to go out again as soon as their vehicles were checked out. She had delayed their departure overnight. Now her fingers drummed nervously on the neatly numbered quadrants of the search area. "I'm not going to send the ground teams out."

Jacqueline only sipped at her coffee.

"If Mr. Lujan sabotaged our hoppers," Gail explained, "and

I don't see any alternative explanation, he does not want us to find our missing craft. And if he doesn't want us to find it, he'll go to whatever lengths necessary to prevent that. I won't put any more of my people at risk."

Jacqueline's eyelids were closed, and Gail wondered what tears were sealed behind them.

"I know it's probably closing the barn door after the horses are out," she went on, "but I'm going to ask Eric Jackson to draft a new security plan. We'll post guards on the equipment, at the perimeter of the compound. See what kind of monitoring equipment we can employ around the mountain. If Mr. Lujan discovers you were not on the hopper, we might have uninvited guests."

Finally Jacqueline nodded, levering herself out of the chair and to her feet. "I'm going to the Infirmary," she announced. "I'm going to see if I can talk Dr. Delacourt out of an office there. With a new class of health techs starting soon, he could probably use an extra instructor."

Gail watched her go, wondering how long the woman's inner reserves would hold up. Surely this was the kind of person who had made up the original contingent at their mountain outpost: people resigned to their destiny, asking only to work at something useful until it overwhelmed them. We have grown soft, Gail thought. We have lost that fibrous inner being. We have lived too long without enemies; we no longer know how to face adversity. All that must change now.

Ruth Anderson poked her head in the door. "Gail?" she asked tentatively. "Eric is here. He wants to know when the searchers can start."

The tiny administrator of the mountain installation took a deep breath. "Send him in," she said. Then Gail Mendoza briskly rolled up the paper maps and closed an era.

"Coconino."

The young hunter was deep in his thoughts and did not hear Nina the first time she spoke his name. He had assumed the Others had weapons; he had not known how powerful they were or how wantonly they might be used. When he destroyed their Sky Ship, they would be angry. What would stop them from turning these heinous devices on the People?

Nina felt the anguish of his thoughts and almost left, but there were things that needed saying, and the time between them was short. She called his name again.

Coconino looked up in surprise. He was sitting on the roof of the Gatehouse high in the Village of the Ancients. His sharp eyes had been sweeping the land to the south; he knew that only a few hilly miles and two river crossings lay between him and the Others. Nina was the last person he expected to disturb his morbid musings.

The sight of her made him immediately uncomfortable. He wondered if she knew it was he who had visited her stone chamber oh, so many ages ago. *I should have married her,* he thought guiltily. *But I couldn't! I still can't. Even in these dark times, even with this pain that will not abate, my sister-brother burns in my soul—*

When she saw his discomfiture, Nina dropped her eyes quickly. "I am sorry to disturb you, Coconino. I know much weighs on your mind. I only thought . . . there would be some comfort in . . ."

Below them a flock of birds rose with flapping wings from the trees along the creek. "Ah, the doves are so beautiful!" she exclaimed involuntarily. Then, aware that he was waiting for her to speak, she forged on. "Once I longed to be such a dove. To preen my feathers and cock my head . . ." She could not resist a furtive glance in his direction. "I am no dove," she said, rubbing unconsciously at her oversized nose.

"A dove is no hawk," Coconino replied self-consciously, "and a hawk no duck. The Mother Earth blesses each differently."

She smiled at that, a wistful smile as she thought of the colorful green-headed ducks the hunters brought back from distant lakes and their dull, unadorned hens. "Yes," she said softly. "And even the plainest of hens can build a nest and care for her young."

Nina felt him jump and knew it was good she had come. In the commotion of the preceding day he had not heard about her joy.

"I am happy for you," he said carefully.

"I am happy for the man who came to my chamber," she replied. "There will be a child to carry his seed among the People." A heavy sigh escaped her. "Much sorrow is coming to us," she told him. "Not all who feasted last night will feast at the harvest."

A chill seized Coconino. "How do you know this?"

For a moment he thought she hadn't heard him. Her eyes were on the horizon, and she rocked herself dreamily as she squatted on the roof beside him. But then her hand strayed to her still-flat belly. ''Since this child was conceived in me,'' she said softly, ''the voice of the Mother Earth . . . I can almost hear . . .''

A long silence stretched between them. They gazed out over the snaking river valley and the fields of ripening squash and sunflowers. Finally Coconino spoke. ''You are right,'' he said. ''Much sorrow is coming to the People.'' Then, after a pause, ''There is a river valley far to the north of here, east of the Black Lands. In it is another Village of the Ancients. It would be, I think, a good place to live someday . . .''

Nodding absently, Nina rose to her feet. ''The Mother Earth has always provided us with a safe haven,'' she said confidently. ''No doubt she always will.

Karen stretched minimally and glanced back at the open door-way and the patch of sunshine spilling onto the floor of the command center. An open doorway! Never had she been any-where where a door could be left open. But the weather was seductive here, warm and dry, with hardly an insect to bother you except down by the river. And as far as the eye could see from their little outpost, there were no other buildings, no sign of human habitation or anything more dangerous than a rattle-snake. Why shouldn't she leave the door open and allow the pure, sweet air to filter in?

Early that day Derek had bounced back into camp in the landcrawler, dirty and unshaven but with a sparkle in his eye. She wondered what he had found. More people? No, that would not make him smile. He did not want to find people. Artifacts, maybe, something of value he could smuggle back aboard the ship. But he had not told her, and she would not ask.

I only hope he'll be here with me tonight, she thought. If the blue sky and soft sunlight were heady, the night had been positively seductive: insects calling softly, the air refreshingly cool after an overly warm day, and a rich blackness so com-plete that she felt as though it protected her from any hurt she had ever endured. She had wandered to the edge of the camp and lain down in the prickly, dried grass, gazing up at a jewel-ridden sky.

Strange, she thought. *I have always cherished nights I could sleep alone. But last night, in the rich womb of the planet that birthed humankind, I felt like the first woman, and I longed for the touch of the first man. I kept hoping Derek would show up and find me.*

Now she turned back to the communications panel, to the

monitors that told her how far and in what direction each of the
search vehicles was. One was straying close to the edge of the
sector Derek wanted unsearched. "Terry, this is Karen. You're
overlapping areas with Jason. There's a sector just south of you
that's only been ground searched. Can you take your heli down
there?"

Karen tried to think of the captain and Dr. Winthrop being on
that mountain to the southwest. She suspected they weren't
really, but it was best not to dwell on that. She imagined instead
that they were there among the survivors they had discovered,
examining ancient towers and office buildings, talking with people who lived a purer, simpler way of life. How primitive were
they? she wondered. Did they hunt and fish as well as raising
their own fruits and vegetables? Did they use projectile rifles, or
had they reverted to bows and spears? Had any horses survived
for them to ride?

With a deep sigh, Karen knew that she would never find out.
The mountain installation was off limits to all, even to her. There
would be no point in asking Derek to take her there. He'd want
to know why, and she couldn't explain it even to herself. It was
just that this was Earth, the world of her fantasies, the place
where her father could never find her, and somehow everything
was more exciting.

Exciting. She looked at the panel of instruments in front of
her. All Earth lay outside that door, and she was chained to this
instrument panel. Things were expected of her. She had a job
to do.

But at least the door was open.

Ben Gonzales was surprised to see Coconino coming out to
the fields. It was well known that Coconino disdained farming
and worked in the fields only at harvest time or when the crop
was threatened by some natural calamity. Ben's first thought was
for the Mother, but so eminent a messenger would not be sent
with news, even great news. Coconino wanted something.

So Ben continued hoeing the squash, waiting until the young
man stopped beside him. Then he looked up politely. "Good
day, Coconino."

"Good day, Teacher."

Ben went on cutting at the stubborn weeds with his tool made
from the shoulder blade of a mule deer. "It looks like a rich
harvest," Coconino observed, then added glumly, "should we
live to enjoy it."

That stopped Ben. He stood up and waited for the young man to continue.

"These Others," Coconino began carefully. "They have weapons of great power. There are such weapons on the Mountain, too, I know, and I wondered if you could tell me about them."

Ben knew something dangerous was afoot here, and he leaned on his hoe, trying to discern what it was. "I'm not a man of weapons," he replied. "Perhaps you should ask Phoenix."

"I have," Coconino told him. "She says that weapons like this need a source of power; our bows and clubs use the power of our arms, but these weapons need some other kind of power which is stored in a container. Is this true?"

"Probably. I haven't seen the weapons."

"But what kind of power is it?" he asked, perplexed. "It has no weight, it has no sharp edge—how does it do what it does?"

Ben saw then why Phoenix had not been able to explain to Coconino even how a disrupter worked, much less the weapons brought from off planet. Which of them truly understood the conversion of mass, the fusing of molecular bonds, the invisible energy that caused such damage? Even if he had understood the principles, Ben could not have begun to relate them in terms Coconino would understand. He only shrugged his shoulders. "It's a kind of magic, Coconino. Very few people understand it. I don't."

Coconino shifted his weight and toed a stone in the shallow irrigation trench that ran between the rows of plants. "This is bad," he murmured, and was silent for several moments, thinking. Then, "If someone threw a knife at me," he said, "I could duck. Or if a puma attacked me with its claws and its teeth, I could wrestle with it and hope to overcome it. But tell me, Teacher, how can I fight what I cannot see?"

The hair on the back of Ben's neck prickled in spite of the warmth of the day. "Why should you have to fight it?" he asked uncomfortably. "The Others are not hostile. They have not come here to harm you."

"Not yet," Coconino conceded. "But something gnaws at me like a rat at a basket. If even one of them should grow angry, how can we withstand their weapons?"

Ben did not like the bent of the conversation and turned angrily back to his hoeing. He did not like the implication; he did not like the kernel of truth in it. Most of all he did not like the fact that since the reported contact with offworlders, no hopper had come to take him back to the Mountain. Why hadn't they called him back?

"Well, you can't wrestle with such weapons, Coconino," he replied testily. "So perhaps you'd better learn to duck."

Tala stood atop the cliff on whose face the Village of the Ancients hung. He did not know that once the last remnant of a band of dreamers had stood here, drenched in torrential winter rains, despairing of any haven from the slashing storm. He did not know that once a boy of seventeen had clawed his way to the edge, hoping against hope that this was, indeed, the mountain in which was the cliff dwelling he had sighted two days earlier and that he had brought his girlfriend, her sister, and the other few survivors to a place of refuge and not death. Tala did not know, nor did he care, about the faith professed but not felt, the optimism that was only bravado, the quiet resolution that if he was wrong, the boy rappelling his way down the cliff face would simply let go of the rope rather than bear the responsibility for his error.

No, Tala felt only the Evil in the ground and smelled the Wrongness in the air.

I would be away from this place, Tala thought as he stamped the ground uneasily. I would return to the pure air of the Black Lands that is untainted by the smell of human beings, any human beings. I would run and soar and trumpet to the wind—

But it will follow me, this Evil. It will creep even to the Black Lands, and I must stop it. We must stop it, Coconino and I.

Again Tala tested the wind, and this time he detected a scent that puzzled him. There was something else afoot here, something that stirred his curiosity. In the collective memory of his kind there was the scent of another place . . . What was it? Somehow there was a coming and going by the Others that he did not understand—but that was not new . . .

Come, Coconino, brother of my soul. Let us draw closer to the camp of the Others that I may see this thing—before we destroy it . . .

"Look, it's like a wrinkle," Phoenix tried again. "Like they took all the space between here and their Sky Ship and folded it so they can pass from one to the other."

"I do not understand," Coconino repeated, shaking his head. The pain grew worse when he tried to comprehend this Place That Bends Space. "I see no fold."

"You don't see the wind, either."

"Do the people become birds and fly?" Coconino asked hopefully.

"No, no, the people don't change," Phoenix replied in exasperation, "the space between objects changes. It becomes time. I think."

"Is time bent, too?" Coconino wanted to know. "Can they make today tomorrow?"

"Yes. No." Now she was totally frustrated and more than a little confused herself. Finally she fell back on her standard explanation for things he couldn't grasp. "It's magic. They step into the Magic Place here and step out in the Magic Place on their Sky Ship."

"Today or tomorrow?" he wanted to know.

"Forget what I said about time," she growled. "That only happens if there's a terrible mistake."

He shifted to a new line of thinking. "How can we destroy this Magic Place?"

Phoenix rubbed at her forehead, trying to erase a dull ache that she had put down to lack of sleep but that had not gone away overnight. "We don't want to destroy it, Coconino," she explained. "We need to use it to get up to the Sky Ship so we can destroy the Sky Ship."

"But if we destroy the Magic Place, the Others will not be able to get from the Sky Ship to the Mother Earth. That is what we want."

"But the Sky Ship can fly away," Phoenix growled, "back to the Sisters of the Mother Earth, and tell them there really is no disease. Then they will come back and bring another Magic Place."

Finally Coconino nodded. "Yes, I understand," he said. "I had hoped—but it is not to be so easy. So, first we speak to the stars, our false message of disease; then we destroy the Sky Ship, and then . . ." His voice trailed off. Mother Earth, why did you send me the dream, the dream where I was swallowed by a great burning thing? The words of Black Elk came back to him: *It is a good day to die . . .*

"Then we use the Magic Place to come back to the Mother Earth," Phoenix finished evenly, her eyes fixed on his face. If he had voiced his fear, it could have been no plainer to her. "We come back, and we return to the People. And you have sons and daughters, and we teach them how to hunt together and tell them of the great day when Coconino destroyed the Sky Ship and ended the threat of the Others.''

"With the Mother Earth's help," he corrected, gazing out over the Village that was so dear to him. *Take courage, boy. The Earth is all that lasts* . . . "Only with the Mother Earth's help. I cannot stand alone."

She touched his arm, and he looked into a face that for once was as open and unclouded as a spring sky. "I stand with you, Coconino," she whispered. "Now and always. I stand with you."

In that moment he knew he could reach her, knew she would put no obstacles in his path, but in that moment his half brother Flint came pounding up to them. "We are ready, Coconino," the boy cried, flushed with excitement. "All wait by the creek for you to tell them the plan."

Coconino sat back from the map he had made in the sand and looked at his boyhood friend as though for the first time. He saw a wiry man with a gaudy red headband and a wide grin, a nose that dipped down toward his upper lip, and bright, dark eyes with permanent smile creases etched around them. Juan was ever confident, ever unperturbed. *We have grown to manhood, you and I,* Coconino thought; *I am twenty, and you are twenty-two. If we do not live beyond tomorrow, at least we have lived fully.*

He turned then to his brother-in-law, Falling Star. *Come back to my sister,* he willed the younger man. *You are seventeen, and you have but one child; come back and give her another.*

Then his eyes fell on his half brother. Flint was twelve, just coming into his manhood. The gangly youth squatted in the circle of hunters, intently studying the marks in the sand that would lead them to a rendezvous with Phoenix and Coconino. Coconino's eyes darkened. "Flint," he said.

The boy looked up eagerly, surprised to be noticed by his illustrious half brother. When he saw the look in Coconino's eyes, however, his heart sank. "We cannot leave the village unprotected," Coconino began.

"All the farmers are staying here!" the boy protested. "And Lookout and Fire Keeper and Three-Legged Coyote—you need every bow you can get for the battle!"

"There will be no battle!" Coconino snapped. "We would lose. We are to steal their fireshooters—no more. Our arrows are only to defend ourselves."

"Dreamer," Phoenix muttered under her breath.

"Then you need someone small and quiet, like me," Flint pressed. "I can steal a quail's egg from her nest while she sits on it. I can be of best use to the People with you."

Coconino balked, but he knew the boy was right. He could not save his brother any more than he could save himself. They were all servants of the Mother Earth.

"That is the plan, then," Coconino said, turning back to the others. "We meet before dawn in the hills north of their camp. Phoenix and I will tell you what we can about where their fireshooters are to be found and when we will need to make our raid."

"But what do these fireshooters look like?" Falling Star asked in perplexity. "How will we know them from the many other tools the Others use?"

Coconino scowled and scratched his head thoughtfully. He had not seen Lujan's weapon clearly since most of it had been concealed in his hand. He looked to Phoenix, but she hesitated and he knew she was not sure, either. "It's a piece of plastic," she began. "It's . . ." her voice trailed off uselessly.

"Is it the thing he wore on his belt?" Flint piped up.

Coconino turned to stare at the youth. "You saw this thing?"

"It looked like two sticks that meet," Flint continued, illustrating by putting his fingers together in a T shape. "I wondered what it was, since it was too small to be a canteen and had no sharp edge for cutting. I thought it must be some tool like the Men-on-the-Mountain carry sometimes. When he was nervous, he would touch it. Is that the fireshooter?"

Coconino and Phoenix exchanged a look. Both of them had watched Lujan like a hawk, yet neither had noticed in their scrutiny of the outsider what this boy in his curiosity had observed. "That is the thing," Coconino agreed. "You must—" Here he hesitated again, but there was no help for it. "You must show Juan what they are. And you and he must watch the village to see which of the Others carry such fireshooters in their belts. Of them you must beware."

"With luck, we'll be able to learn more from inside their camp," Phoenix put in. "We will tell you when we meet you before dawn."

"If we do not meet you—" Coconino began, then broke off. "If we do not meet you, then you must learn all you can by hunter's stealth and—and do what you can. Just do what you can."

He glanced up at the sun, which was slipping quickly behind

the cliff wall. "Go while you still have daylight," he bade them. "As the Mother Earth wills, I will meet you before dawn tomorrow."

With murmurs and quiet jests and the sound of Juan's laughter, the hunters trotted away. Coconino turned back to Phoenix. "Once we have spoken to the stars, you will join them," he instructed. "Juan is a good hunter, but he has not your strength of will. You must lead with him. You must make sure the fireshooters are thrown in the river and not one of them is kept."

"And just where will you be?" she demanded, wishing the answer she feared did not have the feel of truth.

A wry smile twisted Coconino's lips. "I will be where the Mother Earth wants me."

"Well, that's all right for today," she said grudgingly, "and maybe tomorrow. But when this is over, I've got a claim on a few of your nights."

Coconino caught his breath, believing for the first time that his dream might have some other meaning. "My nights?" he stammered.

Make me this promise, Mother Earth, Phoenix prayed. If you can hear me, make me this one promise. "Hell, if Lujan can take a Chosen Companion, so can I. I deserve it, don't you think?"

Coconino caught her arm as she started away. His head was full of images of the two of them cloaked in darkness in her tiny chamber within the Village of the Ancients, and he did not want to risk its never coming to pass. "Now," he whispered hoarsely.

"No." His eyes were compelling, but Phoenix stood her ground. "When this is over, Coconino. Not until this is over."

Behind the resolution in her eyes he saw a quiet despair, and he understood then the bargain she was making. It would get her through all of this. Perhaps, he thought, it will get me through as well. Her body gleamed bronze and smooth in the sun, and he longed to caress it, feel it hard and warm beneath his hands now, before it was too late, but he knew she would never agree. "This pledge is made," he said finally. "I will hold you to it."

Lujan squatted beside Karen at her comm station. Showered and shaven, he felt a world better than he had when he'd trundled into camp that morning. Outside, the sun was dipping toward the horizon; soon the search parties would be returning empty-handed and discouraged. "What's the crew situation on the *Homeward Bound*?" he asked.

"Optimum," she told him. "We could go any time in the

next four hours; otherwise we'll have to wait an additional eight hours to get the same shift on duty without suspicion.''

Lujan rubbed his chin thoughtfully. Four hours; four hours to come up with a cover story, a reason for marooning the bulk of the crew. He had ruled out radiation as a possible reason; new sophisticated equipment could confirm or deny such an allegation. Continuing global disasters were his best alternative so far, but they would spark interest in the geological community. They'd want to send probes. What he needed was for everyone to forget about Earth, to write it off as a dead planet of no possible use. As long as he had something to account for the ''deaths'' of his crew.

Suddenly Karen gasped. "Derek, there's something coming down from the northwest. By air. We don't have any helis in that section; it must be—I don't know, a bird, I guess. But a huge bird. Maybe my equipment's malfunctioning.''

But Lujan was on his feet and headed for the command post door. "It's not your equipment," he snarled. "And it's no bird. It's that goddamn aborigine on his goddamn unicorn!''

CHAPTER TWENTY-THREE

Wings backflapping furiously, Tala alighted with a majestic trumpet in front of the openmouthed offworlders. That an animal of such size should have survived on Earth amazed them. That it flew was more wondrous still. But that seated regally upon its back were two humans in royal array absolutely astounded them.

Both wore ceremonial shirts of white cotton richly embroidered with black, red, and yellow. Across the chest and back yoke of the shirts, ribbons of colored cloth had been painstakingly sewn, their ends dangling some twelve inches from the shoulders. Soft buckskin leggings encased their lower legs, adorned with fringes and feathers, and moccasins covered their feet. Their headbands, like their loincloths, were of simple muslin, unadorned.

At Lujan's elbow, Karen watched in fascination as the woman slid down first, the freshly polished silver of her medallion catching the sun. But it was the man who held her riveted as he sat astride the great beast, eyeing the crowd severely. Here is what I came to Earth to find, she thought. Truly, in this man is personified the ancient home of humankind in all its fierce and rugged glory. The fragile could be dashed against the harshness of that face—or borne by its strength forever.

Slowly, deliberately, Coconino looked over the offworlders. He was taking in their numbers, the drabness of their dress. How pitiful we must look to him, Karen thought; how plain, how sterile!

"Stay back!" Lujan called imperiously to his crew. Then, stepping forward, away from sharp eyes and ears, he nailed Coconino with a glare that would have melted steel. "What the hell do you think you're doing here?" he demanded under his breath.

"I am visiting your village," Coconino replied with great dignity and a trace of innocence. "I came for a feast, some dancing, and a Chosen Companion."

"I thought we agreed that no one but me should know about your People!"

"You agreed that," Coconino told him. "I agreed only that no more Others may come here."

"And where am I supposed to tell these people you came from?" Lujan grated through clenched teeth.

"Tell them anything you wish," Coconino said. "I do not wish to disturb any plans you have made." Lujan sputtered and barely controlled his temper. "I wish only to make merry with my new friends and to see the amazing magic of your machines. And perhaps," Coconino added, "to solve your problem of what to say to the Sky."

Alarm bells sounded in Lujan's head, but there was little he could do. In truth, it didn't matter what these people saw or heard of Earth; they were not going back. He turned to the knot of gaping technicians at his back. "He says his name is Coconino," Lujan told them. "He and his friend have come from a small village near here. Ladies and gentlemen, we have discovered native Terrans."

Turning back to Coconino, Lujan flashed him a frozen smile. "Just do me a favor," he said tightly. "Don't mention the Mountain or anything connected with it. Okay?"

Coconino inclined his head slightly.

"Well, let's not just stand here!" Lujan's manner was suddenly warm, exuding his radiant charm. "This is a great event! A great discovery! Tony, assign a detail to set up some long tables outside. We'll have a banquet to celebrate! Oh, and get Anasiah to run the commissary; he's an absolute genius at it. This is incredible! Karen, come on, we'll show our guests around the camp."

Coconino tossed his leg over Tala's head and slid gracefully to the ground. Several people were scurrying away; most remained to gape at the great beast and the riders he had brought. With a gentle crooning and a slap to the withers Coconino bade the unicorn depart, which Tala did with alacrity and a trace of disgust. Trotting sharply away from the crowd, he shook himself once, put forth a sudden burst of speed, then snapped open his wings and was airborne.

In the hush of amazement at his departure, an older woman stepped forward and challenged Lujan. She was heavy-set with dark skin, her mechanic's protective glasses pushed back into tightly curling black hair. "What about the search, Mr. Lujan?" she demanded.

Lujan turned to face the chief engineer. His eyes were hard at first, but the woman would not give ground before him. So he smiled indulgently and drew himself up importantly. "The search goes on, Rita," he answered. "I'm not calling any teams back. But the captain and the good doctor would want us to celebrate this occasion, to entertain our long-lost kindred. As long as I'm in command, this mission will be conducted in the spirit in which Captain Winthrop would have conducted it."

The woman smiled back at him, but it was an acid smile and the hatred still burned in her eyes. Lujan turned his back on her and led Coconino and Phoenix toward one of the domes.

Coconino saw that Phoenix was wearing her mask, the one she used when she wanted no one to know what she was thinking. That is good, he thought. We must both wear masks in this place. "The Winthrops are missing?" Phoenix asked Lujan, her tone noncommittal as well.

"Not exactly," Lujan replied, "but it keeps the crew occupied."

She made no response; the mask did not slip.

"The people of your camp," Coconino said. "They do not all heed your every word."

"They follow me," Lujan hedged. "Some like it less than others."

Coconino studied the man from the corner of his eye, wondering if Lujan thought he was really that stupid. "If they return to the Sky Places, you cannot keep them from speaking to others about us."

"You're the idiot who showed up here."

There was a slight pause. "That was unfortunate," Coconino said. "Now they will have to stay."

"Yes," Lujan agreed quietly. "They will have to stay."

Coconino fastened his eyes on the ugly white domes of the camp. "The People are at peace with that."

Why, you sly bastard, Lujan thought. You had that planned, didn't you? What else do you have planned? And does it truly coincide with my interests?

"Now, what were you saying earlier?" Lujan asked casually. "About what to say to the Sky?"

"To speak of that now would be bad manners," Coconino told him as casually. "Later, after the feasting and the dancing.

And perhaps—'' Here he cast an appreciative glance at the woman beside Lujan. ''—there will be a Choosing?''

Lujan bit down on his tongue, then pasted the smile back on his face. ''Well,'' he replied evenly, ''we must all mind our manners, mustn't we?''

Walking at Lujan's elbow, Karen felt her heart skip as Coconino looked at her. Magnificent, she thought. Like an Arabian sheik, or a medieval knight, or a Cossack warrior. She did not know what a Choosing was, but she felt that she had been complimented. Were all the men of his village so striking, she wondered, so colorful? Or was Coconino the king, the leader of his people? Yes, yes, such a man must be at the very least a prince.

They were approaching the shuttle now. Lujan waved to a dome near it. ''This is the command center,'' he said. ''Karen, you'd better get back to the comm station. Get in touch with the search crews; tell them we have a little surprise for them when they get back to camp.''

Karen balked; no, no, don't send me away! Let me stay with you. Let me stay with him . . . just a little while longer.

''May she not come with us?'' Coconino asked.

He wants me along, her heart sang. He wants me to come—

''She'll join us later,'' Lujan promised. ''At the feast. For now, she has duties to attend to.''

''So you're a comm tech,'' Phoenix observed.

''Yes.'' The woman made Karen nervous. Her English was better, with less of an accent than Coconino's, but there was something cold about her. There was nothing cold about Coconino.

Phoenix nudged Coconino. ''This woman is the one who speaks to the Sky.''

''Many of us do,'' Lujan interjected. ''But Karen is the best. And the most trustworthy.'' He nodded to Karen, and she started inside.

''Karen,'' Coconino said, savoring the quality of her name. She stopped, arrested by the richness of his voice. ''I look forward to seeing you again at the feast,'' he told her. He held out his hand to her in the manner he had learned on the Mountain.

Karen struggled for breath as she reached to take his hand. It was brown and rough and dwarfed her own dainty one. A thrill shot through her as they touched, and she dared not look into his eyes for fear she would be lost. But Coconino's grip was surprisingly gentle, and she glanced up to see a boy's smile on the man's face. Only when he let go of her hand could she shake herself free of the paralysis that gripped her; she retreated hastily into the command center.

"I think I frighten her," Coconino observed with a wry smile as they started away.

"Strong men frighten her," Lujan replied.

"And you do not?"

Lujan smiled sardonically. "A strong hand can wear a silk glove."

The allusion was lost on Coconino; he had never heard of silk. But Phoenix spoke softly at his ear. "I think he means," she said in the language of the People, "that she is his woman."

"Ah," Coconino acknowledged wisely. Then he turned his attention to the business at hand. "What is inside these strange wickiups?" he asked Lujan. "May we see?"

Lujan flashed his cold smile and led them to another nearby dome. He placed his hand on a marked panel, and a door slid open. Phoenix took note of the mechanism; there were few such locks left on the mountain, but she understood their operation. They were keyed to the lines and whorls of the handprints of authorized persons.

Inside, the dome had a spacious feeling. Twice Coconino's height, it held four bunks, storage compartments, and a few personal effects. "Crew quarters," Lujan told them.

Coconino glanced around, trying to ignore the stale smell that pervaded the air. How could the Others stand it without the scent of the Mother Earth to refresh them? He had noticed as soon as he had slid from Tala's back that the Mother Earth was withdrawing from this place. His pain was less troublesome here, but neither did he have the feeling of closeness that had been his all his life. Inside the buildings the effect was even worse, as though the Earth were developing a callus in this place. He smiled and nodded politely to Lujan but escaped back outside as soon as he could.

Phoenix paused in the doorway as she followed him, bending to adjust her leggings. Surreptitiously she checked the latch. It was essentially tongue and groove, with a portion of the door panel sliding inside the frame. It would be virtually impossible to force entry to one of these domes.

Lujan led the way between the scattered domes, and Phoenix saw that they were numbered. "This is the commissary," Lujan said, waving his hand toward one. "We use a food synthesizer to make various things out of generic proteins and carbohydrates. Those two are supply huts." Phoenix noted their numbers: ten and eleven. "The two largest ones there are the motor pool. I'd show you our vehicles, but they're all out on the search right now, except for the one I had. They'll come back about dark."

"Empty-handed?" Phoenix asked.

"I told you," he replied easily, "the Winthrops aren't really lost."

Phoenix smiled benignly. "Where are they?"

"On the mountain, of course. But I can't really tell people here that. Karen and I are the only ones who know about the settlement there. At this point, it needs to stay that way."

Just sitting quietly on the mountain, waiting—impossible, Phoenix knew. But why are no hoppers coming here? And what happened to the one I saw leaving there just after we left? If the Winthrops were on board—

Suddenly Phoenix knew, and she slammed all her defenses into place. Don't let on that you know! she screamed at herself. Don't give yourself away! Don't— Damn you, Lujan. Damn you! She was a nice lady. And a doctor.

With great difficulty she forced herself to focus on the more immediate problem. "Could we have a look inside the motor pool, anyway?" she asked. "I'm a mechanic by trade, and I'm a bit curious."

Lujan considered. What was she up to, this steely woman? "You mustn't let on that you know anything about mechanics," he cautioned.

She forced a smile. "Don't worry. Your tools are probably so far advanced from what I know that I won't have any idea what I'm looking at."

It proved to be quite true. As they entered through an open bay door, the shocking whiteness of the interior struck Phoenix like a blow. No greasy lubricants, no gritty dirt on the floor, no racks of tarnished metal tools. Everything here was clean and dust-free. In one corner a woman in a gray coverall turned from a workbench to stare at them. It was Rita, the woman who had challenged Lujan earlier.

Phoenix nodded at her, then began to stroll the perimeter of the huge dome with Coconino and Lujan following. Here and there she spotted something familiar: a rack of hammers, a set of wrenches, a sonic cleaner. But there were workstations with screens, boxes of sterilized gloves, and containment chambers that seemed to her more the province of hospitals than that of a garage. Nowhere did she see anything that might help Juan break into the supply huts.

Ever the genial host, Lujan spouted off names of the various devices, occasionally explaining in insultingly simple terms the gross use of something. Phoenix smiled and nodded in imitation of Coconino's undiscerning response.

They came in due course to the workbench where Rita directed the movements of a tiny tool by means of a light pen on a computer screen. Phoenix watched in fascination as the instrument, the size of a sewing needle, probed a jumbled mass of crystals.

"The sounder from my landcrawler," Lujan told them. "There's a short in it somewhere; it's been driving Rita crazy trying to find it. Right, Rita?"

"These switches don't slip, Mr. Lujan," Rita replied coldly. "If one of them does prove to be set wrong, it will be because of willful sabotage."

"Yes, well, we've had more than our share of that on this trip, haven't we?" Lujan muttered darkly. "Don't worry, Rita; we'll find out who did this." Then, quietly, he added, "Just between you and me, I've got it narrowed down to about four people with access and skill."

Phoenix picked up a sonic wrench that lay on the workbench and twirled it idly, watching the ease with which Lujan lied to the woman. She could almost believe him herself. "I intend to have the culprit's head on a platter for the captain when he's found," Lujan finished.

But Rita was not fooled. She parted her lips in a grimace that was more sneer than smile. "I'm sure you will, Mr. Lujan. I'm sure you will."

"And here we are back at the command center," Lujan concluded, ushering them inside that dome. "Karen, is everyone back now?"

"All except one heli, and it's due momentarily," she replied. She rose and turned her seat over to a young man who stood waiting.

"Is this where you speak to the Sky?" Coconino asked her.

Karen quieted her fluttering heart. "I can't send messages to Argo from here, if that's what you mean. It has to be done from the *Homeward Bound*, where we have the equipment to warp them . . ." She paused, sure he would not understand that terminology.

"Ah! You have a Magic Place that Bends Space on your Sky Ship," he surmised, "so that the messages may pass from this place to that."

"Yes." She was startled at his comprehension, limited though it was. "Yes, we have a Magic Place, and once a day I take all the dispatches—all the messages—and send them back to our home planet."

"The Sister of the Mother Earth," he said.

Mother Earth! she thought. How poetic, how beautiful.

"Well, let's go on to our feast," Lujan prodded jovially. "Everyone is waiting for the guests of honor."

Phoenix lagged behind the others as they left the dome and started for the long tables set up nearby. Their message had to be sent from the ship; that was a bad stumbling block. Lujan was not likely to allow them up there, and if he did, he most certainly would not allow them back. Such a consequence would not deter Coconino, of course, but Phoenix intended for both of them to come through this alive.

If Lujan had summarily dispatched the captain and Dr. Winthrop, he would not hesitate to dispatch the two of them when they were no longer needed. They needed another ally in this camp, needed one badly. So far, there was only one logical possibility.

Karen. She walked at Lujan's elbow, seeming to shrink from Coconino and toward her protector, but Phoenix knew why. Hadn't she built walls around herself when she had first met the young hunter? "I think I frighten her," he had said. Oh, yes, she is frightened, Phoenix thought, but not of you. She is frightened by the way she feels when she looks at you. She has her nice, safe, comfortable relationship with Lujan, and you threaten that safety. You threaten it by stirring up her desire.

But we can use her desire, Phoenix thought. We can play on it to lure her in, to gain her help. We must get her to the point where she will do what you ask just because you ask it, as she does with Lujan. But that won't happen through your casual flirtation.

Yet even his casual flirtation was painful to her, but if they were to carry this off, they must have Karen's help. So she must control her jealousy and let Coconino go this one last time . . .

They feasted on strange stuff that Phoenix found tasteless and unsubstantial after the diet of the People. On top of that, she was uneasy with the feeling that someone was watching her.

Everyone was watching them, of course, but Phoenix felt sure there was one pair of eyes somewhere . . . Stabbing a piece of simulated fowl with her knife, she turned casually and surveyed the crowd of people at the long tables. Most of them were watching Coconino, which did not surprise her. He certainly had Karen's attention, though she tended to watch from the corner of her eye or from under half-lowered eyelids.

Still Phoenix felt the eyes boring into her. Was it only Juan or one of the other hunters watching from the darkness? Or was it—

There! Her eyes fastened on the dark-skinned woman from the motor pool, met the cool, level gaze that was surveying her. Rita did not turn away, nor did she reveal surprise at being caught. Then slowly, deliberately, Rita shifted her gaze to the bonfire Lujan had ordered—''for atmosphere,'' he'd said. When Rita turned her eyes back, Phoenix nodded. ''My brother, I will tend the fire,'' Phoenix told Coconino. ''These Others do not know how to keep a steady blaze.'' Then she slid back from the table and made her way to the flames.

Rita had positioned herself on the far side of the fire from Lujan. Phoenix crossed carefully to a point that was within Lujan's sight but from which she could see and hear the older woman. There she squatted with a large stick, poking at the burning logs, adjusting their positions.

''You speak English better than he,'' Rita said flatly.

''Quite a bit better,'' Phoenix acknowledged.

''You also toyed with that sonic wrench like someone who handles one every day.''

Phoenix gave a start, then covered the telltale movement by brushing at an imaginary cinder. She poked at the fire again. ''It's funny,'' she said. ''I don't even remember picking one up.''

''Which means this village Coconino is from is not the only village on the planet.''

Phoenix hesitated. ''That's one explanation.''

Now Rita was silent for a moment, and Phoenix was nearly ready to return to the long tables when she spoke again. ''Where are the captain and the doctor?''

Phoenix exhaled deeply. ''I don't know,'' she replied honestly. ''But Lujan does.''

Rita swore under her breath. ''Have you seen them?''

''Two days ago.''

''Where?''

Again Phoenix hesitated. If this woman went off half-cocked, if she contacted her home world or stirred up the rest of the crew, it could spoil any chance of keeping Earth quiet with a minimum of violence. "Just let the search continue," she said finally. She had picked up the gist of Lujan's fable over dinner. "If they don't turn up in another day, I'll help you."

"When you saw them, were they—" Rita licked her lips. "Were they alive?"

"They were."

Even in the veiled answer Rita discerned Phoenix's fears. "You don't think they still are."

Phoenix arose and tossed her stick into the fire. Brushing off her hands, she asked, "Do you think they would voluntarily stay away from their crew for this long?" Then she turned and walked back to where the tables were being cleared away in preparation for further festivities.

As the Witch Woman rejoined Coconino, he excused himself from Lujan to go to the river and wash. Without comment Phoenix followed him, and he was glad of the chance to drop his facade and speak openly with the Witch Woman.

He began by spitting on the ground and using several of the words he had learned from Phoenix. There was mild amusement in her eyes as she looked at him. "You're picking up bad habits," she said. "You should stop hanging around me."

Unexpectedly he drew her close, his arms locked around her slender body. "I will do more than 'hang around,'" he promised. Phoenix resisted gently, but he had had enough of Others and their callous disregard for the soil on which they had erected their ugly, smelly little village. "I will not sleep in their place tonight," he hissed. "It will stifle me. I will sleep here by the river." The pain was stronger here, but he could keep it pushed back, out of the way. Urgently he pulled her tighter to him. "Come spread your blanket with mine."

But Phoenix shook her head. "Not tonight," she hissed back, forcing the screaming of her blood to quiet so she could think clearly. "You must spend this night with someone else."

Startled, he pulled back to search her face.

Phoenix forged on. "We need help to finish this, Coconino. We need to make sure the right message is sent to the stars. And we need to destroy the Sky Ship; you know that. No Others may leave this place, especially not Lujan. We need someone who will take us up to the ship, someone who will let us return after we have crippled it. We need Karen."

Coconino frowned. "She is Lujan's woman."

"So Lujan thinks."

"But if he thinks I have stolen his woman—"

"He doesn't have to know." Damn it, Coconino, don't make this harder for me. "I'll fix it. Somehow. Leave it to me. I'll get you two alone together. I'll—" Her voice caught. "Just know what you have to do."

Still he resisted. "I do not understand why that would help," he persisted. "She is afraid of me. I will only make her more afraid."

But Phoenix shook her head. "She fears the confusion she feels, but that confusion can be useful to us. Trust me on this one. Go slowly, but go surely."

"Even if it is so and she desires to be my Chosen Companion," he said, "why would my joining with her convince her to do what we ask?"

Phoenix gave a short laugh that was dangerously close to a sob. "If I knew the answer to that," she told him, "I'd be the greatest psychologist the world has ever known."

Coconino saw then how it hurt her and knew that it was something she would not suggest if she did not feel strongly that it was necessary. "All right," he said finally. "I will do as you ask. But only because you say so. And every moment I will wish I were with you instead."

CHAPTER TWENTY-FOUR

The Others were unaccustomed to dancing, but they sang some songs for Coconino. There were nonsense songs and folk songs, some bawdy and some sweet. One woman brought out an instrument and sang a ballad about the hills of her home planet, Quince, and Coconino was moved. Poor woman, he thought. Soon you must learn to sing songs of the Mother Earth instead.

Then they called on him to sing for them, but he declined. "The songs of the People are all of the Mother Earth and her creatures," he said. "When you know Her better, we will sing them for you. As for me, I am more storyteller than singer."

At that, they would have no refusal, and with feigned reluctance Coconino agreed to tell them one of the Stories of the People.

"Once," he began, "in the Times that were Before the Times That Are, there lived among the People a great Shaman. He was a fierce man, full of magic and the knowledge of the Mother Earth. At times he would speak so fervently with the Mother Earth that his spirit would leave his body and sail with the hawk or burrow with the hare into Her very bosom. Then would his spirit return to its body, and he gave good counsel to the People.

"Yet he was a cruel man. Because of his knowledge of the Mother Earth the People had great respect for him. Because of his powerful magic they had great fear of him. But no one had love of the Shaman, for his ways were not loving and his heart was tinged with black. Beware, O People, of the powerful leader whose heart is black!"

Phoenix shifted uncomfortably, and she saw several of his listeners exchange glances, but Coconino continued smoothly on.

"The Shaman had three wives in his lifetime, for when one

died, he would take another. Even as an old man, his woman would swell with child and the People were blessed. So it was, when the third of his wives died, he sought another to increase the number of his children among the People.

"The maiden he chose was fair and young, having only just celebrated her Womanhood. But when he brought his gifts to her door, her mother refused them. Though she feared him beyond any in the village, yet she would not let him take her daughter to wife.

"The Shaman was angered. He called down the curse of the Mother Earth on the woman, and the next day her husband, whom she loved beyond measure, was bitten by a rattlesnake and died. Then came the Shaman to the woman's wickiup and dragged her daughter out, but instead of taking her to a Wedding Chamber in the Village of the Ancients, he forced her back to his own wickiup to lie with her. This is a shameful thing among the People, and there was great murmuring against the Shaman. But the People feared him, and they feared their own fate, for if the Shaman were gone, who would speak with the Mother Earth as he had spoken? Who would bear Her service and instruct the People?"

Coconino looked out at their enrapt faces. He saw Karen hanging on his words, saw the hungering in her eyes. "Then the mother of She Who Was Shamed cried out to the Mother Earth. 'Vindicate your daughter!' she cried. 'I will take your service. I will bear the burden among the People; only strike this evil man and blot him out from among us!'

"Then did the Mother Earth hearken to this mother's plea. She revealed to the woman the secret of the Shaman's visions, a root which, when chewed, opens the mind to the voice of the Mother Earth. This the woman mixed with other plants of which she knew and made a potion for the Shaman. She told him it was full of great power and presented it as a gift of atonement for refusing him. The Shaman drank it greedily.

"When he had done so, his spirit took flight in the form of a wren, swooping and gliding through the air. But as the People watched, a hawk came shrieking after the wren and crushed it. Then the spirit of the Shaman came no more to his body."

Coconino surveyed the faces that surrounded him, strange faces, not faces of the People. "It is not the Way of the People," he told them, "for one to take the life of another. And it was not the way of the young woman's mother to do such a thing; she was a kind and gentle woman, wanting only peace. Yet when she took up the service of the Mother Earth, she was forced to do a thing she did not like, a thing she hated, and the People did not condemn her. When one serves the Mother Earth, one does what one has to do.''

There was a long, uncomfortable silence. Phoenix stirred and rose. ''I am tired, my brother,'' she said pointedly. ''Let us rest by the river tonight, where we can see the stars from our beds. Then in the morning Lujan will show us how he speaks to those stars.''

''Coconino,'' Lujan said as his crew began to drift away toward their sleeping quarters, ''shall we talk now?''

But Coconino yawned and stretched luxuriously. ''Tomorrow is soon enough. I am tired. Since it is not your custom to grant the Right of a Chosen Companion, my sister-brother and I will go make our beds among the cottonwoods.''

''What is the Right of a Chosen Companion?'' Karen asked innocently.

Lujan glared at her. ''It's their custom to offer a stranger a sleeping partner. Any other questions?''

Karen drew back.

''It is a great honor among the People,'' Coconino told the slender, dark-haired girl. ''The maidens all vie for the privilege of being the Chosen Companion and perhaps bearing a child.'' But instead of enticing her, this information seemed to make Karen shrink farther away, back toward Lujan. You are wrong, Phoenix, Coconino thought. She will not come to my bed this night.

But as they started for the cottonwoods that lined the river, Phoenix stopped and turned back. ''The night breeze is cool,'' she said. ''Perhaps you have some spare blankets . . .''

''Of course,'' Lujan replied. ''Karen, get our guests some blankets from the supply shed.''

''Thank you. We will be by the river building a fire to ward off the mosquitoes.'' Then she and Coconino melted into the darkness.

Watching them disappear, Karen slipped her arm around Lujan's waist. ''Oh, Derek, aren't they . . . fascinating?''

Derek studied her in the starlight, then on impulse pulled her close and kissed her intimately. She responded with a passion he had never felt in her before. Indeed, he had thought real passion beyond her.

"Hon, I've got a lot on my mind tonight," he told her, pulling carefully away. "Take the blankets down to them, will you? I'll see you in the morning."

Karen watched him go into his dome and close the door. For a moment she simply stood there, alone in the vast velvet night, listening to the call of night birds and feeling the kiss of the breeze cool on her hot flesh. In the air was a scent of pine, a pungent odor that fed her longing.

The one night I really wanted you, Derek Lujan, she thought, you closed your door on me. And if I didn't know better, I'd swear you did it on purpose.

From the cracked door to his quarters Lujan watched Karen as she carried her bundle toward the direction of the river, wondering if she would actually stay the night. But the truth was, it didn't matter. What mattered was what he had felt in the kiss they had shared.

He's gotten to her, Lujan thought. I didn't think it was possible, but somehow that half-savage, half-naked primitive has gotten to her. If he can stir her that way, he can control her and if he can control her, so can someone else—that monster of a father of hers or some other man.

He closed the door, cursing himself for his stupidity. He had been so sure he was her ultimate manipulator, the one she would betray all others to please. But now— She knew all about his tampering. She knew about the falsified reports, the phony log entries, and the mountain. He might even have mentioned Dillon's name.

Throwing himself on his bunk, Lujan kicked his shoes off and stared at the domed ceiling. Sloppy! he thought. Not like me at all. One could almost imagine that I actually cared . . .

But he shook his head to banish the notion. At least his mistake would be easy to correct.

Coconino was alone by the river, his face illuminated by the small blaze he had just kindled in a small sandy pit. Karen stopped, suddenly afraid to go on.

Then he lifted his face, a face filled with pools of darkness and craggy firelit features. The nose was too large, the brow too sharp—but it didn't matter. He reached out to her across the fire; like a zombie, Karen moved forward.

He took the blankets from her arms; she had forgotten about

them. "What are these?" he asked in curiosity, not recognizing the thin, crinkly material.

"Blankets," she managed. "Special blankets; they hold in your body heat." She stopped short as even that benign phrase took on sensuality.

But Coconino only grunted and shook out one of the sheets. He spread it carelessly on the lush grass that grew here at the river's edge. "Come," he said, patting the blanket. "Sit with me."

Mesmerized, Karen dropped to her knees. There was no breeze here among the trees; the ribbons of Coconino's shirt moved only with the rippling movements of his body as he reached down and drew off his moccasins and leggings. She felt her face flush and knew it was not from the heat of the small fire.

He stretched out casually beside her, propped on one elbow. For a moment he only looked at her, studying her face in the firelight. "You have such round eyes," he said finally. "And such a tiny nose."

"I must seem very plain to you," she blurted.

"Ah, no," he replied, smiling. His teeth glinted white in the firelight. "You seem very beautiful to me. Small and delicate, like a finch."

Karen blushed and could not meet his eyes.

Coconino reached out and brushed her cheek. "Your skin is soft," he remarked. Then he twined his fingers in her dark curls. "Your hair is soft, too. Much softer than the hair of maidens in my village."

With a start Karen remembered the other woman. "Where is your—your friend?"

"My sister-brother?" he asked. "She stands watch. She will let us know if someone else approaches."

The color drained from Karen's face as she realized what Coconino meant.

Coconino saw the change in her and hesitated. Slowly he untangled his fingers from her hair and rose to his knees in front of her. Taking her face in both hands, he looked deeply into her eyes. "Do you wish to go?" he whispered sincerely. "No one will stop you if you wish to go."

Transfixed, Karen found herself unable to answer.

Finally Coconino rose and stood towering over her. His face was concealed in shadow; she could see only his well-muscled legs and his plain muslin loincloth and the gentle movement of his shirt ribbons. Karen closed her eyes, but his image was stained on her memory. She opened them again, gazing up the length of his body.

With a shrug of his shoulders Coconino drew the ribbon shirt off over his head. He folded it carefully and laid it aside with his moccasins and leggings. In his movements Karen saw again a youthfulness that surprised her; he was not much more than a boy, after all. And yet no boy on Argo had ever possessed the dignity and strength that marked Coconino's bearing.

Once more he knelt in front of her and took her face in both his hands. Karen's heart pounded wildly as his face drew nearer to hers. The touch of his lips on hers was the gentlest she had ever known; she trembled at its sweetness.

"Do you wish to go?" he asked again.

"No," she whispered. Then she gave herself up to feelings she had fled since childhood.

In the darkness before dawn Coconino found Phoenix asleep in the lee of a foundation where she had spent the night. Karen had gone while he slept; he had heard her go but had pretended he did not so there would not have to be any awkward words between them. Now, as Phoenix rose heavily to her feet, he saw the pain in her face and regretted again that she had refused to spend this night with him. *It would have been our Fulfillment*, he thought. *It would have been reward for this service we bear . . .*

Wordlessly they stole into the hills, waiting until they were well away from the camp of the Others before they spoke.

"The supply shed is going to be a problem," she told him. "I don't know any way to open it short of a disrupter fired at the lock."

"You and Juan can bring our men in to hide among the other buildings," Coconino suggested. "Then, when someone goes to get something from it, you will gain entrance."

But Phoenix shook her head. "Juan can't wait for us, Coconino. Once we go up to the Sky Ship, they must look for an opportunity. Anything that distracts the attention of the Others. Then they must take one hostage—"

"Hostage?" He frowned. "What is hostage?"

"They must capture one of the Others," she explained, "and force him or her to open the doors to the supply sheds. I saw the markings on the sheds: a stick and a circle on one, two sticks on the other. I don't know which one the fireshooters might be in; they will have to check both."

"Are you sure throwing them in the river will destroy them?" he asked.

Now she frowned. "I don't know. The water's not very deep, and I'm not sure how watertight the cases of the fireshooters may be."

"Deeper water would be better?" he asked.

"Deeper water where they could not be seen would be best," she replied.

"Then we must carry them to the Well."

Phoenix balked. "That's a long way. The Others can move very swiftly in their Machines; our men might be caught."

"Only if they are found," Coconino reminded her.

Still she was troubled by the plan. "Look, Coconino, we have to make very sure our men understand that they are not to try using these fireshooters themselves. Especially that braggart brother-in-law of yours. And Flint—God, I can just see Flint trying to be a hero and using one of those things on the Others!"

"Do not worry," Coconino assured her. "These fireshooters are evil; they are a sin against the Mother Earth. The People would not think of using them."

"I'm not worried about 'the People,' " she retorted, "I'm worried about Flint!"

"I have told him," Coconino replied simply. "He will not try."

Oh, he'll try, Phoenix thought bitterly. When he sees his companions being burned down like dead trees, he'll forget all about sin or the Way of the People or anything but revenge. And me—oh, God, what will I do? If they hurt you, Coconino, if they take you from me, how do I know what I will do?

In the pleasant coolness of early morning Lujan stood outside his quarters, staring down toward the riverbank. He had slept badly and he told himself it was because he was unaccustomed to sleeping alone. That was all. After all, Karen wasn't really important to him, only useful.

As though conjured by the thought of her, she appeared at his side. "Good morning," she greeted him tentatively.

A sharp reply was on his tongue, but he curbed it carefully. "Good morning."

"Waiting for our guests?"

Again he had to bite back a caustic response. "I think they're bluffing," he said. "I don't think they have any intention of helping with our problem." *My* problem.

His attitude didn't surprise Karen; that he had voiced it did. At any rate, she was prepared. She brushed a lock of hair back from her face and drew a sliver of metal from behind her ear. "Aren't you cold?" she asked, rubbing at the short sleeve of his uniform and leaving the metal sliver in his cuff.

He shrugged, eyes on the cottonwood grove. "It'll be hot soon enough." It had the ring of a double entendre. Karen was glad she had planted the transmitter; she wondered what Derek had in mind for Coconino and his friend once he had decided they were no longer useful. Not that she would try to intervene, but somehow it mattered to her. She wanted to know.

Just then the two primitives appeared, walking up the slope from the river.

Coconino and Phoenix had waited until the Others had begun stirring, setting off for another day of searching the desert to the south. Now they sauntered up the hill from the cottonwood grove as though they had never been absent.

"Good morning," Lujan greeted them mirthlessly. "I trust you slept well." Coconino noted the odd tone in his voice. "Have some breakfast. The commissary line is short this early in the day."

"Time for food later. We should talk now," Coconino said expansively, trying to ignore Karen's presence and his own guilty feelings. To lie with a woman only to gain her loyalty was not good even if she had been willing. It was not *moh-ohnak*, and his spirit felt uneasy. "The feasting is done, and with the new day we should set about our task."

"Come into my quarters, then," Lujan said quietly. "Karen, take your watch at the command center."

Karen looked startled. "It's oh-seven-forty; the watch doesn't change till—"

"I want you at the comm station, Karen," he snapped. "The search parties are rolling out again. I want you to know where every one of them is."

In the brief pause that followed, a look of confusion darted across Karen's face; then it was gone. "Aye, sir," she replied simply, and headed down the path that had been beaten to the command center.

With an icy smile Lujan turned back to his guests. "This way," he said, and ushered them to his quarters.

The interior of this dome had off-white walls and a gray floor, seeming all the more Spartan because it housed only one occupant. A single bed stood on one side; a desk and chair stood across from it, and a small bistro table stood by the single window near the door. Lujan invited them to sit with a wave of his hand.

"I do not like your buildings," Coconino observed as he slid reluctantly into one of the plastic chairs. Phoenix declined to sit but stood behind Coconino, her arms folded, a stern look on her face. "They remind me of the Before Times. They block out the scent of the Mother Earth."

"No one asked you to come."

Coconino's neck prickled at Lujan's tone. There was a hostility that hadn't been there the night before or even when they had arrived unexpectedly. Somehow Lujan must have found out about Coconino and Karen. "This is true," Coconino continued, trying to sound calm and sure. "But as you said, we both want the same thing: to keep Others from coming back to the Mother Earth. And so I have come to suggest how we may do that."

Lujan slid into the chair opposite him, facing him coldly across the table. "I'm listening."

"You Others have great magic," Coconino began. "It is far beyond the Magic of the People. Some of it is pleasant. Some of it is useful. Some of it is terrifying. There seem to be few problems that your magic cannot solve."

"Get on with it!" Lujan barked.

Coconino studied his opponent a moment, then smiled coldly. Although he himself was subject to fits of temper, it was the first time he had seen Lujan lose mastery of his feelings. There was a perverse pleasure in pushing this man to the edge. "Now, I am only a hunter," he continued innocently, "and a storyteller. I have no great magic. Neither is it the Way of the People to deal in untruths. But to save Mother Earth—"

"Yes, yes, I know," Lujan interrupted testily. "You will do what needs to be done. What great untruth is it that you think will keep my people from coming back to Earth?"

"We must convince them an Enemy lies here whom their magic cannot defeat."

"You don't know my people; they live to conquer enemies, the nastier, the better. They're not going to be afraid of your People or your Mother Earth."

"That much I know," Coconino replied, keeping a tight grip on his own temper. "I do not suggest that they would be afraid of the People."

"Then what?"

Coconino leaned back in his chair. "It seems to me," he drawled deliberately, "that you Others greatly fear sickness."

For a moment Lujan only stared at him. Then his face broke into a humorless grin. He gave a sharp laugh, the cold cracking of a whip. "Brilliant!" he cackled. "By God, man, that's brilliant!"

On the far side of the command center Karen relaxed in the sun, ostensibly savoring its early morning warmth, but she held a monitoring device to her ear. From the transmitter in Lujan's sleeve she heard every word of their conversation.

"Disease!" Lujan was saying now. "That's the answer. We contact Argo, tell them the landing party has come down with a deadly disease, origin unknown. Only a few of us escaped. It's perfect! Earth becomes immediately deadly and in the long term costly. Do you know how much it costs to fund research to stamp out a new disease? Hell, we can't even conquer the ones we've got!"

Karen heard his chair scrape as he rose and strode toward the door. "I'm going up to the *Homeward Bound* to send the message. I'll 'speak to the sky,' as you say. Go back to your people and tell them I've taken care of our problem!"

Inside the dome, Coconino was on his feet in a flash. "The People will know soon enough," he assured Lujan. "I have no reason to rush off. Perhaps I will come with you and watch how you Speak to the Sky."

"Sorry, Chief," Lujan replied. "Watch changes in fifteen minutes, and when it does, I've got my handpicked skeleton crew and I'm gone. I'll give you a tour next time I come."

Coconino's mind raced. Fifteen minutes! It was all happening too fast. Somehow he had to get onto the Sky Ship and stop it from leaving. "May I at least say farewell to your Karen?" he asked, hoping fervently that Phoenix was right and Karen would get him up to the ship despite Lujan. "She has been gracious and—"

"Gracious!" Lujan barked. "We have another word for it. But there's no need for farewells; she's not coming with me."

"Karen, are you okay?" Mike Thornton asked. The young woman's face was ashen, and her lips trembled.

"I—I—" she stammered. "I just—don't feel well, suddenly."

"Here, step into the command center and—"

"No!" Karen resisted his guidance. "I—I need air. Please, just let me—stand here—"

Lujan strode across the compound toward the shuttle, and she shrank back against the wall. If he should see her—but no, he was intent on where he was going. He had already written her off.

"Can I get you something?" Thornton asked solicitously. "A drink of water or—"

"Yes," Karen gulped as Coconino and Phoenix came into view not far behind Lujan. "Yes, please, get me a drink. From the commissary. Some tea. It always helps settle my stomach." Then she sagged against the building and willed him to go away quickly.

As soon as he had rounded the corner, she staggered toward Coconino. Her knees were weak, threatening to buckle with every step. Just when she thought she could never make the short trip on her own, Coconino turned and saw her.

How he got to her so quickly she didn't know, only how grateful she was to sag against him, feel the strength of his arms supporting her. "Karen—Karen, are you hurt?" he asked anxiously. Behind him hovered the worried face of Phoenix.

"He's—going to leave me," she sobbed, giving in for a moment to the pain of desertion.

Coconino held her, but over her head he exchanged a look with Phoenix.

"Karen," Phoenix intervened with more gentleness than Coconino had ever heard from her. "We can stop him."

Karen straightened up, brushed at the tears that had escaped her, tugged the wrinkles from her clothes. "No, you can't," she said simply. "No one can stop Derek. Not when he's made up his mind."

"We can't make him take you back," Phoenix agreed, "but we can stop him from going. We can serve him up the same fate he has planned for all of you."

For a long moment Karen only stood there, eyes downcast, face hollow and worn. Too many years, she thought, too many power plays. Too many men who had battered and abused her—one way or another. Derek had been gentle, at least. Now there would be no gentleness in her life. No gentleness and no peace.

"What good would that do me?" she asked from her own very real apathy for her plight. "I don't want revenge." She started to turn away.

But Coconino stopped her. "Karen," he said softly, his eyes boring into her. What compelling eyes they were, full of purpose, full of fire! "We must deal with him," Coconino told her. "My sister-brother and I. We cannot let him go. He must not bear tales of the Mother Earth to her sister planets, and so we must stop him. But we need your help."

Karen looked at him, just another man who had used her, and at what cost? She had lost Derek whether he stayed or left, and with him her fragile peace. But as she met Coconino's eyes, she could feel his will like a tangible thing, trying to bend her to itself. Briefly she fought it but she was no fighter, had found nothing worth the pain of the struggling. Slowly she let herself succumb. Why not do as Coconino asked? With Derek gone, Coconino would dominate. He could smooth her path.

"What do you want?" she asked finally.

"We need to get up to the ship," Phoenix told her. "We need you to run the controls for the warp terminal."

Karen sighed. "It won't do any good," she told them. "There's no way you can stop him from—"

"Leave that to us," Coconino assured her. "We have a secret weapon."

Now Phoenix looked at him blankly. "We do?"

"Will you kill them all?" Karen asked quietly, and wondered if she really cared.

"We will kill no one," he answered, "if it can be avoided. That will take your help, for we do not know the workings of your ship or how your friends may escape from it."

Karen nodded then. "I'll help you."

"One more thing," Phoenix said. "Lujan was going to send a message."

"I know," Karen said. "I was listening."

"Can you tell us for sure that the message was sent?"

"I can check from the comm center here before we go up," Karen said listlessly. "The watch changes shortly; that'll be the best time to sneak you aboard. We'd better hurry."

Although the computer had reported that Dillon was in the American Heritage section of the Earth Room, Camilla did not find him there. Instead she found a handsome young man in his early twenties gazing in fascination at Fraser's *End of the Trail*. If the brave in the painting was aged and weary, the young man who studied him was fresh and youthful. His dark hair rippled in waves away from a striking profile that was accentuated by a cleft chin. Involved in the painting, he seemed to have a depth to him that caught her attention, and she paused.

He looked up then and smiled, a dazzling, guileless smile that made her heart flutter. His eyes shone with genuine pleasure, and he said, "I like this one."

It was not a remark she expected, and her curiosity was piqued. "What do you like about it?" she asked.

He shrugged. "I don't know. I just like it." His voice was childlike not in timbre but in inflection. "It tells a story."

Camilla perceived then that the young man was not as blessed mentally as he was physically. But he was charming nonetheless.

"This is from Earth, isn't it?" he asked.

"Yes, it is," she replied. "Everything in this gallery is from Earth."

"My dad's on Earth," he asserted, looking again at the painting. "And my mom. I wonder if they'll see any people like this?"

Camilla jumped and with an effort kept the shake out of her voice. "Your dad? Is he on the *Homeward Bound?*"

Now the young man grinned even more broadly. "He's the captain. And my mom's the ship's doctor." He thrust out his hand. "My name's Cincinnati."

Camilla shook his hand, her heart twisting inside her. "Pleased to meet you, Cincinnati, I'm Camilla."

"Do you know my dad?" he asked hopefully.

"No," she admitted. "No, I don't. I don't know anyone on the *Homeward Bound*. But I have heard of it."

"They should come back soon," Cincinnati told her. "My sister says they aren't finding much. She talks to the people at TRC every day to see how they are. That's where she is now."

Dillon arrived then from an adjoining gallery. "Ah, Camilla. Were you looking for me?"

"Yes, sir," she replied, wishing she did not have to report what she had to report. "Mr. Dillon, this is Cincinnati. Cincinnati Winthrop."

She saw the look of recognition flash in his eyes, but his voice and movement betrayed no trace of it. "How do you do, Cincinnati?" he greeted him politely, giving a half bow. "Are you enjoying the Earth Room?"

"Oh, yes, sir," Cincinnati replied enthusiastically. He pointed to the Fraser painting. "I especially like this one."

"Yes, that one is from the American Southwest," Dillon told

him. "So are these things." With a wave of a hand he indicated a glass case.

Cincinnati peered at the artifacts intently. "Are those arrowheads?" he asked. "They're awfully big."

"Actually, they're spear points," Dillon replied.

"Are they sharp?" Cincinnati wanted to know.

"Not by our standards," Dillon demurred. "But they were effective. Here, let's have a closer look at these replicas."

Camilla watched as he nonchalantly thumbed the lock and lifted the cover on one side of the case. *How can he be so calm?* she raged inwardly. *How can he stand there showing off his artifacts for Winthrop's son and—but he doesn't know. I haven't told him yet; he doesn't know.*

"These are rawhide thongs," Dillon was explaining as he showed Cincinnati the short shaft with its demonstration stone point. "See how the end of the wood has been split and the base of the spear point inserted. Now, rawhide shrinks as it dries, so when it's wrapped around the shaft—"

"It presses the wood together and holds the point there!" Cincinnati exclaimed, his face aglow with sudden insight.

"Mr. Dillon," Camilla whispered.

"Hm?" Dillon turned from the young man with an inquisitive look.

"If you please."

With a barely perceptible sigh Dillon turned back. "Excuse me a moment." Then he followed her to a discreet distance.

I shouldn't have disturbed him, Camilla thought. *He's upset now, I know he is, but I can't bear this. I must tell him.*

"Chelsea!"

Cincinnati's pleased cry arrested Camilla. She looked up to see a young blond woman approaching.

"Look what he was showing me," Cincinnati called out, waving the replica. "It's a spear, and it comes from Earth— What's wrong?"

He had stopped suddenly as he saw her face. Chelsea had plainly been crying. At his question, tears trickled once more down her cheeks. "Give it back, Cin," she told him in a choked voice. "We have to talk."

Without a word Cincinnati held the replica out in Dillon's general direction. Camilla hurried to take it from him. *He knows,* she thought. *His sister hasn't told him yet, but he knows. He knows something's gone wrong.*

Clutching the crude spear, she watched as the two young

people left the gallery. Just before they passed through the doorway she saw Cincinnati reach for his sister's hand.

Camilla felt Dillon hovering at her shoulder. "The TRC got a message," she whispered. "From the *Homeward Bound*. There's—there's some kind of disease. It spread through the landing party. Dr. Winthrop tried—" Her voice broke off. "Only a handful survived. The Winthrops are both dead."

"Yes, I know," Dillon murmured.

She turned on him in surprise. "You *know*?"

"I have many sources, my dear," he replied with that bemused smile. "You realize, of course, that this is probably a ruse."

"A ruse?" she repeated numbly.

"We'll know better when they return, but my guess is that Earth holds some secret we wouldn't want bandied about, and that is why only a few will return. Undoubtedly there are treasures to be had, and my agent will bring us a few samples. Excellent ploy, this plague. It will keep everyone else far away until I can establish a claim." He looked down into her disbelieving face. How beautiful she was, how full of emotion! Impulsively he touched her face, brushed his fingers across the silken hair at her temple. "How would you like to be Queen of Earth, my dear? My lawyers tell me the planet is technically abandoned and not covered by any existing colonization agreements. What irony, don't you agree?"

Camilla stared at him numbly, at the cool, unaffected face of Argo's finest art connoisseur, her employer and sometimes lover. Then she tightened her grasp on the replicated spear and thrust it into his heart.

CHAPTER TWENTY-FIVE

Tala hesitated at the foot of the ramp that led into the cargo bay. Inside, soft colors pulsed and glowed, beckoning to the animal, and there was a smell . . . yes, his kind had been in such places before.

"Come, my brother," Coconino coaxed. "We need your lightning once more. Only step with me into this Machine." Here he suppressed a shudder. "We will go together. I will not leave you."

Tala felt the fear in his friend, and that disturbed him more than the strange Machine. He was seized with a sudden impulse to flee—but that smell . . . what was that smell? Cautiously he placed one foot on the ramp.

Karen and Phoenix waited at the top. Phoenix had never seen a warp terminal. It looked like a crazy cage except that the bars jutted out from the walls, and only two walls, at that. She knew that streams of energy crossed between their tips, setting up a net that somehow invoked the fifth dimension. But at the moment she was only dazzled by their colors.

Tala was coming up the ramp now, sniffing curiously, his ears cocked forward. He's less nervous about this than Coconino, Phoenix thought. Tala was taking on the gray color of the ramp, as he always took on the color of his surroundings unless he was disturbed. But Coconino was a bit gray, too, and it had nothing to do with the ramp.

As they reached the top, an owl hooted nearby and Phoenix knew that Juan and the others were close at hand. Owls were nocturnal, but the Others wouldn't know that, and they would attribute the noise to the local fauna. Phoenix was both comforted and terrified, knowing they were ready. When she and

Coconino returned from the ship—yes, *when* they returned—what would they find? Pandemonium, surely—they would need it to escape among the domes and trees that seemed suddenly too far from the cargo bay doors. But what else? How would Juan and his followers fare?

With an effort Phoenix pushed those thoughts away. She took one last look at the surrounding buildings, fixing their position in her mind; the closest was a good sixty feet to the left. Then she turned her attention back to the warp terminal.

The others were waiting for her between the bristling ranks of tubes. Coconino continued to cling to Tala's neck. "Don't worry," Karen tried to assure him. "It's perfectly safe, not a cloud in the sky."

Yes, thought Coconino. It is a good day to die . . .

Karen spoke to the computer. "Ivan. Transport. Destination: *Homeward Bound.* Set sequence for mark." She glanced once more at Coconino, who was ashen despite his coppery skin. "Mark."

There was a roaring in Coconino's ears, and panic welled up as he felt himself falling, falling, falling . . .

Abruptly there was a hard deck under his feet and he thought his knees would buckle, but he fought to maintain his balance, clinging to Tala's strong neck. The animal was wild-eyed, but he held very still, and no electricity spouted from his twined horn.

This place is sick, it's evil! Coconino wanted to shout. But he kept quiet, breathing deeply to keep his stomach from revolting. Mother Earth, where are you? Can you hear me, even up here in this Ship-in-the-Sky?

Phoenix cleared her throat. "That's a little unsettling for those of us who aren't used to it," she said with forced calm. Her own stomach was churning. "I hope it's a little while before we have to do that again."

The terminal on the *Homeward Bound* was deserted. It looked like a duplicate of the one in the cargo bay except that there was no gaping door to the outside. Instead, a series of sealed hatches separated this compartment from the rest of the ship.

"They'll all be on the bridge," Karen told them. "Derek needs everyone there to execute the launch from orbit. There are only five of them, I think. Maybe six."

Still Coconino stood unmoving, sweat standing out on his forehead. Phoenix eyes him critically. "You're going to be a lot of fun at this party," she grumbled.

At her remark Coconino stirred. "I will do as the Mother Earth bade me," he flared. Then, lost, "But where is She? I cannot feel Her here . . ."

Phoenix turned to Karen. "Take us to the bridge," she said softly.

Lujan whistled idly as he considered his report to the venture's Board of Directors. He would give it in person, of course—suitably grave, fighting for control of his voice as he told how the captain and his landing party had been stricken and the doctor had warped down to try to assist . . .

"Mr. Girard," he said, "prepare to take us out of orbit. Then as soon as we are away, set up the warp sequence to take us back to Argo."

"Are you sure there will be no further trouble with the navigational computer?" Girard asked, a trace of sarcasm in his voice.

Derek grinned at his friend. "We'll just have to take our chances, won't we?"

Then they both jumped as the hatch door slid open.

Dumbfounded, Derek watched as the tall, lithe form of Phoenix sprang through the hatchway. He reached for his disrupter, but her bow was drawn and a deadly flint-tipped arrow was aimed squarely at his heart. He froze.

"Wise decision," she told him, stepping sideways into the room, the wall always at her back.

He clenched his teeth. "What the hell do you—" But his protest died on his lips. In the hatchway stood Coconino, his arm around the neck of the monstrous unicorn.

Coconino looked pale, daunted. Derek remembered well the attack on the mountain tower and knew he dared not let man and beast onto the bridge. He decided to ignore Phoenix and take a bold step forward.

Her arrow tracked him but did not sing from the bow. "What is it you want?" Derek demanded of Coconino, hoping to intimidate the primitive, who was obviously not at his best.

But Derek's tone seemed to rouse Coconino from his uncertainty. His eyes glittered with determination as he stepped forward into the room. "For the Mother Earth to be free," Coconino said, "from the likes of you."

Derek took a deep breath, forcing himself to relax somewhat. "Very well, then," he agreed with what he thought was a measure of grace. "If that's what you want, if that's what your people want, then I will leave and not return."

"You will not leave."

Derek's mind raced. What to do now? How to reason with the man, how to trick, how to manipulate . . .

"Tala!" Coconino called, and the beast moved into the doorway. It ducked its great head and surged through, withers and wing sock scraping the sides. Then it was on the bridge, and the five crew members at their controls cringed away.

"Coconino," Derek said softly, reasonably, "there is another way. I can erase the record of our landing and program in false information. I'll say we landed somewhere else, that we never saw you or your people. When we come back, we'll go to a different place, nowhere near you. We'll stay away—"

"Lies!" Coconino hissed. "Your words burn my ears with their falseness. Lies!" he cried again, raising his arms high in a gesture of invocation. "Let your black heart wither in your chest!"

Tala snorted, his color changing from gray to a fierce brown. "Lies!" Coconino shouted, and the madness in his eyes was reflected in Tala's. "Hear him, Mother Earth; hear the evil words of my enemy. Lies!" His cry was a wail punctuated by the crashing of his foot on the deck. "How long will you bear the insults of this deceitful one?"

Coconino fell to his knees, and Tala jumped, small sparks flaring from his horn. *"Aiieeeee . . . !"* The mournful sound echoed through the bridge, twisting Lujan's gut into a knot of despair. *"Aiieeeee . . . !"* Tala added his trumpeting to the eerie serenade, stamping his forefeet on the textured planking.

Now Coconino began to chant, rising slowly to his feet. The crew stared in fascinated horror as he began to pound out a rhythm in measured steps. The words were unknown to them, but there was no mistaking the harsh, condemnatory tones.

Fire and Ash!

Tala crashed his forefeet against the deck in an echo of Coconino's jerking steps.

Lightning and Wind and Quakings of the Ground!

Hooves and feet beat out a fearful tattoo.

Aiiee, Mother Earth, how all have learned to fear your wrath—!

Suddenly Coconino gave a great cry and smashed his fists against one of the control panels that lined the walls. Lujan flinched, but there was nothing he could do. Phoenix's arrow was still trained on his heart.

Girard, however, made a dive for Coconino. Coconino threw him roughly back, and Tala, carried by the intensity of their shared dance, trumpeted and discharged his horn. Girard reeled back, smashing into his own controls.

Coconino advanced, flinging the dazed man aside. Desperately, Girard clutched at the primitive, succeeding in dragging him away, but the unicorn had located Coconino's target. Once more he unleashed his electrical charge, this time directly at the control panel. An acrid stench filled the air as circuits exploded and crystals fried. Small wisps of smoke curled up from the shiny controls.

Lujan stared blankly at the damage; his mind balked at the truth it implied. At the comm station, Nigel Smith rose shakily to his feet. "My God, he's done it," Nigel breathed, staring at the battered navigational controls. "That's it; we can't go home." His voice was edged with hysteria as he turned burning eyes on Coconino. "We can't go home! We can't—"

Nigel took one step to charge Coconino, but Phoenix dropped him screaming with an arrow through his lung. Before she could nock another, Lujan launched himself at Coconino. They hit the hard deck and grappled there while Tala discharged his horn time and time again, maddened beyond all control. All around them control panels sizzled and arced.

Then Phoenix had her arrow in place and stood near the wrestling men, daring anyone to interfere. Behind her, Karen stepped onto the bridge from the companionway. For a moment Phoenix thought they were betrayed. But the woman only spoke. "Stop them," she pleaded.

"When hell freezes over," Phoenix growled back.

"You've got what you wanted," Karen told her. "No one can leave now. Please, let's just get off the ship before the orbit decays and we all die."

Phoenix hesitated. "How long will that take?"

"I don't know. I don't know how much damage there's been."

Phoenix wet her lips. "I can't stop them. Not unless you tie up all the others."

Coconino heard their voices, but their words could not penetrate his fury. Lujan was slippery and sly, a cunning opponent, but Coconino had had too much experience wrestling to be beaten even on this unfamiliar surface. With a final lunge he had

Lujan pinned; his hand flew to his moccasin, and then he had a knife at Lujan's throat.

Lujan stopped struggling. "You don't want to kill me," he panted. "You need me."

But Coconino did not move his hand. Need this filth? Need this monster who lied with each breath, who destroyed the Mother Earth's creatures for target practice?

"You need me for a hostage," Lujan urged.

Rage burned in Coconino's heart as he remembered the blackened lump that had been a hawk. He thought of the Flying Machine and wondered if, as Phoenix had told him she suspected, it had met a similar fate at Lujan's hands. Desecration! Abomination! Like the people of the Before Times—

"Please," Karen said softly. "For me."

Her voice penetrated his madness like a star breaking through night clouds. If she could plead for him, who had been so betrayed— But what would happen to her if he let Lujan live? Did this carrion deserve her kindness?

"Not for you," Coconino grated through clenched teeth. "You are better off without him." The stone knife was sharp, honed to slice the thick hides of animals. One quick movement—

Coconino exhaled deeply. "But he is a child of the Mother Earth," he said. Reluctantly he shifted his weight off the defeated man, though the knife stayed at his throat. "It is for the Mother Earth to deal with him."

From the corner of the bridge a woman sobbed. "Stop that thing, please," she pleaded as Tala continued to discharge his horn.

Cautiously Coconino rose to his knees while Phoenix backed off to include Lujan in the threat from her bow. Finally Coconino drew back from his adversary, turning to the unicorn but keeping his knife in hand. "Ho, Tala," he called softly. "*Aiee,* my brother. Peace."

The unicorn stopped his reckless attack and stood panting, watching the man.

"Peace, my brother," Coconino crooned, approaching the animal carefully. "It is over now; it is all over. Now we can return to the Mother Earth. Now you can return to your home."

It's over! Phoenix's heart sang as they marched Lujan and the others, hands bound by leather thongs, down the corridor. The message had been sent, the ship was disabled, and they were still alive.

Yet even as her joy kindled, it grew cold. Hostages would

only buy them time. The Others were not going to take kindly to being marooned; there would be reprisals. If they could hide somewhere in the hills, or if they could fly Tala to the north . . .

Just one night, she pleaded silently. One night with Coconino. Oh, Blessed Mother Earth, I ask no other reward for my service but one night, one night with my beloved . . .

But they were too far above the Earth, and She did not hear.

Once again there was the roaring in Coconino's ears and the feeling of falling, falling, falling . . .

An explosion greeted their ears as the shuttle bay solidified around them. Coconino jerked back, sure it was some treachery of the Others, but it was only the urgent, lingering cry of thunder. Rain slashed against the shuttle, the incredible downpour of a late season thunderstorm. The sky, so clear when they had left, was dark with storm clouds.

Crack! Another clap of thunder rent the air, and Tala reared wildly, flinging Coconino against the back wall of the shuttle. Bright sparks arced from his horn as the unicorn trumpeted loudly and crashed his forefeet against the deck. Coconino recovered and tried to reach the frenzied animal, but a jolt of electricity caught him full in the chest and he reeled backward.

Desperately Coconino fought back the blackness that threatened to overtake him. He heard a cry from Phoenix, then the sounds of a scuffle. Someone fell. "Ivan!" he heard Lujan shout to the computer. "Transport. Destination—"

But there was a loud grunt as Lujan was cut short and the scuffling resumed. Coconino staggered to his feet, trying to clear his head. Sounds filtered through to him: Tala trumpeting, Karen shouting— Someone was flung up against him.

Then suddenly Coconino was falling again. Falling and falling and falling into the great burning star of his dream, and there was no bottom, no sides, only emptiness and pain and falling and falling and pain and painandpainandpainand—

Slowly consciousness seeped back into Coconino. He tasted dirt in his mouth, felt the scratchy softness of dried grass beneath his cheek. Birds called, and a soft breeze dried the sweat on his back. His muscles would not respond.

Finally he forced his eyes open, but the landscape spun so crazily that he closed them again, breathing deeply of the sweet freshness of the air. There had been blue sky and—

Blue sky? But the storm, he thought. What happened to the

storm? Has it passed as quickly as it arose? The ground was not wet, though. How long have I lain here? And the shuttle, the Magic Place that Bends Space and trades one place for another. Where is it? I was inside, and then—

Suddenly he realized the pain was gone. His muscles ached from the electric shock they had endured, but the other pain, the pain he had borne in his soul ever since the Others had landed, was gone. We won! he thought dizzily. We have defeated the Others! They are gone from the Mother Earth!

But how can they be? There were so many, and Lujan had knocked Phoenix down and—

Phoenix!

Now he forced his eyes open again. The land still spun, but he forced his arms to push him up into a sitting position, forced his eyes to focus as he looked around him.

The faces he saw nearly rocked him back to the ground. They were faces of the People, round and dark and comely, but he did not recognize a single one of them. Four men and one young boy stared at him in wonder. They wore headbands of cord and breechclouts of woven yucca fibers, their eyes and hair as dark as those of the People should be.

"Who are you?" he demanded. "I do not know you. Where is Phoenix? Where is my sister-brother?"

The men looked at each other in amazement. "We are the People," one said finally. "I am Climbing Hawk; this is Red Snake, my son. Who are you?"

Coconino straightened himself proudly, hiding the terror he felt. "I am Coconino."

There was a collective gasp, and the men backed off involuntarily. "It cannot be," one said. "He lies," challenged another. "The legends are true," said the third. "The great god Coconino has returned to his People."

Now more frightened and confused than ever, Coconino staggered to his feet. "What do you mean by this?" he demanded. "I am no god, I am only a man, but I am Coconino, and I am of the People. Who are you? What is this nonsense you speak?"

"Our legends say," Climbing Hawk told him, "that the great god Coconino once walked the Earth like a man. He rode Tala, the winged antelope, and restored to us the great saguaro. He spoke the language of the Men-on-the-Mountain, and it was he, yes, he, who first fought the Others and flung their Sky Ship back into the heavens whence it came."

Coconino's head reeled. He tried to remember what Phoenix

had explained to him about the Magic Place that could Bend
Space—or time. It wasn't supposed to bend time, but sometimes, if something went wrong . . . Could it be that such a thing
had happened and that somehow its magic had thrown him into
the Times That Are to Come?

"How long has it been since Coconino walked the paths of the
People?" he asked.

Climbing Hawk shrugged. "I do not know. It was before the
time of my grandfather's grandfather. I do not know how long."

Slowly Coconino turned, taking in the landscape, the vegetation, and all that the eye could see. He was no longer in the river
valley. Yet the terrain looked somehow familiar, as though they
might be near the Well. And the season—it was late winter here.
The cacti were only beginning to form buds.

"How long have I lain here?" he asked.

"My other son, Tree Toad, saw you early this morning. He
said he saw two men fall from the sky, so he ran back to tell us.
He thought you were Others."

"Two men?" Coconino seized upon this with hope. "Where
is the other man?" Dressed in her loincloth and ribbon shirt,
Phoenix looked very much like a man.

"We do not know. You were alone when we came."

Still trying to clear his head, Coconino began searching around
him for some trail, some sign of another person's passage. "How
was he dressed, this other man?"

Climbing Hawk eyed the man-god cautiously, trying to read
the truth in him. "Tree Toad did not say. He has gone ahead
with the rest of our group." He did not act like any god. He
acted like a young hunter seeking his *may-ohkha,* his Special
Quarry. But his eyes burned as a god's eyes might— "Are you
truly Coconino?" Climbing Hawk asked.

Coconino stopped and with a great effort pulled himself
erect. "I am Coconino," he said fiercely, "son of a Man-on-
the-Mountain—" He faltered, forcing away an image of Dick
McKay. "—by his Chosen Companion, Two Moons, who is
high in the Council of the Mother—" Ah, Mother, are you
free now? Have you returned to the bosom of the Mother
Earth? But of course you have. They have all returned now, all
those I knew—

Except one. He turned back to his search and found a stone
freshly kicked from its place—the depression where it had lain
was still clear. Then his sharp eye picked out broken branches on

a creosote bush—someone had come this way, and none too carefully. But the ground revealed no footprints, no way of knowing whom he followed.

"Your legends," Coconino said hoarsely as he followed the weaving, almost imperceptible trail of his fellow time traveler. "What do they say of Phoenix?"

The men looked at each other quizzically as they tagged along, helping to pick out the path. "Who is this Phoenix?" Climbing Hawk asked. "A man? A beast?"

Hope pounded in Coconino's heart. If the legends did not speak of her— "A woman," he replied. "A Witch Woman. Your legends say nothing of the sister-brother of Coconino?"

"I have not heard," Climbing Hawk ventured, "but many of our legends have been lost. Twisted Stick would know. Come with us to our village and we will ask him."

"How far is it to your village?"

"Three days to the north, perhaps four with the packs we carry."

But Coconino shook his head peremptorily. "That is too far. She may be here; I must search for her." He tried to remember what had happened in those last few confused moments. Had Phoenix been knocked from the Magic Place? Had Lujan?

"I will help you search," Red Snake volunteered, and his father scowled at the boy.

Coconino scarcely heard them. The trail was leading up a hill; his head pounded from the exertion, but he climbed doggedly, eyes darting across the ground for further evidence.

Red Snake tagged along, pretending to look for tracks but always keeping Coconino in his peripheral vision. It was wonder enough that he, not even in his twelfth year, had been allowed to come south with his father to trade with the mysterious Others. But on this journey to meet the great Coconino returned to his People! Surely the Mother Earth had blessed him above all other boys—above some men. He was favored indeed!

"Was the Sky Ship larger than our whole village?" Red Snake blurted.

Coconino grunted. "I do not know how large your village is."

"Well, it is—" But the boy stopped. "It is not as great as the Village of Coconino was," he deferred. "That must have been a great village—to think of all the heroes that lived in it! Juan and Loves the Dust and—"

Coconino stopped short. "What do you know of these men?" he demanded suddenly.

"That—that they were great men of the People," Red Snake stammered.

Coconino fought against a grief that was too large to be comprehended. They were dead, all dead. Juan, Falling Star, his mother, Corn Hair—even Castle Rock. All gone to the bosom of the Mother Earth, and long since. And yet . . .

"What happened to them?" he asked quietly.

The boy was nervous, uncertain how he should answer. "Don't—don't you know?" he asked. Surely the great Coconino knew that—

"I do not know what has happened to me; how could I know what happened to them?" Coconino snapped, and immediately repented. "I have—I have been asleep," he said. How else could he explain what he himself did not fully understand? "Tell me, what happened to my friends? To my village? What happened on the day that—that the Sky Ship of the Others was destroyed?"

Red Snake gulped and glanced at his father for support but found none. He plunged on alone. "The Others were very angry and rose up against the People," he said. "But Coconino— you—had foreseen this and wisely sent Juan and the men of the People to lie in ambush. There was a great battle; many were killed."

Sudden chains bound Coconino's chest against the expanding grief, grief he had no time for yet, not yet. But how many lives had been wasted in battle, how many cut short in violence? "Who were they?" he asked in the same calm voice. "Do you know their names?"

"Some of them," the boy replied. "Juan, of course."

Juan! Coconino stifled a cry as a single arrow of pain pierced him. Juan, my friend, my brother— Your smile was your greatest treasure. But your sons had to grow to manhood without you—

"And the brother of Coconino," Red Snake continued.

"Flint?" Coconino demanded, a second shaft cutting through him.

The boy looked puzzled, frightened. "No, Falling Star."

What mercy is this? Coconino wondered, feeling himself run through a third time. My brother spared but my sister bereft . . . He turned away and continued to search for tracks. "Juan, Falling Star—who else?" he demanded harshly.

"Very many. I do not remember their names, but Twisted Stick will."

Now Coconino recognized the terrain. They were indeed near the Well, approaching it from the west. The river would be just beyond this hill. Phoenix would know to find water here; that would explain her leaving him, to find water. If it was Phoenix. If she had not . . . "Did they defeat the Others, these brave men of the People?" Coconino asked.

The boy was a moment in answering. "No," he replied sadly. "In those days the Others had weapons which could burn from great distances. We could not defeat them. But through the wisdom of the She Who Saves, the People were able to escape and hide until the wrath of the Others had subsided."

"She Who Saves?" Coconino's heart skipped a beat. They were near the rim of the Well now, the large flat stones where once a skinny Witch Woman had collapsed, exhausted. He remembered still how she had plunged her head into the cold water, flung it back, her long hair spraying droplets in every direction. Perhaps she was there now, kneeling on the rock ledge below . . . "Who is this woman? Did she have another name?"

"Twisted Stick would know," Climbing Hawk interjected. "You must ask him these questions."

"This is her place, though," Red Snake told him. "This is the Sacred Well of She Who Saves."

No! he raged inwardly. It is the place of some other. The place of Two Moons or perhaps Ernestina. Either had the strength of will to save the People. "Why is it her place?" he heard himself ask.

"Here she descended to the bosom of the Mother Earth," Red Snake explained. "She went down into the Well and returned no more. It was said that she—" Here the boy blushed. "That she was Coconino's lover, and she went to be with him."

Corn Hair, Coconino thought desperately. Or Castle Rock. No, Nina! Yes, that was it. Nina had borne his child. Nina was She Who Saves—

"See?" the boy was saying. "She left this here as a sign and a charm, that none should disturb her in this place." He pointed to a large rock on which hung a leather thong. The thong was new, but the medallion was old, tarnished, yet its shape was recognizable. It was a bird made of blue-green stone.

And all the men were astonished that the great god Coconino sank to his knees and wept.

EPILOGUE

Twisted Stick laid the bundle in Coconino's hands. "We have kept this," he explained, "for the Time When Coconino Comes Again. If you are he, you will know the meaning of it."

With trembling hands Coconino folded back the well-oiled hide. The rough parchment inside was old and brittle—the edges flaked in his hands—but the writing was still clear. It was in the language of the Mountain.

"I am Phoenix," it began, "sister-brother of Coconino: He Who Was and Will Be Again. At his coming, give these words to him.

"I had hoped you would return during my lifetime, Brother. But now the Mother Earth calls me to her, and I prepare to go. I wanted to tell you how I served her and the People for your sake. Yet perhaps you will know this because of the name by which the People now call me: She Who Saves.

"Know this, my brother: Our sacrifice for the Mother Earth was not in vain. The Others remain, but they are docile and grow to live in harmony with Her. No more have come in these twenty-five years.

"Know this also: As you boasted, your seed was strong like the Grandfather's, and both were sown in fertile ground. Nakha-a was born of Nina; he has your gift of speaking with the Mother Earth. Michael came from the Mountain to become one of the People. And your daughter, Sky Dancer, who was born of the Other, I have raised as my own.

"So you have given me, Beloved, what no one else could: you have given me a child."

338

Slowly Coconino crumbled the paper to dust, but the tears that mixed with it were not bitter. A child for the Witch Woman! At least he had brought her that much joy. Carefully he touched the medallion he had taken from the Well and hung once more around his neck.

He would carry Phoenix with him always.

About the Author

CATHERINE WELLS grew up in North Dakota, a product of her rural environment and the television generation. She obtained a Bachelor of Arts in Theater from Jamestown College (Jamestown, ND) and a Master of Library Sciences from the University of Arizona.

Ms. Wells currently resides in Tucson with her husband, two daughters, and a dalmation named Daisy. She is devoted to her church, her family, and U of A Wildcat basketball.

DEL REY BOOKS

ANNE McCAFFREY

Available at your bookstore or use this coupon.

____ **DINOSAUR PLANET**   31995   4.95
Kai and Varian, in search of new energy sources, get stranded on a strange planet . . . a sudden change comes over them that leads them into the primitive darkness of a future world.

____ **TO RIDE PEGASUS**   33603   4.95
Five extraordinary women who could read minds, heal bodies, divert disasters, foretell the future . . . out to save mankind in a world decidedly unready for salvation.

____ **RESTOREE**   35187   4.95
An exciting existence in another body on another world awaits a "plan Jane" who is kidnapped by aliens.

____ **GET OFF THE UNICORN**   34935   4.95
Marvelous stories and novelettes of romance and wonder by the "Dragon Lady" of science fiction.

____ **THE SHIP WHO SANG**   33431   4.95
Helva had the brain of a woman, the body of a spaceship . . . and the wiles of a siren born in the stars.

____ **DECISION AT DOONA**   35377   4.95
A fateful encounter teaches two star-roving races—considered mortal enemies—how to co-exist in peace!

____ **ALCHEMY & ACADEME**   34419   4.95
Enchanting tales of some sorcerers and their apprentices . . .

____ **NERILKA'S STORY**   33949   4.95
A warm, charming and unusual love story.

BB   **BALLANTINE MAIL SALES**
Dept. TA, 201 E. 50th St., New York, N.Y. 10022

Please send me the BALLANTINE or DEL REY BOOKS I have checked above. I am enclosing $............(add $2.00 to cover postage and handling for the first book and 50¢ each additional book). Send check or money order—no cash or C.O.D.'s please. Prices are subject to change without notice. Valid in U.S. only. All orders are subject to availability of books.

Name_____

Address_____

City_____State_____Zip Code_____

08   Allow at least 4 weeks for delivery.   **4/91**   **TA 22**